FORGOTTEN REALMS®

R.A. SALVATORE
NEVERWINTER

THE **NEVERWINTER**™ SAGA
BOOK
II

COVER ART
TODD LOCKWOOD

The Neverwinter Saga, Book II
NEVERWINTER

©2011 Wizards of the Coast LLC

Published by Wizards of the Coast LLC.

PRINTED IN THE U.S.A.

Cover art by Todd Lockwood
First Printing: October 2011

9 8 7 6 5 4 3 2 1

ISBN: 978-0-7869-5842-9
ISBN: 978-0-7869-5939-6 (ebook)
620-28362000-001-EN

Library of Congress Cataloging-in-Publication Data
Neverwinter / R.A. Salvatore.
    p. cm. -- (Neverwinter saga ; bk. 2)
  ISBN 978-0-7869-5842-9 (hardback)
I. Title.
PS3569.A462345N48 2011
813'.54--dc22

2011023670

U.S., Canada, Asia, Pacific, & Latin America, Wizards of the Coast LLC, P.O. Box 707, Renton, WA 98057-0707, +1-800-324-6496, www.wizards.com/customerservice

Europe, U.K., Eire & South Africa, Wizards of the Coast LLC, c/o Hasbro UK Ltd., P.O. Box 43, Newport, NP19 4YD, UK, Tel: +800 22 427276, Email: wizards@hasbro.co.uk

Visit our web site at **www.wizards.com**

Welcome to Faerûn, a land of magic and intrigue, brutal violence and divine compassion, where gods have ascended and died, and mighty heroes have risen to fight terrifying monsters. Here, millennia of warfare and conquest have shaped dozens of unique cultures, raised and leveled shining kingdoms and tyrannical empires alike, and left long forgotten, horror-infested ruins in their wake.

A LAND OF MAGIC

When the goddess of magic was murdered, a magical plague of blue fire—the Spellplague—swept across the face of Faerûn, killing some, mutilating many, and imbuing a rare few with amazing supernatural abilities. The Spellplague forever changed the nature of magic itself, and seeded the land with hidden wonders and bloodcurdling monstrosities.

A LAND OF DARKNESS

The threats Faerûn faces are legion. Armies of undead mass in Thay under the brilliant but mad lich king Szass Tam. Treacherous dark elves plot in the Underdark in the service of their cruel and fickle goddess, Lolth. The Abolethic Sovereignty, a terrifying hive of inhuman slave masters, floats above the Sea of Fallen Stars, spreading chaos and destruction. And the Empire of Netheril, armed with magic of unimaginable power, prowls Faerûn in flying fortresses, sowing discord to their own incalculable ends.

A LAND OF HEROES

But Faerûn is not without hope. Heroes have emerged to fight the growing tide of darkness. Battle-scarred rangers bring their notched blades to bear against marauding hordes of orcs. Lowly street rats match wits with demons for the fate of cities. Inscrutable tiefling warlocks unite with fierce elf warriors to rain fire and steel upon monstrous enemies. And valiant servants of merciful gods forever struggle against the darkness.

A LAND OF
UNTOLD ADVENTURE

PROLOGUE

The Year of the Reborn Hero
(1463 DR)

DAHLIA'S LIPS CURLED INTO A SMILE AS SHE WATCHED THE DARK elf dance. Stripped to the waist, Drizzt Do'Urden moved through his attack and defense routines, sometimes slowly and sometimes with blinding speed. His scimitars spun gracefully, deceptively delicate, then darted with sudden, straightforward power. They could strike from any tangent, stabbing often at unexpected angles, and more than once, Dahlia found herself startled and blinking at a clever twist or turn.

She had fought beside Drizzt on the road to Gauntlgrym and inside the dwarven complex, so she thought she had come to understand the extent of his martial prowess. But now, on this moonlit night, she could truly appreciate the grace and coordination of his movements and reminded herself that such perfection in battle didn't come easily.

She marveled at the drow at work, at his slim form, his tight muscles so apparent, and so appealing.

He was always on the balls of his feet, never on his heels, she noted, and his every turn ended in alignment and balance. She noted, too, that Drizzt's neck did not strain with his sudden stabs and swings. So many lumbering human warriors kept all their power up high, above their shoulders, and so their strength seemed to increase in proportion to the decrease of their balance and swiftness.

But not Drizzt.

His neck was loose, his shoulders nimble. His strength came from his belly and the muscles lining the sides of his ribs. How many opponents, Dahlia wondered, had been comforted by the drow's slim neck and flat shoulders, by his apparent lack of strength, only to have their weapons smacked from their hands or cut in half by the power of his blows? His blades hummed with amazing speed as he fell deeper into his dance, but weight, balance, and strength hid behind every cut and thrust.

Dahlia's hand instinctively went up to her right ear, empty now of diamond studs, and her smile widened further. Had she at last found the lover who would end her pain?

Drizzt was sweating, his dark skin glistening in the moonlight. He stabbed out to the right with both blades in a parallel thrust, but deftly turned his feet opposite the attack and flashed away to the left, using his upper body turn to gain momentum for a somersault, one that landed him back on his feet. A mere heartbeat later, he slid down to his knees as if forced low by some imaginary blade coming in from the right. A blue-glowing scimitar stabbed up that way, then Drizzt was moving again, back on his feet so smoothly Dahlia hadn't even noticed the transition.

The elf woman licked her smiling lips.

"I can ride him," Dahlia insisted. "I'm a skilled horseman."

"Andahar isn't a horse," Drizzt replied from his seat on the unicorn's back. The drow reached down to offer his hand to Dahlia once more. Still she resisted.

"Or are you afraid that Andahar will come to prefer me?" she replied.

"It wouldn't matter. I have the whistle."

"I could take that whistle."

"You could try." With that, Drizzt retracted his hand, shrugged, and clucked softly, starting Andahar into a slow trot. They had only gone a single stride, though, before Dahlia planted the end of her eight-foot staff and vaulted up onto the unicorn's back behind the drow.

"Why do you think I need your hand, drow?" she asked. "Why do you believe I need anything from you?"

Drizzt kicked the mighty steed into a faster canter, tugging Andahar's flowing white mane around to steer the unicorn through the brush.

"We'll break early for a midday meal, and make the road soon after," Drizzt said.

"And then?"

"North," Drizzt answered, "to Port Llast, perhaps Luskan, to learn what we may."

From his tone and posture it was obvious he expected an argument. Dahlia had expressed her eagerness to go south to Neverwinter Wood, where she could be rid of the Thayan wizard Sylora Salm and her Dread Ring.

Surprisingly, though, Dahlia didn't object. "Luskan, then," she agreed. "But with all speed, then just as fast back to the south. I'll let Sylora Salm gnash her teeth in dismay over the failure of the primordial, but not for long."

"And then we'll kill her," Drizzt said, as much a question as a statement.

"Second thoughts?" Dahlia asked.

Drizzt steered Andahar toward a copse of trees then, and brought the unicorn back to a slow trot. "I said I wouldn't join you in a quest merely for revenge."

"Sylora isn't finished here," Dahlia said. "She will seek to again free the primordial—raining catastrophe on the North to fuel her Dread Ring—and you think all I seek is revenge?"

Drizzt pulled Andahar to a sudden stop and slowly looked back to stare straight into Dahlia's blue eyes. "I said that if it was no more than your personal quest for revenge, I wouldn't join you."

Dahlia grinned at him, the movement causing the intricate blue and purple dots of the woad on her face to form the hint of an image of a hunting cat poised to strike. Drizzt couldn't miss it, and his expression reflected his intrigue. Dahlia tilted her head to the right, then swayed it back left, and the drow blinked in amazement. In the woman's movement, the cat seemed to spring.

And with Drizzt still obviously mesmerized, Dahlia leaned forward and brushed his lips with her own.

It took several heartbeats, but that at last seemed to break the spell and the dark elf leaned away from her, staring at her with puzzlement.

"Why did you do that?" he asked in a voice that seemed hard to find.

"Because I don't believe you," she replied.

Drizzt cocked his head curiously, and when he started to protest, Dahlia put a finger over his lips to silence him.

"Don't be a fool, drow," she said with a wicked grin. "Don't deny me my fantasy out of some chivalrous notion of the importance of truth."

Drizzt just looked confused, and that made Dahlia laugh aloud at him. Finally he surrendered and turned back, urging Andahar into motion once more.

Andahar didn't tire through the rest of the day and long into the night. Unlike Guenhwyvar, the magical unicorn could be summoned at any time, and could remain for as long as Drizzt needed him. But also unlike the panther, Andahar could be wounded, if not outright slain, and such wounds would take as long to heal as those of a mortal creature. So Drizzt took care to involve Andahar in as few battles as necessary, and only rarely kept the unicorn around when danger was afoot.

They had hoped to make Port Llast that night, but the weather turned foul and it was not to be. They set their camp under an overhang of rock on a high bluff some distance from the road, but in sight of it. Chill rain poured down, and an occasional streak of lightning split the sky. Drizzt managed to get a campfire burning, though it stayed low and sputtering. Whenever the wind swirled, both he and Dahlia found themselves coughing in the smoke.

But still, it was not so bad for Drizzt. How could it be? He was on the road again, and with the promise of adventure awaiting him at every turn. The road was filled with danger, the forests full of wild things, and the land untamed. Even the cities ahead, first Port Llast then Luskan, would keep him on his edge, would keep his hands in easy reach of his blades.

He sat with his back against the stone and stole glances at Dahlia as she ate, as she paced, as she stretched her road-weary muscles. . . . She was out near the front edge of the overhang, her back to him, the swirls of rain catching her just a bit. She stood on her toes and peered into the distance, her diagonally-cut skirt riding up high and affording Drizzt a long look at her shapely legs.

The drow smiled and shook his head. She knew he was watching her. Dahlia played a game, like the kiss when she sat behind him on Andahar, or the way in which she'd wrapped her arms around him for the hard ride.

"Douse the fire." Dahlia glanced at him over her shoulder.

Drizzt's smile disappeared and he stared at her curiously.

"We're not alone."

With a single slide of his boot, Drizzt pushed a mound of dirt that had been strategically placed for just this purpose and killed the flames. He scrambled to his feet and stared into the rain, but saw nothing. Dahlia reached her arm out in front of him and guided his gaze.

A torch's glow flickered from behind distant trees, down along the road.

"They're moving," Dahlia said.

"Along the road, at night, in this deluge?"

"Highwaymen . . . or soldiers of some warlord or another," Dahlia reasoned. "Or some monstrous group, perhaps."

"Perhaps it's only a merchant caravan seeking shelter?"

Dahlia shook her head. "What merchant would so imperil his wagon or his team by moving along a muddy and unstable road in the dark? If he broke a wheel or hobbled his horse, it would likely prove fatal."

"Unless they're fleeing from trouble already found," said Drizzt, and he scooped up his weapon belt.

"You intend to go out to them?" Dahlia asked in an almost mocking tone.

Drizzt looked at her as if the answer was, or should be, obvious.

"To right all the wrongs of the world, Drizzt Do'Urden?" she asked. "Is that your purpose for being? Is that the only motivation that drives you?"

"You would not aid a helpless innocent?"

"I don't know, and I highly doubt that's what we see on the road below," Dahlia countered. She gave a little laugh, and Drizzt knew he was being mocked. "That's all there is for you? Black and white, right and wrong?"

"There's a profound difference between right and wrong," Drizzt replied grimly, and he strapped on his weapons.

"Of course, but isn't there more to the world?"

Drizzt paused, but only for a heartbeat before he produced the onyx feline figurine and called Guenhwyvar to his side. "A light on the road," he explained to the panther. "Find it, watch it." With a low growl, the panther leaped away, disappearing into the night.

"Don't you believe that there are instances where both sides believe they're right?"

"Remind me to tell you the tale of King Obould Many-Arrows some day," Drizzt replied and walked past Dahlia. "For now I'm going to learn what I may. Are you joining me?"

Dahlia shrugged. "Of course," she replied. "Perhaps we'll find a good fight."

"Perhaps we'll rescue an innocent merchant," Drizzt countered.

"Perhaps we'll rescue the ill-gotten booty from an undeserving, self-appointed lord," Dahlia said as soon as the drow turned away.

Drizzt didn't look back at her. He didn't want her to see the unintentional grin her unrelenting sarcasm had brought to his face. He didn't want to give her that satisfaction.

He moved swiftly down the rise and into the trees, pushing himself hard because he wanted to push Dahlia even harder. With his magical anklets speeding his stride, he knew she couldn't pace him. So every now and then he slowed just enough to make her think she was catching up. Long before he neared the road, however, he was only guessing as to how far behind Dahlia might be, if she was still behind him at all.

Drizzt forced his focus in front of him, to the road and the torches down to his right, approaching quickly. He nodded in recognition as a wagon came into view, driven hard by an obviously flummoxed man. His companion crouched beside him, bow drawn, looking behind over the back of the bench seat. Behind the wagon came three other torches, all carried by men running hard to catch up—no, not to catch up, Drizzt realized, but to keep up. These were not the enemies from which the wagon fled. If that had been the case, then surely the archer would have had little trouble in knocking them down.

Barely thirty yards away, one of the trailing torch carriers went down.

"Shoot them! Shoot them!" another of the trailing runners, a woman, shouted desperately.

Drizzt's hand went to Taulmaril, his bow. He gave a little whistle, one Guenhwyvar knew, and the panther revealed herself on a tree branch across the road from him. Drizzt motioned to the path of the oncoming wagon.

Out leaped the panther to the middle of the road, to face the approaching wagon.

The horse team started to veer.

Guenhwyvar roared, like the rumble of boulders, the sheer strength of that call echoing throughout the forests and hills for a league. The horses skidded to a stop, rearing and neighing and kicking their forelegs in terror.

The jolt almost knocked the archer from the bench seat.

"Shoot it!" the driver yelled, working furiously to control the shuddering wagon. "Shoot it dead! Oh, by the gods!"

The archer managed to swing around, his eyes going wide as he spotted the source of the roar. He brought his bow up, his hands shaking.

A streak of silver, like a small bolt of lightning, cut the air right in front of the two men, startling them further, so much so that the arrow slipped from the bowstring. Oblivious to the disarmament, the archer let fly, and the arrow tumbled harmlessly. The man shrieked and the bow jumped, nearly tumbling from his grasp.

The horses continued to rear and whinny, even after the panther jumped back into the brush, disappearing from sight.

"Bowman to the side!" yelled one of the trailing runners, at last nearing the wagon, and both she and her companion veered Drizzt's way in a brave charge.

He wasn't going to shoot them dead, of course, for he still had no idea if these were friends or foes. So he dropped Taulmaril to the ground and drew forth his blades defensively.

He needn't have bothered.

The nearest attacker, a tall and gangly man still many strides from Drizzt, gave a howl and lifted his sword up over his head. Then a lithe elf form swung down agilely from the branch above, her legs hooked and secure. With the momentum of the movement, Dahlia smacked the charging man on the forehead with her long staff and sent him to the ground, his sword flying away.

Dahlia came forward, letting go with her legs to spin down in a landing so balanced that it seemed somehow casual. Even as she touched down, she gracefully sprang right over the sitting and dazed man. The woman, just a couple of strides ahead, tried to get her spear in line, but Dahlia slipped down low as she swept past her, her staff sweeping in to take the woman's feet out from under her.

Back on the road, the archer cried for the driver to ride on. But just as the horses began to run, Guenhwyvar leaped into the middle of the road and roared again. The terrified team reared and shrieked in protest.

From the edge of the road, Drizzt noted the third of the trailing runners—the one who had gone down hard—stumbling in the darkness, his torch sputtering in the rain far behind on the road. Drizzt paid him no heed and sprinted for the wagon, which had gone past him to his left. Though it was no longer moving, Drizzt saw the archer come up facing him, bow reset and drawn.

Drizzt dropped to his knees, sliding across the mud as the arrow went harmlessly above him. He came up right behind the wagon bed and leaped high with his momentum, easily clearing the low tailgate. As soon as he set his feet firmly, he leaped again, tucking his legs to clear the bench and the ducking drivers, and turning as he went so he landed at the base of the yoke, facing the two men. The team continued to rear and struggle, but the jostling didn't bother the agile drow at all. He held his scimitars level in front of the faces of his captives.

"Take it all, but don't ye kill me, I beg," the driver desperately pleaded, his open palms waving and shaking up beside his wide, wet face. "Please, good sir."

The other man dropped his bow, covered his face with his hands, and began to weep.

"Who is chasing you?" Drizzt asked the drivers.

They seemed flummoxed by the unexpected question.

"Who?" Drizzt demanded.

"Highwaymen," said the archer. "A foul band o' ne'er-do-wells thinking to steal our goods and cut our throats!"

Drizzt looked at Dahlia, who had come out on the road to face down the third runner, who stood with his hands up in surrender, obviously wanting no part of a fight with her.

"Who are you and where are you from?" Drizzt asked.

"Port Llast," answered the archer, at the same time the driver said, "Luskan."

Drizzt eyed them suspiciously.

"Out o' Luskan, but coming back on our way through Port Llast," the archer explained.

"Commissioned by the high captains," the driver quickly added, and he seemed to gain some confidence.

"Carrying?"

"Food, wine, goods," the driver said, but the archer tried to halt him, putting his hand out across the man's chest.

"Carryin' what we're carryin' and what business is it o' yer own?" the archer asked.

Drizzt grinned at him wickedly and the man seemed to deflate, perhaps reminded that the high captains wouldn't offer him much of a defense against a simple thrust of the scimitar that hovered barely a hand's-breadth from his face.

A ruckus farther down the road indicated that the pursuit was nearing.

"If I find you're lying to me then know we will meet again long before you see the lights of Port Llast." Drizzt withdrew his blades and flipped them over before neatly sliding them back into their scabbards. "Now be gone!"

He tipped a salute and leaped between the men, over the back of the bench. He helped the three stragglers up into the wagon then watched as it sped on its way.

"Letting them go?" Dahlia came up beside him. "How noble of you." She handed him Taulmaril and the quiver Drizzt had dropped before his charge at the wagon.

"Would you have me steal their goods and slay them?"

"The first, at least."

Drizzt stared at her. "They're simple merchants."

"Yes, from Luskan, I heard. Simple men in the employ of the high captains—pirates one and all, and they who destroyed that city."

Drizzt tried to hold steady against that truth—a truth that he, who had been in the City of Sails during the fall of his dear friend Captain Deudermont, knew all too well, and all too painfully.

"So what they're carrying is ill-gotten from the start, then, and which highwayman is which, Drizzt Do'Urden?" said Dahlia.

"You twist everything to suit your conclusions."

"Or everything is twisted to begin with, and few are what they seem, and a good man does evil and a beggar is a thief."

More noise sounded from down the road.

"We will finish this discussion later," Drizzt said, and he motioned for Guenhwyvar to take a position in the brush.

"To no conclusion that will satisfy the idealist drow," Dahlia assured him, and she too sprinted off into the brush at the side of the road.

Drizzt thought to follow, but the sound of galloping horses, and Dahlia's words stabbing at his thoughts, changed his mind. He lifted his bow, setting an arrow and leveling it.

A quartet of riders came into view a moment later, tightly grouped and leaning low against the driving rain.

Drizzt drew back, thinking he could strike down two with a single shot, for it would take more than a man's girth to halt a bolt from Taulmaril.

"Beggar man or thief?" he whispered.

The riders neared, and one held a sword up high.

Drizzt dipped the angle of the bow and let fly. A sizzling blue-white flash rent the air, momentarily stealing the night, and the arrow burrowed into the road in front of the riders, blasting through cobblestone and dirt with a thunderous report.

The horses reared and bucked. One rider went tumbling, and hung desperately from the side of the saddle. The other two fared better, until Dahlia came soaring out of the trees to the side. Her staff clipped one hard as she stretched out and double-kicked the other.

And then came Guenhwyvar, and the horses spun and bucked and reared in terror.

Dahlia hit the ground with a twist and roll, came right back to her feet, and swung around. She planted her staff to vault up high once more, this time kicking the female rider she had struck with her staff. To the woman's credit, she still held her seat, but Dahlia wasn't done with her. As she landed, the elf whipped her staff out to strike the rider again, and this time sent a burst of magical lightning through the metal pole. Shaking uncontrollably, her hair dancing, her limbs waving wildly, the woman had no chance of remaining on her turning, terrified horse, and down she tumbled.

Three of the horses rushed away, riderless. Guenhwyvar kept the fourth turning and turning, the poor rider hanging on to the side.

"More are coming," Dahlia called to Drizzt when he joined her above the three prone highwaymen, his scimitars informing two that they would be wise to lie still.

"But don't ye kill me, Master Do'Urden!" one middle-aged man whimpered. "Be sure that I ain't no enemy o' yers!"

Drizzt looked at him with puzzlement, not recognizing the man at all.

"You know him?" Dahlia asked.

Drizzt shook his head and demanded of the man, "How do you know my name?"

"Just a guess, good sir!" the man cried. "The cat, the lightning bow, the blades ye carry . . ."

"Guen!" Drizzt called.

Off to the side, the panther was getting a bit carried away with her game, and had the poor horse spinning furiously. As the panther backed off and the horse stopped its spinning, only then did the dizzy highwayman fall to the ground.

"Ye're Drizzt?" the fallen woman asked, her teeth still chattering from the residual lightning.

"That a highwayman would find that a comforting possibility perplexes me," the drow replied.

The woman gave a snort and shook her head.

"They have friends approaching," Dahlia warned. "Finish them or let's be on our way."

Drizzt considered the ragtag group for a few heartbeats then flipped his scimitars into their scabbards. He even offered the man who'd recognized him his hand and hoisted him up to his feet.

"I've no love for the high captains of Luskan," Drizzt explained to the highwaymen. "Only that fact spares you the blade this day. But know that I will be watching you, and any assault upon an innocent will be viewed as an attack upon my own body."

"And that's it, then?" asked the woman, looking miserable and beaten. "We're to forage and starve so as not to offend the sensibilities of the great Drizzt Do'Urden?"

Drizzt looked at her curiously, but for just a moment before he noted Dahlia's superior, knowing smile.

"I was a farmer," explained the man Drizzt had just lifted. "Right near Luskan. Goodman Stuyles at yer service." He held out his hand, but Drizzt didn't take it. "My family worked the land since before the fall o' the Hosttower of the Arcane."

"Then why are you here?" the drow asked suspiciously.

"Ain't no use for farms around Luskan no more," the man replied. "Folks're trading for their food now, and most by ship, or by the wagon like the one that just passed."

"And most of it stolen food, don't ye doubt!" another man interjected. "They got no patience for a farm, nor no means to protect one."

Drizzt glanced over at Dahlia, who merely shrugged as if it was all quite expected.

"We grew it, they stole it, and burned that what they couldn't take," said Stuyles.

Down the road, more of the highwaymen came into view, but only briefly before scattering into the brush, no doubt to try to flank the newcomers.

"Go," Drizzt bade the four, waving them away.

A couple moved to do just that, one going over to help the woman to her feet and calling for the nearest horse as he did.

"I would think you would offer a meal and a dry bed for the two of us for letting you go," Dahlia said to the group, drawing surprised looks from all four, and most of all, from Drizzt. "Weary travelers, rainy night. . . ." she went on.

Drizzt's jaw hung open, and didn't begin to close when Goodman Stuyles answered, "Join us, then."

"We have other business," Drizzt said rather sternly, aiming his remark squarely at Dahlia.

But Dahlia just laughed and followed the four highwaymen. With a great sigh, Drizzt did, too.

The bandits had set up several wide lean-tos among a row of thick pines just off the road, affording them a comfortable enough camp despite the driving rain. They proved to be surprisingly hospitable, offering a warm meal and some good, strong drink.

Goodman Stuyles stayed with Drizzt and Dahlia through the meal and afterward, prodding Drizzt for tales of Icewind Dale—old adventures that had apparently become legendary in these parts so many years later. Drizzt had never fancied himself a storyteller, but he complied with the requests, and soon found quite the audience—a dozen or so—sitting around him and listening intently.

Most of those drifted off to sleep as the fires burned low, but a couple remained, enjoying the banter. "And what business might you have now that brings you south of that forsaken land?" asked one of them, a tall man named Hadencourt, after Drizzt had finished the story of battling a white dragon in an ice cave.

"We're on our way to Luskan," Drizzt answered, "to inquire after some old friends."

"And then to Neverwinter Wood, eh?" Dahlia added, and Drizzt couldn't react fast enough to suppress his surprise at her inclusion of that tidbit.

"There's a great battle raging there," farmer Stuyles remarked.

"Neverwinter Wood?" Hadencourt pressed. "What would bring a drow elf and a"—he looked rather curiously at Dahlia, as if not quite knowing what to make of her—"a lady such as yourself to that war-scarred place?"

Dahlia started to reply, but Drizzt spoke over her. "We're adventurers. It would seem that Neverwinter Wood is now a place of adventure!" He ended by lifting his cup of brandy in a toast. "Though in truth, we haven't decided our course after Luskan, and in truth, we are not even certain that our road will take us all the way to the City of Sails. I've been thinking that it's far past time for a return to Mithral Hall."

The whole time he spoke, the drow stared intently at Dahlia, warning her to keep silent. When he looked back at Hadencourt, he noted that the man wore a smile that seemed a bit too informed for his liking.

"Call it personal," Dahlia said, and she never stopped looking at Hadencourt.

The discussion ended there, abruptly, with Drizzt commenting that it was past time for them all to get some rest. As the others dispersed, Dahlia watched Hadencourt head off to his lean-to for the night.

Goodman Stuyles stepped away to speak with several others of the band. "We'll be moving tomorrow," he reported back to Drizzt a few moments later. "That wagon will soon enough reach Port Llast and we're thinking a garrison'll come looking for us. Are ye to be coming with us, then? We'd be glad to have ye along."

"No," Drizzt stated flatly, over Dahlia's opposite response. "I cannot."

"We're just surviving, is all," Stuyles said. "A man's a right to eat!"

"That you didn't feel the bite of my blade is a testament that I don't disagree," Drizzt told him. "But I fear that traveling along beside you would show me choices with which I cannot agree and of which I cannot abide. Would you enter every adventure unsure of my allegiance?"

Stuyles took a step back and eyed the drow. "Better ye go then," he said, and Drizzt nodded coldly.

"So the world is too dirty for Drizzt Do'Urden," Dahlia mocked when Stuyles had gone. "What rights, what proper recourse, for those who have not, when those who have keep all?"

"Waterdeep is not so far to the south."

"Aye, and the lords of Waterdeep will throw open their gates and their wares to all those put out in the chaos."

At that moment, Drizzt didn't find Dahlia's sarcasm very endearing. He calmed himself with memories of Icewind Dale, memories nearly a century old, of a time and place when matters of right and wrong seemed so much more apparent. Even in that unforgiving frontier, there seemed a level of civilization far beyond the current drama playing out along the Sword Coast. He considered the fall of Captain Deudermont in Luskan, when the high captains had seized full control of the City of Sails and thus, the surrounding region. A Waterdhavian lord had fallen beside Deudermont, and the other lords of that great city had surely failed in their subsequent inaction.

But even in that dark moment, Drizzt understood the fall of Luskan to darkness was just a minor symptom of a greater disease, as was the fall of Cadderly and Spirit Soaring. With the advent of the Shadowfell, the patches of shadow were both literal and figurative, and in those vast areas of darkness, anarchy and chaos had found their way.

How could Drizzt fight beside men like Stuyles and these highwaymen, however justified their ambushes, when he knew that those they ambushed would very often be men and women, like this band, simply trying to find a way to survive and keep their families fed?

Was there a "right" and "wrong" to be found here? To steal from the powerful or to toil for their copper coins?

"What are you thinking?" Dahlia asked him, her voice having lost its sharp edge.

"That I am one very small person, after all," Drizzt replied without looking.

When he did at last turn around to regard the woman, she was grinning knowingly—too confidently, as if she was working some manipulation on him he didn't yet understand.

Strangely, that notion didn't bother Drizzt as much as he would have expected. Perhaps his confusion when faced by such a reality as the tumult of the Sword Coast was so profound that he would accept a hand, however offered, in lifting him from the darkness.

PART I

LOOSE ENDS

And now I am alone, more so than I've been since the days following the death of Montolio those many years ago. Even on that later occasion when I traveled back into the Underdark to Menzoberranzan, forsaking my friends in the foolish belief that I was unfairly endangering them, it was not like this. For though I physically walked alone into the Underdark, I didn't go without the emotional support that they were there beside me, in spirit. I went with full confidence that Bruenor, Catti-brie, and Regis remained alive and well—indeed, more well, I believed, because I had left them.

But now I am alone. They are gone, one and all. My friends, my family.

There remains Guenhwyvar, of course, and she is no small thing to me—a true and loyal companion, someone to listen to my laments and my joys and my pondering. But it is not the same. Guen can hear me, but is there anything I would hear from her? She can share my victories, my joys, my trials, but there's no reciprocation. After knowing the love of friends and family, I cannot so fool myself again, as I did in those first days after I left Menzoberranzan, as to believe that the wonderful Guenhwyvar is enough.

My road takes me from Gauntlgrym as it once took me from Mithral Hall, and I doubt I shall return—certainly I'll not return to stand and stare at the cairn of Bruenor Battlehammer, as I rarely visited the graves of Catti-brie and Regis during my years in Mithral Hall. A wise elf lady once explained to me the futility of such things, as she taught me that I must learn to live my life as a series of shorter spans. It is the blessing of the People to live through the dawn and sunset of centuries, but that blessing can serve too as a curse. Few elves partner for life, as is common among the humans, for example, because the joy of such a partnership can weigh as an anchor after a hundred years, or two hundred.

"Treat each parting as a rebirth," Innovindil said to me. "Let go of that which is past and seek new roads. Perhaps never to forget your lost friends and family and lovers, but to place them in your memory warmly and build again with new friends those things that so pleased you."

I've gone back to Innovindil's lessons many times over the last few decades, since Wulfgar left Mithral Hall and since Catti-brie and Regis were lost to me. I've recited them as a litany against the rage, the pain, the sadness . . . a reminder that there are roads yet to walk.

I was deluding myself, I now know.

For I hadn't let go of my dear friends. I hadn't lost hope that someday, one day, some way, I would raze a giant's lair beside Wulfgar once more, or would fish beside Regis on a lazy summer's day on the banks of Maer Dualdon, or I would spend the night in Catti-brie's warm embrace. I tasked Jarlaxle with finding them, not out of any real hope that he would, but because I couldn't bear to relinquish the last flicker of hope for these moments, these soft joys, these truest smiles, I once knew.

And now Bruenor is gone and the Companions of the Hall are no more.

I watched him take his last breath. There is closure. There is finality. And only through Bruenor had I kept the dream of Catti-brie and Regis, and even Wulfgar, alive. Only through his determination and steadfastness did I allow myself to believe that somehow, some magical way, they might still be out there. Our journey to Icewind Dale should have disavowed me of that notion, and did so to some extent (and also pushed Bruenor, at long last, into a state of resignation), and whatever little flickers remained within my heart were snuffed out when I watched my dearest friend breathe his last.

So I am alone. The life I had known is ended.

I surely feel the sadness, the regret at things that couldn't be, the loneliness. At every turn, I want to call out to Bruenor to tell him my news, only to remember that, alas, he is not there. All of it is there, all of the pain that one would expect.

But there is something else, something unexpected, something surprising, something bringing with it more than a bit of confusion and even guilt.

True guilt, and I feel, and fear, myself a cad.

Yet I cannot deny it.

As I turned my back on Gauntlgrym and the grave of King Bruenor Battlehammer, pushing up in my emotions beside the pain and the rage and the helplessness and the replaying of the scenario over and over again to wonder what I might have done differently, was . . . a deep sense of relief.

I am ashamed to admit this, but to deny it would be to lie, and worse, to lie to myself. For at long last I have a sense of finality. It is time for the past to rest and for me to move forward. It is time, as Innovindil explained to me in a forest far from here, for me to begin anew.

Certainly I'm not relieved that Bruenor has passed. Nor Thibbledorf Pwent, for that matter! A better friend than Bruenor I have never known, and I would wish him back to my side in an instant, were that possible.

But in the larger sense, the greater perspective of my life, there is a sense of relief. I have been ready to let go of Cattibrie and Regis and Wulfgar for a long time now—not to forget them! I'll never forget them, never want to forget them! They are embedded in my heart and soul and walk with Drizzt Do'Urden every step of his road. But I accepted their loss—my loss—years, even decades, ago, and it was only the stubbornness of an old dwarf, refusing to let go, insisting that they were still to be found and that our wondrous years together would be restored, that forced me, too, to hang on.

I am alone now. I am free? What an awful thought! How disloyal am I, then, to feel any eagerness in looking forward, to a new road, a third life, taking the painful lessons of my first existence in Menzoberranzan along with the wondrous joys of my second life beside the Companions of the Hall. Now I am hardened by the whips of the drow matrons, and softened by the honest love of friends, and settled in what I know is, what should be, and what should never be. As my second life so exceeded my first in joy and purpose, could my third not climb higher yet?

I don't know, and truly I understand how fortunate I was in finding these four amazing companions to share a road. Will I find such friends, ready to sacrifice all for me, again? Will I love again? Even if I do, will it be the same intensity of that which I knew with Catti-brie?

I know not, but I'm not afraid to find out. That's my freedom now, to walk my road with eyes wide and heart open, without regret and with a true understanding of how blessed my existence beside these companions has been.

And there is one other freedom now: For the first time in decades, I awaken to discover that I am not angry. Strangely so. I feel as if the rage that has for so long kept my muscles tightened has at last relaxed.

This too stings me with pangs of guilt, and I am sure that those around me will often hear me muttering to myself in confusion. Perhaps I am simply deluding myself. Perhaps the loss of Bruenor has pushed me past the bounds of sensibility, where the level of pain has become intolerable and so I trick myself into something wholly converse.

Perhaps.

Perhaps not.

I can only shrug and wonder.

I can only feel and accept.

I am alone now.

I am free.

—Drizzt Do'Urden

CHAPTER 1

A PROMISE OF CARNAGE

SYLORA SALM STOOD OUTSIDE THE ASH CLOUD OF THE BUDDING Dread Ring, shifting from foot to foot. She knew the stakes. Her scouts had returned confirming her fears: The primordial had been trapped once more by a host of water elementals and the residual magic of the fallen Hosttower of the Arcane. There would be no second eruption of primordial magnitude. The ground was no longer trembling daily beneath her feet.

Her enemies had averted catastrophe.

Sylora stared into the ash and could almost feel it diminish. She had been counting on a volcanic cataclysm to strengthen her magical beast, this Dread Ring that fed upon death.

She continued to shift from foot to foot. If she understood her failure, then so did the being approaching her behind the gray-black veil.

Sylora could hear her heart thumping in her chest. Behind her, Jestry Rallevin, the Ashmadai zealot who had become her closest advisor, swallowed hard.

"I feel him," he whispered. Jestry Rallevin was no ordinary Ashmadai. Though young, barely into his twenties and quite inexperienced, the man still commanded the attention and respect of all the other zealots, both because of his striking appearance—with his large shoulders, dark hair, and brooding dark eyes—and his willingness to throw himself into the cause with absolute abandon. And he could fight—so perfectly in balance, striking with precision and power. If only she had known of his prowess before the few recent skirmishes with the Netherese forces, Sylora silently lamented. She could have used Jestry to tempt that vile Dahlia and then destroy the witch altogether.

That notion reminded Sylora of Temberle, another strong male consort whom she had shared with Dahlia, and one Dahlia had slain before coming west. She glanced at Jestry, measuring him against Temberle.

No comparison, she believed. This one, a true zealot, would have carved Temberle to pieces had they come to blows. Might he have done, might he do, the same with Dahlia? It was a pleasant and intriguing thought, to be sure.

"Sylora, he's coming," Jestry repeated.

Sylora nodded but didn't reply, afraid to break the muted silence of the dead ash. She had understood the coming of Szass Tam from the moment he had focused his magical energies on her Dread Ring. She slumped her shoulders and waited outside the edge. She wouldn't go in there to meet him. Within the Dread Ring, the power of Szass Tam was simply too terrible to behold.

Behind her, she heard Jestry licking his lips nervously. She wanted him to stop, desperately so, but she couldn't bring herself to tell him.

An emaciated humanoid under a heavy black hooded robe approached. Somehow he was darker than the Dread Ring through which he glided.

"I haven't felt the pleasure of a thousand souls crying out their last," the lich said in his uneven and scratchy voice. Two dots of angry fire within the shades of blackness stared at Sylora and his form wavered, blurred by the swirl of magical ash. "I haven't felt the strengthening of my new domain, as you promised."

Sylora swallowed hard. "We have encountered enemies—"

"I know of your failure," Szass Tam's voice reached out like a claw for her heart. "I know of the battle in the dwarven mines. I know it all."

"There are many reasons," Sylora blurted. "And the fight is not yet lost!" She paused then and grimaced, thinking her last word choice to be truly foolish.

"I was there," Szass Tam assured her. "Looking through other eyes. The magic is restored. The primordial of fire is recaptured. It will not be freed again, soon or easily."

Sylora lowered her eyes, her shoulders slumping further. "I have failed you," she said. She stood there for many heartbeats, awaiting recrimination, awaiting a terrible death.

"You have," Szass Tam finally said.

"It was but one battle!" Jestry cried out from behind.

A bolt of black energy flashed out of the Dread Ring, crackling the air beside Sylora. Jestry flew backward to the ground and there he squirmed, his limbs trembling in agony, his hair dancing.

"Is he valuable?" Szass Tam asked Sylora, which was his way, she knew, of asking her if Jestry should be fed to the Dread Ring.

She spent a few moments sorting the riddle. She could throw Jestry to the lich here in the hopes that his sacrifice would suffice . . .

"He has proven his worth many times over," she heard herself replying instead. "Jestry Rallevin has slain many Netherese, and has led my warriors to many victories here in the forest. I should like to keep him beside me."

"You should like to keep him?" Szass Tam retorted. An invisible hand reached out from the ashes to grab Sylora by the throat. She clawed at it, but there was nothing to grab, and yet as insubstantial as it seemed, that magical grasp lifted her up on her toes and began pulling her into the blackness. Suddenly it stopped and she hung there in the air, still scratching, still squirming. Her bulging eyes widened even more when Jestry came up beside her, similarly choked and floating.

"Do not blame me for your doom, poor Ashmadai," Szass Tam whispered from inside the Dread Ring. "Sylora Salm requested your presence."

As he spoke his last word, another voice rent the air, a keening sing-song cry of "Arklem! Ark-lem! Greeth, Greeth, oh, where are you! I don't see you, Arklem. Ark-lem! But you see me . . . oh, I know you see me! Of course you see me. You see all."

Sylora dropped to the ground and barely held her balance. Beside her, Jestry crumpled to the ground and lay groaning, still shaken from the black lightning. From within the Dread Ring, Szass Tam laughed.

Continued babbling drew Sylora's gaze behind her. The lich Valindra Shadowmantle glided among the skeletal remains of many fruit trees. Her half-rotted fingers tapped her chin and she rambled to this unseen companion Arklem Greeth, as if sorting out some deep secret of the world that no one had yet deciphered.

She moved right up beside Sylora before she even seemed to notice the sorceress, the Ashmadai, or even the Dread Ring and the great being standing within.

"Oh," she said to Sylora. "Well. Good afternoon. Well met. And it is a good day! Have you seen Arklem?"

Szass Tam cackled.

"And who is that? Who is that?" Valindra asked. "Is that you, Arklem?"

"It's Szass Tam, Valindra," Sylora said quietly. "The archlich of Thay."

"There is no introduction necessary," Szass Tam said. "Hello again, Mistress Shadowmantle. I did so enjoy our communion in the dwarven halls."

Sylora started to question that, but bit her words back and turned a disbelieving stare over Valindra, Szass Tam's spy.

"Oh, hello and well met, again!" Valindra replied. "I used it!"

"How?" Sylora asked, looking from Valindra back to Szass Tam. "Used what?" she added, twisting her head back to regard the elf lich at her side.

"I still have it," Valindra assured Szass Tam, and she opened a fold of her robe and produced the scepter of Asmodeus, a powerful summoning artifact that Sylora had lent her on her journey to the lair of the primordial.

Sylora instinctively reached for the scepter, fearing that the archlich would be outraged indeed that she had given such an item to any of her inferiors.

"Good, Valindra, and well done in bringing forth the pit fiend," Szass Tam replied, halting Sylora's reach. "Valindra commanded the pit fiend with ease. With practiced ease. She is possessed of great power beneath her . . . her condition."

Sylora nodded stupidly.

"Sylora knows—oh, don't be silly!" Valindra erupted, and she laughed wildly. "She is my friend. She has been reminding me of the times . . . oh, why can't I remember those times of power and play, of magic the same and magic different?"

"Before the Spellplague," Sylora translated. "Her affliction has confused her, but it hasn't erased those powers she knew before the collapse of Mystra's Weave."

"And why is that important?" asked Szass Tam.

"I bring the past to the present," Valindra answered before Sylora could, and the female lich's voice was unexpectedly steady.

"You saw the events within the dwarven mines?" Sylora asked Szass Tam.

"Some."

"I was told that great enemies came upon my charges," said Sylora.

"You erred in sending so meager a force," Szass Tam countered.

"The pit fiend," Sylora protested. "Valindra! And Dor'crae, who stood as my second."

"You erred in sending so meager a force," Szass Tam repeated, biting every word off short for emphasis, as if each was a verdict, a sentence and pronouncement unto itself.

Sylora lowered her eyes. "I did, my lord."

"More than ample, were it not for the residual power of the Hosttower of the Arcane," Valindra replied. "The fault is mine, and not Lady Sylora's."

Sylora and Jestry gawked in utter confusion at Valindra's suddenly cogent words.

"I should have known—oh, I should have!" Valindra's fingers began to tap and her head began to shake. She heaved a great sigh. "It was me, of course. I know the Hosttower—none other! So why didn't I think it so powerful there and then, in the halls of the dwarves? Oh, Valindra!" She slapped herself across the face. "Oh Arklem! Ark-lem! Ark-lem! Arklem, where are you? Greeth, Greeth, I need you!"

Sylora turned back to Szass Tam and held up her hands helplessly.

"Valindra!" the archlich roared, his voice magically enhanced so that it sounded like the bellow of a dragon and had both Sylora and Jestry wincing and covering their ears.

"Yes?" Valindra replied sweetly, seemingly unbothered by the deafening volume.

"Your fault?"

"I should have warned Lady Sylora."

"Why didn't you?"

Sylora winced.

"I needed the power!" Valindra shrieked, shaking wildly and waving her emaciated arms. "Greeth! Greeth! For Greeth, of course."

Sylora couldn't tell if she was talking to them, to herself, or to some unseen third party.

"To bring him in. I was a bad girl, not good, not good. Arklem Greeth—Ark-lem! Ark-lem!—in the body of a great fiend. Oh, but how wonderful that would have been!"

"What is she babbling about?" Szass Tam demanded.

"Valindra?" Sylora asked calmly, moving over into the distracted lich's field of view and forcing Valindra to look at her. "You meant to place your beloved into the corporeal form of the pit fiend?"

"Heresy!" Jestry shouted, or almost finished shouting, before another black bolt of energy slammed him and threw him some twenty feet away. He sat on the ground, hair dancing again, teeth chattering.

"Another word and I'll eat you," Szass Tam promised.

"Oh, Arklem in such a mighty body!" Valindra clapped her hands together. "I should have brought him to me, along the Hosttower vines, you know. I had to put him into the corporeal form right as the fiend was weakened. But that Jarlaxle! Oh, wretched drow!"

"Sylora?" Szass Tam demanded.

"She intended to somehow free Arklem Greeth from his phylactery, apparently," Sylora explained. "To possess the form of the devil she had summoned."

"Oh! What a warrior he would have been!" Valindra shouted, and she clapped her hands together again. "Any who fled the volcano would have met a darker death indeed!"

Sylora stepped away from her and glanced over at the Dread Ring, expecting Szass Tam to reach out with some unspeakable power to destroy Valindra then and there.

"And oh, what a lover!" Valindra shouted, and Sylora spun back, blinking.

"My love. My love! How I miss my love!" Valindra rolled off into another of her "Ark-lem" choruses.

"We failed in Gauntlgrym because that mad creature desired a pit fiend lover?" Szass Tam groaned.

"Our enemies in the dwarven halls were powerful," Sylora replied.

"Our enemies, and allies of the Netherese?" Szass Tam asked.

"Nay," Sylora was quick to point out. "Allies of the dwarven ghosts, it would seem."

"Why should I not slay you this instant, and destroy this miserable Valindra creature with you?"

"Dahlia!" Sylora answered. "Because it was Dahlia Sin'felle who led our enemies to defend the mines and recapture the primordial. A useless witch, as I feared. Would that we had destroyed her back in Thay!"

"Valindra!" Szass Tam commanded in his magically enhanced voice.

Valindra stood straight and stared directly at the source of the command, her eyes clear, her babbling ended.

"The blame for our failure was yours?" Szass Tam asked.

"I should have warned Sylora." The lich lowered her eyes.

"Don't destroy her, I beg you," Sylora said quietly.

"I am still pondering whether or not I should destroy you," came the growled response.

"And so I owe to you a catastrophe!" Valindra said. "Oh, and a fine one it will be!"

Sylora could still hardly make out the form of Szass Tam, but she was certain the archlich stared dumbfounded at Valindra.

29

Singing to Arklem Greeth yet again, Valindra Shadowmantle disappeared into the skeletal remains of the forest.

"I had hoped you would have taken the city by now," Szass Tam remarked.

"It is fully garrisoned," Sylora replied, "with hardy warriors."

"Make of them soldiers in your zombie army," the archlich ordered, and Sylora nodded and bowed.

"The Dread Ring will lend you power now," Szass Tam explained. "It is strong enough to enchant, to create, to transform."

"I didn't dare take from it, fearing I would subtract from its power," Sylora replied, her gaze still on the ground.

"Then take from it only to facilitate its strengthening," Szass Tam said. "You need the help, it would seem."

Sylora winced, but she tried not to show any further weakness. Szass Tam didn't tolerate weakness.

"Do you live in the forest?"

She nodded. "We have caves. Occasionally a farmhouse."

"How charmingly primitive. Ah, if only you had conquered the city by now. . . ."

Sylora's eyes flashed with threats despite herself.

Szass Tam laughed. "You are one of my favored lieutenants," he said. "And you would live in a cave?" She heard his raspy sigh, and something flew out of the ash ring.

Sylora winced again, thinking it was aimed at her, but the missile, a small branch broken from a blackened tree, landed harmlessly at her feet.

Confused, she looked back at Szass Tam then slowly bent to retrieve the object. As soon as she touched it, the woman couldn't contain a grin, for she could feel a distinct connection to the Dread Ring, and the powers of the strange scepter flashed clearly in her mind: to enchant, to create, to transform.

"Build a fortress!" Szass Tam yelled at her.

"I didn't want—"

"Do not fail me again!" the archlich commanded. "Either of you!"

There came a crackle and a sharp retort, and a bright flash erupted within the Dread Ring.

And he was gone. The Dread Ring settled into the dull pall of ash once more.

Sylora Salm breathed more easily.

"What just happened?" asked a confused Jestry, daring to move back near to Sylora.

"Valindra just saved our lives," she replied.

"Indeed she did," Valindra called, surprising them both. She seemed to slip out of a nearby tree trunk, as two-dimensional as a shadow. She reverted to full form and looked up at the two of them, her eyes clear, her expression lucid. "And now Valindra must create a catastrophe. Oh, what a pleasure that will be!"

Without another word, her expression locked in a wild-eyed and wicked, even gleeful grin, Valindra Shadowmantle glided away yet again.

Sylora swallowed hard.

"Not so crazy," Jestry whispered after a long, long pause. "Or too crazy."

Herzgo Alegni walked tall this morning, more so than in many troubled days. His scouts had returned with the welcome news: The primordial within the ancient dwarven homeland had been put back in its hole, and a host of mighty water elementals swirled around the walls of the entrapping pit. Sylora Salm's plan had failed. There would be no second volcano to feed her Dread Ring. The tremors would not split the earth beneath his feet, and would not drop his ambitions into a deep black pit.

The tiefling stood well over six feet tall, not counting his curving, ramlike horns. He popped up the stiff collar of his weathercloak, showing its satiny red interior. He liked the way that bright red called out his demonic eyes, and matched, too, the blade of the deadly sword he carried in a belt loop on his left hip. He puffed out his massive chest, pulling wider the ties of his unfastened vest to show off his thick muscles. He let his black cloak fall behind his left shoulder and moved out of his tent with a strong, sure stride.

He strolled across the high bluff and stood in the shadows of a wide-spread oak. There he took note of a group of his Shadovar minions. "Where is Barrabus?" he asked. The three looked to each other, unsure, and obviously fearful.

"Go and find him!" Alegni demanded. "Bring him to me!"

The trio fell all over each other trying to scramble away, and as they scattered, they spoke to other Shadovar they passed, who glanced at Alegni before they, too, ran off.

Herzgo Alegni waited until all were out of sight before allowing himself a grin at the spectacle of his power.

In short order, the one man in his command who didn't scramble at his every word strolled up to him. Fully a foot shorter than Alegni, and with few ornaments on his small frame—just a diamond-shaped belt buckle and a seemingly unremarkable sword and dagger on opposite hips—this black-haired, grayish-skinned man somehow didn't seem diminished in the presence of the mighty Netherese tiefling. He stood with one arm cocked so that his forearm rested on the hilt of his sword, the other hanging at his side, his fingers rolling an unbitten green apple, which he occasionally tossed and caught without even glancing at it.

"The scouts have returned from the dwarven halls," Alegni informed him.

"I know. Our enemies have failed."

"You spoke with them?" Herzgo Alegni demanded, his red eyes flashing with rage and disappointment. "They spoke with you?"

"They usually do," he answered anyway.

Barrabus the Gray could barely contain his smile. It pleased him to know that Alegni would severely punish the returned scouts for such a breach of etiquette—perhaps he would even kill a few of them. The thought of a few Shadovar tortured to death didn't trouble Barrabus the Gray. Quite the opposite.

Of course, he hadn't spoken to anyone. Why would he need to, to deduce such a simple riddle as the one before him in the form of the puffed-up Netherese lord? The failure of Sylora's minions was hardly unexpected. He'd seen her enemies, including Drizzt Do'Urden and Bruenor Battlehammer, in Sylora's own scrying pool.

Herzgo Alegni grumbled a few curses. "The moment is upon us," he said. "Our enemy is reeling, and would be more so if you had not failed in the task I commanded."

Barrabus didn't respond, other than to give a graceful bow. Indeed, he had been sent to kill Sylora, and should have done so, and would have done so had not that image in the scrying pool interfered, filling him with such confusion and rekindling such long-buried emotions that he had nearly dropped from the high branch into the midst of Sylora's encampment.

He shook that image away, not daring to get caught up in the implications with an angry Herzgo Alegni so close at hand.

"Perhaps I should send you back to her, to finish the deed," Alegni said.

"The guard, already impenetrable, will no doubt be redoubled."

"Surely that doesn't frighten one as cunning and powerful as Barrabus the Gray," came the sarcastic, and wholly expected, reply.

Barrabus shrugged. "You would rally your charges instead, and assail Sylora's minions full on," he reasoned.

"The thought has occurred to me."

"And to me, and to Sylora as well, no doubt. The sorceress is no fool."

"You do not think it the time to strike?"

"I think that Sylora must strike, and quickly," said Barrabus. "She has lost her catastrophe and needs to create a new one."

Alegni looked at him, curious.

"She serves Szass Tam, or so you've told me," Barrabus explained. "She seeks to complete her Dread Ring. I've heard it whispered that Szass Tam does not accept failure well."

Clearly intrigued, Herzgo Alegni paced to the oak then moved around its thick trunk.

"She'll attack us?" he asked as he came around to face Barrabus once more.

"And if you were in her position?" Barrabus said. "Your Dread Ring demands to be fed. You need carnage on a large scale, and quickly. Would you attack an army awaiting your ranks?"

A grin spread on Alegni's face. "With a city full of men and women so near . . ." he said, catching on. "Sylora will soon go against Neverwinter."

Barrabus shrugged again.

"Go out and confirm it!" Alegni yelled.

Barrabus the Gray smiled and bowed, more than happy to take his leave. He'd barely gone a few steps, though, when he turned back to regard the tiefling.

"You're welcome," Barrabus the Gray remarked.

"I didn't thank you."

"But you know my worth. Your frustration reveals as much. That's thanks enough."

Alegni scoffed at the notion, and scoffed all the more when Barrabus added, "I will have my dagger back, my master, that I might serve you all the better."

A scowl enveloped Alegni's face.

"You'll come to see the wisdom of it," Barrabus promised, and laughed, and turned away.

The small man's mirth faltered as he moved out of Herzgo Alegni's sight. Truly, he hated that tiefling more than he'd ever hated any living or undead being. But Alegni had the sword, so Barrabus could not go against him. That wretched sword, so attuned to him, knowing his every move before he made it. That vile artifact, so easily dominating him, so easily destroying him if it, or its wielder, so chose.

Were it simply a matter of dying, Barrabus would have forced Alegni's hand long ago and gladly gone to his elusive "reward." The sword, now known simply as Claw, would do more than merely kill him, he knew. It would obliterate him and enslave the fragments of his soul for eternity. It would feed upon his life force, and only grow stronger because of the kill.

Or it would kill him and resurrect him, so that it could torment him yet again.

Yes, Barrabus hated Alegni, and hated the red-bladed sword, and hated most of all his helplessness, his servitude. Only once before in the many decades of his life had Barrabus the Gray known such a feeling of helplessness: in Menzoberranzan, the city of the drow. Upon his escape from that dark place, he swore that he would never again serve in such a manner.

The blade they called Claw and the Netherese lords who claimed the sword as their own had ripped that vow from him along with his freedom.

"For now," Barrabus the Gray promised himself as he wandered through Neverwinter Wood.

He thought of his dagger, a weapon that had been his trademark for most of his life, a weapon that had wrought fear in the hearts of sturdy warriors and other assassins from Calimport to Luskan and everywhere in between. He knew Alegni would never give it back to him—even though he held Claw, Herzgo Alegni was wary of Barrabus the Gray, and wouldn't lend him any assistance in the form of such formidable magic. Still, he entertained the thought of the great struggle should he ever retrieve that blade. He would use it to draw out Alegni's life force even as Claw diminished his own. He would be the stronger, he believed, and even if they both died in the battle, it would be an end Barrabus the Gray would consider most fitting.

"For now," Barrabus said again.

"Sylora doesn't know I have this," Valindra Shadowmantle whispered, giggling.

She held up the fist-sized gemstone, shaped as a skull. The fires of her undead existence flared in her eyes and reflected in the hollowed orbs of the gemstone.

"I took it from her," Valindra explained, apparently to herself, and she giggled all the more.

The skull was her phylactery, her soul's escape from the frailties of her withering mortal coil. Should Valindra's body be destroyed, there she would reside until another body could be found.

But this particular gem was much more than that. It was an ancient artifact, one of a pair, and served as a great conduit of magical power. Arklem Greeth—Valindra's beloved Greeth!—resided in the other, though Valindra knew not where the sister gemstone and Greeth might be.

She had tried to discern that location—that was why she'd dared steal this artifact from Sylora in the first place. She'd looked into the phylactery and her vision had gone forth from there, in the fugue between the lands of the living and the dead, seeking Greeth, but had found someone else instead, a powerful undead spirit, recently disembodied. Fast had that spirit flown, away from this plane of existence, to its just reward or punishment, but faster had Valindra, through the gemstone, reached out to grab the terrified spirit and offer it a home, an anchor, a phylactery.

"Come forth, friend," Valindra bade, and she rubbed the skull gem. "Come, I have need of you. I know, I know—Greeth, Greeth!—that you cannot fly free of the gemstone for long, but long enough, I think!"

Nothing happened.

"Come forth, or I'll come in there to find you," the lich warned, her voice suddenly grim.

The eye sockets of the skull gem flared with red fires and a cold wind blew forth from its skeletal mouth.

The spirit shimmered in the air in front of Valindra, a pitiful thing, terrified and full of rage—helpless rage, for it was just an immaterial ghost, a malevolent, impotent whisper of anger.

"Korvin Dor'crae!" Valindra cackled with glee. "Oh, you must help me!"

Why would I? the disembodied vampire spoke in Valindra's thoughts.

"Because if you do, I'll grant you more of the skull gem's powers," Valindra teased. "And you can use it to possess another, to steal a body and give form to your . . . energy."

The vampire's ghost didn't respond in words, but Valindra felt his eagerness, his desperation. She understood that Dor'crae had seen his just reward, and he would do anything, apparently, to avoid that ultimate fate.

"You are my eyes on the wind," Valindra explained. "Szass Tam demands of me a cataclysm, and so I must deliver one. Seek out Gauntlgrym once more and return to me with word of the primordial."

It is a long way. I haven't much time.

"You travel as the wind," Valindra said with a laugh. "Go! And return! And then you will seek out more. I must know more! Greeth! Greeth! Oh, but I was a bad girl! There is slaughter to be done, so much! I must know more of those around so that I can arrange the cataclysm, and you are my eyes."

She stopped abruptly and looked curiously at the skull gem. Valindra glanced all around. It took her a few moments to realize that Dor'crae had already gone.

Good, she thought.

"What does it mean?" Jestry asked Sylora privately, less than a tenday removed from their encounter with Szass Tam. A group of Ashmadai stood nearby, engaged in their own conversations about the mission.

"Valindra seeks to please Szass Tam, and we will allow her to find her way to do so."

"Why would you trust that mad lich?" Jestry replied, shaking his head with every word and obviously disgusted at even mentioning Valindra Shadowmantle.

"You have forgotten our visit with Szass Tam?" came the sarcastic reply.

"No, but—"

"And that Valindra deflected his ire from us, and to herself?"

"You believe she did that for *our* benefit?" Jestry asked.

Sylora wore a puzzled expression, as if the answer should be obvious.

"I think Valindra is simply insane," Jestry replied.

Sylora seemed for a moment as if she were about to lay him low with a shock of lightning, or some other powerful spell.

Jestry swallowed hard. He realized he was being quite forward. Dare he speak to her in such a manner?

But she quickly relaxed and nodded. Jestry sighed. Sylora must value him as an honest advisor to allow him to speak his mind.

"She has no idea of the danger involved in admitting such a failure to the archlich." He couldn't help but raise his voice for just a moment before catching himself and going back to a whisper. "She was rambling, hardly coherent of her own admission of failure."

"No," Sylora said flatly. "You underestimate Valindra Shadowmantle at your own peril."

"Underestimate? I'm terrified of the creature!" Again his voice rose, and a few Ashmadai glanced his way before wisely turning back to their own conversation.

"You underestimate the power of her mind," Sylora explained. "She survived the unwitting conversion to lichdom and the Spellplague, and that's no small thing. I've spoken with her at length about her early days after the fall of Arklem Greeth. Yes, she was quite insane, but a drow psionicist helped pull her cogent reasoning back to the fore."

"She babbles, she sings, she is . . . inappropriate," Jestry argued.

"She allows the insanity to spill forth. She releases it, and copes with it, and follows it up with reminders of reality. She saved us from Szass Tam, consciously so."

"Why?" he asked.

"Because she knows she's not yet ready to command the Ashmadai of Neverwinter Wood, nor is she capable of bringing the Dread Ring to fruition. Valindra needs me, or she will disappoint Szass Tam far more than did the failure in Gauntlgrym."

"And when she needs you no more?"

"I will be pleased to accept my victory for Szass Tam and return to Thay, leaving Valindra as Szass Tam's commander on the Sword Coast."

"They will destroy you," Jestry insisted, but Sylora shook her head and wore an expression of complete confidence.

"I've spoken to Valindra at length," she repeated with gravity. "And I've studied the history of Valindra Shadowmantle, once a mistress in the fabled Hosttower of the Arcane. She was accomplished in life, and she will become even more powerful in undeath, as her mind heals."

Jestry stepped back and looked Sylora over carefully. "You see her as a conduit to your own immortality," he said suddenly, then he gasped, obviously fearing he'd gone too far.

But Sylora grinned. "You are but twenty years old and I near middle age," the sorceress explained. "You'll one day understand. Now, go." She pointed to the path, which seemed a tunnel through the dark trees lining its sides, branches intertwined so tightly that even the light of the full moon failed to penetrate.

"You're going to perform the summoning of the devils," Jestry said. "I would wish to witness the glory of your call to the Nine Hells."

"No summoning tonight," Sylora assured him. With a knowing smirk, Sylora glanced to her side and nodded as the lich Valindra came drifting out of the shadows, the Scepter of Asmodeus in hand.

"Through some magic I don't know—perhaps with the scepter's ties to the Nine Hells, perhaps with the skull gem I allowed her to take from my tent—Valindra has sensed something unusual on the outskirts of Neverwinter," Sylora announced to Jestry and to the group of Ashmadai standing ready in front of the tree tunnel. "You will escort her as she demands. You will do anything that she demands!" Her voice rose powerfully as she finished, the threat all too clear. Her wide eyes scrutinized each and every member of the party.

"But not you," she whispered to Jestry out of the corner of her mouth. "You are my eyes and ears and nothing more, whatever Valindra demands. Of you, I ask only that you return to me with a full recounting of the night's events." She turned to face him as she stepped back, putting him between her and the other Ashmadai. "I would not have my lover slain by a lich, to be raised horrid and cold and useless to my needs."

Jestry could hardly draw breath. Her lover? Could it be? Was she at last offering him that which he had most desired since the day Szass Tam had put the Ashmadai war party under her command?

Sylora glanced back at him only once. "Don't disappoint me," she whispered in a throaty voice. "We will know great glory here, you and I. And great pleasure."

She crossed paths with Valindra then, the lich drifting past her and tittering quietly, muttering something the distracted Jestry could not discern—not that he was paying her any heed in any case. He just stood there as Valindra floated past him as well, telling him to "Greeth Greeth, move along!"

But he couldn't tear his eyes off the spectacle that was Sylora Salm. The high, stiff collar of her black gown perfectly framed her hairless head, her smooth and creamy skin glistening in the moonlight. That head struck Jestry as the perfect orb, held on the pedestal of that collar, and so entranced was he that it took him many heartbeats to allow his eyes to rove down the curving, shapely form, to the high slit in the back of the dress, and there he stared once more, his heart stopping then leaping at each flash of white skin, catching the moonlight with every alluring step.

Her lover, she'd teased.

Her lover.

He had to succeed, had to survive through this dangerous night. Jestry took a deep breath and steadied himself, finding the control required of an Ashmadai. He even managed to tear his eyes away from the departing Sylora, to spin around . . . and to realize that Valindra and the others had already started away.

He began to sprint, but barely took a step before he found himself glancing back yet again toward the woman he so desired.

But she was not to be seen, having melted into the night.

Jestry Rallevin reminded himself of who he was, and of the danger ever-present around him—danger to him and to his beloved Sylora Salm. They had faced Szass Tam and had barely escaped the archlich's murderous wrath.

They had to start winning. Sylora needed the carnage to feed her Dread Ring. Jestry had to make it happen for her.

For them.

He ran down the dark tree tunnel toward the distant torchlight.

Sylora Salm was glad to be alone, at last. She brought forth the strange scepter of black wood from a fold in her cloak and held it up in front of her glistening eyes.

She could feel the energy in it, vibrating with power. This was a conduit to the Dread Ring, a dark scepter for a dark queen.

She glanced back at the cave complex she and her Ashmadai called home and an image came to her. Just to the left of the opening, up behind the front rocks of the cave, sat a small skeleton of a tree, just a single, twisted trunk with a single broken branch pointing forward, looking out like a sentry beside the cave entrance.

Sylora climbed the stones to stand beside the dead tree. She tapped the wooden scepter against the dark trunk and gasped as a blast of energy flowed through her. Her fingers tingled and a burst of ash came forth from her scepter, spraying the dead tree, covering it in blackness.

The ground shuddered violently and to the other side of the small hill, a boulder broke away and tumbled down.

Sylora looked around, not understanding.

The ground shuddered again, and on the other side of the small hill, another boulder broke away and tumbled down.

Sylora looked around, not understanding.

The ground shook again. The skeletal tree began to grow.

The sorceress backed away, nearly tripping and falling to the ground.

The tree widened, and with a great grinding sound, it climbed upward, ten feet, twenty, thirty. The hill grumbled in protest and stones tumbled. There came a cry from inside the cave, and an Ashmadai man stumbled out of the entrance, coughing and covered in dirt.

"Lady Sylora!" he cried.

She stood in front of a tower of ash, a tower that very much resembled a dead, skeletal tree. High above the clearing, beneath what had once been a broken tree branch, an opening had formed in the tower, creating a covered balcony.

The Ashmadai called to her again, but Sylora paid him no heed. She backed down the hillside, her gaze never leaving the ash tree tower. In her hand, the scepter called for more.

So Sylora, giddy with power, complied. She walked out some fifty paces from the cave opening and drew a line in the earth with the tip of her scepter, her conduit to the eager magic of the Dread Ring. By the time she completed the first half of her semicircle, moving to the side of the rocky hill, the initial points of her scratching bubbled with lava as the Dread Ring reached deep into the ground, bringing forth the residual power of the decade-old cataclysm.

She left a ten-foot gap before marking the second half of her creation, and by the time she was done with that curving line, the first wall had begun to erupt from the ground. Molten stone roiled and fell over itself as the wall climbed higher, to ten feet and more.

Sylora giggled like a child at play, and laughed all the more when the zealot called to her again, begging explanation.

His answer came gradually as Sylora Salm completed the wall, building a narrow channel moving out from the gap, turning boulders into smaller structures and two dead trees into smaller guard towers overlooking the wall.

Other zealots arrived from the nearby forest, all looking on with wide eyes, some falling to their knees to offer prayers to their devil god, others rushing in to see Sylora and to ask the same questions.

But she gave them no explanation and merely disappeared into the cave opening.

A few moments later, she reappeared, higher up in the tower, standing in the opening of the broken branch, her balcony.

"My lady?" the first of the Ashmadai inquired again.

There was reverence in his voice. There was awe showing clearly in all of their upturned faces.

42

Sylora liked that.

"Behold Ashenglade," she said to them, a name that had just popped into her thoughts. "Finish it!"

She disappeared back into the tower and the zealots looked around in confusion.

"Double gates for the entryway!" one offered.

"And a roof!" said another, and so they went to work.

Inside the treelike tower, complete with three stories and a circling stairway, Sylora Salm reclined and listened to them going about their tasks. For a decade, the sorceress had lived in the forest or in the caves or in one or another abandoned house.

Now she understood—Szass Tam had made it clear to her. Since she had come to Neverwinter Wood, more than a decade ago, she had treated her time there as a step to something else, something grander. That had been her mistake. Now the Dread Ring had shown her the error of her ways, had forced her to take ownership of the mission, of the place, and soon, of Neverwinter itself.

CHAPTER 2

BECAUSE HE HAD TO KNOW

DRIZZT AND DAHLIA FOLLOWED THE COASTAL ROAD NORTH OF Port Llast. Andahar's steady gait moved them swiftly toward Luskan, his speed and endurance doubling the pace of a normal mount even though he carried two riders. With less than a day left in their journey, Drizzt surprised Dahlia by veering the unicorn from the road, turning west along a side trail.

Dahlia slapped him on the shoulder and offered him a quizzical look when he glanced back.

"I prefer a different gate," the drow explained.

"Different? They are the same, all three," the elf protested.

"I was in the city only recently. The guards—"

"Are never the same, and could be at any of the gates in any case," said Dahlia. "You have not been in Luskan in tendays, and likely all the ships in her harbor are changed, and thus, most of the guards serving the high captains have rotated ship to dock and dock to ship. What matter then, which gate?"

Drizzt didn't answer, other than to hunch a bit forward and urge Andahar on more swiftly.

Dahlia started to argue once more, but when she looked ahead and saw the rolling farmland, she reconsidered. Given their encounter south of Port Llast, and given what she knew of Drizzt Do'Urden, she could guess why he felt compelled to probe inland, the farmlands, before entering the city.

Even from afar, it was obvious that most of the fields were overgrown with high weeds and grasses. A few trees had even taken root.

Saplings showed in many places, and one field sported a small copse that had obviously been growing for decades.

As Drizzt and Dahlia crested on a high rise, they came in sight of a rickety farmhouse and barn, and at last saw some cultivated land, but it covered far less than a single acre. It seemed more of a garden than a farm.

Drizzt held Andahar there for a bit, surveying the spreading lands below for some time. He kicked the unicorn into a slow trot, veering to follow the remains of a broken post fence.

"Look," Dahlia said, pointing past him, beyond the tall grasses and near the garden to a pair of children. At the same time, the children spotted the riders and split away from each other, fleeing with all speed into the heavy grass. A third child, younger still, came into view near the barn only briefly before crawling into the darkness underneath the low entry porch.

"Not warm to visitors," Drizzt remarked.

"Can you blame them?" Dahlia replied. "I'm sure that most who come this way are the goodly sort who would help with the harvesting, if not the planting," she added sarcastically.

Drizzt kept Andahar moving at a slow and unthreatening pace. With a thought imparted to the magical unicorn, he bade the steed to enact the magic of the bell-lined barding, and each subsequent stride filled the air with the tinkling of sweet music.

"You think to tease them out with a happy song?" Dahlia asked.

Drizzt veered the unicorn through a break in the weathered fence, then cut a straight line toward the dilapidated porch of the farmhouse. On a couple of occasions, both riders noticed movement to the side—the sudden shift of grass and once, the brief glimpse of a mop-haired young boy.

But the drow didn't react to any of it. He just kept his mount walking steadily, kept the bells ringing their song, and kept his eyes straight ahead.

At the base of the porch, he dismounted and casually tossed Andahar's reins back over the unicorn's strong neck. He offered his hand to Dahlia, but she fell away from him, rolling backward off Andahar to back flip to her feet on the other side of the steed.

"Of course," the drow whispered, and lowered his hand. He paused and looked all around, noting some movement in the grass not so far away, and ending with his gaze locked on the eyes of the child under the barn's entryway. He offered a quick smile before turning and walking up the porch steps. He pulled off his black leather glove and knocked on the door.

"They won't answer, even if anyone is at home," Dahlia remarked, coming up beside him. "If anyone even lives here, I mean."

"The garden is meager, but it is tended," Drizzt replied. "And there are animals." He pointed to the side of the barn, to a chicken coop, where a few scraggly chickens walked around, pecking at the dirt.

"Someone might live in a nearby house and come here to reap," Dahlia said. "Safely watching from a distant point when strangers come knocking."

"Leaving their children to the whims of those strangers?"

Dahlia shrugged. Desperate people were capable of many things, she knew from long and bitter experience, even regarding the safety of their children.

The elf closed her eyes and fought the memory. She stood atop that cliff again, that long-ago time, a baby in her arms . . .

"There's no answer to your call," she said, a sudden urgency in her tone. "Let us be gone."

In response, Drizzt pushed open the door and walked into the farmhouse.

It was a fairly large home, with several rooms and even a staircase leading up to a loft. It had once been a decent abode for the floors were not dirt, but made of wide oak planks, which squeaked when he walked into the entryway. A half-burned log lay in the hearth and a metal pot sat on the counter across from a small table. Truly the place had fallen into disrepair, but someone lived there.

"Well met," he called softly, walking in farther and moving from doorway to doorway. "We're travelers from the south, and no enemies of the good farmer folk of Luskan."

No response.

"Let us be gone," Dahlia said, but Drizzt held up his hand and cocked his head. Dahlia followed Drizzt into a side room. The creaking floor surely betrayed them, but once in that room, the couple waited and listened.

They heard the slightest hushed intake of breath, as if a youngster fought hard to not scream out in terror.

Drizzt moved suddenly, bending low and pulling aside the meager bedding, no more than hay and a blanket. He brushed the floor quickly, studying the creases and lines in the wood, then wedged his fingers in one crack and pulled open a secret hatch.

Then he stood, even more suddenly, leaning back as a trigger clicked and a crossbow bolt rose up from the hole, only narrowly missing his chin before finding a hold in the ceiling above him. Without the slightest hesitation, Drizzt rolled forward, reaching down to snatch the feeble crossbow from the hands of its wielder, then to grab the boy as well, by the collar. With frightening suddenness and speed, the drow plucked both from the hole and set the dirty child down on the floor in front of him.

"Quick to shoot," he scolded.

The boy, no more than ten or eleven years of age, stared wide-eyed at the exotic drow, his jaw hanging open, in awe of the intruder's white mithral shirt, the unicorn necklace pendant lying against Drizzt's neck, at the pommels of his fabulous weapons, one gem-encrusted black adamantine fashioned into the likeness of a hunting cat's head and maw, the other with a single star-cut blue sapphire set into its silver. Even wider went his eyes when he looked at the drow's elf companion, with her exotic hair and that mesmerizing woad. He gasped and had Drizzt not been quick to guide him aside, he would have fallen back into the hole.

"Don't hurt him!" came a shout from the crawl space, a woman's voice. "Oh, please, good sir . . . err, good *elf* sir, don't you hurt my boy!"

"Now why would I do that, good woman?" Drizzt calmly replied.

"Because it's all she knows, you naïve fool," Dahlia said from behind. She stepped past Drizzt and offered her hand to the woman, and to another child, a girl. The older woman hesitated and the young girl shied away.

"Take my hand and come out or I'll fill your hole with hay and toss in a torch," Dahlia warned.

Drizzt wasn't sure if Dahlia was bluffing. For an instant, he thought to shove Dahlia aside and reassure the woman in the crawl space, but he didn't act at all. For not the first time, and surely not the last, Drizzt found himself perplexed and strangely intrigued by his new companion.

Whether bluff or honest threat, Dahlia's words worked, and with surprising strength, she tugged the woman from the crawl space.

The woman wasn't as old as she appeared, with her scraggly, thinning hair, tired eyes, and weathered skin. It occurred to Drizzt that she might be quite attractive, had she been among the aristocracy of Waterdeep or some other city. Life, not age, had taken the luster of her youth, for she was likely but a few years past thirty.

"Are those other children outside yours as well?" Dahlia asked, little tenderness in her voice.

The woman looked at her with suspicion.

"We are not here to harm you or your children, nor to rob you of anything, I promise," said Drizzt. "In fact, quite the opposite." He started to reach for a small pouch on his belt, but Dahlia intercepted him with her hand and when he looked at her, she scowled and shook her head.

Drizzt didn't understand, but he could tell from Dahlia's expression that she wasn't preventing his charity out of any selfish reasons, so he held back.

"Your husband is . . . ?" Dahlia asked.

The woman snorted and looked away, giving a quick shake of her head. She didn't have to say any more for Drizzt and Dahlia to understand that he was long gone, murdered likely.

"Five children," Dahlia said with a mocking tone. She reached for the woman's hand and lifted it, turning it as she went so that Drizzt could clearly see the deep calluses, broken fingernails, and seemingly-permanent dirt stains.

Clearly embarrassed, the woman pulled her hand back. Dahlia laughed, shook her head, and walked back to the farm's rickety door.

"I hope some of your children are old enough to help you around here," Drizzt said, trying to put forth a better face. He flashed a stern scowl at Dahlia. She smirked.

"We get by," the woman replied. She squared her shoulders and took a deep breath. "What do you want?"

"Nothing," Drizzt answered. "We saw the garden, and were—"

"So you want my food, then? You'd take it from the mouths of children?"

"No, no," Drizzt assured her. "We . . . *I* was surprised to see that someone was living here, nothing more. We're traveling to Luskan, and I was curious as to the state of the farms."

"Farms," the woman snorted. "There are no farms."

"Do you know a man, a farmer, named Stuyles?" Dahlia asked from the doorway.

"I knew someone named Stuyles. A few of them."

"Oh, and pray tell us what has happened to them."

Drizzt shot Dahlia another angry glance. He turned back just in time to see the woman shrug. "Those that could go, went," she answered. "Some to sail with the pirates, no doubt. Some to their graves at the end of a blade, no doubt. Some to other lands, for good or ill."

"And how many have stayed?" Dahlia asked. "How many like you, living off the land, hoping your garden isn't raided by highwaymen or soldiers—or goblinkin or wild animals—so you go to sleep without your belly growling too loudly?"

The woman, embarrassed, looked away and didn't answer.

"Leave them," Dahlia said to Drizzt. "We've leagues to travel and I grow bored with this nonsense."

Drizzt didn't know where to turn. He felt more completely at a loss than he had for a long, long time. The world, even around the always wild Luskan, had devolved to such a miserable state. It shook the core beliefs and optimism that had guided him for more than a century.

And there seemed nothing he could do about it, and that was the most troubling and terrifying reality of all.

As he stood there in contemplation, Dahlia grabbed him roughly by the hand and tugged him toward the door. As they exited, the woman shouted after them, "Don't you steal my melons!"

"If we did, there would be nothing you could do about it," Dahlia snapped back.

Outside, though, Dahlia didn't go for the garden, but straight to Andahar, offering only a cursory glance at the three children hiding—badly—nearby, gawking at the sight of the magnificent unicorn.

"Did you have to speak to her in such a manner?" Drizzt asked, climbing up on Andahar's strong back.

"I was speaking to you," Dahlia retorted. "I care nothing for her."

"Perhaps that's your problem," said Drizzt.

"More likely it's your folly," said Dahlia.

They rode away from the farm and down the road in silence after that, and Drizzt even stopped the magical bells from singing their sweet song, for it seemed out of place there, as if the music would lend neither hope nor joy, but would instead simply mock the broken country.

More farms came into view around every bend, and none were in better repair than the one they'd just left. Most of the farmhouses and barns were simply burned-out shells, and more than one settlement within a sea of overgrown and ruined fields showed nothing more than a few charred beams and the stones of a lonely, abandoned hearth.

"Farmer Stuyles's home, I wonder?" Dahlia teased at one such ruin.

Drizzt ignored her. On one level, he was angry with Dahlia, but on another level he was worried she was right. He couldn't find any logic with which to argue against her unstoppable cynicism. All of that, of course, led him back to farmer Stuyles and the band of "highwaymen." Could he deny their justifications? The obvious truth lay bare before him now: With the fall of any pretense of civilization in Luskan, the surrounding farmlands, neglected by any organized militia, fell victim to bandits and even to minions of the new powers of the City of Sails. Everything those men and women had worked to build, everything their parents and grandparents for many generations had built, had been stolen away. The idea that they could simply pack up and relocate in the now-wild realms of Faerûn seemed preposterous.

So what were they to do? Depend on the magnanimity of the high captains of Luskan? The emissaries of Bregan D'aerthe? The Lords of Waterdeep?

Was it a crime for a hungry man to steal food, a freezing man to steal clothing, in a world where a destitute man had no recourse to law?

Drizzt was glad that he hadn't exacted punishment on Stuyles and his band, and every former farm they passed reinforced his decision. But that truth did little to dent the pain such a bleak reality presented to the idealistic, optimistic dark elf.

At long last, the walls of Luskan came into view. Drizzt pulled Andahar up and slipped off the side of the unicorn. As soon as Dahlia did likewise, he dismissed the steed, who thundered away, each stride diminishing him by half until he was no more.

"Why did you stop me?" Drizzt asked.

Dahlia looked at him, perplexed, and he tapped his pouch.

"You thought to save the farmer woman with a few gold coins," Dahlia said.

"Help her, not save her."

"Damn her, you mean."

"What do you mean?"

"What might any merchants have thought when a peasant farmer woman or one of her filthy children showed up at market bearing gold?" Dahlia asked.

"I could have given them silver, or copper even," the drow argued.

"Even so, were she to possess coins, then all the thieves of the land would decide she was worth robbing. This land is filled with thieves, and worse. Are you so blinded by your eternal faith in goodness that you cannot even see that simple truth?"

"You're my instructor, then?"

"When you need it," Dahlia quipped.

"And my guardian, my guide to salvation?"

"Hardly that! In truth, given the nature of my lessons, I might be quite the opposite. A demon come to show you the path to . . . entertainment."

Drizzt shook his head and started walking down the road to Luskan, showing little amusement at Dahlia's barbs.

"If you had wanted to help her, you might have hunted a rabbit or a deer for her table," the elf woman said. "Or simply gathered some firewood."

"And you knew that and said nothing back at the farm, when we might have done some good."

"You confuse me with someone who cares."

Drizzt spun back on her, and seemed on the edge of an explosion.

"Drizzt Do'Urden, saving the world one peasant at a time." Dahlia spat on the road at Drizzt's feet, then stood back easily, staff in hand as if inviting him to attack her.

But Drizzt was too buried in the confusion of the day and the shadows of the world. With a helpless snort, he started off again toward the City of Sails. Dahlia caught up to him in but a few strides.

"We'll find a way, our way," she said.

"To help?"

"To entertain ourselves at least. And consider, when Sylora Salm's skull cracks beneath the weight of my staff, the world will be a brighter and better place." She started to grin, but Drizzt shook his head.

"The light will come earlier," he promised. "For Sylora will already be dead by my blades by the time you strike."

"A challenge?"

Now the drow did manage a smile.

"I do so love a challenge, and beware, for I never lose," said Dahlia.

"Even if you have to kill me first to ensure your personal victory, I expect."

"Keep thinking that way," Dahlia played along. "I welcome doubt."

CHAPTER 3

CHERRY PIE

VALINDRA STOOD ACROSS A CLEARING FROM A SMALL HOUSE ON the southern reaches of Neverwinter. The glow from a hearth within whispered warmth against the chill of night, but seemed a solitary thing indeed this far from the returning population of the old city.

"In there?" Jestry asked skeptically. "The one you seek? Alone?"

A deathly cold breeze blew by them, and Valindra's smile widened as she nodded. "Why would she not be?"

"She?" Jestry hugged his strong arms tight to ward off the chill. The path to the cottage could hardly be called a road, and there were no other houses within at least several hundred yards of the place. Neverwinter Wood was in the midst of a war, of course, and the roads were full of bandits—many of the folk who'd come to rebuild Neverwinter were less than respectable. Why would anyone live out there alone? How could anyone *survive* out there alone?

"Sylora Salm values you," Valindra remarked, catching the Ashmadai warrior off guard. "I know not why. You seem . . . dull."

Jestry scowled at her, but quickly reminded himself that he was dealing with a lich, and one considered quite insane.

"So do—Greeth! Greeth!—come in with me to meet my new friend," Valindra said.

Jestry blinked and fell back. Her wild incantation in the middle of the sentence threw him off guard, but he thought he detected a bit of a curl to Valindra's lips. Had she shrieked intentionally to disturb him? That was the thing about Valindra: how could he know?

"I'll send others and coordinate the sentries," Jestry replied.

"You will come in with me," Valindra corrected. "Alive or dead."

Jestry felt that cold breeze again and he sensed a hunger there.

"I know of one who would covet your lifeless body," Valindra teased, and Jestry's eyes widened. It took all of his willpower to stop him from letting out a scream.

"Easy," Valindra said, but she wasn't talking to Jestry. She didn't seem to be talking to anyone! "Even if I kill him, you cannot have him. Not yet."

"What do you mean?" Jestry demanded.

"Alive or dead?" Valindra teased.

Behind them, the other Ashmadai shifted uncomfortably, and Jestry glanced back for support. But Valindra held the scepter of Asmodeus. Sylora had named her the mission's leader, and Jestry understood all too clearly that if he tried to disobey the lich, his "friends" would carry out her orders against him, even kill him if she asked.

"You alone," Valindra said, nodding to herself.

Jestry called back to his fellow Ashmadai. "Guard the path, and all around." They acted as if they looked upon a doomed man.

Without another word, Valindra glided toward the small cottage, the scepter extended in front of her. Jestry caught up with her just before the porch steps. The front door opened.

"May I help you, O wanderers in the dark of night?" she said as she appeared in the doorway, her form framed by the glow of the fire within. Her voice had a sweetness, an innocence that seemed so very out of place in that dangerous land.

"That is the only question I ever consider," Valindra replied.

Jestry thought to glance at the lich, but found he couldn't take his eyes off the woman standing in front of him. She wasn't beautiful, really, though certainly not unattractive, with a slight frame, an open, round face, and curly hair that shone red even in the dim light. A strange sensation came over Jestry just standing there looking at her, just hearing the innocence and warmth in her voice, just in seeing the playful bounce of her thick hair. He thought of cherry pie.

Cherry pie on a comfortably cool autumn night, with the wind blowing off the lake and his mother and two sisters sitting beside him. He thought of the twin girls at either end of the line pulling on one end or the other of the quilt, which was just slightly too short for the job of covering them all.

He shook his head to compose himself, but the woman then said, "Do come in. I wasn't expecting visitors at this late hour, but I've some fine stew still warm in the cauldron."

Jestry found himself back again in that memory, staring across the lake in the hopes that he would be the first to spot the torchlight signaling his father's return from the hunt.

Valindra was almost through the door before the warrior even realized she was moving. He nodded to the red-haired woman and entered the comfortable cottage. As he moved to the hearth, he kept glancing back at her.

Her face and smile were open and warm. There was nothing about her that Jestry would call sexy—certainly she possessed not a single feature that Sylora Salm didn't possess in a more classically beautiful manner. But somehow, all together, it . . . worked.

"And what have I given the goodly gods to be graced with such visitors on a dark night?" She closed the door and motioned for Valindra and Jestry to sit in the chairs in front of the hearth while she went to retrieve a third chair for herself.

It all seemed so perfectly normal and natural: a man and a woman travel a road and find respite in a warm house along the way.

Valindra took her seat and held forth her scepter as the woman came over. The woman paused at the sight of that distinctive item.

Valindra smiled.

The woman grinned.

And then it hit Jestry: Valindra was obviously an undead creature. Half her skin was rotted away! The white of bone peeked out from one wrist and even on one of her emaciated cheeks. There was no way this woman, this innocent and gentle creature, couldn't see that. And yet, she showed no discomfort at all.

Jestry glanced around, searching for an escape.

"My name is Arunika," the woman said.

"Valindra," the lich replied.

"And he?"

"No one worth mentioning," Valindra assured her.

Jestry glanced from the lich to Arunika and saw on her kind face that she didn't share Valindra's assessment. He suddenly found himself feeling much more comfortable.

"Why have you come?" Arunika asked.

"In friendship," Valindra replied. "And you would rather have us as friends!" she shrieked suddenly, and began chirping "Arklem! Ark-lem!" every few beats.

Arunika seemed more amused than frightened. She sat back in her chair and looked at Jestry.

"The Spellplague," he quietly mouthed.

"Valindra?" Arunika asked as the lich finally calmed.

"In friendship," Valindra replied as if nothing had happened. "And in kinship."

"I'm not your kin," Arunika insisted.

Valindra flashed a wicked smile and held forth the scepter of Asmodeus.

Arunika nodded, her light eyes sparkling at the sight.

"It was given to Valindra by Sylora Salm of Thay," Jestry dared interject, "who serves Szass Tam."

"And so you are Ashmadai," Arunika replied.

"As are you?" Jestry dared ask. Why, after all, were they here in the home of a simple woman, a comely and nondescript commoner by all appearances?

Arunika's laughter mocked him, but she held out her hand as soon as he began to recoil from it.

"You could say that I am aligned with the Ashmadai, yes," she admitted.

"And who else?" Valindra insisted sharply.

Now Arunika narrowed her bright eyes and scrutinized the lich. "You have come as emissaries of this Sylora Salm?"

"Yes," Jestry answered even as Valindra launched into a birdlike squeal, "Greeth! Greeth!"

"I'm not alone, I assure you," Arunika said then. "I have friends, very powerful friends, nearby."

Valindra hissed and Jestry thought she might attack Arunika then and there. He resisted the urge to spring up to the woman's defense, or to shout out in frustration against Sylora's terrible decision to ever send Valindra on this mission. And why would Sylora have made such a wrong choice? Arunika was no threat. She was a friend, surely, and she didn't need to be confronted by a powerful and insane lich.

"My friends will be sympathetic to your cause against the Netherese," Arunika went on, calming Valindra before her agitation could truly bubble over. "Go and tell that to Sylora Salm. I'll serve as go-between. She knows where to find me."

As she finished, she glanced at Jestry and motioned to the door, clearly bidding him to be gone. He took no offense, but somehow he knew that Arunika wasn't asking him to leave, she was telling him, and in no uncertain terms. He looked at Valindra then stumbled out into the night.

He dared pause at the door for just a moment, to hear Arunika talking softly to Valindra, assuring the lich that her friends would help—and Jestry got the distinct impression that Arunika spoke in personal, and not just general, terms.

Jestry rushed away, afraid of being caught eavesdropping, but he did catch one more word: "sovereignty."

He didn't know what it meant.

A long while passed before Valindra exited the house. From the porch, she directed the Ashmadai, then floated down behind them on their journey back to Sylora's base. She clutched the skull gem and the scepter close to her heart, continually giving thanks to their magical powers. The scepter had sensed Arunika, and the skull gem had given her Dor'crae—and with him, the eyes to locate Arunika.

Arunika had hinted at that which Valindra most dearly wanted to find: a way to be rid of the demons of confusion haunting her mind.

Kimmuriel Oblodra had done much to help her, and he was but a mere drow psionicist. What was that against the power of one of the Sovereignty? If Kimmuriel's powers could keep her from falling over the ledge, surely Arunika's friend could bring her back from the brink.

Simply discussing the trouble with Arunika now allowed Valindra to keep her focus for a long, long time, all the way back to Sylora's encampment.

All of the returning team walked those last strides with their mouths hanging open in awe. Sylora had been quite busy in the hours since they'd gone off to find Arunika. The treelike tower dominated the scene, sitting on the hill beside the cave opening, but that was only one part of the risen fortress. Two walls had been lifted from the ground, with several smaller towers and structures evident within.

It was a small city, created of black stone, and raised from the ground in a matter of hours.

Jestry had no reservations about the sight in front of him. He knew instinctively that it was Sylora's creation. It carried the color, the texture, the smell of the Dread Ring, and was like some of the structures he'd left back in Thay.

As he neared the outer gate, he saw the guards—both Ashmadai and ash zombie servants. Up high and in the distance, he spotted Sylora herself, standing at the tall tower's balcony, which, now that he considered it more closely, looked much like the stub of a broken branch.

"Go on, go on!" Valindra said, coming up past him.

"Sylora," Jestry said, pointing up to the distant sorceress.

"Go on, go on!" Valindra said again, then muttered something along the lines of "how beautiful, how beautiful," though Jestry wasn't sure if she was speaking of the complex, the tower, or Sylora herself. Nor did it matter, he realized, and he shook all thought of the lich's foolish rambling away and hurried to follow her into the compound and to the tower.

The entrance to the tower lay inside the cave, where a short stone stairwell in the side wall went up just a few steps to a black stone door.

The door opened magically for Valindra and Jestry, who entered the ground floor of the tower to find it complete with a stocked hearth, obsidian chairs, and a small table covered in furs and set with utensils.

Jestry and Valindra continued up the sweeping stair along the far wall of the circular room, climbing up above the hearth to another black stone door. He pushed through the door to find another chamber, this one only partially furnished, but clearly intended as Sylora's workshop. The stair continued to wind around the room, going between the outer and an inner wall. The stairs turned here, crossing high above the room, leading to an open trapdoor. The door fed into a low chamber not quite at the third level of the tower, a room that opened out onto the balcony.

Sylora nodded down at the pair through the trapdoor, and motioned for Valindra to go up and join her and for Jestry to follow the other stairwell to the third level, Sylora's private quarters.

"Well done, Lady," Valindra greeted, her tone wistful. "So much like the Hosttower, it seems!"

"That was not my intent," Sylora assured her. She motioned to the scepter. "Did it lead you well?"

"Oh, well!" Valindra exclaimed. "By Greeth . . . Ark-lem! Ark-lem!"

"Do tell," Sylora prompted, and she heaved a great sigh, understanding well the meandering direction Valindra's story would surely take.

It took some time, but Valindra did at last recount Arunika's words. Then, dismissed by Sylora, the lich wandered the ten feet out along the broken branch balcony to the railing. With a mischievous glance back at Sylora, Valindra lifted herself over the railing and leaped out, floating down to the courtyard below.

"And what did you think of our new friend, Arunika?" Sylora asked when Valindra had gone.

Jestry, crouched in a small hollow just above her, was not surprised at the confirmation that Sylora was aware of his presence. The top entrance of the hollow had been left open, after all, presumably so that he could eavesdrop on Sylora's conversation with Valindra.

Jestry pushed aside a black cloth, which appeared as part of the balcony wall, and dropped down beside the sorceress.

"An interesting woman," he said, trying hard to keep the true level of his fascination out of his voice.

Sylora's grin told Jestry that she recognized his true feelings all too well.

"She is not beautiful," Jestry blurted, and thought himself incredibly inane.

"Seduced by a smile and a word," Sylora replied in a mocking tone that showed she was hardly upset. "Young men are such easy prey."

"No, my lady, my love . . ."

"Hold your tongue, Jestry," the sorceress interrupted. "Or I'll tear it out and hold it for you." Despite the threat, and the fact that Sylora certainly could carry through with it, the timbre of her voice once more conveyed that she was more amused, even pitying, than upset. She walked out to the balcony rail. "You're fond of her, then?"

"No, I mean, I did not—"

"Afraid of her?"

"Surely not!" he protested.

"Good, because you might well be in Arunika's company quite a bit in the coming days," Sylora explained. "That's suitable to you?"

"I do as Sylora asks," the Ashmadai obediently replied. "I do not question Sylora Salm."

"Good, because I tell you this now and do not disappoint me in it: When you're with Arunika, you're to do her bidding. If she tells you to kill yourself, do so."

Jestry swallowed hard, but nodded. Such was his duty as an Ashmadai.

"And if she wishes to couple with you, do so," Sylora added.

Jestry swallowed harder, and tried not to nod too eagerly.

"Do you understand?"

"I do . . ." he started to say, but he couldn't quite get past the words and wound up shaking his head and admitting, "No."

Sylora laughed and reached up to gently stroke his face. "My poor, innocent warrior," she said. "Do you fear that such an act with the likes of Arunika would make me jealous?"

Jestry thought he should say no, and thought he should say he feared to do exactly that, and thought he should blurt out that Arunika was nowhere near as beautiful as Sylora, of course, and that he could only truly love Sylora.

He thought a lot of things.

He said nothing.

She danced away from him then, to the edge of the balcony, where she leaped over, her magical cloak transforming her into the likeness of a giant crow, and she glided down to the courtyard on widespread wings.

Jestry found himself drawn to the railing, watching the woman alight, watching her transform again into the woman he had come to adore.

This was not going well. Evidently Barrabus had underestimated the scouting network of the Neverwinter enclave.

"I have friends in the region," Barrabus said.

"Shadovar?" Jelvus Grinch asked.

Barrabus smiled innocently. He knew the question to be rhetorical. "My friends are enemies of the zealots who have infiltrated Neverwinter Wood. Is that not enough for you?"

Around him, the crowd stirred.

"We have reason to believe that these zealots, who facilitated the cataclysm that destroyed this fair city, are now building the most awful of necromantic facilities not far from your intended city. They've raised an army of the dead culled from the bodies of that cataclysm, and will send them to the"—he paused and glanced around at the rebuilding efforts—"inadequate walls you have constructed."

"We're not simple farmers," one woman protested. "All here can raise a weapon and raise it well!"

That brought a cheer from all around, and Jelvus Grinch, widely considered the first citizen of Neverwinter, couldn't help but puff out his chest a bit.

But if Barrabus was impressed, he didn't show it.

"You will be overrun," he stated flatly. "And even if some of you manage to escape, or somehow hold out, those who are killed will return as zombies to battle from the ranks of your enemies."

That stole some of their bluster, to be sure.

"And you offer your services?" Jelvus Grinch said, and Barrabus nodded. "And those of the Shadovar, your kinfolk?"

"I'm no Shadovar."

"But you're allied—"

"For the time, perhaps. That's none of your affair."

"We have no love for the Empire of Netheril!"

"And they care not for you, or for your city," Barrabus answered. "They have no designs here that concern you."

"The Netherese were known prominently in Neverwinter before the cataclysm," Jelvus argued. "Some have said that a Netherese noble dominated the Lord of Neverwinter in the waning days—"

"That was a long time ago."

"And now they don't care?" the woman in the crowd yelled.

"It's only been ten years!" Jelvus Grinch added.

"Have you seen any Netherese within your walls?" asked Barrabus. "Have they made any advances against any of your citizens?"

"Then why are you here?" asked Jelvus. "If your allies have no designs on Neverwinter, then why do they care at all?"

"My allies battle the zealots—you know this. If the zealots overrun Neverwinter"—he turned to speak to all of the gathering—"if you are all slain that you might join the zealots' undead army, then the struggle of the Shadovar in Neverwinter Wood becomes all the more difficult."

"Allies of necessity, then?" Jelvus Grinch reasoned when the murmurs had died away.

Barrabus shrugged noncommittally. "If allies at all," he said, again with little conviction. "I am here to warn you of the possibility of an assault. I offer my services as scout, and my blades in the battle should it come, nothing more, nothing less."

"Can ye fight, then?" one man called from behind.

Barrabus's smile was anything but innocent. It was a look he had perfected as a child in Calimport, an expression of confidence unshakable and unnerving. There was no boast, no answer, because there needed to be none.

Jelvus Grinch surely knew the truth, simply in looking at Barrabus's face.

"I cannot condone an alliance with the Shadovar," he said.

"But you won't discourage it," Barrabus reasoned from his tone. "And I am not Shadovar."

"Your help would be . . . appreciated."

Barrabus nodded and Jelvus broke up the gathering with a call for all to get to work shoring up the meager walls surrounding their rebuilding efforts.

"You really think the undead will come?" Jelvus Grinch quietly asked Barrabus as the pair walked off alone.

"Likely. The zealots attempted a second cataclysm."

Jelvus Grinch stopped walking and sucked in his breath.

"It was foiled and the volcano put back in its place, by all accounts," Barrabus assured him. "I doubt you have to fear another eruption."

Jelvus Grinch looked at him skeptically.

"If I thought differently, would I be here?" Barrabus said, and when that didn't seem to relax Jelvus, Barrabus the Gray added, "I was here for the first explosion, you know."

"When Neverwinter was destroyed?" Jelvus Grinch balked. "There were no survivors."

"There were a few," Barrabus replied. "The lucky, the quick, and the clever—or, more likely, those who were all three."

"You were here? When the ash fell and the lava—"

"When the gray flow rampaged through Neverwinter and to the sea, taking almost everything with it. I was there." He pointed to the Winged Wyvern Bridge. "I watched the river run with molten stone and ash, and bodies. So many bodies."

"I shouldn't believe you," Jelvus Grinch said. "But I find I do."

"I have better things to do than lie to the likes of you over such an unimportant piece of trivia."

Jelvus nodded and bowed.

"There's one more thing," Barrabus said. "There's an elf about, a drow of some renown. His name is Drizzt—"

"Do'Urden," Jelvus finished.

"You know of him," said Barrabus. "You know him personally?"

"He escorted a caravan here some months ago," Jelvus answered. "He and a dwarf—Bonnego Battleaxe of the Adbar Battleaxes. Would that he had stayed in these dark times! And we asked, do not doubt. To have the likes of Drizzt Do'Urden beside us now would serve us greatly should the attack you expect come to pass."

Barrabus nodded and sighed more deeply than he should have. So, the vision he had seen in Sylora's scrying pool had been accurate, and Drizzt Do'Urden was alive and well and in the North.

"What is it?" Jelvus Grinch asked, drawing him from his thoughts. "Do you know of Drizzt?"

"I do. A long time ago . . ." His voice trailed off. "I would ask you, as a favor, as a sign of our budding alliance, that you would inform me if Drizzt is seen anywhere near Neverwinter."

Now Jelvus Grinch looked at him suspiciously, so Barrabus added, "I do loathe most drow elves, and would hate to kill him by mistake."

That seemed to satisfy the man. Barrabus gave a quick salute and went out from Neverwinter's gate to see what he could learn.

CHAPTER 4

TURF WARS

"THAT GUARD RECOGNIZED ME," DAHLIA WHISPERED TO DRIZZT as they moved into Luskan, past the guards at the gate, all of whom continued to stare at the departing elf. One in particular wore an expression that indeed seemed more than simple lust.

"Did he? Or are you not simply a remarkable sight?" Drizzt replied. "Perhaps he recognized me."

"If he had recognized you, it would have been of no consequence, I'm sure," Dahlia said. "I've warned you I'm not welcome in Luskan."

"Yet you did not disguise yourself."

"My troubles here are ten years old."

"Yet you fear being recognized."

"Fear it? Or welcome it?"

"Perhaps you would someday deign to tell me why you expect trouble here in Luskan," Drizzt said. "I'm curious why you're so unwelcome here."

"I killed a high captain," Dahlia admitted, almost flippantly. "Borlann the Crow. Ten years ago, right before I set out with Jarlaxle and Athrogate for the mines of Gauntlgrym, I killed him."

Drizzt couldn't help but smile.

"Would you like to know why I killed him?" she asked.

"Does it matter?"

"Does it matter to you?"

Drizzt shook his head, and though he was a bit taken aback by the level of his disinterest over the reasons and by his instinctive sense of callousness toward anyone who would have taken the mantle of Ship Rethnor, he found he could only smile wider. "If I had my way nearly a century ago, Borlann's father would never have been conceived, and neither he."

"You've had dealings with the House of Rethnor as well, I see."

"Kensidan, Borlann's grandfather, murdered a dear friend of mine when Ship Rethnor and the other high captains seized power in Luskan and condemned the city to the sorry state we see today. I had no choice but to flee, though I dearly wanted to pay Kensidan back for his efforts."

"Then perhaps I've settled your debt to the family of this Kensidan."

"Only if one believes in generational responsibility, and I don't. I know nothing of Borlann."

"He was a high captain," Dahlia answered. "What more is there to know? He dealt death and misery on a daily basis, and often to those undeserving."

"I need no justification from you. Do you need it from me?"

Dahlia spat on the ground.

Drizzt stared after her as she walked to the side of the road, entering an alleyway. She pulled a small coffer from her backpack and flipped open the lid. Drizzt eased just a bit closer, and glanced both ways along the street to make sure no one paid them too much heed. From this angle, he could see the coffer was comprised of multiple compartments, one of which Dahlia had opened. She pinched the powdery ingredients within and snapped her fingers in front of her face, sending the puff of brown powder all around her.

Then she reached into a different section of the coffer and came back with a silvery hair pick. She pulled off her hat and turned her back to Drizzt, bending low and away from him and flipping her black and red braid forward.

When she came back up and turned around, Drizzt sucked in his breath. Dahlia's woad was gone, with not a blemish marring her perfect skin. And her hair, still that remarkable black and red, was fashioned in a completely different cut, short and stylish with a sharp part, hair angling down in front to almost cover her left eye.

She closed the coffer and tucked it into her pack, put her leather hat back on her head, and walked over to Drizzt.

"Do you like it?" she asked, and the attempt at vanity from Dahlia was as jarring to the drow as the abrupt change in her looks. Her entire appearance seemed softer, less aggressive and threatening.

He considered her question, and realized that he had no easy answer. The Dahlia he had known was not unattractive. Her fighting prowess, the danger of her, her ability to convey her hatred of the high captains by spitting on the road—he couldn't help but be intrigued. But this other side—even her posture seemed somehow more feminine to him—reminded him of the warmth he'd once known—more conventional, perhaps, but no less attractive. Perhaps the greatest tease of all was the hint that Dahlia could be tamed.

Or could she?

Would Drizzt even want to?

"I accept your silence as compliment enough," she teased, starting away.

"If you could so easily disguise yourself then why didn't you do it before we entered Luskan?" Drizzt asked.

Dahlia replied with a wicked grin.

"It's not as much fun if it isn't as dangerous," Drizzt answered for her.

"When there's conviction behind your complaining, perhaps then I'll listen more attentively, Drizzt Do'Urden," Dahlia replied. "For now, just accept that I understand the truth of your sentiments and will welcome your blades when trouble finds us."

"You're walking with purpose," Drizzt said, thinking it wise to change the subject. "Pray tell where you're leading me."

"Pray tell me why you brought me here. My course would've been south, to Neverwinter Wood, remember?"

"There are questions I need to answer first."

"To see if Jarlaxle survived," Dahlia replied, catching Drizzt by such surprise that he stopped walking, and had to scramble to catch up.

"It's obvious," she said when he neared. "Your affection for him, I mean."

"He is helpful," was all Drizzt would admit.

"He is dead," Dahlia said. "We both saw him fall, and witnessed the explosive fury of the primordial right behind."

Drizzt wasn't sure of that, of course, since he'd known Jarlaxle as the ultimate survivor of many seemingly impossible escapes, but he could only shrug against Dahlia's assertion.

"I would know, too, of the power of Bregan D'aerthe in Luskan," he said.

"Diminished," Dahlia replied without hesitation. "It had weakened considerably those ten years ago, and it's unlikely the drow have expanded once more in the City of Sails. What's left here for them?"

"That's what I hope to learn."

"You seek Jarlaxle," Dahlia teased, "because you care."

Drizzt didn't deny it.

Dahlia walked past him out into the middle of the street and motioned toward an inn across the way. "Seeing all of those decrepit farms and famished farmers has spurred my appetite," she said without looking back at Drizzt.

The drow stood there watching her back as she walked away from him and toward the inn. She'd made that statement for his benefit, he knew, just to remind him that they were not alike, to remind him that she had an understanding of the world that was different—and greater—than his own.

He kept thinking that Dahlia would glance back toward him when she noticed he wasn't following her.

She didn't.

By the time Drizzt entered the inn, Dahlia was already seated at a table and talking to one of the serving girls. There weren't many patrons in the inn at this early hour, but those who were, mostly male, focused on the exotic Dahlia. Even when Drizzt entered, he garnered no more than a quick glance from any of the men.

Dahlia waved the serving girl away as Drizzt approached.

"Did you think, perhaps, that I would wish a meal as well?" Drizzt asked.

Dahlia laughed at him. "I expected your sympathies for the poor farmer folk would force your belly to grumble for days to come. So that you might properly sob for them, I mean."

"Why would you say such a thing?"

Dahlia laughed again and looked away.

Drizzt heaved a sigh and started to stand, thinking he'd go to the bar and buy a meal, but before he'd even stepped away from his chair, the serving girl returned, bearing two bowls of steaming stew.

Dahlia motioned for him to sit, her expression conciliatory, and at last more serious.

"It troubled you to see those farms," she said a few moments later, the bowls of stew in front of them, Drizzt stirring his with his spoon.

"What would you have me say?"

"I would have you admit the truth."

Drizzt looked up and stared at her. "I've always known Luskan to be a city of ruffians. I've always found many of the customs here, such as the Prisoner's Carnival, distasteful, and I realized when Captain Deudermont fell that Luskan would know even darker times. But yes, it pains me to see it. To see the helplessness of the commoners trapped in plays of power and a reality made more harsh by the proliferation of pirates and thugs."

"Is that what pains you?" Dahlia asked, and her tone hinted at some clever insight, which drew Drizzt's gaze once more. "Or is it that you cannot make things right? Is it their helplessness or your own that troubles you so?"

"Do you seek to enlighten me or to taunt me?"

Dahlia laughed and took a bite of stew.

Drizzt did likewise and tried to keep his attention focused on the others in the common room—folks who watched him and Dahlia quite intently. He took note of one woman leaving in a hurry, though she tried to appear casual in her departure, and of another man who slowly walked to the exit and never stopped staring at the pair, particularly Dahlia.

R. A. SALVATORE

By the time they had at last left the inn, midday had long passed and the sun was halfway to the horizon. Once more, Dahlia took up the lead.

"How many eyes are upon us now, I wonder?" Drizzt asked, the first words they had spoken since their pre-meal conversation.

"Us?"

"On you," the drow clarified. "Do you believe it's your beauty that attracts such attention, or your history here?"

While her appearance had changed fairly dramatically with her hairstyle and skin alterations, this was so obviously still Dahlia, the one and only Dahlia. Anyone who had ever met Dahlia, Drizzt knew, would not be fooled by such cosmetic changes, nor would anyone who had ever met Dahlia likely forget her.

"Don't you think I'm beautiful?" Dahlia asked with a fake pout. "I am wounded." She stopped abruptly and offered Drizzt a warm smile. "Don't you like my disguise?"

There was a softness to her now that seemed almost magical. Her hair was more cute than seductive, and her face carried a soft glow and an innocence without the magical woad. Perhaps it was the warm afternoon light, the sun sending a warm glowing line across the waters off the Sword Coast. In that glow, Dahlia seemed unblemished, gentle and warm, through and through. It took all of Drizzt's willpower to refrain from kissing her.

"You invite trouble," he heard himself say.

"I'm disguised to avoid exactly that."

Drizzt shook his head with every word. "You're hardly disguised, and were not at all when we came through Luskan's gate. If you truly wished to avoid trouble, you would've changed your appearance much more profoundly back out there, in the farmlands."

"Am I to spend all of my days in hiding, then?"

"Has Dahlia ever spent a single day in hiding?" Drizzt asked lightheartedly.

Dahlia winced, and Drizzt recognized that he'd hit on some painful memory, yet another unknown facet of this elf.

"Come," she said, and she walked away swiftly.

When Drizzt caught up to her, he found her expression very tight and closed, and so he said no more.

From a far corner of the tavern, two assassins watched the couple depart, one rolling a dagger eagerly in his grimy hands under cover of the table.

"Are ye sure it's her then?" asked a skinny fellow with a face full of black stubble and one eye no more than a dull white orb.

"Aye, Boofie, I saw her come through the gate, I did," answered the dagger-roller, Tolston Rethnor, the same guard who had watched Dahlia enter Luskan's gate earlier in the day.

"Hartouchen's to be paying well for she what killed his father," said Boofie McLaddin, referring to the new high captain of Ship Rethnor, the heir of Borlann the Crow. "But so's his anger to be great if we're starting a fight with them damned drow elves over a mistake."

"It's her, I tell ye," Tolston insisted. "She's even got that staff. I'm not to forget Borlann's lady friend—none who seen Dahlia forget Dahlia!"

"Half the reward, ye say?"

"Aye."

"Well I'm wanting half o' th' other half, too." When Tolston balked, Boofie went on, "Ye thinking just the two of us to fight them then? After what ye been telling me o' Dahlia all the way here? She killed yer uncle to death, hey? And he was the boss, and got there by killing all them what stood afore him, hey? I'm to bring in me boys, a whole bunch and a wizard besides. They'll be wanting their cut."

"They'll be buying Hartouchen's gratitude," said Tolston.

"'That and a finger o' silver'll get me a meal," Boofie replied. "And I ain't thinking much o' the gratitude when me belly's growling. Half and half o' th' other half, or go and kill 'em yerself, Tolston Rethnor, and then hope yer bravery puts ye in line for Hartouchen's seat. More likely, though, I'm thinking yer foolishness will just get yer ripped body buried in the family crypt, and a few might call ye brave, but most'll name ye as stupid."

"Half and half o' th' other half," Tolston agreed. "But get yer crew quick afore others figure out that Dahlia's back in Luskan."

Upon the tavern's staircase, not far from Tolston and Boofie, a small girl—by all appearances a human child—played with a wooden doll and only glanced up as Drizzt and Dahlia left the tavern.

Then she went back to talking to her doll, though her words were aimed more directly at the wizard she knew to be watching her in his crystal ball, and with the high captain of Ship Rethnor beside him, most likely.

Dahlia moved with purpose and kept up her pace across the city. Sometime later, she turned down a side street, her swift strides soon bringing them to an unremarkable two-story building.

"Jarlaxle and Athrogate made their Luskan home on the second floor," she explained. "There's a stair behind the building and a separate entrance there."

She started around the building, but Drizzt hesitated.

"Perhaps we should find the landowner to inquire—"

"If you had rented a house to the likes of Jarlaxle and he was late in returning, would you be quick to throw wide its doors and rent it out to another?" Dahlia interrupted.

It was a good point, Drizzt had to admit, and so he shrugged and followed the elf around the back and up the wooden staircase to a porch and the back door. Dahlia fumbled with it for a bit, obviously seeking any traps the clever drow mercenary might have left in place. Finding nothing, she stepped back and motioned to Drizzt.

"Because there might well be magical traps that you could not detect," he reasoned, and she didn't disavow him of his line of thinking.

Drizzt moved up and gripped the doorknob, then gave a twist—it wasn't locked—and he pushed it open. Daylight spilled into the small apartment, a place of sparse furnishings and even fewer supplies.

"No one has been in here for some time," Drizzt said, glancing around. There was a plate on the table, but it was covered in dust.

"Not since Jarlaxle and Athrogate fell in Gauntlgrym," Dahlia replied. "Could we have expected any differently?"

Drizzt's dark face grew very tight.

"You thought they might somehow have escaped," Dahlia remarked.

"Jarlaxle is known for such things."

"You hoped they had escaped."

"Is that an accusation? What a sorry friend I would be . . ."

"A friend?" Dahlia asked, and she didn't hide her amusement in the least. "Drizzt Do'Urden a friend to Jarlaxle? So at last you admit it! How does that comport with those tenets that guide your life?"

"I've shared many adventures with Jarlaxle," Drizzt replied. "And he has proven to be . . . surprising."

"At the least," Dahlia said, still grinning. "But that's all in the past now. He's dead, as we saw."

"I never argued otherwise."

"Not with me," Dahlia replied.

"Not with anyone."

"Not with Drizzt?" She paused and let that hang in the air for a few moments, clearly enjoying Drizzt's obvious consternation. "You knew we wouldn't find him, despite your hopes to the contrary. You owed your friend that much, at least. But take heart, for coming here has not been totally in vain." She pointed to the plate on the table. "We know now that Bregan D'aerthe's power in Luskan has waned greatly, for surely they would've come here to investigate their missing associate."

"We don't know that they haven't come here. They are excellent at their craft—they might be watching us at this very—"

He stopped and cocked an ear.

Dahlia heard it, too, a slight creak like a footfall on an old wooden stair. She slipped silently toward the door. Drizzt pulled an object from his belt pouch and whispered something she couldn't hear. She crouched at the side of the door and cracked it open then fell back fast.

A spinning hammer hit the door with great force and knocked it open wide.

Dahlia broke her staff into flails and moved to exit, thinking to strike before the next missile could come her way, but she fell back again as something flew at her from behind. Six hundred pounds of angry panther soared past and out the door. She didn't yell out, but her eyes opened wide indeed.

But not as wide as the eyes of the two pirates who had the misfortune of leaping to block the doorway at that very moment.

Guenhwyvar sent them flying with hardly a break in her momentum. She skidded out onto the porch, her claws digging in deeply to slow her slide.

Dahlia went out right behind her. She broke fast to the left, away from the stairs, and straight at one of the pirates Guenhwyvar had sent flying. Half over the railing, the man somehow managed to catch himself and come around with a fairly balanced and powerful swing of his sword.

At the last instant, Dahlia managed to duck under the blow. Inside his reach for the moment, she sent her flails out and around, striking him hard in the ribs from left and right. He grunted but kept fighting, retracting his blade for a second strike, but with a deft snap of her wrist, Dahlia sent her left hand up, smacking the pirate's wrist hard with the handle of her weapon. The man yelped, his arm going out wide, but not too far. The momentum of the strike sent the top pole flipping over the pirate's arm.

Dahlia wasted no time in driving her weapon hand straight down, the cord tethering the poles twisting the pirate's arm as the flail's initial momentum battled the reverse tug.

Dahlia went down into a low crouch. When the flail flipped back hard, freeing the man's sword arm, Dahlia leaped high into the air and spun in a soaring circle kick. Her hard boot crunched against the pirate's jaw, snapping his head back and to the side, and Dahlia didn't disengage, extending her leg farther, driving him back and over the rail.

He tried to grab at her, and when that failed, to slash at her. But it was too late. He dropped the dozen feet to the cobblestones below.

Dahlia landed and spun into a defensive crouch, expecting an attack.

And indeed several came at her, but not from across the porch—not from the porch at all but from the roof. A trio of spears flew down.

Dahlia couldn't see them in time to dodge.

"Guen, the roof!" Drizzt yelled, charging out the door. He leaped in front of Dahlia. Icingdeath slashed up high to clip a pair of the falling spears, with Twinkle following fast to clip the third, barely deflecting it.

The spear thumped down hard into the wooden decking just beside Dahlia, the shaft vibrating from the force of the strike.

Dahlia didn't pause long enough to thank him. She dived into a roll right past Drizzt toward a pair of thugs, her weapons working furiously and seemingly independently to parry and counter their sword thrusts.

Drizzt spied Guenhwyvar leaping to the far railing. The drow winced as he heard the crunch of splintering wood, but the railing held enough for the panther to spring away, easily clearing the edge of the roof.

Drizzt charged out to join Dahlia, but then he saw a motion to his side. He dropped his blades and slipped his bow from his shoulder, drawing and setting an arrow and letting it fly in one fluid movement.

He didn't hit the archer on a balcony across the way, but the man was too busy diving aside to make an honest return shot.

Drizzt let another arrow fly, then heard Dahlia cry out, "Leap aside!"

So he did, trusting her.

A pirate crashed down, slamming into the deck with enough force to splinter a couple of boards. He managed to force himself upright.

But Dahlia slipped away from her two opponents long enough to swipe across with a flail, shattering the poor fool's cheek and jaw.

He dropped face down on the porch.

Drizzt ignored the fallen thug in front of him and drew a bead point blank on one of Dahlia's opponents.

The last slanted rays of daylight shone on the pirate's face, perfectly framing his look of sheer terror.

"Run," Drizzt whispered. The man threw down his sword, turned, and fled.

Drizzt swung back around, letting his arrow fly at the concealed archer on the porch across the way. The missile drove into a large water barrel, punching a clean hole in its nearest side. Drizzt could barely see the opposing archer, just his face behind the bow he held atop the barrel, poised to fire.

The twist of his face, reflecting shock and most of all pain, told Drizzt that his arrow had crossed through the barrel and reached its destination.

The archer was trying to shoot—Drizzt could see that—but he couldn't seem to let go of the bowstring. He grimaced and held his pose for a few heartbeats, then just dropped his head atop his drawn bow, the movement knocking the arrow clear.

Water poured out of the barrel in front of him.

They had to move from the exposed porch, Dahlia thought. And how could Drizzt let one of the thugs escape? She wasn't sure which thought made her more angry.

No matter. She made short work of the other pirate, her spinning weapons eluding his defenses left and right, each turn sending a flail smashing into him. His parries hit nothing but air for quite some time, until the cumulative battering of Dahlia's weapons took its toll at last. The poor fool just slumped to the ground, curling up and half rolling aside, where he lay groaning, apparently unaware of his surroundings.

Dahlia had no time to finish him. She turned and flicked her wrists, reverting her weapons to a pair of short staves, and then joined them into a single eight-foot staff as she neared the front railing. She thrust the staff out in front of her, planted the leading end, and leaped out into the growing twilight.

In the alleyway almost directly across from the battle-scarred porch, Therfus Handydoer watched with amusement. The top-ranking wizard in Ship Rethnor, Therfus had served the last four high captains to don the mantle of the Crow—and to don the magical cape—though the current leader, Hartouchen, didn't possess that particular item.

"Because of you, murderess," Therfus whispered, watching Dahlia flip her flails back into a long staff.

So much trouble, this elf woman, Therfus mused, and he thought of Borlann—he'd liked that high captain the most of all.

"I wonder, dear girl," he whispered, though of course she couldn't hear him, "might Hartouchen reward me more greatly if I can bring him the Cloak of the Crow along with your pretty head?"

Seeing Dahlia moving to the nearest rail and planting her staff, Therfus threw a line of lightning from his hand. Rushing the distance to Dahlia, the bolt took the form of a serpent, and just as she reached the high point of her vault, it struck with the force of thunder.

Drizzt saw Dahlia's leap out of the corner of his eye. He knew her instincts were correct. As Dahlia had finished the last of the pirate brawlers, Drizzt had noted more trouble from afar: archers lining the rooftop of the adjacent building.

"Guen!" the drow yelled. He raised Taulmaril and let fly a series of shocking arrows, sparking as they blew away large pieces of the roof's decorative crest. "Guen!" he yelled again. "To my missiles!"

Up above him, the panther roared, and another archer shrieked in reply.

Drizzt glanced to his left, to the front edge of the porch and the vaulting Dahlia—and took in the lightning serpent.

He started to cry out, but his voice was lost in a great blast that seemed to lift the entire porch before dropping it back in place.

Drizzt stumbled into the wall then tumbled through the doorway into the apartment before his legs gave out under him.

"Dahlia," he whispered, his voice thick with pain.

He watched as she hung in midair atop her upright staff for many heartbeats. Forks of lightning arced out all around her. Slowly she descended to the porch, but she didn't fall. Instead she staggered to her feet, holding and waving her staff as if she couldn't let it go.

Dahlia waved the crackling staff and her hair danced wildly. She growled in defiance and denial, but her voice cracked with jolting energy and, Drizzt knew, with pain.

An arrow shot down and grazed her bare thigh, drawing a line of bright blood. She tried to turn away, but she had little control of her muscles. Jolts of electrical energy continued to arc into the air around her. Another arrow whipped past her, barely missing.

"To me!" Drizzt cried. He fell out the door, leveling Taulmaril as he went and letting a barrage of arrows fly at the adjacent rooftop. "Quickly!"

His grimace lessened a bit when he saw a black form leap from his roof to the archer's nest.

Arrows rose up to meet the flying Guenhwyvar, most missing but one pair struck home. They did little to slow the great cat. She hit the tin roof with a scrabble of raking claws, catching a hold on the slope and charging at the scattering group.

One fleeing archer paused long enough to aim at Dahlia.

Just before his arrow left the bow, though, Drizzt's lightning missile blew him backward, lifting him over the crest of the roof to fall to the cobblestones below.

Therfus Handydoer couldn't see all of the unfolding battle from his angle, but he found the whole thing amusing anyway. He didn't really care if some of the mercenary pirates, or even some of Ship Rethnor's crew, were cut down. They were mere warriors, after all, and none of them very good ones at that.

Still, the fight was going on too long for Therfus's liking. Too long and too loud, and that could only attract unwanted attention.

He meant to end it.

He began another spell, pausing only to wince as one of those devilish lightning arrows blasted into an archer and drove him up and over the crest of the roof.

Shaking his head, Therfus released his magic. At the last moment, he added a little touch of his own, planting a black storm cloud twenty feet in the air above the porch.

Still fighting against the jolts of energy, Dahlia heard hail drum against her leather hat before she felt its pelting sting.

A pellet slammed into her shoulder, tearing her skin so deeply she felt it crack against bone. She forced herself toward Drizzt. He stood in the cover of the doorway, driven back by the hail. Another step brought her closer to him. He reached out for her, holding his arm out despite several painful ice strikes.

Dahlia reached for him, but another jolt of energy sent her suddenly flailing. The slick porch threw her off balance and she crashed hard against the corner of the railing where it met the stairs, and slipped down to her buttocks.

More ice pelted her. She tried to get up, but she kept slipping.

More ice bashed against her.

So Dahlia threw herself down the stairs.

As she bounced and tumbled, she grabbed at the railing to try to slow her descent. At last she spilled out into the cobblestone street in a roll, but thankfully, she'd escaped the ice storm.

With great effort, she forced herself back to her feet and managed to stagger a few steps, though she didn't really know where to go.

And then it didn't matter, for out of every alleyway, the pirates came, brandishing swords and axes and gaff hooks.

Dahlia, still fighting simply to maintain her balance, understood she had no chance of defending herself.

Even if Drizzt reached the edge of the porch then, where the ice storm still raged, he couldn't cut them all down in time.

Even if Guenhwyvar leaped down, in all her roaring fury, by the time the pirates even realized their peril, many would already have finished her.

Dahlia resigned herself to death.

It wasn't supposed to end this way.

Drizzt had barely crossed the threshold in pursuit of Dahlia when the pelting ice drove him back.

With a growl he threw up the hood of his cloak and leaped out once more, but the slick ice sent him sliding to the middle of the porch, unable to turn and get to the stairs.

He yelled for Guenhwyvar. He put up Taulmaril and began launching arrows once more.

A pellet of ice smacked him hard and dropped him to his knees, so he continued to shoot from his knees. He searched for the wizard—if he could just get a shot at the wizard!

He looked up at the adjacent roof for Guenhwyvar. An archer was in view, desperately trying to set an arrow as another form, a woman, came running across the rooftop, brandishing a long knife. She barreled into the archer, her leading arm sweeping aside his bow, her knife striking hard.

Drizzt could have shot her down, but was she an enemy or an ally?

He lowered the bow and threw himself into a slide to the railing overlooking the street, overlooking Dahlia, overlooking the thugs closing in on her.

He could only yell out for her. He lifted his bow and tried to decide which one of these killers he would stop.

And, by default, which of the others he would allow to get to Dahlia.

Therfus Handydoer laughed a bit as he watched the scene unfolding in front of him, the female elf tumbling out into the streets, still staggering foolishly from his lightning serpent.

He knew the drow was trapped in his area of icy punishment. He'd defeated the feared Dahlia and her drow companion so easily! He almost pitied warriors.

Almost, but how might he pity one foolish enough to lift a sword when a spell was so much more powerful?

It occurred to him to finish Dahlia then, to take the kill as his own before the surrounding thugs could close in, and so he began to whisper his next spell.

The tip of a deadly dagger came in tight against his throat.

"This is not your time to kill, son of Ship Rethnor," a quiet voice intoned. "Is it your time to die?"

Therfus's mind whirled. How could he escape this? For a brief moment, his sneering contempt for those who chose the blade over the spell was shaken.

"You would kill the noble second of a high captain?" he asked, hoping his station would save him where his spells obviously could not.

The man behind him snorted.

"Do you not understand that significance?" a suddenly defiant Therfus said with strength returned to his voice. "I am a noble second!"

"As am I."

Therfus managed to turn his gaze down to the dagger, along its silvery blade to the beautifully jeweled and distinctive hilt. Suddenly he understood.

"Beniago of Ship Kurth!" he declared. The recognition of his would-be killer brought as much relief as fear, particularly since he knew the reputation of that deadly dagger.

The knife moved away from his throat and the assassin shoved him a step forward. Therfus wheeled around. "This is no business of Closeguard Isle!"

"Obviously, we disagree."

"You walk on dangerous ground, son of Ship Kurth."

He meant to finish with an imposing point of his long and crooked finger, but as he reached out, the ground jolted with such force that it was all Therfus could do to hold his footing. Even Beniago, so graceful and feline in his movements, lurched forward.

Anger rose up to bury Dahlia's fear—anger that her end would come at the hands of such peasants, anger that she couldn't explore this relationship with a companion who, at long last, might prove worthy of her, anger that Sylora Salm would outlive her.

And anger that Kozah's Needle, her powerful staff, had eaten the lightning serpent and was apparently multiplying its power and dumping that power back into Dahlia in a debilitating way. She wanted to throw the staff aside, but she couldn't begin to release her grip on it.

But there was one thing she could do, she realized.

As her attackers closed in, she drove the end of Kozah's Needle down hard upon the cobblestones and bade the staff to release its energy.

An explosion of lightning lifted her up, the ground itself rolling, turning large stones free of their settings and hurling the pirates into the air.

Drizzt yelled for Dahlia as the porch above her came tumbling down. Dahlia couldn't turn to look. She felt the energy flowing through her, focusing through her staff, releasing into the ground. Like a great exhale, the lightning energy drained her as it departed, so fully consuming her every thought that she was hardly aware of the devastation around her.

When it had all died away, Dahlia stood calmly, a solitary figure, her eyes closed, holding Kozah's Needle upright as it continued to throw the occasional spark.

Eventually, she was able to open her eyes. Some of the pirates crawled, others squirmed, one grasped an ankle he'd painfully turned in his fall.

None of them seemed to hold any further interest in Dahlia, unless it was in getting as far away from her as quickly as possible.

To the side lay the ruined porch, a dark form curled under a pile of splintered wood.

"By the gods," Therfus mumbled, staring dumbfounded below.

"I offer you the chance to flee this place," Beniago said.

"In the name of Kurth?" the wizard snapped back at him.

"In any name you please."

"Do you know who this is?" the wizard spat.

"A mercenary of Bregan D'aerthe, I assume," Beniago replied, and his grin showed that he was well aware that he was taunting Therfus.

"Not him, the female," Therfus stated flatly.

"We know."

"Then you know of Dahlia's history with my Ship. She's a murderess, and Borlann Rethnor her victim!"

Beniago nodded.

"She murdered my friend! My captain!" Therfus said with a growl. "You would deny me this retribution?"

Beniago brandished that terrible jeweled dagger, and given the reputation of both the blade and the assassin holding it, Therfus understood well the depth of that threat. Beniago could stab him before he could begin to defend, physically or magically, and with that blade, it would only take one wound to kill him.

Therfus glanced all around. He heard the black panther and followed the sound of the roar to the roof, where new warriors—men serving Kurth, no doubt—had taken control.

He looked back to Beniago and his knife.

"Closeguard Isle will pay for this outrage," Therfus promised as he took several quick steps away from the assassin. "This is a grave betrayal, I warn!"

Beniago merely shrugged.

Dahlia heard Guenhwyvar land behind her as she charged to the porch rubble. She batted aside one loose board before Drizzt began to pull himself up from the wreckage.

He glanced behind her and suddenly stopped moving.

"Stand easy, Guen," he whispered.

The panther issued a low growl in response.

Dahlia slowly turned around.

A group of men stood in front of her, all holding bows, save one who leveled a wand in Dahlia's direction.

"Keep your cat at bay," the warlock with the wand warned.

"Yes, do," added a tall man in a dark cloak, walking out of the alleyway directly across from the fallen porch. "I am Beniago," he explained with a low bow. "Your presence is requested at Ship Kurth, forthwith."

"And I suppose I would have no choice in the matter?" Drizzt asked.

"It would seem not," Beniago replied.

"Better than Ship Rethnor," Dahlia said to Drizzt.

Drizzt stared at her hard, his scowl placing blame for this turn of events on Dahlia's pretty shoulders. But his anger couldn't withstand Beniago's next remark.

"You're both wanted," he said.

Drizzt studied Beniago carefully. He'd never met this one, but the man's easy posture warned him that he was no novice with the blade. He and Dahlia were certainly and undeniably caught.

Still, Drizzt looked for weakness, for some seam in the leather armor, for some option should the need arise.

His scan ended at the man's belt, at the hilt of that distinctive blade. Memories of a distant past flooded Drizzt's thoughts.

It couldn't be the same blade, the drow told himself.

But the enemy he'd known who had carried such a dagger had likely been in Luskan, with Jarlaxle, perhaps even at the time of his death.

It was possible.

"Forthwith," Beniago repeated, forcefully drawing Drizzt from his contemplation. The drow looked up at the tall man, almost expecting to see an old enemy standing in front of him. But this man was taller, lighter skinned, with curly red hair . . . and a hundred years too young!

Beniago motioned to Drizzt to follow Dahlia, who had moved several steps away. He did so, with a grin on his face.

Perhaps one of the problems of living so long a life, he mused, was the jumble of memories—too many memories!—which inevitably found their way to his consciousness at the slightest provocation. He glanced again at the dagger and laughed at himself, certain now that it was a different blade.

But only because it had to be. The world had moved on.

CHAPTER 5

THE MONSTERS WE KEEP

HADENCOURT PAUSED OUTSIDE OF ASHENGLADE TO ADMIRE ITS construction, and though he knew it had been created magically, it still seemed impossible to him that so much had been built in so short a time. Hadencourt wasn't quite as committed to Szass Tam, and by extension Sylora Salm, as he was to the Ashmadai zealots, but he had to give credit where credit was due.

Ashenglade was not the work of Asmodeus or any other denizen of the Nine Hells. It was the work of the Thayan Dread Ring.

As he approached the gates of the fortress, he faced a phalanx of grim-faced Ashmadai guards and a host of zombie minions, but all he had to do was flash his smile—his real smile and not the façade he wore for the peasant bandits in the north. The resistance melted away, and the gates were thrown wide.

"Dahlia and the drow were heading north, to Luskan, they said," Hadencourt reported when he stood beside Sylora Salm on the second floor of her treelike tower.

"Greeth! Ark-lem!" Valindra shrieked from the corner.

Hadencourt stared at her incredulously.

"Ignore her," Sylora told him.

That was no easy thing to do, though, and Hadencourt's gaze lingered over the lich for some time. Valindra stared back at him with a crooked grin.

"The farther they go from here, the better, though I'd love to burn Dahlia to ashes," Sylora Salm replied to the original point.

Valindra's expression disappeared and she cocked her head as she studied Hadencourt. She'd noted the great deference in Sylora's tone, Hadencourt realized, and that, he deduced, was something rarely heard.

"You may get your opportunity," he replied, turning back to the sorceress. "Dahlia made a point to mention Neverwinter Wood as her intended destination, though her immediate road headed the opposite way. She said there was adventure to be found here. I assume she was referring to you."

"And her companion?"

"Tried to deflect her from revealing their future path."

"He was wary of you?" Sylora asked suspiciously, and she turned around to view the hollowed tree trunk she'd excavated and hauled into the back of the chamber. Years before, Sylora had created of the trunk a scrying pool.

Hadencourt shook his head doubtfully. "He was more reserved than she, I would expect. But then, who isn't?"

Sylora turned back to regard Hadencourt directly, her look as suspicious as her previous question. Hadencourt was a newcomer to Neverwinter Wood, one of the more recent Ashmadai reinforcements. He wouldn't have known Dahlia from his time there, as she was long gone by the time he'd arrived—that was why Sylora had chosen him to serve as a scout on the northern road.

"I know all about Lady Dahlia," Hadencourt admitted.

"Who are you?"

The tall man smiled as he'd done outside, revealing long, pointed teeth. He furrowed his brow and a pair of horns sprouted from his forehead.

"I thought you were Ashmadai," Sylora said, trying to keep her calm façade—no easy task when confronted by a mighty malebranche devil.

"Oh, my lady Sylora, I surely am!" Hadencourt replied. "More devoted than these tieflings and humans, of course. After all, they merely worship Asmodeus, while I witness his glory personally. And let me assure you that he's every bit as impressive as his hordes of worshipers would have you believe."

"Does Szass Tam know of your—?"

"Do you think me foolish enough to try to hide something this important from the archlich?"

"And he sent you here anyway," Sylora remarked.

"Fear not, my lady Sylora," Hadencourt said with a deep bow. "In this endeavor, I am subservient to Sylora Salm. I am no spy, unless it's your spy. Such were my orders from Szass Tam, and I honor them with relish."

Her expression reflected her skepticism.

"Greeth! Greeth!" Valindra chimed in.

Sylora looked past the devil to the lich, and Hadencourt turned as well to regard her—fast enough to see a serious and cogent expression on Valindra's face, albeit briefly, before she tittered and floated away.

Grinning knowingly—the lich wasn't as insane as she let on—Hadencourt faced Sylora once more.

"Were I a demon of the Abyss, you would be correct in your doubts, I expect," Hadencourt said. "But consider my heritage. One does not survive the Nine Hells with subterfuge, but with obedience. I accept my place as your second."

Sylora cocked an eyebrow, drawing a laugh from the devil.

"As your primary scout, then?" Hadencourt bargained. "Surely you will not expect me to submit to the commands of one of these mortal Ashmadai."

"You will remain separate from the warriors here," Sylora agreed.

"Well, then, with your leave, I'll return to my duties on the north road." He bowed again, and seeing Sylora's nod, turned to leave.

"If you wish to truly serve as my second," Sylora remarked, stopping him before he'd gone more than a couple of steps, "you will relieve me of that nuisance Dahlia."

Hadencourt turned a sly eye Sylora's way. "Szass Tam was not as definitive regarding her fate."

"Szass Tam didn't understand the depths of her traitorous ways, then."

They exchanged nods.

"With pleasure, my lady Sylora," Hadencourt the war devil said.

Sylora Salm had enough experience with devils to know he meant it.

"You would deny me this glory?" growled the Ashmadai warrior, Jestry. "I have earned this moment, and you would see me stand back and allow . . ." He paused, blowing his breath out in angry gasps as he considered the huddled, ash-covered zombies scrabbling through the forest all around them, heading for the walls of Neverwinter. They were some of the multitudes who had died in the cataclysm—the great volcanic eruption that had buried Neverwinter a decade before. They seemed more like the corpses of halflings, or human children, for the molten fires had shriveled their forms.

"We will not win this night," Sylora replied. "Not fully, at least. All that we send in will be destroyed."

"I'm not afraid to die!" Jestry proclaimed.

"Are you eager to die, Jestry?"

The Ashmadai warrior went to strict attention. "If in the service of my god Asmodeus—"

"Oh, shut up, fool," Sylora said.

Jestry blinked in astonishment, and he seemed wounded.

"If Asmodeus thought you of more service in his presence, then he would drag you to the Nine Hells personally, and immediately," Sylora teased. "He wants you to fight for him, fearlessly, but not to die for him."

"My lady, an Ashmadai must be willing—"

"Willing and wanting are two different things," Sylora interrupted. "Pray do sort out that difference, Jestry. I expect you to die in service to me, if it's necessary. I don't want you to die in service to me—not yet, at least—and surely I don't want you to want to die in service to anyone else, and if you do then know that there will be ramifications." She matched Jestry's dumbfounded stare with a glower. "If you die, I can raise your corpse," she explained, and motioned to the shriveled zombies moving in the forest night. "When I come to believe that you will be of more service to me as such, I'll kill you myself, I promise you."

Jestry paused for some time before speaking, "Yes, my lady." His gaze went back to the northwest, to the distant torch lights marking the low wall of Neverwinter.

"Come along," Sylora bade him, and she started walking the other way, to the south and deeper into the forest.

"My lady?"

"Be quick."

"But . . . the battle against Neverwinter?"

"The servants of Szass Tam know their mission," Sylora assured him, and she kept walking. Jestry, after another longing look to the distant torchlight, scrambled to catch up.

Valindra Shadowmantle's fiery red eyes gleamed with hunger as the scrabbling zombies passed her by.

She held the magical scepter, and through it willed the zombie legions out of the forest and across the small clearing. They ran on all fours to the distant wall, oblivious to the many arrows reaching out at them.

A fireball lit up the night on the middle of the field, consuming several of the hunched forms, but Valindra, so amused by destruction, could only giggle.

A group comprised of living soldiers ran up beside Valindra, but didn't pass.

"Would you have us attack, Mistress Valindra?" asked an Ashmadai woman, a young and pretty thing who had until only recently been the consort of Jestry.

"Let them play! Let them play!" Valindra shrieked in response, and the group of Ashmadai shrank back against the unexpected anger in her voice. "Ark-lem . . . Ark-lem . . . oh, which way was it? He will help us, he will. Greeth! Greeth! Greeth!"

The Ashmadai woman looked to her companions and rolled her eyes.

Suddenly, Valindra's magic hurled the woman up in the air and onto the field, where she stumbled, but managed to hold her footing.

"To the wall!" Valindra commanded her. "Go and kill them!"

Beside the lich, the group of Ashmadai cheered and started to charge, but Valindra turned on them fiercely and held them back. "Not you!" she ordered, and as one, they stopped short.

Valindra turned back to the young woman. "You," she explained, her voice sinister and thick with vicious amusement.

The woman hesitated and the lich leveled her scepter. Whether out of fear or from the simple reminder of her loyalty to Asmodeus, the warrior woman gave a battle cry and sprinted toward the wall.

Then Valindra waved her scepter and drove on her zombie legions. She nodded repeatedly, happily, as hundreds more swarmed out from the forest. She reached into the scepter, feeling its power, calling on that power to increase, to awaken fully. She held it out in front of her horizontally and closed her eyes, trying to find the tunnel gate to connect this place with the Nine Hells.

She imagined the looks on the faces of those fools in the ruins of Neverwinter when a greater devil, a pit fiend, perhaps, walked into their midst.

The ends of the scepter flared to life. Sylora had told her not to summon forth any denizens of the Nine Hells, but Valindra was too caught up in the moment to remember Sylora's words, or to care.

She spoke the name of a fiend, and ended with a great, ecstatic exhale as she closed her eyes.

When she opened them again, she expected to see a great devil standing in front of her, but alas, there was none. Just the scepter, its ends still shining, but hardly with the power Valindra expected. She closed her eyes and redoubled her efforts, demanding that a devil come forth.

But as she looked more deeply into the magic, Valindra realized that there was no tunnel to be found.

"Sylora," she rasped, for Sylora had been in possession of the scepter earlier that day, and had shown some great control over it. Szass Tam had given it to Sylora Salm, not to Valindra, and Sylora had granted it to Valindra for the journey to the dwarven mines. Was it possible that the sorceress knew some other secrets of the item, some internal locks on some of its powers, perhaps?

Valindra tried one more time to bring forth a devil, but she couldn't—not even a minor manes or some other such fodder creature.

"Clever witch," she whispered, and she cursed Sylora a thousand times under her breath.

From across the way came the shouts, and the field near the wall lit up with fire and lightning as Neverwinter's wizards joined the battle. Before the thunderous retorts ended, however, the screams began. Not shouts of glory or cries of rage, but screams of pain.

Zombies wouldn't cry out in such a manner, of course. And other than the zombies, there was only the one living Ashmadai nearing the battle.

Valindra uttered no more curses at Sylora or anyone else. She basked in the screams, found herself growing more animated by their beautiful pitch. If she'd had a beating heart then surely it would have thumped against her breast at that moment.

She turned to the Ashmadai. "Surround me," she ordered, and she, too, began drifting out to the open field to join in the battle.

"This is the moment of our glory," Jestry continued to complain as he and Sylora traveled swiftly south of Neverwinter.

Sylora Salm had heard enough. She stopped abruptly and whirled on Jestry, her eyes and nostrils flaring. "You are my second—and I hold you there above others who are far more powerful than you and quite envious of you."

"Valindra," Jestry said.

"Not Valindra," said Sylora. "Though she could destroy you with a thought. Nay, there are others about, of whom you do not know and will not know."

The Ashmadai brought his hands to his hips. His pout was just beginning to show when Sylora slapped him across the face.

"You are my second," she said. "Act as such or I'll be rid of you."

"The battle is back there!" Jestry argued. "The moment of our glory—"

"That's a minor skirmish to placate Szass Tam," Sylora shot back.

Jestry's eyes widened. "My lady!"

"Are you afraid to hear the truth? Or can I not trust you? Perhaps I should now fear that you will betray me to Szass Tam?"

"No, my lady, but—"

"Because if you so intend," Sylora went on as if not even hearing him, "then you should consider two things. First, perhaps I'm merely testing your loyalty in speaking so candidly to you, when in truth I'm not speaking candidly at all. And second, you should always be aware that I can kill you—too quickly for even Szass Tam to save you. I can kill you and I can deny you a place at the foot of Asmodeus, do not doubt."

"I am loyal," Jestry weakly replied.

"It doesn't matter, as I'm higher in Asmodeus's regard than a mere zealot," she answered.

"I'm loyal to you," Jestry apologized.

Sylora paused and let it all sink in, nodding for a few moments. "Our attack is merely a feint, Jestry," she explained. "We must pressure the folk who attempt to rebuild Neverwinter, as I wish to see the limits of their powers. Valindra commands less than a fifth of my zombies this night, and only a small number of your Ashmadai. She will not risk herself against the walls of Neverwinter, for that's not her mission. Perhaps some of the citizens will die this night, but we will not take Neverwinter, nor tear down her walls."

"But still, I would be there."

"We'll learn—"

"I would learn!" he insisted. "I'm no novice to battle, personal or grand."

Sylora sighed heavily. "It is naught but a prelude," she said. "For we've now been offered the promise of a greater ally by far, one that might produce the cataclysm Szass Tam and our Dread Ring demands."

He looked at her curiously.

"You were there!" she yelled at him.

"The lady Arunika?"

"Lady," Sylora echoed with a knowing little laugh. "Ah, my young zealot, you have so much to learn."

"Do we go to her now?" he asked eagerly. "We can't be far from her cottage."

Sylora grinned, and Jestry stiffened.

"Intrigued?" Sylora asked.

"No," he blurted. "It's just—"

Sylora laughed and started away.

Soon enough, they arrived at Arunika's front porch. The red-haired woman greeted them warmly and invited them in. Never once did she take her impish gaze off Jestry.

He couldn't return the look. Everything about Arunika seemed right to him. He wanted to bury his face in her curly hair. As he passed her by, her scent filled his nostrils, and he could almost imagine a springtime forest on a warm and sunny day following a gentle morning rain.

"Lady Valindra has told you of your, of our, potential ally?" Arunika asked, motioning for the two to take seats. Conveniently—though out of coincidence, magical prescience, or a prearrangement, Jestry couldn't know—the woman had set out three chairs that night, two facing one. Arunika took the single chair, opposite Jestry and Sylora.

"I'm intrigued," Sylora replied. "Such creatures as you described to Valindra are known to me, of course, though I've never dealt with one personally."

"Nor should you," Arunika replied, and Sylora nodded as if she'd already come to the same conclusion.

Jestry had to work hard to keep up with the conversation, for he kept getting distracted by the mere presence of Arunika, by that springtime smell and her thick, curly red locks. Her allure was something unexpected. At one point, he looked from her to Sylora, and by every standard—her height, her form, her jawline, her nose, her penetrating eyes—Sylora had to be considered far more striking. Jestry had already declared his love for her, and none of that had changed, surely.

But Jestry found that he couldn't look at Sylora for more than a few heartbeats with Arunika sitting so near. He turned back to face the redhead, and found her staring back at him, a curious grin on her pretty face.

Arunika knew something, apparently, that he didn't. He tried to break her stare with a look of consternation as she became more intent, but she only grinned more widely.

He felt a bit of panic welling inside him. He looked to Sylora, but found that she wore the same expression as Arunika.

"What . . ." he started to ask as he turned back to Arunika, just as she stood up from her chair.

The rest of the words caught in Jestry's mouth as Arunika stepped right up in front of him and reached out with one hand to gently stroke his thick black hair.

He wanted to say something, but couldn't.

She kept stroking his hair, her other hand working the ties on her plain dress. She loosened it and brought her arms down by her side just long enough to let the dress drop from her shoulders and fall to the floor.

She stood there naked and unashamed, and the incongruity of her actions, of her forwardness, as compared to the quiet temperament she'd shown to this point had Jestry in a near panic.

Not for long, though. He glanced again at Sylora, who smiled and nodded, and turned back to regard Arunika. He could barely keep his eyes open as she again stroked his black hair, her delicate touch sending shivers throughout his body.

She bent down to kiss him and he couldn't resist, and when he tried to press more passionately, she teasingly drifted back from him, and when he tried to stand to pursue, she used but one small hand to easily hold him in place.

Jestry didn't fully comprehend this strange strength. Nor did he notice the small horns that had sprouted on the woman's forehead. Even when her batlike leathery wings suddenly opened wide as she moved down atop him, Jestry took no notice, for it didn't really matter at that point.

He was lost and he didn't want to be found.

Barrabus the Gray watched the approaching zombies with a mixture of anticipation and disgust. He'd seen these creatures many times in his battles with the ridiculous zealots, and remained thoroughly horrified by the undead things.

But he itched for battle, a true battle, chaotic and frenzied, where he could lose himself, where he could forget his plight.

All around him on Neverwinter's wall, men and woman rushed to and fro, calling out orders, organizing their defenses. Archers let fly, which Barrabus considered a waste of time and resources, since those puncturing missiles seemed to have minimal effect on the ashen zombies. More effective were the few wizards, filling the field with fire, lightning serpents, and pelting ice storms.

Barrabus couldn't help but chuckle as he watched a group of zombies rushing across a patch of ground that had just been iced over. The scrabbling creatures flailed suddenly and spun every which way.

"Kill them when they mass at the base of the wall!" cried one of the guard commanders, standing beside Barrabus.

"You won't find the opportunity," Barrabus corrected him.

The man looked at him curiously.

"They'll not pause for a wall," Barrabus explained. "Not these creatures."

"What nonsense are you spouting?" the commander said, staring down at Barrabus with contempt, as if the man had challenged him directly.

Out of the corner of his eye, Barrabus saw a zombie rush up to the base of the wall and climb it so easily that a casual observer might have been shocked to even realize that the plane in front of the running creature had turned vertical. The assassin thought to warn the commander, perhaps even to spring over and push the man out of the way.

But he didn't bother.

The zombie came over the wall in a rush, leaping onto the proud guard commander's back before he could even swing around. Together they tumbled into the courtyard, the zombie raking at the commander all the way to the ground.

Another zombie was right behind the first over the wall, this one leaping for Barrabus.

The assassin's sword flashed, taking off the zombie's hand. His dagger pierced the chin of the creature as it slammed in to bite at him. With barely a twist, not a hint of wasted motion, Barrabus deflected the skewered creature just enough so that it flew past him instead of taking him with it from the parapet.

As soon as the creature had been turned aside, Barrabus paid it not another thought, for, judging by the panicked cries of city defenders, other zombies were pouring over the wall. Barrabus rushed down to the left, wading into a struggle between a pair of zombies and one overmatched guard. A heavy chop of his sword removed the nearest zombie's arm. As it tried to turn, he bulled through it, heaving it into the second zombie. It tried to grab at him, but he swiftly took off its second hand with another sword chop.

Barrabus went into a frenzy, sword and dagger working in fluid, circling motions, battering and stabbing and chopping at the pair of zombies, quickly reducing them to piles of gore on the parapet.

Another undead monster came to the top of the wall, right beside him, and tried to leap on him. But Barrabus the Gray was too quick for that. He dropped to his knees and ducked.

The creature flew right over him and into a guard who had fool-ishly moved beside Barrabus to battle against the other two zombies. Zombie and guard tumbled from the parapet. Barrabus could only grimace that his victory wouldn't be clean, that his rescue of the guard wasn't quite complete. Other city defenders rushed over to the fallen man and quickly dispatched the zombie. The fallen guard would live, at least, and that was more than he might have expected if Barrabus hadn't intervened.

Barrabus took pride in that, and the feeling surprised him. He wasn't the compassionate type and rarely if ever cared about the fate of another.

As his gaze moved back to growing brawl in the courtyard, with zombies and Neverwinter fighters scrambling all around, he shook his head.

He didn't dare climb down to fight beside the settlers. Their techniques were too sloppy and too unpredictable, and his own need for precision and coordination with those around him would likely get him killed among that crowd.

So Barrabus turned the other way, to the field and the forest and the incoming hordes. With a shrug and a grin, he hopped over the wall.

An arrow had painfully grazed her shoulder, but that was the least of the Ashmadai woman's problems. She managed to arrive at Neverwinter's wall, but while the ash zombies simply climbed it with ease, she could not.

She ran up and down the barrier, looking for some handhold to help her scale it. Neverwinter's defenders didn't seem to notice her, for the zombies continued to pour up there for the fight.

In short order, the Ashmadai looked behind her with more concern than when she looked at the wall in front of her. Valindra was there, coming out of the forest with the other zealots. Valindra would see her helplessly, foolishly, running up and down the wall like a mouse lost in a maze.

Desperate, she ran on faster, until she found her salvation in the form of a small man.

He landed from the twelve-foot fall in a beautifully executed sidelong roll. As a group of zombies rushed at him, he rolled over a second time and up he came to his feet, his weapons working with sudden ferocity—so sudden that the hungry zombies hadn't even the time to lift their emaciated limbs to defend themselves.

The Ashmadai assured herself that she wasn't impressed, and she charged.

At another point in Neverwinter Wood, to the north of the battle-field, Herzgo Alegni and his Shadovar forces watched with interest.

Many wanted to charge into the fight, particularly when the Ashmadai came onto the field.

But Alegni held them back.

"Let the folk of Neverwinter know pain and loss," he explained to those nearby. "The later we arrive to rescue them, the more the settlers will appreciate us."

"The undead easily breached their wall," a nearby Shadovar remarked. "Many of Neverwinter's defenders will die."

"They are expendable," Alegni assured him. "More will come to replace them, and those who do will find the Shadovar among the settlers—Shadovar declared as heroes of Neverwinter."

"Perhaps we can greet them on the Herzgo Alegni Bridge?" another Shadovar remarked.

Alegni turned to the woman and nodded.

He hoped for that very thing.

Barrabus rolled and rolled again, taking all the shock from his fall and moving far enough from the pursuing zombies to set his feet properly under him to defend. He came up tall in front of the scrab-bling creatures. His sword drove them back with long cuts while his dagger stabbed hard into any who tried to come in behind that sword.

He was surrounded, but that meant nothing to the agile warrior. He spun left to right, his sword slashing and stabbing, and at one point, he even tossed the blade up a bit and caught it with a reversed grip. He turned his wrist then stabbed behind his back to skewer a leaping zombie behind him.

Again he turned, yanking the sword hilt up high so he could bend back in under it, tearing it free of zombie flesh. He flipped it again, caught it with a normal grip and circled it over his head before slashing it across another zombie, shoulder to hip. The weight of the blow stopped the charging creature cold. It crouched as the blade tore down across its chest. Then the zombie bounced once, to the side, before falling away.

Barrabus couldn't savor the kill, for he stood alone out there and so many zombies sensed him, smelled his living flesh, and came at him without fear.

But he kept moving. He kept swinging. He kept killing.

He couldn't think, and that was the joy. He couldn't think of Alegni or the Empire of Netheril, or Drizzt Do'Urden, or who he'd once been or what he'd now become.

He just existed, simply survived, in the ecstasy of battle, lost on the precipice of death itself. His muscles worked in perfect harmony, honed in the practice of a century. Every strike came at the last possible moment, barely quick enough because of the growing enemies around him.

Eventually, even he wouldn't be quick enough and his enemies would get through to him.

To tear at him. To bite at him. To kill him?

Could they?

Barrabus the Gray was doubly cursed. The years did not diminish him, but he hated his existence.

He couldn't kill himself, for that sword, Claw, was inside of his mind and wouldn't allow it. He'd tried—oh, how he'd tried!—in the early years of his indenture to the Netherese, in his service to Herzgo Alegni, but to no avail. He'd even built a contraption that would drop him on his knife to end his life, but it had failed because he had not properly secured the weapon—because that sword, Claw, had deceived him.

Nor did it even matter when, indeed, he had been killed. For that awful sword and the mighty Netherese had not allowed him to easily escape through death. Even as he drew his last breath, his life was renewed, resurrected, by the awful, unrelenting devil sword.

And so Barrabus the Gray was left with battle, wild and ferocious battle, and he believed that this was how he would eventually meet his end. Perhaps one time, the sword would grow bored enough with him to simply let him go.

Would it be this day?

Did he want it to be this day?

The question seemed ridiculous as he surveyed his work: a handful of destroyed zombies and several more flipping absurdly around on the ground, limbs missing or maimed so badly they couldn't support the creature or answer its crazed call.

Perhaps the curse was his own cowardice, Barrabus thought. Perhaps he couldn't kill himself or even let himself be killed, or even truly put himself in an inescapably deadly position because somewhere deep inside of his heart and soul, his continual declarations that he wanted to die were all a lie. For if he were slain over and over again, if he proved useless in battle, would Alegni not let him go?

Another enemy neared, and at the last moment, Barrabus looked into her eyes—living eyes and not those of a wretched zombie.

Surely Barrabus, who had been battling Ashmadai zealots for so long, recognized the intensity in those eyes, and he knew to take this foe seriously. She came at him with a high stab of her weapon, one of those familiar red-flecked staff-spears almost all of the Ashmadai employed. As Barrabus moved his sword up horizontally to parry, the woman retracted and dropped her spear lower. Sliding her hands along its length, she spun a full circuit and clubbed at him with the scepter's thicker end.

Barrabus expected the move. He'd seen this high-feint, low-club maneuver from every Ashmadai who had initiated battle against him, and none but the initial attempt had ever gotten near to hitting him. Even as his sword started its ascent, Barrabus quietly repositioned his feet, and as soon as the woman began her true move, the assassin charged ahead.

She hadn't even come all the way around when he slammed into her, and in her twisted position, she couldn't begin to hold her balance against his bull rush. She tumbled, and he simply leaped over her, ignoring her attempts to swipe at him with her weapon. He landed standing above her head and facing her.

She recognized the danger and she thrashed, trying to turn at least sidelong to the man. But Barrabus paced her easily, staying above her head, where any swings or stabs she might try had little effect.

He stared into her eyes. Perhaps it was because they looked so different from the soulless zombies' eyes, but for some reason, Barrabus didn't slip his sword past her pathetic defenses and finish her.

She almost clipped his shin with a swing of her scepter but he dropped his leg back in time to avoid it, then kicked out, his boot meeting the club where she gripped it. The Ashmadai howled in pain and the staff-spear went flying.

"Yield!" Barrabus poked his sword tip just below the hollow of her throat. He couldn't believe the word as it left his lips.

"Never!" she hissed. She grabbed the blade of his fine weapon and blood erupted from her hand.

Barrabus retracted fast—against her pull. His disgust for these zealots heightened in that moment, but still, he didn't stab down hard to put an end to her.

He sensed a zombie approaching his back and reversed his grip on his sword, thrusting it out behind him and scoring a solid hit in the creature's gut. He bent down and held his sword firmly, arcing the blade above him. It flew over him, crashing into the zealot as she tried to get away.

Another pair of zombies rushed at Barrabus. He darted forward, sword and dagger thrusting and flashing out to either side, clearing a path so he could rush right between the undead pair. He turned to the left and chopped one to the ground.

His dagger hand worked independently, snapping back and forth to fend off the second zombie's slapping hands. Step by step, Barrabus fell back, and the hungry beast came on. Suddenly Barrabus stepped forward and drove his dagger straight into the zombie's eye, all the way to the hilt.

How the creature thrashed! But Barrabus just left the dagger in place and stepped back. Another stubborn enemy was coming his way.

The female Ashmadai hadn't even bothered to collect her fallen staff-spear. She just came at him with her fists.

Barrabus tossed his sword up into the air, and the woman couldn't help but let her gaze drift up with it.

When she looked back at Barrabus, she saw only his fist, closing fast. Her nose shattered under the weight of the blow and blood gushed from both nostrils. But she held her footing.

Barrabus ducked her grasp and rolled under her arm. She stumbled forward, and sliding beside her, Barrabus captured her in a head lock. He knew how to kill quickly with such a choke, and knew how to shorten it to incapacitate.

The woman struggled for just a few heartbeats before she fell limp in his grasp. He meant to let her fall unconscious to the ground in front of him, but another zombie came in at him, so he threw her at it. He dived out the other way, into a roll, and retrieved his sword.

He came up and reversed his momentum, charging right back in, slashing at the zombie once as it extricated itself from the Ashmadai.

Barrabus's dagger still stuck deep into its eye, the other zombie came at him, too, ignorant of his flashing sword and flailing wildly.

Then flailing without hands.

Then without an arm.

Then its head flew free, spinning up into the air.

Barrabus caught the head as it fell, by his own dagger hilt still deep in the eye, and a flick of his wrist sent the gruesome thing spinning away.

He had both of his weapons again and the immediate threats had been eradicated, but Barrabus knew he was in trouble.

Across the field came the more formidable foes, a host of Ashmadai, and the lich he'd seen beside Sylora Salm herself, the lich he knew to be beyond his power.

He glanced back at the city wall and the distant gate. From inside, the sounds of battle echoed loudly. The defenders had hardly put this first assault down.

Barrabus the Gray had nowhere to run.

A streak of blue-white lightning erupted from Valindra's scepter and sped for Neverwinter. Its glow reflected on the terrified faces of a pair of archers for just a flicker before it struck in a great explosion, blowing the men off the city wall.

The lich wanted to fly up into the air, to get up over that wall and rain death on those inside. She hated them, viscerally. They were alive and she was not, and how she wanted to count them among the ranks of her undead army.

But then Valindra remembered Arunika's words, and the promise of emotional control. This was one of the tests she and Arunika had discussed, where the hunger of lichdom and prudent caution crossed swords.

Still she found herself drifting toward the wall.

She remembered Sylora's orders for her: She would use her army to test defenses and soften up the enemy until Arunika's new allies could be brought in and exploited.

Still she couldn't stop herself.

But then she saw some fighting at the base of the wall. Zombies scrambled to get at some unseen foe. The Ashmadai she'd sent ahead to die, stubbornly still alive, was going in as well. Other Ashmadai began shouting about the enemy on the field, naming him as the Netherese champion.

Before Valindra could even tell them to catch and kill the champion, the furious zealots had taken the task upon themselves. They stretched their line far down to Valindra's left and began approaching, the ends of the line curling ahead to seal off any escape by the infamous Barrabus the Gray.

Valindra turned her attention back to the enemy champion and his battle. The Ashmadai woman was down, many zombies lay scattered around him, and now he saw his coming doom.

He would run for the wall, the lich knew, and perhaps someone there would drop him a rope . . .

Hardly thinking, Valindra reached out with her scepter and a burst of red lights spun across the field. As the last of the missiles flew away, the lich conjured a storm cloud and began pelting Barrabus and the ground around him with ice.

She watched with a satisfied grin as he pulled his cloak tight and hunched low, futilely racing for the wall.

The Ashmadai warriors closed fast from behind.

But then came shouts from the farthest edge of the line, far to Valindra's left: "Shadovar! Netheril is come!"

To the Ashmadai, no battle cry could sound more encouraging. As one, they forgot their enemies in Neverwinter and turned instead to meet the newest force on the field.

Valindra glanced that way, then at the crawling enemy she'd pummeled, then to the city walls and the continuing fracas within.

"It is him!" an Ashmadai tiefling warrior cried. He pointed to the far end of the line, to the battle with the Netherese.

A large form towered over one of her minions, his huge sword shining red even in the dark of night.

"The Netherese Lord, my lady!" the nearest Ashmadai reported. "The leader of our enemies!"

"A great victory awaits us!" another cried, and charged at the distant form.

Valindra studied the fight and it took only a few moments to understand they couldn't win. Most of her zombies were inside the city walls, and her Ashmadai force didn't nearly match up to this approaching enemy. Even worse, the Netherese lord was out in his full glory, his every swing with his large red-bladed sword cutting those nearest zealots apart. The strength of his blows overwhelmed any defenses, swatting scepters aside and driving through skin and bone with ease, and he left a line of severed bodies in his bloody wake.

The lich hissed and turned her attention one last time to the enemy now moving to the base of the wall, the warrior her minions had named the Netherese champion. At least in this, she would claim victory.

She thrust out her scepter and loosed another lightning serpent. Then Valindra, acting so much more like the living, clever Valindra Shadowmantle, Overwizard of the Hosttower of the Arcane, turned and fled the field.

The energy of the missiles took his breath away and nearly knocked Barrabus from his feet as he scrambled for the city wall. All around him, the Ashmadai closed in, and he knew he needed to either find an easy way to climb the wall, as unlikely as that might be, or have someone up there assist him. Judging from the sounds of battle behind the wall, that seemed even more unlikely.

Then came the storm, balls of ice battering him, the ground growing slick beneath his feet. He held his footing but he could barely walk.

He turned to consider his dilemma, to stand and fight, perhaps.

Sounds of battle to his right brought him hope that Herzgo Alegni had at last entered the field, but before he could savor that hope, Barrabus saw the lightning serpent flying across the field.

He flipped over sideways and landed right back on his feet, his hair dancing wildly, but just dodging the magic's stinging bite.

And then the first of his pursuers came in at him. One slipped to his back before he even got close. Another held her footing and slid toward him on the slick grass. She held out her scepter to parry Barrabus's swinging sword.

Barrabus neatly sidestepped and the sword went high above her. In the same movement, he reached his dagger hand through the opening at the crook of the woman's left elbow. She tried to bring her scepter into position for an offensive strike. But as her hand went behind her, he brought it up hard and swung it back over. He turned sidelong to the woman and over she went, unable to resist the throw.

She landed on her feet and even managed to turn enough in mid-air so that she almost faced him. But it did her little good. Barrabus's dagger arm stabbed out, driving the blade deep into her chest.

At the same time, Barrabus aimed his sword down at the second attacker. The sword slipped into the Ashmadai's gut, angled to slice through his diaphragm and into his lungs.

Barrabus didn't pause long enough to consider whether he'd finished either of those opponents. He leaped away in another sidelong somersault, his black cloak flying wide to obscure his form. He landed on slick grass. He leaped again in the same direction then a third time in rapid succession, until finally, he found solid footing.

Another pair of Ashmadai rushed at him, jabbing their weapons, just as the woman he'd stabbed climbed back to her feet and came at him. With a disgusted look, Barrabus brought his sword down and around in front of him, and on the upswing, tossed it into the air so that his hand could grasp and activate his belt buckle dagger.

He flicked his wrist, launching the knife, and caught his sword so fluidly that neither of the two battling him even realized that he'd tossed the sword free of his hand, let alone thrown a knife.

Until the blade stuck deep into the woman's throat. She crumbled to her knees but kept crawling, praying to her beloved arch-devil with every movement.

Barrabus, heavily engaged with the other pair, didn't find her zealotry admirable or amusing. Just stupid.

He worked his new opponents into just the right angle. When the crawling zealot reached him, he simply shifted his foot and half-turned, dropping a heavy sword chop on the back of her head.

She fell to the ground as surely as if a large rock had fallen on her from on high, and Barrabus went back to stabbing and parrying and slashing at the other two.

The woman groaned, pulled herself back to all fours, and started crawling again.

One of the zealots battling Barrabus cried out in ecstasy, "Asmodeus!"

He should have concentrated on Barrabus instead, for his distraction gave the agile assassin all the opening he needed. He darted in between the pair, turned, and shoved out, sending the fool stumbling to the side and right over the crawling woman's back.

He brought his arms back in close, one elbow driving back to hit the other opponent under the ribs, lifting him up on his toes. Barrabus dropped to one knee as the man lurched forward. He brought his dagger hand up over the man's head, driving him down.

Barrabus hopped back to his feet and stabbed his sword into the hollow of the man's throat. Behind the crawling woman, the other Ashmadai tried to spring up, but Barrabus's dagger flew toward him and stuck in his chest, sending him back to the ground, gasping.

The woman stubbornly came at him again. On her knees, head lifted to face the assassin, she cried out, "Asmode—!"

Before she could finish the word, Barrabus decapitated her. Her head spun long into the empty air. It landed facing Barrabus and showed no look of horror there, just defiance.

He rushed past, kicking her kneeling, headless corpse to the ground, and finished off the other attackers. As he bent to retrieve his dagger from the Ashmadai's chest, he spit on the man's body.

He sensed others near him, so he leaped around, landing at the ready.

It was not a group of Ashmadai standing in front of him, but a trio of Shadovar.

"Well done, Barrabus the Gray," one of them remarked. "Master Alegni requests that you return to the city at once, as we will win the field."

Barrabus glanced across at the Netherese lord.

He trotted to the wall, pausing to collect his belt buckle dagger from the corpse of the decapitated woman, then veered over to scoop up the first Ashmadai he'd defeated this night, the woman still very much alive.

He set her over his shoulder and ran to the base of the wall, calling up for a rope.

When he climbed a few moments later, he took the captured Ashmadai with him. He wasn't sure why, exactly, except that he knew he didn't want to leave Herzgo Alegni such a trophy.

CHAPTER 6

THE LUSKAN GAMES

HIGH CAPTAIN KURTH WAS WIDELY REGARDED AS THE MOST impressive of the five leaders of Luskan. Standing in front of him, it wasn't hard for Drizzt and Dahlia to discern why. Unlike the other four leaders of the City of Sails, Kurth had not inherited his station. He'd fought for it and won it, both in a tournament of combat and sailing skills, and in a subsequent vote of the many crewmembers of Ship Kurth. Upon his victory, he, like those before him since the time of Deudermont's fall, had abandoned his birth name and taken the title of the proud Ship.

"An interesting dilemma Beniago has presented me with, wouldn't you say?" Kurth asked Advisor Klutarch, the man he'd bested for the position of high captain.

The older man grinned his gap-toothed smile and stroked the sharp gray stubble on his cheeks and chin, nodding all the while. "Beniago angles for his turn at high captain," Klutarch answered. He turned to face the red-haired Beniago, who stood in front of Drizzt and Dahlia. "Don't ye, ye sea dog? Or might that ye'd've been better off killing the dark-skinned one, as 'twas the light-skinned lady ye was sent to retrieve?"

Drizzt and Dahlia looked at each other with not a small bit of confusion, for the pirates spoke so cavalierly of them, as if they were not present—or still armed.

"Lady Dahlia travels with the drow," Beniago replied. "High Captain Kurth made clear that he wished to engage Lady Dahlia on good terms, and I didn't think that a likely outcome were I to kill her companion."

"Not if all the guards of Luskan fought beside you, idiot," Dahlia muttered under her breath, and Drizzt flashed her a grin. Beniago heard her too. He glanced back and gave the woman a cold stare.

"Better not to anger Bregan D'aerthe," High Captain Kurth remarked. "You are of that band, are you not?" he asked Drizzt.

"I'm a well-known companion of Jarlaxle of Bregan D'aerthe," Drizzt bluffed, the implication a lie though the literal words were true enough.

"Well, where have he and Bregan D'aerthe been?" Kurth asked, not hiding his impatience. "Every month there are fewer sightings, and I fear the whole of the drow presence quickly fades into myth." Kurth came forward in his chair, his face growing serious. "There are rumors that they plot with one of the five, to elevate him as their puppet ruler of all of Luskan."

Drizzt did not reply, for while he had no knowledge of any such thing, of course, he couldn't deny it was a distinct possibility where the drow mercenary band was concerned, with or without Jarlaxle leading them.

"Perhaps you will prove to be an important prisoner, then," Kurth went on. "Or, better for yourself, a fine spy."

"Why would Bregan D'aerthe desire such an outcome?" Drizzt asked innocently.

"Do tell."

"Five weaker high captains are more malleable than a single powerful leader, surely," Drizzt explained. "Too involved in matters of their own Ships to join in common cause. . . . We saw that even in the long-past war against Captain Deudermont, did we not?"

Kurth and Klutarch glanced at each other and smiled.

"A single powerful ruler, or even if the five could be of one mind, would be better positioned to bargain more for the benefit of Luskan, yes?" Drizzt went on. "But fortunately, we outsiders rarely had to fear the five high captains being of one mind or purpose. And always, we can count on one having a price to shift his fealty. Other than the war against Captain Deudermont, I cannot think of a time when they've all come together for anything more than a shared dinner."

"Ah, yes, the Luskan Games."

"And you play a dangerous one now," Drizzt went on, "to hold a lieutenant of Bregan D'aerthe as hostage."

"Hostage?" Kurth said, feigning a great insult, even dramatically bringing his hand up to his heart, as if he'd been mortally stung by the words. "My man Beniago rescued you from the villains of Ship Rethnor, did he not?"

Drizzt was about to deny that claim, to assure Kurth that he and Dahlia would've won the fight anyway, perhaps even that he had other allies lying in wait before Beniago had made his appearance, but he paused when he noted Kurth and Klutarch again exchanging smiles.

"Well played, Drizzt Do'Urden," High Captain Kurth congratulated him, and for the first time in the meeting, Drizzt found himself taken off his guard.

"Are ye thinkin' that ye're not known within the walls o' Luskan?" Klutarch asked. "Yerself, who fought beside that dog Deudermont a hundred years ago, and yerself, who's been in the city many times since?"

"Enough of this foolishness," Dahlia insisted. "To you, I offer my thanks," she said, indicating Beniago. "We would've prevailed in the square, do not doubt, but your arrival was well-timed and appreciated."

"We couldn't let the prized Dahlia and her valuable companion be killed, or fall into the hands of Rethnor," Kurth explained. He stood up, and to the amazement of Drizzt and Dahlia, bowed deeply. "Good lady, on behalf of three of my peers, I wish to thank you for ridding us of the impetuous Borlann."

That stark admission had both Drizzt and Dahlia widening their eyes in surprise.

"Would that I had done the same to Borlann's ancestor, Kensidan," Drizzt said, "that Captain Deudermont might have prevailed."

Dahlia's shocked glance at him bordered on panic, and Beniago and Kurth both shuffled uncomfortably, as did all the other guards in the hall.

"Don't ye be provoking us needlessly, drow," Klutarch warned. "The past's better left past. If we wasn't believin' that, then ye'd've been killed in the street, and Dahlia'd've been taken 'ere in chains, a great bargaining piece in our continuing diplomacy with Ship Rethnor."

Drizzt grinned at them, quite pleased with himself, but said no more.

"You wished me here, and so I am here," Dahlia interjected, "with gratitude for your help in our fight. We have business to attend, however, so if you have anything else to offer, pray do so now."

"I have much to offer, dear Dahlia," Kurth replied, "or I wouldn't have taken such pains to ensure your survival. My actions in the street, with Beniago confronting the second of Ship Rethnor directly, will surely invoke admonitions against me at the next meeting of the five high captains, and perhaps even reparations for those crewmen of Ship Rethnor who were killed or injured due to our interference— and I have no doubt the ever-opportunistic Hartouchen Rethnor will account to me those soldiers you two took down in the battle. But no matter, for I think the gain worth the cost, for all of us."

"Even though I'm not a representative of Bregan D'aerthe?" Drizzt interjected, drawing a glance and shake of the head from Kurth.

"Perhaps I should use you as a bargaining chip in my dealings with the other four high captains, eh?" Kurth replied, and Dahlia stiffened.

But Drizzt remained at ease, for he knew that Kurth was hardly serious.

"Then why did you intervene?" Dahlia asked when Kurth stared at Drizzt for just a moment, then laughed away the whole notion. "What do you want?"

"Allies," Drizzt answered before Kurth could.

The high captain looked once more at the drow. "Do tell."

"By all that I can discern, Bregan D'aerthe has retreated considerably from the day-to-day affairs of Luskan," Drizzt replied. "If true . . ."

"It's true," Kurth admitted. "Jarlaxle has not been seen in tendays."

Drizzt tried not to wince at the added confirmation of Jarlaxle's demise and said, "Without Bregan D'aerthe, there are openings in the commerce and power structures of the city, and no doubt the five high captains will each seek to claim those opportunities for his own. You say I'm known well in Luskan. If that's true, then my reputation with the blade is so known, as are my alliances and acquaintances with the folk of the nearby towns and cities."

"Your arrogance leads you to believe I intervened because of *you,*" said Kurth.

"Dahlia's recent history with Ship Rethnor is why you intervened," Drizzt corrected. "You see her position here as tentative, and so you believe you can exploit it to enlist her to your cause."

When he finished, an uncomfortable silence hung in the air for a short while, and even Drizzt moved his hands near to his scimitar hilts, wondering if he'd gone too far.

"Your companion is wise in the ways of the world." Kurth smiled at Dahlia, relieving the tension.

"In some things, perhaps," she replied. "Not so much in others."

"You will teach him in those, I'm sure," Kurth remarked, the lewd implications drawing more than a few chuckles around the room.

"Enough of this banter," Kurth said as he rose from his chair. "I have no interest in any enmity between you two and Ship Kurth, and indeed, as you both know, I do hope for something in exchange for my assistance in your battle with Rethnor—something more than the mere satisfaction of foiling Hartouchen, I mean, though that itself is no small thing!"

More laughter, louder laughter, broke out around the room, along with a few curses thrown at Ship Rethnor, and even a song the crew of Ship Kurth had composed to belittle their rivals.

"Ship Kurth is ascendant," Kurth assured his two guests. "Allow me to show you a bit of my resources, and perhaps we will reach a bargain for your services."

Drizzt waited for Dahlia to look at him. When she nodded her agreement with Kurth, he didn't argue their course.

Kurth led them to the back of the room, pulled aside a curtain, and threw open the double doors leading out onto a balcony. The porch faced the east, where the morning sun was just rising, and from their perch on Closeguard Island, they were afforded a wonderful view of the city of Luskan.

"The docks," Kurth explained, pointing to the wharves and warehouses. "No high captain has more men along the quayside than I, and even though Luskan sees considerable trade through her land gates, this is the heart of our commerce, and this is where the best deals are to be found. Pirates seeking to off-load booty don't expect market price, after all. So while Rethnor and the others have focused their efforts on the walls and the merchant section, I've aimed at the docks."

He looked at Drizzt directly. "And at the drow," he added, "whenever they deign to grace us with their wares. Perhaps you can help me in that area."

"I know nothing of Bregan D'aerthe's movements or intentions," Drizzt answered.

"And of Jarlaxle?"

Drizzt shook his head.

"Good enough, for now," said Kurth. "They will return. They always return. And in that event, I'll be glad to count Drizzt Do'Urden among my . . . allies."

"And my role?" Dahlia asked. "I am no friend of the pirates or the drow."

"The docks are my focus, but not my only endeavor. My reach extends beyond these walls—far beyond, and farther will it go. If you think I risked so much merely to sting my rival Hartouchen Rethnor, then you underestimate me, dear lady. I wish to extend my enterprise far and wide, and will need scouts and warriors to facilitate my designs. I can think of no better than Dahlia and Drizzt."

The two glanced at each other, working hard to keep their expressions noncommittal.

"Come," Kurth bade them, moving back into the room. "Let me show you other aspects of Ship Kurth, which you might find enlightening, perhaps even enjoyable."

They moved down Kurth's small tower and out the front door. A collection of soldiers rushed out ahead of them, crossing the bridge to the mainland and spreading out left and right. Beniago and a pair of wizards remained right behind them while a handful of light-armored warriors formed a rank directly in front of them.

They went into the city and moved along Luskan's streets, heading toward the merchant section.

"You think it wise to walk with us openly so soon after the fight?" Drizzt remarked.

"Better now than when the extent of it is known to the three uninvolved high captains, and before the fool Rethnor can properly regroup," Kurth replied with a laugh. "You're clearly under my protection, of course, and who would go directly against a high captain, especially when that high captain is of Ship Kurth?"

They moved into the merchant square, where many were setting up their kiosks. The smell of fruits and herbs, thick in the air, mixed with other, more exotic scents.

"What is that?" Dahlia asked, crinkling her nose. "Perfume?"

"Of course, my lady. It's all the rage in Luskan," Kurth said.

Dahlia wore a skeptical expression. "In Thay, I would expect, but here?" Her expression turned to one of disgust as she looked around at the filth and mud so common in the City of Sails, at the dirty commoners and their ragged clothing.

"Have you ever sailed with pirates . . . privateers, I mean?" Kurth asked with a grin. "A truly smelly bunch—so much so that many are insisting that their shipmates mask their natural aroma."

Dahlia returned that grin, though hers was a helpless one, defeated by the high captain's simple logic.

"And I, of course, was first to note that trend," said Kurth.

"Note, or foment?" Dahlia asked.

Kurth grinned and bowed. "And so I dominate the fragrance trade," he said. "Something that might interest you as a benefit of serving in my employ. For yourself, perhaps even for your drow companion." He looked at Drizzt. "No offense intended, of course, but battle does bring forth the body's natural oils, and I'm not the first to note that drow carry their own peculiar scent."

Drizzt remained too incredulous at the entire conversation to take offense.

"Oh, and something else," Kurth said, as if the notion had just come to him. He stopped and turned to face a squat stone building, its windows still shuttered by heavy metal blinds. "I note, pretty Dahlia, that you have a fancy for shiny stones." He tapped her left ear, where the ten diamond studs glittered in the morning light, then motioned to the heavy, iron-bound door.

Beniago stepped up to the spot, rapping out a rhythmic sequence. The merchant inside threw the lock and bolts, and in the group went. On Beniago's warning, they held near to the entrance for a few moments as the merchant picked a careful path across the floor to the side of the room. He pushed through a curtain and the group heard the creak of levers being thrown, followed by the sounds of sliding floorboards.

He was disarming pit traps, Drizzt knew, and the drow looked on slyly, wondering why Kurth had so readily shown them some of the defenses of the place.

As soon as the merchant returned through the curtain and nodded, Kurth led them on a slow walk of the room, showing off rubies and emeralds and many other gems and jewels. Flickering candlelight bathed the room in a soft glow, and the stones glittered in their many glass cases.

"You fancy diamonds, I see," Kurth said, directing them to one particular case.

Dahlia moved up beside him, her icy blue eyes glittering with their sparkling reflections. She didn't hide her fascination with one stone in particular, prominently displayed in the center of the case.

"Another benefit," Kurth offered. "Go ahead, lady, take any one you wish."

Dahlia looked at him with open suspicion.

"Free of any cost to you," Kurth assured her.

"Free, other than my agreement to be indentured to Ship Kurth?"

Kurth laughed aloud. "Lady, please," he said, motioning to the case, but then he paused and motioned again to the shopkeeper, who rushed over and reached under the case to shift a few unseen levers, no doubt incapacitating a trap or alarm of some sort.

Then he motioned again to Dahlia as he opened the hinged top of the case.

Dahlia looked at Drizzt, smiled, and shook her head. "No," she replied. "But you have my gratitude for your offer."

"You will not be indebted," Kurth assured her.

"I'll feel indebted, and that's not so much of a different thing."

"My lady," Kurth said with exaggerated exasperation.

"Perhaps you would care to purchase an item instead," the merchant remarked, and the poor man knew as soon as the words left his mouth that he should have remained quiet. Dahlia looked at him incredulously, but that was by far the most benign of the looks coming his way. Kurth and all of his soldiers stared hard at the diminutive man. Beniago even took a step closer to him. The merchant made a little mewling sound and seemed to shrink, appropriately hanging his head.

Dahlia's gaze went to Drizzt, who moved slightly back and slid his hands to his weapon belt. She nodded.

"Perhaps I shall do so, good jeweler," she said in a light tone to pierce the tension. "Sadly, however, I'm short of funds at the moment." She tapped Kurth on the shoulder. "Though that situation might soon be remedied."

Her teasing hint that she might be open to some employment took the high captain's mind off the merchant quite readily, something that was not missed by his obedient soldiers.

"He'll give you the finest deal possible," Kurth said, casting one disconcerting glare at the small man for good measure.

"You have given me—us—much to consider," Dahlia said to Kurth. "Will we find you on Closeguard Island tomorrow at midday?"

"This day is only just begun," Kurth reminded her.

"And I have not rested at all through the night," Dahlia replied. "Drizzt and I will take our leave here."

"You may reside on Closeguard Island," Kurth said. He looked past Dahlia to a pair of burly soldiers, who quickly shifted to block the exit. "I insist."

"We have much to consider," Dahlia replied. "You understand that we prefer to discuss our plans in private, of course."

"You will not be safe anywhere in Luskan, outside of my protection, lady," the high captain said. "Do you think one minor failure will put off Ship Rethnor?"

"But now we know of the threat," Drizzt said. "And so we're not worried."

"Then you're a fool."

"Then why would you want me in your employ?"

That set Kurth back on his heels, and for many heartbeats he just stared at the drow, as if trying to decide whether to lash out or back off.

"Midday tomorrow, then, on Closeguard?" Dahlia asked, and she pressed the point by walking over to Drizzt, who stood closer to the door.

High Captain Kurth looked to Beniago, to his wizards, then to his soldiers, and finally nodded his agreement. The burly soldiers moved clear of the door.

"He's used to having his way," Drizzt whispered to Dahlia when they were back on the market square.

"And yet he allowed us to leave, not even knowing our course."

"Do you think he's punishing the poor merchant now for daring to speak up?"

Dahlia looked at Drizzt skeptically, as if the notion was ridiculous, which of course, she knew it was not. "Why would he? What would be his gain?"

"His pleasure, perhaps," said Drizzt.

"Finding one with a good jeweler's eye is no easy task, particularly this far north."

"But were it to his gain, he would beat the man to death with nary a concern."

Dahlia could only shrug.

"It matters," Drizzt remarked as they walked away.

Drizzt was speaking as much to himself as to her—trying desperately to hold on to beliefs that had carried him through a century of fierce battle, beliefs that shielded him from the grief and pain of so much loss.

He saw the pity in Dahlia's pretty eyes. But was there something else there, as well?

Envy?

They went to the Cutlass to get some food and drink, but didn't remain there for their meal, taking Kurth's warning to heart. Moving carefully through the shadows of Luskan, they went back to the scene of the fight, and stood in front of the wreckage of the porch, below the door of what had been Jarlaxle's apartment.

"How strong and agile are you?" Dahlia asked with a wry grin. "You control your blades so well, but can you also control your body?"

"How so?"

"Beyond the practiced movements of swordplay, I mean?"

Drizzt stared at her as if he had no idea what she was getting at, so Dahlia moved through the broken boards to the base of the wall below the door and planted the end of her eight-foot metal staff on the ground. With a nod to Drizzt, the woman leaped up, hands climbing the staff to its top end as she rose, and there she caught a firm hold and rolled her body, inverting at the top of the staff. She pirouetted just a half turn, lining her legs up perfectly with the open portal, and rolled into the room, letting go of the staff as she did.

Drizzt caught it before it fell aside.

"Bring it up with you, if you would," Dahlia said, poking her head out the door.

Drizzt tightened his belt and his backpack and took a firm hold of the staff. He looked up at Dahlia, thinking to go even higher in his leap, to get all the way into the room standing, perhaps.

Up he leaped, reaching higher on the pole, grabbing hold and inverting . . . almost.

Before he went over, the drow caught himself, his instincts fighting against his intentions, and he didn't quite invert. He managed to break his fall by continuing his hold on the staff, and he landed with some measure of dignity back where he'd started.

Dahlia looked down at him from the doorway, obviously quite amused.

Drizzt frowned and leaped again, this time with a growl, throwing himself even higher and with more speed.

But once again, as he neared the break point of his inversion, his instinct resisted, and even though he fought through it this time and forced his upending, that slight break in his movement altered his momentum and his angle. He went upright, feet high in the air, but fell against the wall to the side of the door and failed miserably to grab on.

With great effort, Drizzt managed to catch enough of a hold to spin him back upright before he crashed down. The staff clanged down to the side.

"Do you intend to inform all the city of our whereabouts?" Dahlia teased.

Drizzt pulled himself up to his feet, rubbed a sore elbow, and glared at the smiling elf.

"It's not unexpected," Dahlia offered.

But to Drizzt, it surely was—unexpected and disconcerting. He was a warrior who had ridden an avalanche down from the top of a mountain by staying atop the tumbling stone, a warrior not unaccustomed to doing free somersaults in the air in battle, even to leaping over an opponent and turning around to strike as he landed.

This movement didn't look difficult to him. Dahlia had executed it brilliantly and easily.

"With a running start, you'd have no trouble," Dahlia remarked.

Drizzt looked around at the broken porch. "I would have to spend an hour clearing the way," he replied, and with a shake of his head, he went to his pack. "I'll throw up a rope for you to secure."

"No," Dahlia answered before Drizzt had even untied the backpack. He looked up at her curiously.

"You're strong enough and more than agile enough," Dahlia explained. "Only your fear holds you back from completing the movement." She smiled even wider. "And what you fear is being embarrassed, and failing where I succeeded," she added, and with a laugh, she disappeared into the room.

Drizzt grabbed the staff and leaped with all his strength, catching his high hold and spinning his legs up and over, so high he had but one hand on the very top of the staff, the other out beside him, controlling his balance. He balanced like that, inverted and eight feet above the ground, for several heartbeats before leaning toward the door and pushing off again to gain speed.

He landed on his feet, facing out from the door, the staff in his hand.

Behind him, Dahlia laughed again and slowly clapped her deceptively delicate hands.

"Not so difficult with a bit of practice," Drizzt remarked, tossing Kozah's Needle back to Dahlia. He walked past her, pulling off his gloves and undoing the neck tie of his cloak.

"I've never attempted anything like that maneuver before," Dahlia stabbed at him as he walked by her. He stopped and slowly turned on her, unblinking, his violet eyes matched her blue orbs.

Dahlia smiled and shrugged.

Drizzt grabbed her and pulled her close, and she gasped in surprise, just for a moment before her smile returned, and this time, it was an inviting look.

Drizzt moved his lips toward hers, but he hesitated at the last moment. That didn't stop Dahlia, however, and she fell over him, pressing him in a tight and passionate kiss. She brought her hands to the sides of his head, pulling him tighter, holding him closer. She moved her face back just a bit, just enough so that she could bite at his lower lip then, with a groan, went right back in tight against him, this time with her mouth opened just a bit, just enough for her tongue to tease him.

Finally, suddenly, Dahlia broke the clench and jumped back from Drizzt, moving to arms' length. She stared at him, her breathing heavy.

Drizzt, hair tousled, stared back. He chewed his lip where Dahlia had nibbled it.

He glanced at the open door.

Dahlia reached out with her staff and used it to push the door closed—as tightly as the damaged threshold would allow. Then she tossed the staff expertly so that one end caught under a raised plank in the door while it fell diagonally, its nearer end settling on the floor. Staring at Drizzt once more, her grin returning, her blue eyes sparkling with anticipation, the elf took one step to her left and stomped down suddenly on the butt end of Kozah's Needle, the weight of her stamp crunching the metal edge down into the floorboards, firmly securing the door.

She turned back and flicked off her cloak with a snap of her finger, then strode to one of the small beds in the room and sat down facing Drizzt.

She lifted one leg his way, inviting him to help her remove her high black boot.

Drizzt paused—for a moment, it seemed as if he would just fall over, but Dahlia didn't laugh at him.

He came to her and took her boot in his strong hands, and Dahlia just lay back on the bed, inviting him.

"They'll join us," High Captain Kurth insisted to his gathered commanders.

"Lady Dahlia, perhaps," replied one, a wizard named Furey, though he shook his head even in partial agreement. Furey served as Ship Kurth's historian, which was no small role. "This other one, Drizzt Do'Urden . . ." He shook his head more forcefully.

"It's true that he fought beside Deudermont?" Beniago asked.

"Indeed," Furey answered. "Drizzt played no small role in the fall of the Hosttower of the Arcane."

"Something for which we should be grateful, in the end," Kurth said with a lighthearted chuckle.

"Indeed, in his own convoluted way he facilitated the rise of the five high captains unbridled," Furey said. "And from what I've been able to garner in the old records and in the stories passed down through the decades, Drizzt tried to warn Deudermont against his course."

"But not out of any favorability toward the high captains," Kurth put in. "I've spoken with some of my elderly minions and they assure me that Drizzt Do'Urden has never been known as a friend to Ship Kurth or any other Luskan Ship."

"Drizzt understands the power of what is," Furey remarked, and Kurth looked at him curiously.

But Beniago caught on to the logic and added, "He realized that Deudermont would create instability, and that there were others ready to leap in and assume the power when the cloak of the Hosttower was cast aside."

"But he hated the high captains," said Furey.

Kurth sat back in his chair and lifted his glass of whiskey for a deep swallow as he tried to sort it all through. "Perhaps enough years have passed," he remarked, his voice barely above a whisper.

"And we now are, after all, what is," Beniago added.

"He's an idealist, who served a goodly dwarf king," Furey said. "He's the enemy of thieves and rogues."

"And yet he's often seen in the company of Jarlaxle," Beniago put in, and the others looked at him curiously. "I have friends at the Cutlass," the assassin of Ship Kurth went on. "When Drizzt and King Bruenor were assailed in there a couple of months ago by some band of ruffians, Jarlaxle and his dwarf friend Athrogate intervened, and joined in the fray. When Drizzt and King Bruenor left Luskan soon after, Jarlaxle and Athrogate went with them."

"You're certain of this?" Kurth asked, and Beniago nodded. Kurth looked to Furey.

"It could be true," the wizard admitted.

"If Drizzt will conspire with the likes of Bregan D'aerthe, what might his objections be to the practices of the high captains?"

"Because we're not as vile as the drow?" Beniago asked with a laugh.

"Not for lack of trying, I hope," Kurth replied, and joined in the jollity.

"And Lady Dahlia should welcome our protection," Furey admitted.

"Then there is hope!" Kurth announced, and lifted his glass in toast. The others all did likewise, and with enthusiasm—except for Beniago, who remained caught by the improbability of Furey's last proclamation. "Truly I would value their addition to my network."

"We'll be knowin' in the morning," remarked Klutarch, who had remained silent since their departure from the jeweler's shop. Klutarch's role was, after all, to be a second set of ears for Kurth.

"We'll know their answer first," Kurth said. "And if it's not one we wish to hear, we'll use Ship Rethnor's designs on the pair to convince them further that our alliance is in their best interest—in fact, that it's their only hope."

"Easily enough accomplished," Furey assured his high captain. "Though I fear we may lose a considerable number of potential recruits manning such a ruse against the drow's blades and Dahlia's deadly staff."

Normally, such a lead would have prompted Beniago to offer similar assurances to Kurth, but the assassin was still caught up mulling Furey's remark that Dahlia would welcome their protection, trying to figure out why that seemingly obvious conclusion rattled so clumsily in his thoughts. He looked up at long last to consider Kurth, Klutarch, and Furey, all plotting about where and when they might launch their phony ambush to further entice Dahlia and Drizzt.

No one in Ship Kurth knew the city better than Beniago. He should have taken the lead in the plans. He was, after all, the Ship's assassin, the warrior who knew the shadows and the streets, the disposition of the rival ship forces, and the pulse of the City of Sails. But he couldn't. Something bothered him. Something wasn't quite right.

Dahlia looked down at the sleeping Drizzt Do'Urden, at the moonbeam playing on the sparkles of perspiration dotting his muscular back. She told herself that he was merely another in her long string of encounters—well-played, to be sure, but nothing extraordinary.

She told herself that, but she didn't believe it.

There was something very different about that passionate night compared to the dozens Dahlia had experienced before, and the distinction lay in the lead-up and not merely in the act itself.

She didn't have the time to pause and consider all of that, however. Dahlia reminded herself that she had work to do, that she had alliances to smash to pieces, that she had a road to blaze before a different trail was forced upon her.

She dressed quietly, staring at Drizzt the whole time. She left her boots off, lacing them together and flipping them over her shoulder, then quietly padded to the door. She held it firmly in place as she gently lifted the staff out of its locking position. Then, with a last glance back at Drizzt, Dahlia eased the door open.

She stepped to the threshold, and seeing no one about—it was past midnight, after all—she bent low and set the end of her staff down to a spot amidst the rubble. Dahlia took a deep breath and swung herself out past the broken porch, landing lightly on the cobblestones of the empty street.

She quickly pulled her boots on, broke her staff into flails so she could more easily carry it, and ran on through the moonlit streets of sleeping Luskan.

She stood outside the small jewelry shop for quite a while, noting the sparse movements on the street, looking for any patterns she might exploit. There were a few city guards in the area, but of course, Dahlia could expect that most of them wouldn't care at all about Ship Kurth's jeweler. That was the way of Luskan: City guards were Ship guards, with loyalty to one high captain alone.

Using the same maneuver that had brought her into the second-story apartment above the broken porch, Dahlia was soon atop the shop's roof. She picked her way to the apex and from there calculated the area that would be above the case of diamonds. Using her staff, she prodded the slate tiles and found, to her satisfaction, that more than a few had loosened in the harsh sea air of Luskan. Always wet, always windy, often icy, the City of Sails felt the cold ocean's bluster keenly.

Dahlia tied off her coil of rope around the brick chimney and eased her way down to the spot. Using a two-foot section of her staff, she pried off tiles then poked at the rotten boards beneath them. Soon she'd removed enough of the roofing to poke her arms and head through the hole. She lit a candle and nodded in satisfaction when she noted that she was directly above the case. With the rope secured around her waist and looped through a metal eye-hole in her harness, she gradually released the rope and lowered herself into the room, head down.

She came to a stop just above the case and set the candle atop the glass. She had a glass-cutter and a suction cup in her pack, and was considering whether to use it or take a more straightforward route when a voice made up her mind for her.

"You so disappoint me," Beniago remarked, coming out of the shadows at the side of the room.

Dahlia reacted as soon as the first word had left his mouth. She poked down with Kozah's Needle in one hand, shattering the top sheet of glass on the case. At the same time, she flipped the latch on the eye-hole of her harness, freeing herself from the rope, and caught the rope enough with her free hand to spin herself over, dropping to straddle the case with one foot atop either side of its metal skeleton.

"I'll try to do better," she replied coolly, as if she'd expected the man all along. She went into a defensive crouch, setting her boots more firmly on the narrow rim of the case and turning her eight-foot staff slowly in her hands in front of her.

Beniago came closer, walking a zigzag path as if expecting Dahlia to throw some missile his way. Barely five strides from her, he looked at her then down at the broken case, and shook his head.

"The diamond," he said, "offered to you by High Captain Kurth as a gift."

"There's no such thing as a gift."

"Cynical, pretty lady."

"Taught by bitter experience. Gifts have conditions."

"And would those conditions have been such a bad thing, particularly in light of your relationship with Ship Rethnor, a formidable foe?"

"They don't frighten me."

"Obviously not."

"Nor does Ship Kurth."

"But still, I would be remiss in my duties to High Captain Kurth if I didn't once more put forth our offer. Take your chosen diamond—"

The words had barely left his mouth when Dahlia exploded into motion. She pulled her staff into two four-foot lengths and turned them down like great pincers. With practiced control, she squeezed the velvet wrapping and the diamond between them and with a flick of her wrists, sent the stone flying up into the air in front of her. She snapped her staff back together, let go with one hand, and deftly used her free hand to redirect the stone as it descended right into her pocket. And all the time, even in the moment it took to execute the entire maneuver, Dahlia kept her gaze locked on Beniago.

The assassin showed his amusement, and perhaps amazement, with a grin and a shake of his head.

"Take your chosen diamond," he repeated, chuckling beneath the words, "and I'll even pay for the repair of the case—and glass is not so cheap in Luskan this time of the year! So you see? You have created a better bargain for yourself already. Join us . . ."

"No."

"My good lady . . ."

"No."

"Then I must take back the diamond."

"Please try."

A sword appeared in Beniago's left hand, his jeweled dagger in his right—and for a moment, Dahlia thought that a strange combination, since her previous observations of Beniago had made her think him right-handed.

"No matter," she whispered.

She leaped from the case, landing halfway between it and her opponent, setting her feet as she touched down perfectly to sweep her long staff out in front of her. She halted her subsequent backhand mid-swing, retracted it, and stepped forward, thrusting the staff as a spear for Beniago's belly.

A lesser opponent might have been clipped by the swing and prodded hard by the thrust, but she got nowhere near to hitting Beniago—nor did she expect to. What Dahlia had hoped was that Beniago would slap at Kozah's Needle with his sword perhaps, so that she could share a bit of lightning energy with her opponent, perhaps even jolting his sword from his grasp.

But Beniago not only avoided any such incidental contact, he smiled at Dahlia as if to show her that he knew what she was trying to do.

That didn't concern Dahlia, though. Quite the opposite. She preferred her opponents capable and well-schooled. She stabbed again with the staff and jumped forward to drive Beniago back, and indeed he did retreat, but the aggressive elf warrior discovered something in that attack: Beniago had not disabled the floor traps!

The floorboards collapsed beneath Dahlia's lead foot and only her agile reaction stopped her from sliding into the suddenly-revealed pit. Still, her foot did go in enough to tap the nearest of the many spikes within, wicked and pointed things that easily punctured the hard sole of her boot and pricked at the bottom of her foot.

She felt the slight puncture, almost immediately accompanied by a burning pain. She had no doubt that the spike was poisoned, but could only hope it hadn't penetrated her flesh enough to deliver a killing dose.

Beniago seized the opportunity to charge forward, leading half-heartedly with his sword, and the off-balance Dahlia did well to slap it aside, though she couldn't focus her energy enough to apply the weapon's signature lightning blast. She did even better in her subsequent retreat, just barely avoiding the brunt of the man's main attack with his jeweled dagger.

Dahlia fell away and turned her head, but still got scratched by the small blade. Just scratched.

And in that moment, thinking to reverse and press the man, Dahlia found out the awful truth.

She'd been barely nicked, a slight scratch across her cheek, but in that contact between Beniago's blade and her flesh, Dahlia knew doom. True doom. She sensed her soul being pulled forth, as if the dagger drank of her very life essence. She felt the coldness of utter obliteration, the emptiness of nothingness. She felt as violated as she had on that long-ago day when Herzgo Alegni had assaulted her village and torn asunder her childhood.

She retreated as fast as she dared, not wanting to put her feet down with any weight on a floor lined with deadly traps.

And they were deadly, she knew now, for her punctured foot began to grow numb, and it took considerable concentration with each step for Dahlia to stop it from rolling under and buckling.

Beniago pursued, smiling as if his kill was surely at hand.

Dahlia forced herself through it all and shook her head against the unnerving and unholy power of that wicked dagger. She broke her long staff into two, then snapped those two four-foot lengths into flails and sent them immediately spinning, up and over and out at her pursuer.

With her wounded foot, time was against her, she feared, so she went on the attack, striding forward, lashing out with the flails one after the other. Her assassin opponent ducked and dodged left and right, and tried to keep her at bay with his long sword, all the while holding that awful dagger cocked at his side, ready to strike like a poisonous serpent. Dahlia quickly realized that Beniago was making the same mistake of so many before: He was trying to parry her spinning sticks in such a way as to cut the ties between the poles.

She launched her right-hand flail in an arcing, downward-diagonal attack, and Beniago backhand parried with his sword, forcing the blade in against the handle-pole of Dahlia's weapon. As she followed through, Beniago slid his sword quickly up and out, hoping that the countering weight of her swing would create enough resistance for him to slice the binding tie cleanly.

But this was Kozah's Needle, imbued with great and powerful magic, and no blade in existence had the edge to accomplish such a feat. To his great credit, Beniago was quick enough not to fall into the obvious trap, at least, retracting his blade before Dahlia could catch the swinging pole of her weapon and twist his sword from his grasp.

Instead the elf shifted her left foot forward and turned her hips, her second weapon coming in hard, driving Beniago back in full retreat.

Dahlia shadowed his every step, imagining his boot prints and filling them with her own feet.

"Well done!" Beniago congratulated after a few such rounds had him all the way back near the shadows where he'd first appeared. He'd barely finished speaking, though, when he darted out to the side, springing away and even turning his back on the pursuing Dahlia as he executed a series of darts left and right, combined with seemingly wild leaps. He jumped up onto the broken diamond case and sprang far away, and with that visual barrier between himself and Dahlia, he moved even faster, spinning sidelong in one leap so that he could disguise his landing.

Dahlia came over the case as quickly as she could manage, but there was too much room between her and Beniago now, and she couldn't gauge his exact steps.

"Have you discerned the pattern of the floor traps?" Beniago teased. "But wait, how could you, since there's no pattern?"

As he continued to laugh at her, the woman glanced, ever so slightly, over her shoulder, back at the broken case and the hanging rope. Her punctured foot throbbed, and the burning sensation began creeping up her leg.

Beniago grinned, apparently catching on to her distressed look, and he moved into position to intercept should she try to escape up the rope.

"You disappoint me," he said. "You would leave our well-fought battle?"

"Well fought?" Dahlia echoed. "On this field of your choosing? In this place of devilish traps, which you know and I do not?"

"You will learn it soon enough," Beniago taunted her, and Dahlia came on then fiercely.

Beniago had moved, seemingly inadvertently, to a place where she could get at him over floorboards she'd already tread.

Her flails worked in wide circles, diagonally, her momentum growing, and Beniago didn't retreat. He fell lower into a crouch, blades ready to defend. Dahlia flipped a forward somersault, just to hide her attack angles, and landed in a full sprint at the man.

Or tried to.

The floorboards were no longer solid, no longer safe, and as Dahlia touched down, a board beneath her boot gave way. She managed to hold her footing and felt no sting of a spike this time, and hoped she'd passed it by quickly enough.

But something lashed out at her, whipping at her trailing ankle and wrapping around it. Unable to stop, she wrenched her hip and knee, and went down hard.

And Beniago was moving as well, leaping back up to the case, towering over her and coming down hard from on high.

Dahlia rolled to her back and kicked up with her free foot, and untangled her flails to ward away the assassin's blades, particularly that awful dagger. She had no choice now and unloaded Kozah's Needle's pent up lightning energy with each connection, buying herself time by forcing Beniago back and away, stinging him with sharp crackles of power.

She tried to get her free foot under her, but the leathery lash snaring her trailing foot more than held her, it was dragging her! She heard a grinding sound from the displaced floorboard behind her.

"It's not too late, Lady," Beniago said, his teeth chattering with Kozah's Needle's residual energy. "Ship Kurth desires your services."

Dahlia threw herself into a sitting position and grabbed at the lash, to find that the obviously magical cord had wrapped over upon itself, knotting around her ankle. She thought to go for her small knife, but her instinct told her that her meager utility blade would be of no use against the tendril. She flipped the end of one flail up high and snapped her wrist hard, flipping it and driving it straight down. She released lightning energy as it connected on the floorboard and blew a clean hole with the force and the magic, sinking the pole deeply into the wood. She threw herself against that pole, gripping and pulling for all her life.

But the gears of the trap kept turning, kept dragging her. She wriggled her foot, trying to extricate it from the boot. Her arms stretched out inexorably from her body, and she hadn't the strength to resist the pull.

Her arms stretched above her head as she stubbornly held on to her anchoring flail pole. She wriggled and jerked her foot every which way. Her frustration mounted—she almost had her foot free when Beniago's dagger flashed in front of her eyes.

"Last chance, Dahlia," he said, the blade poised to strike and with Dahlia having no way to prevent it.

So Lady Dahlia did the only thing she could: She spat in his face.

With a growl of protest, Beniago slashed that awful knife toward the woman's extended arms, and Dahlia instinctively recoiled, letting go.

"The pit take you then!" the assassin said, and there seemed as much regret in his tone as anger.

As if on cue, the grinding stopped.

Dahlia didn't waste a heartbeat in rolling around and up to her knees, facing the assassin, her remaining flail whipping wildly as if she expected him to come charging in.

He didn't, though, apparently too perplexed by the failure of the trap.

The riddle was soon answered as a dark form moved out from the side of the room, from the same area where Beniago had first appeared. The newcomer didn't waste a word of introduction, just came out hard and fast, curving blades leading the way in a mesmerizing, dizzying dance.

Beniago turned and fled. He reached into a pouch and pulled forth some small ceramic globes and began throwing them down with each step. They hit and exploded with brilliant, blinding flashes, one after another, allowing Beniago to get to the door and out into the street.

Drizzt lost ground with each blinding flash-bomb. As Beniago shouldered his way out, the drow swung around and rushed to Dahlia. He leaped past her and drove Twinkle down hard on the magical lash, severing it cleanly.

He reached for Dahlia, but she didn't take his offered hand. She leaped to her feet and kicked away the remaining length of enchanted tendril then strode indignantly to her planted flail and pulled it free of the floorboard. Her proud demeanor took a bit of a misstep, though, as she moved toward the broken display, for she stumbled on her now fully numb foot and burning leg, and nearly pitched headlong into the case.

Drizzt was right beside her, propping her.

She cast him a hateful look and pulled away, and indeed, Drizzt fell back a step, caught by surprise.

"I'm sorry," Dahlia said, shaking her head against the wounded expression on her lover's face. She reached out for him and tugged him to her. "I feel so much the fool," she whispered into his ear as she hugged him tightly.

"Let us be gone," Drizzt replied. "Don't underestimate these people." He reached for the rope hanging over the broken case.

"Without securing enough treasure for our life outside the city?" Dahlia quipped, and Drizzt turned back on her, his expression hard.

"Why, are you afraid of these foolish high captains and their scalawag armies?" she asked with feigned surprise.

Drizzt spent a long while digesting that, his expression moving to an inquisitive one, prying into Dahlia to discern her intent. The elf also noted a flicker of pain on the drow's strong features, a revelation and a reminder to her—he was saying, clearly but without words, that he'd fought these men before, their ancestors at least, and to great loss and pain.

Dahlia didn't want to push it any further. Drizzt's pain resonated with her and she found, to her surprise, that she didn't want to inflict any more on him.

"I had a plan to escape the lash," she said, taking the rope from Drizzt and lifting herself up to the top of the case, and trying, unsuccessfully, to hide her unease as she planted her wounded foot on the metal rim. "I would have escaped, and Beniago would have dropped into the pit."

Drizzt nodded, but obviously only to grant Dahlia her pride.

"I straightened my leg and felt the grip of the lash lessen," the elf explained. She hooked her flails into her belt and began to climb. "When Beniago came back at me, I would've moved to the pit, freeing my foot." She left it at that, for even in her ears, her words sounded inane.

Up on the roof, the couple scouted the city, looking for their best route out. All around them came sounds not typical in the sleeping city: doors creaking open, footfalls on a slate roof, a sharp whistle badly disguised as the call of a night bird.

Ship Kurth had awakened.

They climbed down and sprinted from shadow to shadow across the marketplace. At first, hints of pursuit came in the same curious sounds, the footsteps and the creaking doorways, but very soon, they could hear their pursuers clearly behind them, chasing them stride for stride.

Drizzt reached into his pouch and produced the onyx figurine, calling Guenhwyvar to his side. The panther, though tired from her exploits of the previous day, didn't growl, but took his orders and leaped off into the shadows.

A chorus of shrieks informed Drizzt and Dahlia that Guenhwyvar had greeted the minions of Ship Kurth.

By the time they made the city wall, many enemies had revealed themselves, left, right, and behind. Up on the city parapet a handful of pirates raced to guard the ladders they could use to climb the wall. Drizzt started to pull out Taulmaril, his intent clearly to shoot those enemies blocking the ladders, but Dahlia held him back.

"Do you think I trained you at the apartment balcony for no good reason?" she asked, and when Drizzt looked at her quizzically, she executed her pole vault, easily bringing herself to the eight-foot parapet, though she nearly tumbled right back down when she tried to plant her numb leg.

She dropped the staff down to Drizzt and he wasted no time in joining her. When he got up beside her, he pulled out Taulmaril and skipped an arrow along the wall to the left and to the right, driving back the closest pursuers.

Someone from the shadows below responded with an arrow that nearly hit Dahlia. Drizzt replied with a shot of his own, the lightning arrow of the Heartseeker lighting up the man's horrified expression just an instant before it blew him to the ground.

Drizzt and Dahlia ran off into the night, just a short way to the trees, where Drizzt called forth Andahar. He pulled Dahlia up behind him, and off the unicorn thundered, hooves pounding and bells singing a teasing melody to pursuers who couldn't hope to catch them.

They kept up a swift pace down the south road, and when Drizzt finally slowed Andahar to a brisk trot, he struck up a conversation about the road ahead, about Neverwinter Wood and their waiting adversary, Sylora Salm. It didn't take him long to recognize that it was a one-way dialogue.

He pulled Andahar up to a walk and felt Dahlia lean more heavily against him.

He turned to look over his shoulder, to stare into Dahlia's open, empty eyes. She slid down, rubbing her face against his shoulder, leaving a trail of vomit. Too shocked to react, Drizzt didn't catch her before she tumbled hard from Andahar's back. She landed heavily upon the hard ground.

Drizzt leaped down beside her, called to her frantically, cradled her head, and stared into her eyes only to realize that she was not looking back.

Small bubbles of white foam rolled out her open lips.

CHAPTER 7

OF LUST AND HUNGER

ARRABUS, HIS FEMALE PRISONER SLUNG ACROSS HIS SHOULDERS, moved around the courtyard within the walls of Neverwinter. The battle was fast ending, the defenders victorious. Out in the field behind him, however, the fight raged in full force. Though with Valindra gone and the Ashmadai caught by surprise, it had become more of a massacre than an actual battle.

The city gates swung open and those warriors freed of defensive duties moved for the portal, hungering for more blood.

"Who are these shadow warriors, Barrabus?" one voice rose above the others of the Neverwinter garrison as they poured through the gates onto the field.

Barrabus met the gaze of Jelvus Grinch. "Keep your forces within the city," he warned. "Secure your walls and seal your gate."

"Who are they?"

Barrabus cast him a disapproving glance and walked past into Neverwinter. He felt Jelvus Grinch's hard stare following him every step.

"Heed my words," Barrabus warned one last time, and he nodded only slightly when he at last heard Jelvus Grinch recalling his forces and ordering the gate closed and barred.

Barrabus moved to a pair of guards inside and near the closest structure, a barracks. He rolled the unconscious Ashmadai off his shoulder, easing her into the grasp of two soldiers nearby. "Chain her in a secure cell," he said.

One soldier nodded, his smile revealing much—too much.

Barrabus's sword flashed out, its tip landing against the soldier's chin. "If you harm her in any way, I will find you," he promised. "You will chain her and lock her cell so she cannot escape. And then you will stand guard outside that door."

"I'm no filthy gaoler!" the man replied.

"Would you prefer to be a gaoler or a corpse, because either path is within your grasp?" asked Barrabus, quietly, evenly.

The soldier looked to his companion, who took a step away. They had just witnessed Barrabus the Gray at play on the field of battle, after all, and the whispers of his prowess had echoed across the battlefield. No one in Neverwinter was eager to witness his prowess from the perspective of an enemy.

The first soldier turned back to glare at Barrabus for just a moment, then slung the woman over his shoulder and started away, his friend in tow.

"When I seek her out, presently, if she reports any wrongdoing on your part, we will speak again," Barrabus said.

Barrabus heard a chuckle behind him. He turned to face Jelvus Grinch.

"You presume much in this city, which is not yours," Jelvus Grinch said, his burly arms crossed over his chest, and half the Neverwinter garrison standing behind him.

"She's my prisoner, fairly taken in defense of Neverwinter," Barrabus answered without a flinch. "It would disappoint me greatly to learn that Neverwinter would not allow me the use of a single prison cell—"

"And a pair of guards."

"You should thank me for getting those fools out of your sight."

Jelvus Grinch couldn't hold his defiant pose or his stern expression. A great smile widened on his bearded face and he reached out and slapped Barrabus on the shoulder. "Well fought, Barrabus the Gray!" he cheered, and the garrison behind him erupted into a great "huzzah!" for the hero of the battle of Neverwinter.

The whole thing, of course, did nothing more than annoy and perhaps embarrass Barrabus. He was only there, after all, on behalf of Herzgo Alegni, who in turn was only there because of his master's nefarious designs on Neverwinter, and he cared not a whit about the city or any of its inhabitants.

"I'll interrogate my prisoner after she has sat in the darkness, and in fear, for some time," Barrabus explained to Jelvus Grinch, and started away.

Jelvus Grinch held out an arm to stop him. "Master Barrabus," he said politely, withdrawing the arm as the gray man fixed him with an icy stare.

"We're fighting for our lives out here, for the very existence of Neverwinter," Jelvus Grinch went on. "Against the forces of chaos and . . . insanity, it seems! Against these wretched and shriveled undead, who rise unbidden against us."

"Not unbidden," Barrabus assured him.

"You know!" Jelvus Grinch cleared his throat, composing himself. "You know," he said more quietly. "You know what's been happening here. You understand our plight . . . more than we do, perhaps?"

"Surely," Barrabus corrected.

Jelvus Grinch started to laugh. Then, in front of scores of warriors and battle mages who looked to him for leadership, the first citizen of Neverwinter bowed low before Barrabus the Gray. "And that's why we need you," he said, coming out of the bow.

Barrabus stared at him noncommittally.

"You helped us defend the city this night. You have come to us in a dark hour and helped us carry on. Without your warning, without your blades—"

"My blades were inconsequential," Barrabus said. "I would be dead on the field, with only minor victories to show for my efforts, had not that other force, who still battle beyond your walls, arrived."

"And you know of them, too," Jelvus Grinch said wryly.

Barrabus nodded. Jelvus Grinch grinned from ear to ear and held his arms out wide.

"What do you want?" Barrabus the Gray asked.

"Join us," Jelvus Grinch replied. Behind him, many cheered again and echoed that sentiment.

"I just did."

"No," Jelvus Grinch replied, shaking his head emphatically. "Not just for that one battle. Join us in our efforts to give rise to a new and greater Neverwinter. Work with us, protect us."

Barrabus the Gray laughed as if that notion was absurd.

"What tribute would you like?" Jelvus Grinch asked. "A statue?" He waved his arm out to the main market square. "A statue of Barrabus the Gray, blades in hand? A tribute to the warrior who kept watch so the new residents of Neverwinter could raise the city anew from the ashes of the cataclysm."

"A statue?" Barrabus echoed incredulously. "You would carve me in stone?"

Jelvus Grinch held up his hands. "What man . . . what man of rotting flesh and blood, after all, would not aspire to achieve a measure of immortality in stone?"

"Or perhaps you might employ a medusa," Barrabus teased, "and save your artisans for work on your buildings." Suddenly a perfectly wonderful, perfectly cynical, perfectly wicked thought came to him. "Or your bridges," he added.

"Our bridges?"

"The Winged Wyvern Bridge," Barrabus said.

Every head in the crowd turned to regard the distant structure, just the tips of the wyvern's wide-spread wings visible from that vantage point.

"Yes, what of it?"

"It was not always called that," Barrabus explained.

Jelvus Grinch looked at him curiously.

"For a brief time only," Barrabus elaborated. "The Lord of Neverwinter renamed it in the days before the cataclysm—perhaps that's why the angry volcano unleashed its rage on the city."

"We know nothing of—"

"Of course you don't," said Barrabus. "For everyone within the city at that time was killed . . . everyone but one." As he ended, he turned to face the first citizen directly, his expression explaining much.

"You?" a thoroughly confused Jelvus Grinch asked.

"I was here," Barrabus replied. "When the volcano blew, I was in Neverwinter."

"There were no survivors," someone behind yelled.

"Then how do I stand before you?" Barrabus said. "I was here on that fateful day."

In the crowd beyond came many gasps.

"Master Barrabus, you already have our gratitude," said Jelvus Grinch. "There's no reason—"

"I'm not lying. I was here." He pointed down at the Winged Wyvern Bridge. "I was down there, actually, standing atop the Winged Wyvern when the first explosions rolled the ground beneath the city, when the first fireball punched into the sky. I was there when the mountain leaped from afar, charging down from the Crags, through that valley. I watched the river run gray and red with molten rock and ash. I heard the thunder of every roof being shattered by great boulders, tumbling from on high."

"You'd be dead!" one woman in the crowd shouted.

"I should be, many times over," Barrabus said with a helpless laugh.

"You have spoken of this before," said Jelvus Grinch.

"You have no reason not to believe my words."

"How, then?" Jelvus Grinch asked.

"Go to the center of the Winged Wyvern," Barrabus said. He reached down and flipped his belt buckle, turning it into a knife. He held the blade up in front of the surprised Jelvus Grinch. Many in the crowd gasped once more.

"Climb under the bridge," Barrabus bade him.

"Under?"

Barrabus laughed. "You will find it, 'BtG,' scratched in the stone with this very knife on the day I was certain my life was at its end."

"You weathered the storm of the volcano under the Winged Wyvern Bridge?"

"Can I say it any more clearly?"

Jelvus Grinch started to respond, but simply couldn't find the words. He glanced back at his comrades, who shrugged, nodded, or shook their heads.

"The Winged Wyvern Bridge," Jelvus Grinch muttered in disbelief.

"A fr— An enemy once claimed that to be a stupid name," Barrabus said. "Though I loathe him, I cannot disagree."

"What do you want?"

"You wish me to work with you, to help keep you safe while you rebuild your city," said Barrabus.

"Yes."

"Rename the bridge."

"Barrabus?"

"The Walk of Barrabus," the grayish man replied. He easily envisioned the froth coming from the lips of Herzgo Alegni when he learned of it.

"It's possible," Jelvus Grinch said after glancing around to determine the mood of the crowd. "And you will join with us and serve as captain of the Neverwinter Guard?"

"No," Barrabus answered without the slightest hesitation, and that, of course, drew more than a few whispers.

"I've already served you well," Barrabus said. "And I'll continue to be around—perhaps I'll choose to help you again when the need arises, as it surely will."

Jelvus Grinch blew a heavy sigh. "So much like the drow," he said, and Barrabus perked up at that reference.

"Do tell."

"Heroes wander through Neverwinter and aid in our plight, but none will stay," one woman said.

"That's my bargain," said Barrabus. "And know that I'll be more inclined to aid in your cause, whatever that cause may be, should I learn of the Walk of Barrabus." With a curt bow and a little grin, the small man took his leave.

"Would that Drizzt Do'Urden had kept his swords in Neverwinter," he heard one man lament as he moved toward the gate.

The name stabbed at the heart of Barrabus the Gray.

"Is he dead?" Sylora Salm asked, only half-jokingly. She looked at Jestry, splayed head down over the arm of a couch. His hand hung down and his fingers barely brushed the floor. His naked back showed bright lines of blood from many deep scratches.

"I've been known to kill a few," Arunika replied with a laugh. She walked over and slapped Jestry hard on the side of his head, and he stirred and coughed. "But not this one. Not your pet. Not yet."

"Not at all, I beg," Sylora replied, reaching for her own clothes and wincing at a few of her own scratches. "When Jestry is of no use to me, I'll take that pleasure as my own."

"You believe he'll live that long?"

"He's a fine warrior."

"You just told me that you intend to pit him against Lady Dahlia," Arunika said, for indeed the two had shared much in conversation these last hours, their words punctuated by the heavy snoring of the exhausted Jestry. "How many times did you mention her prowess with that unusual weapon of hers?"

"Not enough times to do her justice, I admit," said Sylora. "Kozah's Needle is a mighty weapon indeed, and none have ever mastered it to compare with Dahlia's proficiency."

"And this one?" Arunika asked, and she grabbed a clump of Jestry's hair and pulled his head up so that Sylora could see his face. The sight had both females smiling. Jestry's lips were wet with spittle. Arunika let him go and his head dropped and bobbed. "Do you believe that he can stop her?"

"I hope it won't come to that, but should it, I intend to offer him every advantage."

Arunika smiled and headed for a dresser across the room. Sylora watched her, enjoying the view, her perfect humanoid form not blocked, but somehow enhanced, by those leathery devil wings.

Arunika reached into a drawer and fumbled with some ties. Then she reached in farther, up to her elbow, up to her shoulder, though there was no way the drawer could be nearly that deep. She felt around for a bit and retracted her hand from the obviously extra-dimensional bag, holding a small box. She moved back to stand in front of Sylora.

"A gesture of good will," she said. "To seal our alliance."

"I thought we'd just done that," Sylora replied seductively, and Arunika laughed.

The succubus bent low in front of the sorceress and slowly opened the box, revealing a copper ring with an empty gemstone setting.

"A stormcatcher band," the devil explained.

Sylora looked at it, and back at Arunika.

"It will catch the magic of Kozah's Needle and turn it back on Dahlia," Arunika explained.

Sylora's smile widened. She gingerly reached for the band and pulled it from the box, holding it up in front of her eyes.

"I'm sure that my alliance with Brother Anthus will provide more to help you build your champion," Arunika said.

The devil was right, Sylora knew. She wasn't looking at Jestry as a man, a free-willed human being. He was her champion, or soon to be, and she would construct him as such, with armor, with a superior weapon, with this stormcatcher ring. He was an instrument, not a companion. Even in their sexual encounters, Jestry was no more to her than a means to an end, and woe to him if he failed in that role. He had purpose only in those goals Sylora determined.

Something stirred deep within the sorceress, some regret that she'd allowed herself to move to such a place of callousness. What forks in her road had she chosen? What decisions might she have made to alter this destination in her life?

Sylora let these questions fly away as she glanced back at the ring, reminding herself of how badly she wanted to see the corpse of Lady Dahlia. Perhaps she would raise the witch as a personal zombie servant. Perhaps, with Valindra's help, she might even be able to allow Dahlia to retain enough of her former self so that her continuing torment at Sylora's hand would wound her all the more profoundly.

Sylora peered through the ring at Jestry and considered the many tools she could bestow upon him to give him the edge he needed. What a fine beginning this ring would offer! Sylora grinned wickedly as she imagined Dahlia hurled backward by the lightning burst of Kozah's Needle. She remembered the elf's pretty face so very well, and in her mind, she twisted it into a look of sheer shock and stinging pain. That was how Dahlia would recognize the last moments of her life.

Delicious.

"So, once again, I'm needed to save the pitiful Barrabus the Gray from certain doom," Herzgo Alegni announced loudly when Barrabus entered the Netherese encampment not far from the gates of Neverwinter.

"All hail Herzgo Alegni!" one of the Shadovar saluted, and others took up the cheer.

Every laughing face that met the gaze of Barrabus went stoic immediately, though, for the assassin obviously wasn't taking the joke very well.

"Saved me?" Barrabus remarked to Alegni, stepping up in front of him.

"Why, my small friend, it was obvious," the tiefling replied. "They had you flanked—an army of zealots against one small man."

"Do you believe that I would've been foolish enough to go out amid that swarm had I not known of your impending arrival?" Barrabus replied.

"You deny your predicament?"

"I served you up a feast of zealots," Barrabus said, and he took great satisfaction in seeing the doubt spreading on the faces of the gathered Shadovar—and all of Herzgo Alegni's charges had gathered and were listening intently by this point. "I could have remained within the city walls, of course, destroying zombies. But to what end?" He turned around, appealing to the crowd as if they were a greater and more important judge than Herzgo Alegni.

"To what end?" he said again, more loudly. "The zealots had recognized that they couldn't breach the wall, and seemed content to let their zombie fodder do what damage they may. But I, of course, could not allow that, and so I ventured out. I knew that the zealots couldn't resist the chance to defeat the Gray. I knew they would find comfort in their numbers and would come forth from the forest. What a prize they might have scored—"

"Enough!" Herzgo Alegni shouted.

"And this is the gratitude I'm shown for taking such a risk?" Barrabus continued, spinning back on Alegni. "You mock me when I'm the cause of your vic—"

He ended with a growl of pain as Herzgo Alegni drew his red blade just enough to tap the tuning fork in his hand. Answering the call, Claw sent forth its devastating magical energy—powers attuned to the life force of Barrabus the Gray.

"This . . . is the . . . gratitude . . ." Barrabus the Gray said through teeth clenched so hard the veins on his neck stood out clearly.

Herzgo Alegni leaned in close and whispered, "You would mock me in front of my minions?"

Barrabus growled in response, and Alegni gripped his sword tighter, bidding it to greater intensity.

Barrabus went down to one knee. He lowered his head, trying to fight the pain, but a cough escaped his lips and it carried with it bright red blood.

"Why do you force me to treat you this way?" Herzgo Alegni asked, walking around him. "Certainly you did your job . . . acceptably, though I'm surprised that you put yourself into such a situation that required me to rush my counterattack in order to save your life. Perhaps I should have let the zealots slaughter you."

Barrabus thought that a preferable choice, indeed.

A few heartbeats slipped past, and finally Alegni called to his sentient sword and the vile blade released its grip on Barrabus the Gray. It took all of his willpower to keep from toppling over. He slumped down to both knees, but he wouldn't give Alegni the satisfaction of seeing him lying on the ground.

"You let her escape," Alegni said.

Barrabus managed to turn his gaze up to the tiefling.

"The witch, Valindra," Alegni explained.

"The lich, you mean?"

"She's both. Our victory would've been complete if we'd taken her down. And if you had fought better against the worthless zealots, I could have delayed my charge and the lich would have more likely been lured into the battle."

Barrabus rose to one knee, letting the waves of anguish pass. He tried to ignore Alegni's preposterous claims, because he knew that otherwise he would surely say something the Netherese lord would make him regret.

"So I had to choose . . . because of your mediocrity," Alegni went on. "But in the end, I had nothing to gain by delaying. The lich would've destroyed you from afar and would have remained beyond my grasp anyway."

Alegni's gloved hand appeared in front of Barrabus's face, and the assassin knew better than to let that invitation pass. He took the hand and the powerful tiefling roughly hoisted him to his feet.

"So, as I explained, I saved you, and for no reason other than my generosity," Alegni insisted, and he ended with a prompting stare at Barrabus.

"Thank you, my lord," said Barrabus. "I'm not worthy."

"No," Alegni agreed. "Not unless you can assure me that your efforts in the battle, and indeed your warning to the Neverwinter settlers of the coming storm, has put you in proper standing among them."

"They begged me to stay," Barrabus said.

Herzgo Alegni considered that for a short while. "You can gain access to the city whenever you choose?"

"They will throw their gates open wide for me."

Alegni nodded, taking his time as he considered the words. Finally, he started walking away. "Then perhaps you were worth the effort of my rescue," he said without looking back, "despite your ineptitude."

"You got your prize!" Barrabus dared yell after him.

"The lich escaped."

"The prize was the defeat of the Thayan forces, and they are defeated," Barrabus insisted. "The prize was my foothold into Neverwinter, and they are ready to celebrate me as their first citizen!"

Herzgo Alegni stopped walking away and a hush fell over the gathering, with many Shadovar actually falling back a few short steps. Slowly the Netherese lord turned around to face the impudent Barrabus.

"So I have," he said with a wry grin. "So I have."

Herzgo Alegni turned away and walked off, leaving the sputtering Barrabus alone in the cul-de-sac of the encampment. All of the other

Shadovar dispersed, many of them looking at Barrabus and shaking their heads, as if to scold him for his ridiculous pride.

And truly Barrabus the Gray felt ridiculous at that moment. Ridiculous and helpless. Trapped as he'd never been trapped before, not even when he'd lived among the city of drow elves in the Underdark enclave of Menzoberranzan.

He took a deep breath and stood straight, denying the remnants of the wracking vibrations of pure agony.

He took some comfort in imagining the expression Herzgo Alegni might wear when he learned of the Walk of Barrabus. Alegni had long coveted that crafted bridge as his own tribute.

Barrabus the Gray would take his small victories where he could find them.

Jestry stumbled down the steps of Arunika's front porch and staggered off after Sylora Salm. It took him a long while to compose himself enough to actually catch up to the sorceress, and when he did, she stopped short and turned a scrutinizing eye upon him.

"I don't know what to say," Jestry remarked.

"Gratitude?" Sylora prompted, and Jestry looked back through the trees to the small cottage, and rubbed his face.

"Yes," he managed to whisper after a few heartbeats, and he turned to stare back at Sylora, this woman he so adored. "Surprise?"

"Why?"

He looked back to the cottage, holding up his hands to indicate to Sylora that the answer should be obvious. Among Jestry's male peers—even some of the female zealots—discussions of such escapades were fairly common, the typical bonding and bragging of strong young warriors living on the edge of disaster. But how could Jestry even begin to brag about this night? Who would believe him?

He looked back at Sylora and couldn't help himself. "I love you."

She hit him so hard that his weakened legs wouldn't support him and he tumbled sidelong to the ground.

"Why?" he cried, looking up at her. "What?"

"Do you think Asmodeus would approve of such idiocy? Love? There is no love. There is only lust."

"But—"

"You disappoint me," Sylora interrupted and started away, and Jestry pulled himself to his feet and scrambled after her. Again she stopped just as he neared, turning an even sharper stare over him.

"That is the truth we know!" Sylora said, and she poked her finger hard against his chest. "And in that truth, we are stronger. There is no love. Our enemies are weak because they delve into such nonsense. There is no love, only lust. There is no warmth, only heat. There is no friendship, only alliance. There is no community, only self. These are the tenets of your existence. These are the truths to which you gave yourself. Would you deny all of that because your loins itch?"

As she finished, she reached down and grabbed Jestry's crotch hard and twisted. The man grimaced but held his ground.

"You desire me," Sylora whispered, moving very close to the man's face. She held her grip as she did, and twisted a bit more.

"You desire me," she said again, more intently, and Jestry realized that there was a question in her tone. He nodded.

"You must have me," she said. "You seek to possess me."

Again he nodded.

"What I just gave to you with Arunika will only sate you temporarily," she whispered. "And then you will need me again, even more, and you will beg me to show you even greater pleasure."

Jestry was breathing too hard to respond.

Sylora let him go and shoved him back a step.

"I'm glad of that," she said, suddenly calm. "And the promise of greater pleasures, pleasures beyond your imagination, is not a hollow one. I have a purpose for you, Jestry, and when you fulfill it, I'll show to you a level of ecstasy that will probably kill you. You would like to die like that, wouldn't you?"

Jestry found himself nodding before he even considered the implications of her promise.

"But woe to you if your death is not found in service to Asmodeus."

"What do you mean?"

"The devil lord would frown on love, don't you think?"

The words hit Jestry hard and he lowered his gaze with embarrassment. "Yes," he admitted softly.

"There is no love, only lust," Sylora instructed yet again. "Our enemies don't understand that, and so they are soft."

"The Netherese?" Jestry asked, looking up.

Sylora shook her head. "Not the Netherese. They, too, understand, and that's why they are dangerous. Our other enemies—the humans, the dwarves, the elves, the halflings—they are weak."

"But we're human," Jestry said before he could bite back the words.

"We have ascended, because we know the truth. And what is that truth, Jestry?"

The man swallowed hard because within Sylora's words there loomed a clear threat should he fail this test.

"There is no love, only lust," Jestry recited.

"But you said that you loved me."

Jestry took a deep breath and squared his shoulders. "Only because I desire you. I'd tear off your clothes and throw you down before me!"

"You said that you loved me."

"I've been taught that women wish to hear those words, so I said them that I might more fully possess you," Jestry insisted. He tried to sound convincing, but knew the lie to be so obvious as to be ridiculous.

"And now that you know that I reject those words, and that I desire you in the same way as you do me?" Sylora teased, coming forward to stand very near to him again, letting him feel her hot breath on his neck and chin.

"I hunger for you even more," Jestry said. He was glad that he'd paused long enough to consider his response before blurting it out, for he'd almost said that he "loved" her even more.

Sylora grabbed him roughly by the chin and tugged him closer. "Fear not, my champion, for I will feed you well."

She moved as if to kiss him, but instead bit him hard on the lower lip, drawing blood.

CHAPTER 8

THE MIDNIGHT RIDER

Drizzt guided Andahar as fast as he dared while trying to keep Dahlia steady. He'd slung her over the back of the unicorn, and had stopped no less than three times in the first twenty strides to make sure she was still breathing.

She was, but barely. One of her thighs had turned an ugly blue and spittle flowed from her lips.

Drizzt didn't dare stop to more closely inspect her wound, though he figured it had to be on her lower leg. He spurred Andahar on, trying to figure out where to turn, or if he was even going in the right direction.

With the delays and indecision, and the futile attempts to ease Dahlia's suffering, it was long past midday when Drizzt at last arrived at the farmhouse south of Luskan, where the dirty woman eked out a paltry existence with her five children. They weren't hiding this time. The children and the woman came to the doorway and watched him slip down from Andahar and gently pull Dahlia off the unicorn's back. He draped her across his shoulders and moved toward the doorway. The woman crossed her arms and wore a profound scowl.

"She dead?" the woman asked. Her expression went from sour to surprised when she looked upon Dahlia . . . because Dahlia's hair and facial skin didn't appear the same as she had when they came through there, Drizzt realized.

"Not dead, not dying," Drizzt answered defiantly. "But she's gravely ill—poisoned. I need to leave her here. I need you to watch over her while I return to Luskan."

He moved to enter the doorway, but the woman didn't immediately step aside. She stood there staring at him.

"Please, will you tend her?" Drizzt asked.

"I'm not knowing much about poison."

"Just keep her as comfortable as you . . ." Drizzt started to explain, but the woman yelled past him suddenly, to her children.

"Go and fetch Ben the Brewer!" she ordered sharply. "And be quick!"

The children ran off down the dirt path.

"Ben the Brewer?" Drizzt asked.

"He has many herbs," the woman replied.

"He can cure her?" Drizzt asked, and he was surprised by the desperation in his tone.

The farmer woman looked at him and scoffed, but finally stepped aside so he could bring her into the house. He lay Dahlia down gently on a bedroll and moved immediately to her boot, unstrapping it and pulling it off—or trying to, for her leg was thick with poison.

After some time and more than a little grease, Drizzt at last managed to get the boot off. Dahlia's foot was horribly swollen and discolored, blue and red and yellow.

He winced and brought a hand up to his face to try to compose himself. The farmer woman moved past him and studied the foot. "Looks like the bite of a tundra viper," she said.

"And Ben the Brewer can cure that?" Drizzt asked.

The woman cast him a pitiful glance and shook her head.

Drizzt took a deep breath. He couldn't lose Dahlia. Not now. Not with the loss of Bruenor so raw, not with his sudden loneliness, the realization that all of his friends were gone. He fell back from the bed, surprised by that revelation, by how much he needed Dahlia, by how frightened he was that she, too, might leave him.

"This is no snakebite," the farmer woman said, inspecting the single puncture in the bottom of Dahlia's foot.

"A poisoned spike."

"Then you should seek the one who coated the spike," the woman said. "Few would play with such a mixture if they had no antidote, eh? Or get us a dose, aye, for we . . . *you,* will need the poison to counter the poison."

Drizzt nodded and spent a long moment staring at Dahlia. Other than the angry leg, she looked quite serene, though very pale.

"I'll return before the next dawn," the drow pledged.

He started for the door, but even as he reached it the farmer woman cried out. Drizzt spun around to find her backing away from Dahlia, her hand over her open mouth, a look of horror on her face. The dark elf rushed to Dahlia, but found nothing amiss.

"What?" he asked, turning to their host.

"Her face!" the woman cried. "It's bruising again, like before!"

Drizzt looked back to the elf and he understood. The magical powder Dahlia had applied was wearing off, and her woad was returning. He breathed a sigh of relief and gave a little laugh.

"It's all right," he explained, standing back up and moving for the door. "Beware that her hair might change as well."

"She's a doppelganger, then?" the woman asked with horror.

"Nay, just a bit of magical disguise."

The woman, a simple creature, shook her head at such nonsense, and Drizzt managed a smile, then ran out of the house, leaping onto Andahar's back and setting the unicorn off in a full gallop along the road to the north.

Images of Dahlia's foot haunted him with Andahar's every running stride.

They stood around her in a circle, bloody and battered. All of them, from Bengarion to Dor'crae, the nine lovers she had killed.

"You cannot escape us," Dor'crae promised her. Half of his skin was missing, blasted free from the force of the rushing water. "We await you."

"You think we have forgotten you?" asked another.

"You think we have forgiven you?" asked another.

They began to laugh, all nine, and to pace in unison, circling Dahlia as she spun around every which way. She had nowhere to run. Kozah's Needle could not help her this time.

A tenth form joined the marching nine; a tiny form; a baby, half elf and half tiefling. He didn't say anything, but stared at Dahlia hatefully then smiled a wicked smile to show a mouth full of sharpened teeth.

Dahlia cried out and fell away from him, but that only put her closer—too close!—to those on the other side. She cried out again and stumbled back to her original spot.

They taunted her and laughed at her. Desperate, she charged at the line, fists balled, determined to fight to the bitter end.

But she was grabbed by others, by Shadovar, and was thrown down and held.

Her mother cried out for her.

Herzgo Alegni fell over her.

When he finished, he walked away, laughing, along with his guards. To kill her mother, Dahlia knew, but Dahlia was not there anymore, was back in the midst of the circling ten she'd murdered.

She was naked, and she fell to the ground, crying.

They laughed at her all the more.

"We have not forgotten," they chanted.

"We have not forgiven," they chanted.

"We await you," the baby taunted. "The time is near."

Drizzt went over Luskan's wall with no more noise or notice than a shadow in the starlight. He knew the city well, and made his way from structure to structure, alley to alley, roof to roof, to the base of the bridge to Closeguard Isle.

He could see the balcony where he and Dahlia had stood beside High Captain Kurth, as Kurth had explained to them the layout of the city. After a short while, watching the movements of the soldiers on Closeguard, Drizzt figured he could get to that balcony unnoticed.

But then what?

Was he to put a scimitar to the throat of a high captain? Would the man then surrender the antidote? Did Kurth even have any information regarding the poisoned traps in the jeweler's shop?

Frustration almost had Drizzt stomping his boot. His thoughts wrapped in on themselves, leading nowhere. He knew that time was against him, was against Dahlia, but what was he to do?

"Go to Kurth," he whispered and nodded, for that seemed the only option. He crouched beside the railing and took his first step on the bridge, but slipped back quickly when he saw several forms approaching from the other end.

The men and women walked right past him. He heard their general comments, talk of trouble with Ship Rethnor, and with one woman blaming Beniago for the current state of affairs.

"Beniago was so taken with that murderess," she said.

"The trouble with Ship Rethnor will pass," another woman insisted. "None o' their leaders were killed by Beniago's group— just a pair o' hired scalawags. All the rest fell before the elf and the drow."

"And when Ship Rethnor decides to kill a few of us?" the first woman replied angrily.

"Ye'd do well to temper yer wrath when it's aimed at Beniago," a man said.

"Bah, but he's out drinking and whoring." The first woman waved her hand.

"He has eyes," the man said, and the woman glowered at him.

The group moved away and Drizzt let them go, reconsidering his own course. He glanced back at Closeguard Isle and the tower, but went the other way, into the city, heading for the dock section, where ruffians roamed for their "drinking and whoring."

He knew that he'd need luck on his side, but knew, too, that this was not a section of indoor taverns behind closed doors. Most of the establishments near the docks were open-front bars, with patrons wandering up and down the street.

Drizzt paused again when he neared the area, which was well lit and quite boisterous even at this late hour—particularly at this late hour. Some of the many people on the street would recognize him, and given his recent encounter with both Ship Rethnor and Ship Kurth, that might not be such a good thing. He wouldn't be the only drow down there, at least, he noted, as he spotted one tattooed dark elf walking with others of his crew.

Drizzt pulled the hood of his forest-green cloak up over his head and pulled the cowl low. He wrapped the cloak around his body, as well, to hide his distinctive blades.

He went down among the crowd, keeping his head low, his eyes constantly scanning.

He caught more than one man staring at him curiously, and knew that his time here would be short indeed when one such fellow then turned to a companion and whispered something, and the companion rushed away. To gather allies, no doubt.

Drizzt shook the notion away and focused on Dahlia, reminding himself that she needed him here and needed him to be quick. He picked up his pace, moving along, studying the faces.

Beniago.

The man seemed to be alone, walking with a mug of ale in one hand, a half-eaten loaf of bread in the other. Drizzt surveyed the area then moved fast. He cut across Beniago's path, perhaps ten strides ahead of the man, and only briefly glanced at him, making sure that Beniago noticed him as well.

But only for that fleeting instant.

He didn't want the assassin to be sure that it was him. The hint was his tease.

He crossed the narrow street and moved between a pair of taverns and down a shadowy alley, picking up his speed as soon as he was out of sight. The drow skidded to a stop and picked his way up the side of a building to a rooftop. He crept along the alleyway, and he watched.

Beniago turned into that alleyway a few heartbeats later, drink and bread gone, weapons drawn. The assassin of Ship Kurth moved down cautiously, twenty steps into the alley, then around a corner at the backside of the building into a shorter alley that exited onto a far less bustling street.

The man stayed near to a wall, his gaze darting all around. He was out of sight of the street now.

Drizzt dropped into the alley behind him, his cloak open, his hood back.

Beniago spun to face him, gave a gasp, and thrust his sword at the drow's midsection.

A scimitar picked it off cleanly, and even as Beniago brought his long weapon back to bear, the drow came on fiercely, both of his blades out and high in front of him, his wrists rolling over each other in a devastating and straightforward assault.

Beniago fell back and repeatedly batted his sword up horizontally in front of him. He kept his other arm, holding his prized dagger, cocked at his side.

Drizzt noted it, of course, and so he pressed all the harder, his scimitars beating a steady rhythm against Beniago's sword. He found an opening, Twinkle hitting the sword at just the right angle to move it aside, and Icingdeath coming in right behind, with an open path to Beniago's shoulder.

But Drizzt didn't take the opening to score a hit, and altered his angle just enough so that Beniago could adjust his sword and block that blade, too.

Drizzt came on harder, recklessly it seemed, and he stumbled past and crashed hard against the alleyway wall as Beniago threw himself to the side.

With a growl, apparently thinking victory imminent, Beniago's other hand stabbed out, but that growl turned to a gasp as Drizzt's blade came down in a swift backhand slash, intercepting the thrust and gashing Beniago's forearm.

The assassin cried out and his dagger went flying away.

Beniago turned to his right and leaped away, his left sword hand, slashing back to fend off the drow.

But the drow dropped below the swipe, executing his own cut, and Beniago had to leap up to avoid getting his ankles chopped out from under him. He landed off-balance, trying to throw himself back against the wall enough to catch his balance, but that twisting movement slowed him.

Drizzt tumbled past him with amazing quickness, his magically-enhanced anklets providing a burst of speed. He came to his feet farther along the first alleyway, blocking the escape.

Beniago skidded to a stop, his cut arm tucked under his sword arm, his blade waving defensively in front of him. He began to backstep immediately, and glanced over his shoulder.

"My panther is out there," Drizzt warned—and lied, for he'd already overtaxed Guenhwyvar and had not dared summon her back to the Prime Material Plane. "If you try to flee, she will destroy you."

"I'm second to the high captain of Ship Kurth," Beniago warned. "If you kill me—"

"They will seek to kill me in response?" Drizzt mocked him. "Is that not already the case, Beniago?"

"More so!" the assassin promised, and he seemed to grow more confident then, for a din had begun on the street behind them.

Drizzt heard it, too, and he reached into his innate powers, last remnants of his days in Menzoberranzan, and placed a magical globe of darkness halfway down the alley between himself and the street.

"Ship Kurth will hunt you to the ends of Faerûn!"

Drizzt put up his blades. "If I wanted to kill you, you would already be dead," he said. "You left an opening against my overhand spin. Don't deny it, for you noted it and tried to correct your block, and only were able to do so because I allowed it."

Beniago fumbled for a response, but had none.

"Dahlia is poisoned," Drizzt went on. "I need the antidote to the jeweler's trap, and I need it now, or she will surely perish. I go now to that shop." He started to climb the wall, for now a shout went up from the street behind him. "Come to me with the antidote."

"Why would—?"

"You will be high captain one day," Drizzt said as he neared the roof. "You'll want allies."

"You ask me to trust you and Dahlia?" Beniago asked incredulously, but Drizzt was already gone from his sight.

Not gone from the alleyway, though, as he found another perch and watched Beniago.

A gang of pirates finally prodded through the darkness globe, then came charging down the alley as Beniago moved to retrieve his dagger. The assassin regarded his allies with a disgusted shake of his head and roughly shouldered past them.

A semi-conscious Dahlia thrashed as Ben the Brewer's hot knife cut deeply into her foot. The farmer woman holding her down nearly got a knee in the face for her efforts.

"Ah, but it's an ugly thing," she said as green and white pus flowed from the wound. "Viper juice?"

"Aye, and we've all seen the withering o' that bite."

"Then she's a dead one."

"Should be already, but not a lot went in," Ben the Brewer replied. He cut again, drawing an X on Dahlia's foot, and more pus flowed forth. "And she's a tough one, I'm thinking."

Dahlia cried out, perhaps in pain, but it wasn't a response to his knife, they both knew. She was lost in her fevered dreams once more, and obviously, those dreams were not proving to be a pleasant experience.

Ben the Brewer reached up to Dahlia's thigh and pulled tighter on the slip-knot he'd set there. "I'd take her leg," he said. "The foot at least. But I'm not thinking she'd live through the cutting."

"She's doomed anyway," the farmer woman replied, and she looked to the wide-bladed axe and the long serrated knife he'd brought.

"If High Captain Kurth learns of this . . ." Beniago started to say, holding his hand out to Drizzt.

Drizzt took the phial. "He'll thank you when Dahlia and I offer him our allegiance," he finished for Beniago. "If Kurth is still high captain when we meet again, I mean," the drow added, a clear implication that he believed that Beniago might find a way to rise to that seat of power.

As he heard the words leave his mouth, Drizzt had to work hard to hide his own surprise. Though born in Menzoberranzan, Drizzt was hardly a master of subterfuge, hardly a player in the realms of shadow and murder. When before would he have even considered such an interaction with a man like Beniago? When before would he have even considered any alliance with one of the high captains of Luskan? Drizzt wasn't merely tossing that possibility out in order to garner the antidote, he was actually thinking that he and Dahlia might do well to ally themselves with Kurth, or Beniago. There was, after all, a practical side of the matter: He had the antidote in hand!

A shout came from one of the nearby alleyways.

"Ship Rethnor has awakened to your presence," Beniago warned.

"And Ship Kurth?"

"Possibly, but I can stand them down," Beniago replied. "There's little I can offer you against the rage of Ship Rethnor."

Drizzt lifted the whistle on the end of the chain and blew into it, and with great running strides, Andahar came to him, leaping through the dimensions. Drizzt motioned for the unicorn to keep running past him.

"Farewell, Beniago," the drow said, grabbing Andahar's flowing mane and leaping up atop the steed. "If this is the antidote, know you have made a friend. If not, then know without doubt that my blades will find your heart."

And with that warning, Drizzt Do'Urden was gone, Andahar galloping across the market square, hooves clap-clapping on the cobblestones. A shout came up from a rooftop and Drizzt turned the unicorn sharply down an alleyway. He dodged a crate, leaped another, and swerved hard at the last instant to avoid some rubble.

In full gallop, Andahar came out onto the next street over, and cries went up and faces appeared in darkened windows. Drizzt heard the shouts along the rooftops, trying to track his progress, no doubt in an attempt to ready some archers or some other ambush up ahead.

So Drizzt turned Andahar again, and again, street by street, alley by alley. Galloping hard, he took out Taulmaril and set an arrow to the magical bowstring.

Movement on the roof ahead and to the left caught his attention, so he put up the bow and drew back. His legs clamped hard around the unicorn, holding him steady as he let fly, again and again, a barrage of lightning arrows streaking for the roof's facing, blasting holes in the wood and shale, and brightening the night in a shower of multicolored sparks.

On they ran, Drizzt bending low over Andahar's strong neck, whispering encouragement into the unicorn's ear. He knew that enemies were all around, intent on stopping him. He knew that if he failed, Dahlia was surely doomed.

But he wasn't afraid. There wasn't the slightest fear in him that he wouldn't get there in time, that these thugs would stop him. He couldn't believe that, or fear that, not at this moment, not in this . . .

Exhilaration.

That was the word for it, the only word for it. He was alive, his every sense honed and sharp-edged, relying on his warrior instincts.

Exhilaration. Drizzt had no time for fear or doubt.

Andahar snorted as if sensing the drow's thoughts, and ran on harder, plowing along the lanes and alleyways in the zigzag maze Drizzt had determined to get them to the gate.

An arrow reached out from the side, grazing Andahar. Drizzt responded with a lightning missile that revealed the archer, who promptly ran away.

To the other side, a large pirate rushed out of a doorway, spear in hand, and aimed for the approaching unicorn.

Drizzt's arrow threw the fool back through the door before he'd even cocked his arm.

Unicorn and rider thundered down a decline and turned a sharp corner, heading up another street, this one leading straight to the opened west gate. Arrow after arrow reached out from Taulmaril, streaking the night with silver, slamming against the walls of the guard tower or slashing into the cobblestones at the feet of the wide-eyed guards. They shouted warnings and they called to each other for help.

And Drizzt kept shooting, arrows slamming into stone and wood, showering sparks and lighting beams with licks of flame. He scored no further hits on the scrambling guards—he wasn't trying to cut any of them down—but he kept them running and diving and shouting for help, too confused and surprised to organize a valid counter, or even to shut the gates.

Andahar never slowed, thundering up the road, and finally, a sentry found his wits enough to rush to one of the gates.

Drizzt's arrow splintered the wood barely a finger's breadth from the sentry's face, and he shrieked and fell away.

Out into the night leaped Andahar, charging down the road.

And off they went, the wind blowing in Drizzt's white hair, and he felt free and alive. He knew that Dahlia would survive—he simply knew it in every corner of his soul. He couldn't be wounded again, body or heart, so close to his most recent, brutal loss. Nay! He denied the possibility. He was free and he was running through the chill night on his mighty, magical steed. He was alive, the warrior, the thief, who had slipped into the heart of hostile Luskan and pulled from their foes the answer to Dahlia's dilemma.

"On, Andahar!" he cried, and he fired an arrow high into the night sky, a sizzling silver streak, an expression of his leaping heart.

He set the bells of the barding to ringing.

Exhilaration.

They never slowed, running hard for hours, all the way back to the distant farmstead. Drizzt noted a single candle glowing from within as the structure at last came in sight, and he took that as a hopeful sign that Dahlia was still alive. He skidded Andahar to a stop and flung himself over the unicorn's back as if it was all a dance.

Just then, a murderous scream came from the farmhouse.

He froze in place, his world collapsing, his mood, his feeling of invincibility, seeming so suddenly, a cruel joke. He was invincible or he was doomed, and the choice didn't feel like his own, not that night, not then, not with Dahlia beside him.

The scream—it had to be Dahlia's scream—reminded him all too clearly of his own cry those many years ago when he'd awakened to find his wife lying cold beside him, his friend screaming, too, in the hallway for another lost to the mists of time.

Drizzt crashed through the door, drawing his blades.

The farmer woman huddled in the corner, her hand still muffling the last gasps of her scream.

Dahlia half-sat, half-knelt on the bed, sweating and swaying side to side as if she would fall to the floor at any moment. She held Kozah's Needle in tri-staff form, one end out in front of her and swinging back and forth like a pendulum.

Drizzt stared at the floor in front of Dahlia, where a serrated knife lay, then kept turning to see a man sprawled upon the floor, face-down.

"She killed him!" the farmer woman cried.

"He tried to cut off my foot!" Dahlia yelled back, in a voice surprisingly strong.

Drizzt ran to the fallen man. He groaned as soon as the drow touched his shoulder. "He's alive." Drizzt gently rolled Ben the Brewer over onto his back.

"Give me a moment to find my balance and I'll rectify that," Dahlia said.

Drizzt shot her an angry glare and motioned for the farmer woman to join him. She ran a wide circuit around Dahlia and fell down to the floor beside her wounded friend.

Ben the Brewer opened his eyes and shook his head.

"Now, that'll leave a mark," he said, rubbing the lump on his skull.

Dahlia swooned and fell back on the bed, banging her head on the wall as she tumbled.

Drizzt and the farmer woman helped Ben the Brewer to his feet.

"Thought she was near dead," Ben explained. "And she might well be. We'll need to take that foot, but I'm not going near to that one unless she's tied well!"

In reply, Drizzt held up the phial. He rushed to Dahlia and cradled her head.

"Kill him," Dahlia whispered, opening one eye.

"Drink," Drizzt said. He knew that Beniago might have double-crossed him, might have given him nothing other than more of the same poison.

But it was too late for him to change his mind.

Dahlia began to cough and tremble almost immediately. She pulled herself away from Drizzt with a sudden convulsion and rolled to her side, where she vomited over the edge of the bed.

Drizzt fell over her and tried to hold her still.

"What did you do?" the farmer woman asked.

"The antidote," Drizzt tried to explain. His thoughts were whirling as he wondered if he'd just finished off his lover.

"Aye, that's what I'd expect," said Ben the Brewer. "It'll clean 'er out, but won't be a pretty sight."

He staggered over and picked up his knife, but when he stood straight, he found Drizzt staring back at him hard.

Ben the Brewer dropped the blade back to the floor.

"I just realized that I don't even know your name," Drizzt said to the farmer woman a couple of mornings later. They stood outside the house. It was his first time away from Dahlia since administering the antidote. The elf rested easily, at last, her fever broken, the swelling in her foot and leg at last receding.

"Meg," she answered.

"Meg?"

"Just Meg. I had more of a name once, when it mattered. Now I'm Meg, just Meg, and Ma to my kids. Nothing more."

"We owe you much," Drizzt said.

"You owe me a clean floor, to be sure!" Meg said with a sad laugh.

Drizzt smiled at her. "Your generosity . . ."

"I did what any person would do, or ought to do, or once upon a time outside Luskan would do," Meg replied, her voice sharp.

"Still, I would like to show my appreciation, to you and to Ben the Brewer."

"I want nothing from you, other than that you'll be long gone from my house, not to return."

The chill in the woman's voice surprised Drizzt. He thought perhaps their time there had forged a bond. He thought wrong, apparently.

"Firewood, at least," said Drizzt. "Or perhaps I can hunt a boar for your table." She involuntarily licked her lips, and he smiled, thinking he'd tempted her.

Her face turned stone cold. "You get your lady elf and be gone," Meg said flatly. "She'll be fine to travel this day, so you're going, both of you, and don't you come back."

"Because people will talk and the high captains will hear," came Dahlia's voice from the doorway. She walked out on surprisingly steady legs.

Drizzt looked at Meg, but her expression didn't change.

"Call your steed," Meg said. "You've a road worth riding." She turned away and walked past Dahlia, and shut the door behind her.

Drizzt stared after her, even started after her, but Dahlia grabbed him by the arm and held him back.

"Summon Andahar," she said quietly. "It will be best."

"They saved you."

"You saved me."

"They did—they helped us greatly!"

"They tried to cut my foot off."

"Only to save you."

"Better to die, then."

The way she said it struck Drizzt profoundly, because he knew she meant it. He wanted to chastise her, wanted to tell her to never speak like that.

But then he thought of his midnight ride, of his exhilaration, of his sense of control, of confidence, of his sense of sheer joy in the adventure, whatever the stakes. It was a feeling Drizzt Do'Urden had not known in a long, long time.

He blew the whistle for Andahar, and he set the bells of the barding to ringing as they charged away, down the southern road.

PART II

THE ENEMY OF MY ENEMY

Long has it occurred to me that I am a creature of action, of battle and of adventure. In times of peace and calm, like my friend Bruenor, I find myself longing for the open road, where bandits rule and wild orcs roam. For so many years, I stubbornly clung to the battle and the adventure. I admit my thrill when King Bruenor decided to quietly abdicate and go on his search for legendary Gauntlgrym.

For in that quest, we found the open road, the wilderness, the adventure, and indeed, the battles.

But something was missing. I couldn't quite place it, couldn't quite articulate it, but for a long while now, indeed back to the early days of King Bruenor's reign of reclaimed Mithral Hall, there remained a sharp edge missing, a necessary edge scraping my skin and keeping me wholly alive.

Anyone who has ever stood on the edge of a cliff understands this. One can bask in the views, and with such a wide panorama, one cannot help but feel the thrill of being a part of something bigger and grander, much like the manner in which the stars pull a soul heavenward to join with the incomprehensible vastness of the universe.

But amid all the beauty and awe-inspiring grandeur, it is the feel of the wind that completes the sensation, particularly if it is a swirling and gusting breeze. For then comes the greatest affirmation of life: the sensation of fear, the recognition of how fleeting this entire existence can be.

When I stand on the edge of that cliff, on the precipice of disaster, and I lean against that wind, I am truly alive. I have to be quick to realign my balance and my footing as the wind swirls; if I wish to stay on my perch, indeed to stay alive, I have to remain quicker than the whims of the wind.

In the past, I stubbornly kept tight the battles and the adventures, and ever turned my eye to the open and dangerous road, but it was not until very recently that I came to understand that which was truly missing: the thrill of the risk.

The thrill of the risk. The edge of that high precipice. Not the risk itself, for that was ever there, but the thrill of that risk . . .

In truth, it was not until my midnight ride back from Luskan that I realized how long I'd been missing that thrill.

When first I left Dahlia, I was afraid for her, but that fear dissipated almost immediately, replaced by a sense of invincibility that I have not known in decades, in a century perhaps! I knew that I would get over Luskan's guarded wall, that I would find Beniago, and that I would bend him to my need. I knew that I would win out. I knew that I would be quicker than the gusting wind.

Why?

The risk was ever there, I now understand, but for so many years, the thrill of that risk was not because of the untenable price of defeat. For the price of having friends so dear and a companion so beloved is . . . vulnerability.

I can accept the wind blowing Drizzt Do'Urden from the cliff. Such a price is not too high. But to watch Catti-brie fall before me?

Then I am not invincible. Then there is simply the risk, and not the thrill of living on the edge of that dangerous cliff.

No more.

For when I rode to Luskan, I was invincible. The walls could not stop me. Beniago could not stop me.

And now I understand that when I lost my friends, my family, my home, I lost, too, my vulnerability, and gained back in return the thrill of danger, the freedom to not only walk on the edge of that high cliff, but to dance there, to taunt the wind.

What a strange irony.

But what, then, of my growing relationship with Dahlia?

She fascinates me. She teases me with her every movement and every word. She lures me—to where I do not know!

On my ride, in my unbridled joy, in the thrill of adventure and battle and yes, risk, I knew that she would survive. I knew it! Even when all reason warned me that the poison would take her long before I could return from Luskan, somewhere deep inside of me, I just knew she wouldn't be lost to me. Not then, not like that. Her fate could not be written such; her death wouldn't be so crude and mundane.

But what if I was proven wrong? What if she had been taken from me, like those before? Surely Dahlia dances more wildly on the edge of that cliff than I do. She is fearless to the point of utter recklessness— in the short time I have known her, I have seen that all too clearly.

And yet, that risk does not frighten me.

I don't want her to die. The fascination, the attraction, is all too real and all too powerful. I want to know her, to understand her. I want to yell at her and kiss her all at once. I want to test her in battle and in passion.

She is as erratic as she is erotic, changing her tone as easily as she alters her appearance. I think it a game she plays, a way to keep friends and enemies alike off-balance. But I cannot be sure, and that, too, is part of her never-ending seduction. Is she teasing me with seemingly erratic behavior, or is Dahlia truly erratic? Is she the actor or the role?

Or perhaps there is a third answer: Am I so desperate to know this unpredictable doppelganger that I am reading too much into her every word? Am I seeking, and thus seeing, deeper meaning than she intends as I scour for clues to that which is in her heart?

A carefully guarded heart. But why?

Another mystery to unravel . . .

I knew she wouldn't be lost to me, but how? How did my instincts counter my reason so fully? Given all that has passed in my life, shouldn't I have expected the worst outcome regarding Dahlia? Given the losses I have endured, shouldn't I have feared exactly that in a desperate situation?

And yet I did not. I reveled in the midnight ride, in the adventure and the thrill of the risk.

Is it Dahlia's competency, her swagger, her own fearlessness, affecting my heart? Or is it, perhaps, that I do not love her—not as I loved Catti-brie, or Bruenor, Wulfgar and Regis?

Or is it something more, I wonder? Perhaps Innovindil's lesson reached me more deeply than I had known. Logically, rationally, I can see Innovindil's viewpoint, that we elves have to live our lives in shorter segments because of the short-lived races with whom we naturally interact. But could it be that Innovindil's lessons have sparked within me a confidence that I will go on, that there is more road in front of me? Though those I deeply loved are removed from my side, I will find others to share the leagues and the fights?

It is all of that, I expect, and perhaps something more. Perhaps each loss hardened my heart and numbed me to the pain. The loss of Bruenor stung less than those of Catti-brie and Regis, and less than my knowledge that Wulfgar, too, has surely passed on. There are other reasons, I am confident. Bruenor's last words to me, "I found it, elf," reflected a full life's journey, to be sure! What dwarf could ask for more than what King Bruenor Battlehammer knew? His final battle alone, his victory over the pit fiend while immersed in the power of dwarven kings of old, would surely fill to bursting the heart of any dwarf.

So I did not cry for Bruenor, though I surely miss him no less than any of the others.

There is no one answer, then. Life is a complicated journey, and few are the direct lines from feeling to consequence and consequence to anticipation. I will try to unravel it all, of course, as that is my nature, but in the end, I am left now with only one inescapable truth: the joy of that midnight ride, of bargaining with Beniago at the end of a scimitar, of reckless adventure.

The thrill, the edge of the cliff.

This is your promise to Drizzt Do'Urden, my lady Dahlia the erotic, the erratic.

And this is your legacy to Drizzt Do'Urden, my old Companions of the Hall.

Do you see me now, Catti-brie?

Do you see me now, Bruenor?

Do you see me now, Regis?

Do you see me now, Wulfgar?

Because I see you. You walk with me. You are in my thoughts every day, all four, and I see you smile when I smile and frown when I hurt. I believe this, I sense this.

I pray for this.

—Drizzt Do'Urden

CHAPTER 9

BLACK DIAMOND

D RIZZT MOVED TO THE BACK OF THE SMALL ENCAMPMENT, coming to the edge of the bluff overlooking the riverbank. Dahlia was at the cold stream, her boots and black leather hat on the ground beside her. Her black hair was still in its fashionably shoulder-length cut, swept forward, and her woad remained hidden by the makeup . . . or was it the other way around, where the woad was the makeup and this was the real Dahlia?

Drizzt chuckled as he considered that, for the illusion that was Dahlia resonated with him on many more levels than her physical appearance. It was a helpless chuckle, for he held no hope that he would unwind the mysteries of Dahlia anytime soon.

She slipped her shapely leg into the stream, then drew it forth and rubbed at her sore and still discolored foot. She looked at the unsightly puncture and shook her head with obvious disgust.

"Which is real and which the illusion?" Drizzt asked, skipping down the steep incline to stand beside her. He noted that she wore a new piece of jewelry, a black diamond in her right ear, complimenting the ten diamond studs in her left.

"Both and neither," Dahlia answered dismissively. She grimaced as she squeezed her foot, bringing forth some pus and blood from the wound.

"Are you so afraid that the truth of Dahlia will be revealed?"

Dahlia looked up at him sourly, and shook her head as if his question wasn't worth her trouble.

"We owe a great debt to Meg the farmer woman and Ben the Brewer," Drizzt remarked.

"You would start babbling about them again?" Dahlia snapped back. "Had you returned to the farmhouse a few moments later, I would've been one foot lighter. Or both of them would've lain dead at my feet."

"They would've taken your foot only because they thought it the only way to save your life."

"They would've *tried* to take my foot and I would've killed them both," Dahlia insisted.

"You would've killed a mother in front of her children?"

"I would've asked the children to turn around first," Dahlia sarcastically replied.

Drizzt laughed at her unrelenting sourness, but Dahlia only glared at him all the more. For a moment, just a heartbeat, Drizzt almost expected her to jump up and attack him then and there.

"Damn you, Beniago," the woman muttered, squeezing her aching foot yet again.

"He provided the antidote," Drizzt said.

"Then he's a fool, because he saved the life of one who will kill him."

"It wasn't Beniago who set the traps," Drizzt reminded her.

"It was Beniago who forced me from the rope to the floor."

"He defends the wares of Ship Kurth."

"And you would defend him?"

"Hardly. Didn't I arrive to chase him off?"

Dahlia spat on her foot and squeezed it again. A dribble of blood and greenish-white pus slipped out. "Killing him will wound Ship Kurth, and make it clear that I'm not one to be toyed with."

"Ah, that's it, then," Drizzt said with a grin. "It's your embarrassment at being outfoxed."

Dahlia narrowed her eyes threateningly.

"High Captain Kurth, or yes, perhaps Beniago, understood that you would return to the jewelry shop to appropriate the piece, and so they were quite ready for you," Drizzt said. "In fact, I suspect that the only reason they even took us to that particular merchant was because of your obvious fondness for sparkling gemstones."

"I knew they'd know," Dahlia insisted. "I wanted them to know."

"And you wanted them to defeat you and kill you?"

Dahlia's blue eyes threw imaginary darts into his face, Drizzt knew, but he grinned all the more, enjoying having the upper hand against Dahlia for once. For all of her stubbornness, she couldn't, with true conviction, claim she'd expected the trap.

"I already told you I'd sorted out the design of the trap and deduced how to defeat it," Dahlia said, biting each word off short for emphasis. "I would've slipped free of the lash and Beniago would've died if you hadn't intervened."

"With poison in your foot?"

"I would've stripped Beniago's corpse naked and found the elixir. And had it not been for your foolish intervention, I would have had the time to tend the wound then and there, before the poison had spread up my leg."

Drizzt laughed, shook his head, and let it go at that.

"We will return to Luskan," Dahlia announced, standing and facing to the north up the road.

"To repay Ship Kurth?"

"Yes."

"What of Sylora? I thought it was she you hated above all others."

Despite her stubbornness—and she was possessed of great quantities—Dahlia couldn't resist glancing back over her shoulder, back to the south.

"I go with you now to find Sylora," Drizzt stated flatly, "as I committed to do when we left Gauntlgrym. I, too, would like to repay her for her actions that have so devastated Neverwinter. But I won't return to Luskan beside you, should you choose that course."

"I wouldn't have gone to Luskan at all had it not been for your insistence," Dahlia reminded him.

"But not to engage Ship Kurth or any other of the high captains."

"No, to find Jarlaxle, because you cannot accept that he's gone," Dahlia said, for no reason other than to sting him, Drizzt realized.

"To Neverwinter Wood?" he asked. "Or do we part ways here?"

Dahlia's glare abruptly turned into a wicked smile. "You'll not abandon me. Not now."

"I won't go to Luskan," Drizzt said flatly.

Dahlia held her stare for a few moments, but then it was she who blinked and nodded. "Ship Kurth will still be there when we're done with the witch of Thay," she decided. "And perhaps we would do well to let a few tendays pass, so that Luskan forgets about Drizzt and Dahlia."

"And then we kill Beniago?"

Dahlia nodded and Drizzt shook his head.

"Let it be," the drow advised.

Dahlia's sigh showed more contempt than resignation.

"Kill Beniago?" Drizzt went on skeptically. "He who is powerful within Luskan and Ship Kurth? Beniago, who I spared at the end of my blade?"

"You think him an ally?" Dahlia asked incredulously.

"I think that perhaps the past is better left in the past," Drizzt replied. "Beniago gave me the elixir knowing I would use it to save you. He was grateful that I didn't kill him, because I surely had him dead, had I so chosen. He will soon enough be a man of great power within Luskan, and within the whole of the region, and he has shown himself to be no enemy of ours."

"Drizzt Do'Urden bargains with murderers now," Dahlia said with a wry smirk.

She meant the remark as another jab, obviously, but it struck Drizzt as more of an honest question than that. It was a question that he'd asked himself many times in his past. He thought of Artemis Entreri, his long-time nemesis, and undeniably a killer. Yet Drizzt and Entreri had struck a bond beneath the tunnels of Mithral Hall when it was still in the hands of the duergar dwarves. And Entreri had fought beside Drizzt and Catti-brie during their escape from Menzoberranzan. Drizzt and Entreri battled side-by-side, because it had been in their best interests. And on more than one occasion, Drizzt had not finished off Entreri, had not killed him, when he'd found the opportunity.

His thoughts also fell to Jarlaxle, of course, the drow to whom Drizzt had run when he'd lost Catti-brie and Regis. Was Jarlaxle not a killer?

"He thinks these killers potential allies," Dahlia went on.

"Better, perhaps, that they are not overt enemies," he quietly replied.

Dahlia couldn't let it go without one last stab. "And thinks these killers perhaps even lovers, yes?" She gave a little laugh and limped back up the grassy banking toward the camp.

"This is what I've come to know," Drizzt stated flatly, halting Dahlia in her tracks. "There is right and there is wrong. There is good and there is evil, but rarely are either of these concepts fully embodied in any one person. Life is more complicated than that; people are more complicated than that. Not all allies will prove of similar weal and not all enemies will be so different from me. I wish this weren't true." He gave a resigned, almost hopeless smile. He thought of Captain Deudermont, then, his old friend who had placed principle over pragmatism in an untenable situation, the result of which had been the fall of Luskan to the nefarious high captains. Drizzt had not agreed with Deudermont's designs, had warned against them, to no avail.

"Or perhaps I don't," he admitted. "Perhaps it is, after all, that complexity that makes life interesting."

"The complexity you find in others, which doesn't exist in the pure heart of Drizzt Do'Urden?" Dahlia teased.

Drizzt laughed and shrugged. A million retorts flitted through his thoughts, but in the end, Drizzt had no response. Dahlia had weighed her words and her tone perfectly, he realized. She knew him, his reputation and his soul, and obviously she had no hesitation in flicking her finger against his heart. He watched her diminish into the shadows, reminded again that this was not Catti-brie beside him, not a rock of conscience, not even a dependable friend. What might Dahlia do to help Drizzt if her own life was on the line? Would she flee and leave him to his fate?

He played through their many battles at each other's side in Gauntlgrym. Dahlia had fought valiantly, fearlessly. He could count on her in matters of the sword.

"Will you join me tonight by the fire?" Dahlia asked from beyond the bluff.

But could Drizzt count on her in matters of the heart?

Drizzt shook it all away with a little laugh. What did it matter? He pulled himself up and brushed the dust of the road from his pants and cloak, then went to the river and quickly splashed his face.

Then he went to Dahlia's lair.

With Andahar keeping a swift pace, Drizzt and Dahlia passed Port Llast the very next night, giving the town a wide berth for fear that some of Kurth's agents might be among the visitors. Not far down the road from there, Drizzt realized that they were not alone.

"In the tree to the left," Dahlia whispered back when he informed her.

Drizzt pulled Andahar up to a halt and turned the steed sidelong to the road, his eyes focusing on that inhabited tree.

"Must I shoot you from your perch before you admit your presence?" Drizzt called out, bringing Taulmaril across his lap.

"Please, not that, good sir Drizzt," came the reply from within the shelter of the boughs—the fast-browning boughs, for the summer season was beginning its turn to fall.

"Stuyles's man," Dahlia remarked, and Drizzt nodded.

"Would you break bread with us again?" the drow called out. "Entertain us with tales of the north while we repay the bards' debt?"

"We should just ride past them," Dahlia said. "Or do you feel the need to tell them of the farmer woman and the brewer?"

"Perhaps many would be interested, including Stuyles."

"To what end?" Dahlia asked. "Do you hope that they will lay down their knives and swords and return to the plow? Will Drizzt Do'Urden fix the world?"

Ahead of them, the would-be highwayman dropped down from the tree's lowest branch and waved them on, and Drizzt, not bothering to answer Dahlia, spurred Andahar forward. Dahlia kept her sour expression all the way to the bandits' encampment.

They were greeted warmly, and offered food and a seat by a warm fire. Stuyles was there, and prodded Drizzt for his latest tales, and the drow obliged by telling him of their meetings with Meg the farmer woman and Ben the Brewer.

They all laughed when Drizzt recounted Dahlia's defense of her foot at the expense of poor Ben, and indeed, any here knew the man.

Even Dahlia couldn't resist a bit of a grin.

One by one, the bandits drifted away to their respective cots, until only the tall bandit named Hadencourt remained. "Now you go to Neverwinter Wood to repay Lady Sylora?" Hadencourt asked.

Dahlia, half asleep by that point, perked up immediately and stared at the man.

"We hear much," Hadencourt explained. "And surely the tale of Dahlia Sin'felle is one of note, as were her two journeys to Gauntlgrym."

The matter-of-fact manner in which he spoke made Drizzt uneasy. He looked to Dahlia, who seemed on the verge of throttling the man.

"Pray tell us what you've heard, good Hadencourt," Drizzt prompted.

"More than any of the others here, of course," said the man. "But then, I knew much more about the situation long before I met up with Farmer Stuyles and his band of misguided heroes."

Dahlia and Drizzt exchanged suspicious looks.

"I'm not a former farmer," Hadencourt flatly declared. "Nor a peasant, nor a commoner, nor a true member of this ridiculous band, in any manner they would accept."

"Do tell," said Dahlia.

Hadencourt stood up—Drizzt and Dahlia were quick to do likewise. "I'd prefer to show you," Hadencourt said, and started off into the dark night.

Drizzt and Dahlia exchanged glances yet again, and Drizzt recognized the murderous hints on her face. He called forth Guenhwyvar, sent her on a roundabout path, and they set to follow the man.

In a moonlit lea, they caught up to Hadencourt. He stood easy, staring up at the stars and the lunar orb.

"Are you an agent from Waterdeep?" Drizzt asked.

"Or from the high captains of Luskan?" a more suspicious Dahlia added.

Hadencourt laughed and slowly turned to face them. "Hardly," he said, "to either."

"You serve Sylora Salm!" Dahlia accused, and she brought her staff in front of her in a powerful and aggressive movement.

Hadencourt laughed all the louder. "Serve?" he echoed, and his voice took on a different timbre, deeper and more resonant, full of something . . . darker.

Horns wormed out of his head, spiraling up above him. His mouth elongated, widened into a devilish grin of long and pointed teeth. His skin darkened, midnight blue, black perhaps, and he grew in stature, his clothing tearing, his enlarging and cloven feet bursting from his boots as he stood towering over the couple. With fiendish, clawed hands, he ripped the remainder of his clothing aside, his spiked tail waving out behind him.

A great inhalation lifted the fiend's massive chest and a pair of leathery wings sprouted behind hm.

"By the gods, is the world full of devils?" Drizzt asked.

"It's a malebranche," whispered Dahlia, who was quite knowledge-able of the denizens of the lower planes.

As if in answer to Drizzt's rhetorical question, two more fiends leaped out from the brush to either side. These were smaller than Hadencourt, each wielding a shield and a long sword. While Hadencourt's skin was cool and dark, like a long dead coal, theirs was fiery red, peeking at Drizzt and Dahlia in stark stripes through the leathery wrapping of hellish armor. Each wore a bronze helm, but the horns showing through those headpieces were surely their own and not ornamental.

"It's a world more to our liking now," Hadencourt started to reply to Drizzt, but the drow cut him short by bringing up Taulmaril and shooting an arrow right into Hadencourt's chest. The enchanted missile slammed in hard, burning and sizzling, and knocked the malebranche back several steps, and before he could even bellow in rage, the other two leaped at the companions, long swords flashing.

Dahlia's weapon pointed forward like a spear, and out flashed Drizzt's scimitars, coming up in front of him in an underhand cross that slapped aside the legion devil's thrusting sword. He followed through hard, left and right, wanting to get past this lesser fiend to get to Hadencourt.

But this one was quick, whipping its shield around in time to block the chopping blades, and even as Drizzt retracted and re-aligned, two more legion devils leaped out from the side to join their embattled companions, one coming in hard to Drizzt's left, the other to Dahlia's right.

Drizzt started to yell out to warn his companion, but he bit off the first word, realizing that Dahlia didn't need his shout. She stabbed her staff straight ahead, driving back the legion devil, then swung it down and to the side, planting against the ground beside Drizzt's feet. Up she went, high into the air, and she drove out to the side, double-kicking into the second charging fiend. One foot slammed against the shield block, but the second slipped past and cracked the devil in the face, halting its charge and nearly dropping it to the ground. The devil tried to swipe at her with its long sword, but Dahlia was too agile for that and rolled her legs up high, the sword harmlessly slashing nothing but air beneath her.

She flipped over into a somersault and landed in a crouch beside Drizzt.

He wasn't watching. He couldn't be. His scimitars flashed left and right, thrusting ahead and lifting vertically to defeat the surprisingly well-coordinated attacks of the devils. He worked purely on instinct and the fast fiends came at him, sword, sword, shield, and shield. Metal rang out against metal as scimitar met sword, then came the dull thuds as Drizzt's attack met a heavily-padded shield.

The devil to his right came in aggressively, leading with its blade forward then swinging around for a shield bash. Its companion, working in perfect unison, tried to trap the drow by luring him farther to the left. But Drizzt recognized the maneuver.

As the devil to his right swung around to shield rush, Drizzt broke off fully with the other and turned a fast backspin over to his right, coming ahead in a rush behind the thrusting shield. He got a clean strike in, Icingdeath slamming hard against the devil's back, tearing a few of the leathery armor bands and bringing hot blood over the fiend's red skin.

The drow started in, thinking to drive the wounded devil into its companion and score many hits on both as they tangled, but again their coordination proved too clever, for both devils scrambled away as both of those facing Dahlia rushed off to the side as well.

After a single step of pursuit, both drow and elf skidded to a stop and swung back on each other, then turned as one to face Hadencourt.

He stood a few long strides away, holding a large black trident in one hand. He still stood straight, but the wound of Drizzt's missile was clear to see, fetid smoke wafting out of the hole in Hadencourt's right breast.

Drizzt glanced left and right, but the four legion devils showed no sign of returning. He looked to Dahlia and then both turned once more to Hadencourt.

"Come on, then," Dahlia dared the fiend.

Hadencourt's mouth widened into a feral hiss and he spun around, pirouetting around his planted trident. He free arm led the way around, crooked at the elbow, a large black metal bracer on that wrist glowing with sudden power. The malebranche snapped his hand forward and from that bracer came a host of spinning disks—shuriken—flying out at Drizzt and Dahlia.

Both went into a fast defense, Drizzt with his scimitars and Dahlia breaking her staff immediately into flails, whipping them back and forth to block and deflect as many of the multitude of missiles as she could.

And so they did, both of these superb warriors, but the sharp edges of the shuriken proved the least of their troubles. The missiles held a vicious secret, an explosive secret, and every block resulted in a small blast that drove the respective defender back in surprise and in pain as showers of tiny shards washed over them.

Now came the legion devils once more from the sides.

Hadencourt snapped his arm again and another volley of spinning missiles flew out at the disoriented pair.

They fell back. The legion devils charged in to finish the task.

Drizzt reached into his innate powers, back to the magic of the deep Underdark, and summoned a globe of impenetrable darkness, filling the area. He put one scimitar away as he did, his free hand grabbing Dahlia by the arm and tugging her along.

But they hardly got out of the globe when they were fighting again, a legion devil shield-rushing them and knocking Drizzt back, stumbling, while Dahlia fell to the ground.

Drizzt went back in hard, drawing his second blade, slashing ferociously to try and end the battle quickly. The legion devil didn't cry out, but its fellows apparently heard its silent call, for soon they appeared around the globe.

"Run! Go!" Drizzt cried to Dahlia.

He didn't have to ask her twice. Off stumbled Dahlia, a legion devil in close pursuit. She rushed from the lea and into the cover of the forest.

Drizzt forgot about her the moment she started away, because he had to. His focus became the three foes in front of him and the fourth, infinitely more dangerous, on the other side across his magical globe. He put his scimitars up in a flashing flurry, spinning and striking furiously. He dived down to the side, into a roll, and came up charging forward at the nearest devil, who threw its shield across to block.

And Drizzt stutter-stepped, stopping just for a moment, just long enough for the shield to whip past before lunging ahead with a vicious thrust. The legion devil managed to bring its sword around in time to partially block that stab, but only partially, and still the tip of Twinkle punctured its leathery skin. Better-aimed, the real attack of Icingdeath knifed in over the sword and scimitar, driving right into the howling devil's mouth, breaking teeth and twisting into the throat and skull.

The blade reversed almost the moment it went in, for Drizzt had no time to tarry.

He couldn't have asked for a better moment for Guenhwyvar's arrival—how many times in his life had the drow experienced exactly that? The speeding panther flew in front of him, driving back the three legion devils.

Drizzt turned and he ran, full speed, his magical ankle bracelets speeding him along. He veered and paused only long enough to retrieve his bow, then tried to approximate where Dahlia had entered the forest—perhaps he could catch her pursuing devil and down it—but she was long gone.

Behind him, he heard Guenhwyvar roar out, and he knew there was pain in that call, but he knew that he couldn't turn and fight.

Not here. Not now.

Hadencourt was still grimacing in pain, rubbing the hole in his chest, as he came around the globe to rejoin the three legionnaires. They had not pursued Drizzt, or the panther that was now limping into the brush, for the malebranche had instructed them not to do so.

No, Hadencourt had better allies for that task.

One of the legion devils growled in response and clapped its sharp teeth together and banged its sword on its shield, each strike drawing a pained grimace. The line of blood on its back thickened once more as the crease Icingdeath had put there opened wide.

The second wounded devil seemed less eager to chase off after the drow. It worked its serpent's tongue over its broken teeth, each flicker bringing forth gobs of blood. The movement seemed to feed on itself, growing more ferocious with each flicker, becoming a convulsion, becoming a seizure.

Hadencourt looked at the pitiful thing with disdain, and when it fell to the ground and began thrashing, blood now pouring more freely from its mouth, the malebranche snorted in derision, kicked the sputtering legion devil in the face, and told it to be silent.

And when it was not, when it kept thrashing and gurgling and spitting, Hadencourt drove his trident down into its chest.

A few more thrashes and the legion devil lay still.

The other two nodded their agreement.

A handful more devils joined them then, smaller and lighter creatures hardly as tall as a short dwarf, though quite unlike a dwarf, they had wiry bodies and thin limbs. They scrabbled on all fours as often as they walked upright. Their actions were more primal than those of their more cultured devil companions, more feral and vicious, with their tongues constantly flicking out from their canine snouts and their wild eyes darting around hungrily.

Most notable of all, they were covered, tailbone to skull, in a coat of quills, red-tipped and blue like veins near their base.

The remaining two legion devils crinkled their expressions in disgust and tried to avoid looking at the spined devils.

"You know what I seek," Hadencourt instructed them.

The five spined devils scrabbled off into the forest, a pair running up the nearest tree as easily as if they were skipping across a fallen log.

Tearing aside brush with his sword, the legion devil charged through the forest. The creature knew the elf woman was just ahead. It knew that it had her!

The devil burst through one thicket, stumbling onto clear ground, then skidded to a stop. The path ahead was clear, the brush thinner, and the elf nowhere in sight. The devil moved more cautiously then, remembering the lessons Hadencourt had imparted when it had been summoned forth to wage this battle.

The devil nodded its horned head. It considered again the female's departing move. Before it, left and right, stood a pair of tall trees and in the path directly between them lay the tell-tale imprinting of the butt end of a long staff, a depression in the ground, and there, the elf's footprints ended.

Forked tongue flicking past its long teeth, the devil leaped up and hooked its sword arm over the lowest branch.

Hanging there in mid-air, its focus above, sword arm looped, shield arm reaching, and kicking one leg up repeatedly, the legion devil presented the most appealing target.

Dahlia, who had not climbed the tree and had only made it look like she might have vaulted up there, rushed out from around the tree trunk to the devil's right, staff in hand. The devil saw her at the last moment and threw its arms back over the branch, but its descent was not in a straight line as the staff jabbed into its midsection hard, driving it back.

As Dahlia let the devil fly free of the strike, she released a measure of lightning, further throwing the beast aside. Head over heels, it tumbled into the thick trunk of the other tree. With a howl of pain and outrage at being so deceived, the legion devil spun around to regain its footing, and just came up straight when the elf waded in.

Her flails spinning in a blur of motion, Dahlia cracked one after another off the devil, hitting every vulnerable spot. She had the beast off-balance, lurching every which way, but always just a fraction of a heartbeat slow in trying to block the next crushing blow.

The devil threw up its shield arm, but Dahlia's flail whistled in behind the block, cracking hard into the beast's elbow. The shield arm slumped and one-two went Dahlia's strikes over the top of the shield and into the devil's ugly face.

In desperation, the devil lunged forward with its sword, slashing wildly. But Dahlia danced to her left and forward, moving right past and snapping the flail in her right arm up under her left armpit. She turned as she passed, pulling hard with her right, and just as the devil turned to keep up with her, the elf warrior released her armpit hold.

The front pole of the weapon shot forth like an arrow, blasting into the devil's face, snapping its head back, shattering its nose and cheekbone.

Dahlia leaped and spun, a high pirouette, and she came around with a backhand right and a forehand left. Up again she leaped and turned as the now-staggering devil tried to keep pace, and yet again, she scored two clean and powerful hits.

Up and around she went again, but this time in the opposite direction. The devil, blinded by rage and by its own blood, stumbled along the same way, though, and so when Dahlia landed, she was behind the battered beast.

Her first strike proved a glancing blow, and was intended as such, for while it inflicted little damage, it moved the devil's helm to the side. The following strike found that very spot, cracking the devil's skull, snapping its head to the side. It stumbled a step, then another, then did a weird hop, landing on its feet for just a heartbeat before falling over to the dirt.

Her staff reassembled by that point, Dahlia leaped over to straddle it. She drove it down with all her strength, and all the magic of Kozah's Needle, the lightning curling aside the devil's leathery armor and leathery skin as the weapon slid into its muscular chest.

How the beast thrashed.

Dahlia leaped up and inverted herself over the staff to avoid the wild slashes of sword and shield. But she held on, calling upon every bit of Kozah's Needle's lightning magic, jolting and burning the beast inside and out.

Finally it lay still.

In the distance, she heard the cry of a great cat, Drizzt's panther, pitiful and agonized. Dahlia ran toward her.

Guenhwyvar's wail pierced Drizzt's heart as surely as the flash of barbed quills pierced his skin. He managed to get his cloak around in time to block some, but this was not a magical garment like his old *piwafwi*, and as thick as the cloth was, it proved little defense against the insidious spines.

How they burned, the fiendish poison lighting a thousand little fires within!

Drizzt grimaced and stumbled aside, diving behind a tree just as another volley chased after him. He tried to focus, knew he had to focus.

Guenhwyvar cried out again in pain.

The drow dismissed his own discomfort. He charged back out from behind the tree, Taulmaril in hand, and let fly arrow after arrow into the boughs. Leaves flew, wood splintered and cracked, and the whole of that tree shook under the weight of the enchanted missile barrage. As he cleared a patch of the foliage, Drizzt caught quick sight of the devil, scrambling nimbly along a branch.

He couldn't react quickly enough to get a clear shot, so he took the next best course and aimed his missile at the branch itself. The sizzling bolt blasted in, showering white-blue sparks every which way and splintering the branch.

Out of the corner of his eye, the drow caught another flicker of motion, and he dived aside just in time to avoid the rain of quills from a second devil.

He shouldered Taulmaril and sprinted for the tree, leaped up, and grabbed the lowest branch. He rolled right over that one, coming to his feet and springing up yet again to the next branch in line. He spotted the spined devil and ducked behind the trunk, going for Taulmaril.

A large form passed right by him, nearly dislodging him, and he almost lashed out in surprise before he recognized his treasured companion.

"Guen!" he called after the running cat, and surely Drizzt's heart sank at the sight. For Guenhwyvar's flank was stuck full of diabolical quills, and when she turned to angle after the spined devil in this same tree, Drizzt saw more of the barbed and painful darts pinned around her face, including several caught around her mouth, and one that had sunk deeply into her eye.

Drizzt tried to align himself for a shot—he didn't want the panther fighting another of these porcupine-like devils. But he was too late, and by the time he held forth Taulmaril, Guenhwyvar had made the leap, recklessly burying the devil under her great girth and weight. The branch bent and broke under that momentum, and down went the devil and the panther, tumbling to the ground. But Guenhwvyar, loyal Guenhwyvar, never let go, accepting the vicious sting of so many more quills while finally getting her powerful jaws around the devil's small head.

The devil thrashed beneath the cat. Another volley of quills sailed forth from the other tree, where the second fiend lurked, and Drizzt winced and gritted his teeth at the sight of Guenhwyvar's beautiful black coat being so violated.

The panther merely roared and bit down, and the devil's skull collapsed beneath the weight of that crushing jaw, and the wretched creature suddenly lay very still.

"Guen, be gone!" Drizzt commanded as he began to fire his missiles at the second tree. He felt the panther's resistance, and despite her pain, Guenhwyvar didn't want to leave him. But he yelled again, compelling the cat, and he nodded grimly as the corporeal form became an insubstantial gray mist below him. A hundred quills or more dropped to the ground, or atop the lifeless body of the spined devil, as the panther dematerialized.

That sight, all of those spines that had so pained poor Guenhwyvar, enraged Drizzt even more and he let fly more and more arrows, blowing apart branches in the other tree and clearing great swaths of leaves with every shot. A volley of quills came forth in response, but Drizzt avoided the surprisingly accurate missiles by simply dropping from his perch, landing on the ground softly and hardly slowing his withering fire.

He soon had the devil pinned behind the tree trunk, ducking for cover that the mighty bow, Taulmaril the Heartseeker, would not afford it. As he walked past the devil Guenhwyvar had killed, it occurred to him that he'd rarely seen Guenhwyvar so resist his command that she return to her Astral home.

He let fly another arrow, this one blowing right through the trunk and stabbing at the spined devil behind it. Now the beast came forth in a charge, its quills glowing a fierce red in its agony and outrage. It ran along the branch leading nearest to Drizzt, who calmly kept approaching, and leaped out at him.

He took the creature out of mid-air with his next explosive missile, reversing its flight and throwing it to the ground. A second arrow drove hard against the resilient fiend as it tried to stand, though still it managed to get upright.

Drizzt's expression didn't change, his movements remaining slow and deliberate as he stalked his prey. He drew back again on Taulmaril, trying to dismiss a nagging discomfort: why had Guenhwyvar resisted his demand that she return home?

Surely this devil, as vicious and cunning as it was, would prove no match for him.

The spined beast howled at him. He put his arrow right into its open mouth.

But then Drizzt understood Guenhwyvar's reaction. Suddenly, and on instinct, he whirled around and dropped his hands down low on the bow, swinging it around like a club just in time to ward the legion devil rushing in at his back.

Even with his maneuver, though, the drow was at a disadvantage, for the agile devil easily dodged, throwing shield and sword out wide to either side, but then coming right back after the drow.

Drizzt dropped Taulmaril and retreated as fast as he could, desperately reaching for his scimitars as he came up hard against a tree. He saw the devil's sword rushing quicker, though, and knew he was going to get stabbed, and only hoped that he could bring his blades around enough to minimize the blow.

Time seemed to slow as the sword thrust forward at him, inside his reach as Twinkle and Icingdeath slid free of their scabbards. Drizzt drew in his breath, trying to make himself smaller, trying futilely to keep himself moving ahead of that wicked blade.

He hardly registered the movement as a metal pole came down hard atop that sword, as a second metal pole, joined by a fine but strong line, wrapped down and under the sword, and as a third part of that staff, similarly fastened to the end of the mid-piece, wrapped up and over to smack the surprised devil across the face.

With the tri-staff wrapped around the sword, Dahlia yanked hard, turning the thrust and bringing the devil's arm out wide. The beast responded with a roar and accepted the turn, twisting its shield horizontally and trying to jam its edge sidelong into Drizzt's face.

Too late.

The drow dropped low, under the second attack, and both his blades thrust forth in front of him, double-stabbing the legion devil in the chest.

The devil tried to back off those scimitars, but Drizzt dug in his heels and pressed forward, holding faith that Dahlia would keep the sword trapped out wide.

She did, running beside, pacing the drow and his victim for several long strides until at last the devil slammed its back into a tree and Drizzt drove his blades right through the beast. They held that pose for a long while, the devil with its arms out wide, twitching as it tried desperately to hold onto the last moments of its life on the Prime Material Plane.

Then its shield slumped to its side, and Dahlia yanked the sword free of its weakened grasp.

Drizzt held the scimitars in deeply for several more heartbeats, then, with a sudden and fierce growl, he shifted the angle and dragged the dying beast out from the tree, turning as he went to throw the devil aside, and twisting his scimitars to rip open more flesh.

The drow stood tall as the devil spilled face-down into the dirt.

"You didn't think I would desert you, did you?" Dahlia asked innocently.

Drizzt looked at her, but no smile came to him, and Dahlia's confused responding expression lasted only the moment it took her to notice his right arm, stuck full of quills and swelling from the poison.

"Where is your cat?" Dahlia asked, coming to his side, for it became obvious that only his adrenalin in the rush of battle had kept the drow upright this long. She steadied him as he swayed.

"Gone," Drizzt answered in a whisper, and he closed his eyes and fought back against the waves of pain.

As soon as he was steady on his feet once more, Dahlia moved to collect Taulmaril. "We'll find a place to rest," she explained, "so I can cut out those spines . . ."

"Do you think you can elude me?" roared Hadencourt's booming voice, and it seemed to be coming from every direction at once, with echoes both near and far away.

Dahlia drew Drizzt's gaze to the dead devils. "He knows where we are," she explained. "He's a malebranche, a war devil—his sight extends through the eyes of his minions."

She was moving as she spoke, and so was Drizzt, neither wanting to face Hadencourt or any of his remaining soldiers just then.

"I will find you!" the unseen war devil roared with an accompanying burst of laughter. "You cannot hide!"

Drizzt and Dahlia stumbled off through the brush.

CHAPTER 10

THE MISSHAPEN WARLOCK

AN UNEASY HERZGO ALEGNI PACED AROUND A DARK THICKET in Neverwinter Wood. He knew another Netherese lord had come through the shadows. He could feel the presence. And the sickly sensation accompanying that feeling gave him a good indication of who it might be.

He was hardly surprised, but still dismayed when the withered old man made his appearance, his mottled robes masking his frame—a body that had once, long ago, rippled with the muscles of a warrior.

"Master," Alegni said humbly, bowing his head and lowering his gaze to the ground.

"So you remember," the old man said with a snort.

Alegni glanced up to look into the warlock's face. How could he not remember such a thing? This man, Draygo Quick, had sponsored Herzgo Alegni into the Circle of Power, and had recommended Alegni specifically to lead the expedition in Neverwinter Wood.

As soon as he realized his *faux pas,* Alegni dropped his gaze back to the ground, but Draygo merely laughed.

"How many more decades will you need, my protégé?" the old warlock said, and the twist of sarcasm he put on that last word made Alegni wince.

"Oh, look up at me!" Draygo Quick insisted. When Alegni complied, he continued, "I didn't sponsor you for this task so that you would forever live in Neverwinter Wood."

"I know, Master," Herzgo Alegni replied. "But much has happened here, much unexpected. We were on the verge of victory—the city's main bridge had been named in my honor."

Draygo laughed again, a wheezing sound that showed how his years of playing with diseases and rot had exacted a toll on his lungs. "I cannot deny that the cataclysm of the volcano was unexpected."

"Once more, I make gains in Neverwinter," Alegni assured the warlock. "And I've dealt the Thayans a vicious blow."

"I know, I know," Draygo said dismissively. "And not so vicious. You destroyed a few zombies and murdered a few zealots, who will no doubt rise as undead to fight you once more."

"More than that!" Alegni insisted, but when Draygo's eyes widened at his tone, the tiefling warrior sucked in his breath.

"I know . . . everything," Draygo assured him. "I've had my understudy spying on our enemies quite thoroughly. This sorceress, Sylora Salm, who rises against you, is no small opponent."

"She has begun a Dread Ring," Alegni said.

"Nearly finished one, you mean," said Draygo. "Fortunately for us, for you, there aren't enough living beings to feed it properly, to give it full power. But that's not the extent of your trouble. This lich who has joined with her . . . ?"

"We chased her from the field," Alegni dared to interject.

Draygo nodded, though his expression showed that he didn't appreciate being interrupted by his lesser.

"She's formidable, and grows more so by the day," Draygo said. "I don't know how, but she came through the Spellplague and as her mind clears, she seems possessed of magical dweomers from both eras. Sylora Salm has undoubtedly surrounded herself with powerful allies."

Herzgo Alegni nodded.

"Too powerful for your forces, I fear," Draygo added.

"I'm not without resources," Alegni insisted. "I will defeat Sylora Salm."

Draygo was shaking his bald head with every word. "Too many Shadovar have fallen. Too many years have passed."

Herzgo Alegni stiffened and squared his shoulders. "You would take me from the field of battle?" he asked.

"I would bolster your cause."

"More soldiers?" Alegni asked hopefully.

Draygo shrugged as much as nodded. "A few, perhaps. More importantly, I will bolster your ranks with one who better understands the way of the sorceress."

Alegni's eyes widened again and he started to shake his head, though he dared not openly oppose Draygo's words. "Him?" the tiefling angrily retorted, and stammered, because he knew who Draygo Quick had in mind and it was no one Herzgo Alegni wanted anywhere nearby.

"Him," Draygo calmly replied. "And I need not explain to you the pain should you not properly protect this one."

Behind Draygo, the shadows coagulated and a thin form appeared, blurred by dark mist.

"He should be with Argyle in study—that was our bargain."

"Our bargain?" Draygo laughed. "Our bargain is whatever I tell you it is. Your title is wholly my doing, and so I can undo it. I can undo everything . . . with a word. You wanted him. Indeed, you went to great lengths to bring him along."

"That was a long time ago." The regret rang thick in Alegni's voice.

"Yes," Draygo replied, "a long time ago, when you thought he would be strong of arm and a great warrior. Your contempt for warlocks—"

"Not contempt," Alegni interrupted. "Nay, I understand and appreciate the power of dark magic."

"But you relish the power of the sword. That is your failing, I fear. Ah, but it matters not. You're being watched very carefully now, Herzgo Alegni, and by powers who grow more impatient with you than I. Secure the whole of Neverwinter Wood, and drive out the forces of Thay."

Alegni knew he couldn't push further, that there was no debate to be found here, and he bowed and accepted the edict.

"He's smart, he's powerful, and he knows your enemy," Draygo assured him.

"He's . . . I cannot look upon him."

"Does he disgust you? Does his infirmity insult the great Herzgo Alegni, who could surely take him in his bare hands and snap his spine in half?"

Alegni ground his teeth and tried hard to steady his breathing.

"You will consult with him. You will listen to his words of wisdom. You will complete this mission successfully and soon. We have other business to attend, and I'll not hold my forces here in Neverwinter Wood another decade. Nor will I have Sylora's Dread Ring come to fruition. I hold you personally responsible to stop it. Know that most of all."

"Yes, Master."

Draygo Quick stared at him for a bit longer then slowly turned and walked away, the shadows gathering around him as he went. Barely a few strides away, his form became so blurred as to be indistinguishable, and he was gone, melting back into the Shadowfell.

Herzgo Alegni closed his eyes and brought a hand up to rub his face, feeling weary.

"You truly can't even bear to look upon me," came a scratchy and whiny voice from the same area where Draygo Quick had disappeared.

Alegni didn't have to open his eyes to know the identity of the speaker. It was Effron the Twisted, of course, Draygo Quick's understudy, who should have been at study with Argyle—at study with Argyle forever, or at least until Herzgo Alegni was dead of old age.

"Can you not even look upon me?" the newcomer asked, and Alegni opened his eyes to regard the young tiefling, who firmed his chin and lifted it.

Alegni knew him to be more than twenty years of age, but he looked like a young teenager. Frail and thin, so very thin, his eyes, one red, one blue, barely reached the top of Alegni's broad chest. He sported ramlike horns, like Alegni's, lifting from mid-scalp forward then rolling around in a tight outside circle and looping back, tapering to a point that just jutted forward of the front bend. His hair was black, shot with purple, swept back and hanging scraggly around his painfully thin and twisted shoulders. This battered creature had suffered great trauma, and just looking at him now reminded Alegni that he should not be alive. His left shoulder jutted out behind him, his useless and withered left arm hung limply down his back, swaying as he walked.

He wore what seemed more like a woman's slip than a wizard's robe. The clingy material emphasized his bony frame, his jutting ribcage, his narrow hip bones. He carried a black bone wand in his right hand, and constantly worked it in circles around his fingers. Yes, Alegni remembered that, too.

"I do so always enjoy the look upon your face when first you glance upon me," Effron the Twisted said. It was obviously a lie, for the young tiefling struggled to hold his composure and keep the pain from his thin face.

"I have not seen you in three years, and only a few times, and a few short times, since you were a boy," Alegni replied.

"But you recognize me!" the emaciated warlock replied, and he jerked left-to-right so that his withered and useless arm would swing around enough for him to clap his left hand with his right.

"Don't do that!" Herzgo Alegni warned through clenched teeth.

Effron laughed at him. It was a sad laugh.

"Go back to Draygo," Alegni said. "I warn you, there's no place for you here."

"Master Draygo thinks there is."

"He's wrong."

"You underestimate my powers."

"I know your skill."

"You underestimate my knowledge of your enemies, then," Effron insisted. "Knowledge that will give you the victory you desire." He widened his red eyes and gave a crooked grin, revealing a mouthful of straight white teeth that seemed so out of place with the rest of the twisted tiefling. "The victory Master Draygo orders you to complete, and in short time. Without me, that will not be achieved. Do you so loathe me that you would accept failure and the consequences of Master Draygo's rage rather than accept my help?"

"Your help," Alegni snorted.

"You're not winning here," Effron insisted.

"Perhaps you were so deep in your studies you missed my victory outside Neverwinter's wall."

"If you think that a victory, then you're more in need of me than even Master Draygo believed—and he believed it quite strongly, I assure you."

Alegni glowered at him.

"Was Sylora Salm on the field?" Effron asked.

Alegni narrowed his eyes.

"Was her champion? The elf warrioress with the mighty staff?"

"She has not been in these parts for years."

"She returns," Effron assured him, and Alegni couldn't hide his surprise.

"I know your enemies," Effron said. "I'll help you win here, and then I'll be gone." He paused and considered Alegni, who could barely hide his contempt. "Which would be the more pleasing to you?"

Herzgo Alegni scowled and turned away, and Effron slumped, a bit of moisture glistening in his strange eyes.

Intrigue overwhelmed caution in Valindra's thoughts as she glided past the umber hulks lurking at the wide entrance to the underground cavern. The young monk, Brother Anthus, who led their troop had been here before, several times, and yet his skittishness couldn't be denied. His breathing was so labored that Valindra expected him to topple over into unconsciousness.

And the lich certainly understood why.

Valindra didn't breathe, of course, but no matter, for this spectacle of power—a dozen mighty umber hulks lined up in perfect order and discipline—would have intrigued her in life as much as now. With that thought, the lich looked to Sylora, a sorceress not so unlike herself in her former life. The Thayan seemed composed enough, but surely there was a bit of hesitation in her step.

And why not? The cavern beyond reeked of slime and the murky pond illuminated by the underground lichen wasn't the most inviting of sights.

Valindra, Sylora, and Brother Anthus entered, moving between the lines of umber hulk guards, the loyal and fanatical Ashmadai contingent dutifully following.

The water stirred. Brother Anthus, a scrawny young man whose brown hair was already thinning from his constant fretfulness, shifted nervously and glanced back at Sylora and Valindra.

"The Sovereignty ambassador," he whispered reverently.

The water stirred and the ambassador's head appeared, an oblong mound on the water, two black eyes staring at the visitors.

A second form rose up out of the water as well, walking out of the shallows nearest them. It was a man, or had been a man, naked and wearing a perfectly blank expression on his face and in his strangely distant eyes. His skin was nearly translucent and covered with a slimy, membranous substance.

"Welcome," he said in a voice that seemed to come from somewhere else, almost as if it was being channeled through him. Behind him, the aboleth stirred, rings of water rolling out from its large form.

The ambassador's mind slave, its servitor, then spoke the creature's name, and it was surely unpronounceable by any of those listening— and surely would have been unpronounceable to the speaker if he was trying to form those sounds all on his own, with combinations of consonant sounds that no human or elf tongue could hope to replicate. Still, despite the stark reminder of how foreign an entity this type of creature truly was, they all, from Sylora to the Ashmadai soldiers, felt a sense of calm, of warmth, of *home*.

Despite her eagerness and curiosity, Valindra didn't share that warmth, and she couldn't help but feel a bit of disgust as the aboleth's piscine head rose up from the water. Rounded on top, flat underneath, not unlike a bottom-feeding catfish, the large mottled head climbed up several feet. Limp whiskers, like lines of black rope hanging below, dripped fetid dark water back into the pond.

"You are the one of whom we were told," the servitor said, aiming the words at Valindra.

"Yes," the lich hesitantly replied.

"We sense your confusion," said the slimy man.

He bowed, and somehow that movement made Valindra much more comfortable.

"Welcome to all of you," the servitor went on, and he began speaking to each of them individually, conveying great knowledge of who they were and why they had come.

Valindra tried to listen at first, very curious to get as strong a read on this strange creature as she could. The ambassador was the promise to her, the potential way through the fog that continually clouded her thoughts, or twisted them in directions she never desired. But soon into the remarks by the servitor, the lich felt something else, something too personal for her to ignore.

She felt the creature—not the servitor, but the aboleth itself—probing her thoughts. She "heard" its vibrations and instinctively hesitated and threw up mental barriers. Only for a moment, though, for in truth, the lich feared her continuing mental affliction more than she feared the aboleth. She consciously let her guards down, inviting the creature in.

"Ark-lem!" she called out, her natural reaction to stressful situations. "Ark-lem! Greeth! Gree . . ."

She bit off the last word as a moment of clarity invaded her confused mind. And not just simple clarity of thought—Valindra had experienced those brief moments, of course, particularly on the battlefield—but clarity combined with insight and memory, and more importantly still, a true memory of the former Archmage of the Hosttower of the Arcane. Suddenly, and for the first time, Valindra remembered the disembodied spirit of Arklem Greeth after the Spellplague, and recalled the sister skull gem, Greeth's multi-dimensional and magically multi-faceted phylactery. Greeth's essence remained within that gem, trapped and helpless, but in there nonetheless. Valindra had only begun to understand the true powers of those wondrous gems, and in this one moment of clarity, she considered Dor'crae, who was grounded to this plane of existence through the power of her own skull gem.

She could trap Dor'crae fully with the power of her gem, as Greeth was trapped by his own phylactery. She'd understood that from the first time she'd encountered the disembodied vampire. But if that were true, might she not, therefore, find a way to loosen the other skull gem's hold on her beloved Arklem Greeth? Free him to possess the corporeal form of another so that he wouldn't be lost to her any longer?

Valindra's lies to Szass Tam regarding her desires with the pit fiend had been grounded in some measure of truth, after all. She grinned then at the possibility of putting her beloved Arklem Greeth into such a magnificent corporeal form.

But where was that other gem? It had been in the room, her room, in ruined Illusk beneath Luskan! Yes, she remembered that.

Where had it gone?

A name flashed in her thoughts, that of a particularly resourceful and self-serving dark elf . . .

All of that flashed through Valindra's mind in a matter of a living creature's heartbeat, a brief moment in which all the reasoning she should have been doing for months and years now had coalesced suddenly to create a great stream of possibility.

The lich stared out at the aboleth with awe, reverence, and hope. For even as the ambassador left her, then, it left behind the unspoken promise that it could indeed help her through her plight.

The meeting lasted only a few moments longer, with the servitor assuring Sylora Salm that this was the first of what might be a fruitful alliance. That strange slimy man also took a moment to assure Brother Anthus that the road for him would be long and glorious, and he ended with a smile and knowing nod at Valindra, who had been promised, perhaps, the most of all.

When they left the aboleth's chamber, Sylora was smiling indeed. "The people of Neverwinter will pay dearly for their partnership with the Netherese," she said.

"Because you have struck an alliance with . . ." Valindra paused and tried to figure out how she might speak the aboleth's name, but quickly gave up on that idea and simply referred to their host as "the Sovereignty ambassador."

"Informal, but to our mutual gain," Sylora replied.

"Truly? Then what did you offer in return?"

"To allow the Sovereignty to exist here without our interference," Sylora replied, and she looked at Valindra curiously.

"They don't care about our designs here," Sylora explained. "Unlike the Netherese, our ambitions for dominance do not include dominance over the living. The Sovereignty understands that we can coexist without ever crossing paths, they in the land of the living, us in the realm of the dead. Our friend, Brother Anthus, did well in preparing them for our visit."

The young monk bowed stiffly and uncomfortably, as was his wont.

"An alliance of convenience," said Valindra. "My favorite kind."

"You will meet with the ambassador again. He . . . it, told me as much," Anthus remarked.

Valindra nodded and smiled, her eyes flickering with hope.

"And you concur with the . . . speaker?" Sylora asked.

"He's the ambassador's servitor," Brother Anthus explained. "Anything he says comes straight from the aboleth."

"He assured me that the aboleth would help me elevate Jestry to become my champion," Sylora reminded them.

"Then rest assured that it will be a promise fulfilled," Brother Anthus replied without the slightest hesitation.

Valindra started cackling then with laughter. "It shall be so," she said in her own voice, between giggles, and she stared long and hard at Anthus.

"Indeed, you are quite the proponent of our new friend," Sylora remarked.

"You don't have a spy in your midst," Brother Anthus assured them. "There would be no point, since the Sovereignty can scour our very thoughts. Why waste time and effort and risk discovery with such subterfuge when the ambassador can go straight to the source . . . at will?"

"Who is that?" Barrabus the Gray asked Herzgo Alegni when he caught up to the tiefling outside Alegni's tent. Not far away, the twisted newcomer lurked around a copse of trees, fiddling his fingers in apparent spellcasting practice.

"No one of any concern to you," Alegni answered, his voice rough-edged and clearly filled with aggravation.

"Good. I detest wizards."

"Warlock," Alegni corrected.

"Even worse," said Barrabus, taking no pains to hide the utter contempt in his voice.

He noted that his response brought a strange look to Herzgo Alegni's face, as if the tiefling was suddenly pondering something in a different light.

"No," Alegni said, and his smile unsettled Barrabus. "Perhaps I spoke too hastily."

"What does that mean?"

Alegni ignored him and walked past him. "Effron!" he called out to the warlock.

The young tiefling looked over, then began shambling awkwardly his way.

Barrabus couldn't hide his disgust at the infirm being. "Shall I kill him and end his misery?" he asked, in jest of course, but the angry glare from Alegni, a flash of pure outrage beyond anything Barrabus had ever seen from the tiefling—and he'd seen, and evoked, more than his share of Alegni's unrelenting anger!—told him he'd hit a peculiar nerve with his off-hand comment.

"Effron," Alegni said when the warlock approached, "this is Barrabus, your new partner."

"You can't be serious," Barrabus said.

"Oh, but I am."

"He's a child."

"You're an old human," Effron countered.

"One to learn from the other, then," said Alegni, clearly pleased with himself. "I expect that your respective skills will complement

207

each other." He turned to Barrabus. "Perhaps you will gain an appreciation of magic."

"Only if it twists over itself and destroys its caster," Barrabus muttered.

"And you," Alegni continued, addressing Effron, "will perhaps come to understand the true power of the sword, the nobility and courage of he who confronts his enemies in mortal melee."

"I understand the value of fodder," Effron replied, turning a narrow-eyed stare at Barrabus, and only then did Barrabus notice the young tiefling's weird eyes: one red, one blue.

"And woe to either of you if the other is killed," Alegni finished. "Now be gone, the two of you. Find your place together and do not disappoint me."

He turned on his heel and headed back to his tent. Barrabus glared at him, emanating hate with every step. When Alegni reached the tent flap, Barrabus glanced over at his new partner, and realized that this warlock, Effron, watched Alegni with equal consternation.

Perhaps they had a bit of common ground after all, Barrabus thought.

Sylora continued to stare at the surprising Brother Anthus for just a few moments longer then finally relaxed in acceptance at the undeniable truth of the young monk's reasoning. Why would the Sovereignty need any spies? Sylora had witnessed telepathy often in her time beside Szass Tam, of course, and, since she often dealt with the undead, including powerful liches and vampires, she knew the dangers and powers of possession as well. But she'd never seen such a display of psionic strength to equal that single example offered by the aboleth ambassador and its servitor. The aboleth could do more than impart its thoughts to her through its slave, and relay back her responses with perfect translation.

She, too, had felt an intrusion in their time in the cavern, very brief, a mere flicker of invasion, hardly more than an introduction.

But in that mere heartbeat of intrusion, the aboleth had stripped her emotionally naked. Sylora hadn't tried to deceive the ambassador because she'd known from the instant she felt the intrusion that there was no way she could possibly do so.

She'd heard the rumors of the power of aboleths—the mighty umber hulks obediently lining the walls only served as a reminder to the creature's ability to dominate—and now that she considered it, Sylora was relieved that she'd gotten out of that chamber without being enslaved.

She had no intention of returning to the underground pond and its otherworldly inhabitant. She looked at Valindra.

"Yes, Sylora, I'll serve as your ambassador to the Sovereignty," the lich said, as if reading her every thought.

Perhaps she was, Sylora feared. Perhaps the ambassador was even then scouring her mind, through Valindra's eyes.

It occurred to Sylora Salm then that the sooner she completed the Dread Ring and moved on to a different mission in a far different location, the better off she would be.

"When you return to the cavern, take Jestry with you," Sylora said.

Valindra's laugh caught her off guard. "Your plaything is strong of body, but not of mind," the lich explained. "He will likely be overwhelmed by the wondrous ambassador."

"In that instance, he's no use to me anyway," Sylora replied. "Dahlia will soon return to Neverwinter, I am informed. I do not wish to waste my energies upon her. Jestry will be recreated to defeat her. The ring is the first piece only—now I need that which Arunika promised me."

Valindra offered a bow in response, an awkward, stiff movement that created more than a bit of crackling noise in her dry skin.

CHAPTER 11

DEVILISH PURSUIT, DEVILISH DECEIT

DAHLIA CRAWLED THROUGH THE BRUSH. SHE WAS QUITE FAMILIAR with forests, having grown up in the thick boughs of one, and with her fine elf eyes, she was able to penetrate the darkness quite well, to separate flora from fauna and rocks from enemies. And her enemies were out there, she knew, probably in the trees, some crawling around the ground, sniffling for any scent of her and Drizzt. She had no idea how many minions Hadencourt might be able to summon from the Nine Hells, but she couldn't deny the effectiveness of those he'd already sent against them.

She glanced back from where she'd come at that thought. She'd escaped the sting of the spined devils, but Drizzt had not.

Dahlia knew she might have to leave him to Hadencourt. He'd taken a vicious barrage of those poisoned quills, and when Dahlia cut them out, despite the drow's stoicism, she'd seen the profound agony on his face, and the green poison flowing from his wounds.

The elf closed her eyes at that thought. Drizzt had saved her from the traps of Ship Kurth, and had saved her again in the fight with the legion devils and Hadencourt—she couldn't deny that truth. They had been caught by surprise, and nearly overwhelmed, and the drow's daring maneuver had given her room to flee. And now she might have to abandon him to his doom.

She didn't like it, but she saw no alternative.

Dahlia hoped they could stay hidden long enough for Drizzt to recover.

I will tell the devil where you are, witch, came a voice in her head, a familiar voice, but one Dahlia had never expected to hear again. *I will lead him to you and watch him devour you. Perhaps I will even possess your lifeless body, and torture it through the years.*

"Dor'crae," Dahlia spat, glancing around in horror.

She had no idea how the spirit of her vampire lover could speak to her. She had not only watched, but had ushered in the vampire's seemingly utter destruction in the rushing wave of water elementals back in Gauntlgrym. But the voice in her head was that of Dor'crae! She knew it without doubt even then as she heard the vampire spirit's taunting laughter.

You thought me destroyed, but I remain, the voice went on. *I am more than my mortal trappings, you see. And indeed, I will need a new body. May I have yours, Dahlia?*

Dahlia brushed away the taunts, and her surprise at realizing that Dor'crae survived, pressed by the importance of the actual threat he'd uttered. Could Dor'crae, apparently a disembodied, free-floating spirit, do as he'd suggested? Could he lead Hadencourt to Dahlia and Drizzt in their hiding place, a shallow cave, which was no more, really, than a narrow crevice between a pair of out-leaning boulders?

The elf rose from her crouch, turning slowly as if expecting the vampire to appear suddenly and strike out at her. Her finger went to a loop on her belt, where she kept a wooden finger-spike, a subtle stake to drive into Dor'crae's black heart.

She waited a bit longer, concentrating to try to catch any hint of Dor'crae's telepathy. Had she imagined it? Was this one of the devil's tricks? Or was this, perhaps, a manifestation of her normally dormant conscience because she'd considered leaving Drizzt to die?

When she heard nothing more, Dahlia crept back through the brush to the overhang. She expected to see Drizzt lying on his back, sweating profusely and near delirium.

She didn't understand Drizzt Do'Urden.

He was sitting up, and though his hair was disheveled and a bit matted from sweat, he managed a wry smile at Dahlia as he dug one last quill tip from his arm.

"I may need a new cloak," the drow lamented, and poked his finger through one of the holes in his forest-green weathercloak.

"The poison?" Dahlia asked.

"By my word, it hurts," Drizzt casually replied. He clenched his right fist, the muscles on his swollen arm tightening and forcing more blood and pus from the many wounds on his arms.

"Can you fight?"

Drizzt looked up at her. "Have I a choice?"

"Likely not," said Dahlia. "I suspect we have a spy among us."

Drizzt glanced all around.

"A spirit," Dahlia said. She sighed deeply and looked around at the forest. "Dor'crae came to me."

"The vampire?"

"Corporeally destroyed, but with a stubborn spirit, it would seem. And he mentioned our devil pursuers."

Drizzt crinkled his brow.

"I think Hadencourt may soon come calling," Dahlia said. "Can you bring back your panther?"

"No, Guenhwyvar needs to rest on the Astral Plane. The magic of the figurine can be broken if it's sorely overused. It will be days before I summon her again—a tenday if there's any way I can manage without her."

Dahlia considered the odds. "Hadencourt has at least three legion devils remaining at his side, and perhaps some more of the spiny creatures."

"The battlefield has to be of our choosing," Drizzt explained.

Dahlia glanced back over her shoulder at the dark forest. "We should be gone, then, and soon."

Soon after, Dahlia crouched in the brush atop a small hillock, looking down over their previous encampment, and indeed, Hadencourt's minions were there, crawling all around the boulders.

Had it truly been Dor'crae who had come to her, and done as he'd promised? Was it possible?

She lay still and closed her eyes, listening to the wind and the rustle of leaves, trying to sense something more.

She felt it, then: a titter of mocking laughter—not aloud, but in her thoughts. Dor'crae had found her again.

The elf warrior got up and walked to a small clearing. She broke Kozah's Needle into two four-foot lengths and set them to spinning and swinging. She knew this dance, had used it many times before to gather the weapon's inner strength. Now she spun, bringing the poles together hard, a crackling blue bolt arcing out just briefly before being caught by Kozah's Needle and sucked back in. And so it went, around and around, the staves clapping together and creating a jolt that Kozah's Needle immediately absorbed.

She could feel the weapon's power gathering within, the metal tingling in her grip. She chanted to the ancient, forgotten Netherese god that lent the weapon his name as she performed the ritual. The stars above her dimmed, their sparkles stolen by a concentrated black cloud.

They came at her all at once, all three of the legion devils charging from the brush, waving their swords and howling at the sight of their prey.

Dahlia spun to meet them, her two staves becoming flails, which she immediately put up in a furious routine, spinning them out left, right, and in front of her to keep the three at bay.

The legion devils seemed more than content to fan around her and come at her with measured strikes instead, their caution allowing Dahlia only a couple of hard hits against raised shields. In came their swords, in fine concert, and Dahlia had to work wildly to bat those strikes aside. Trusting her companion, she turned her attention to the devil in front of her and the one to the right, a move that surely gave the legion devil on her left flank an easy opening.

That beast howled as it moved to exploit the exposed elf, but it howled all the louder when a streaking magical arrow slammed into its chest, driving it back. A second followed, then a third, which clipped off the shield the devil tried to bring forth and exploded right in the fiend's face.

"Down!" Drizzt yelled in the tongue of the surface elves, and Dahlia, without breaking her flowing routine, dropped to her knees.

Right over her head came the next arrow, aimed squarely at the center devil's chest.

And so it would have struck the beast, except that Dahlia's spinning flail whirled too near it and the weapon drew the arrow's lightning energy into it, stealing the weight of the blow.

Dahlia looked at her flail with true surprise, and she could feel the power swelling within it. A second arrow followed the first and this time she purposely intercepted it.

Her hand burned with the power contained within that metal weapon, and she wasted no time in slapping it across to her right. The devil there got its shield up easily to block, but no matter. As Kozah's Needle struck that shield, the added energy of two of Taulmaril's missiles burst forth, hurling the fiend several strides away. Down went the devil, jerking in spasms, head shaking violently, jaw clenching, snapping and biting at the empty air.

In the span of a few heartbeats and a few launched arrows, Dahlia found herself one-on-one with the remaining devil, and she went on the offensive, brutally and almost recklessly, determined to bring the fiend down before its companion could return to its side. Her flails spun up and around, to the side and in at the legion devil from every angle, again and again. The devil tried to counter through one of the obvious openings left by the aggressive attacks, but Dahlia wouldn't relent long enough for that, and anytime the devil tried to go on the attack, it got hit and hit hard, and hit repeatedly.

Drizzt understood his companion's strategy, and knew that the fiend Dahlia's lightning magic had thrown to the ground wouldn't be out of the fight for long. He couldn't get a clear shot at that one, though, so he turned his bow to her current opponent.

Again the drow felt that invincibility, that sense of living on the edge and the confidence that he wouldn't tumble over that edge. By any reasonable measure, he should not dare this shot with Dahlia engaged in such close and furious combat.

But he knew he wouldn't hit her.

He let fly his well-aimed shot, skipping an arrow beneath the legion devil's shield to blast and burrow into its leg. How it howled!

Somehow, though, the stubborn creature held its balance and its battle posture.

No matter, though, for Dahlia's spinning weapon hit it again, even harder.

Drizzt changed his focus immediately, going back to the first devil he'd shot. He calmly walked forward, missile after missile flying forth from his enchanted bow, sizzling darts blasting into the devil's shield, burning devil flesh and driving the fiend ever backward.

Drizzt sensed a powerful presence at his side. He kept walking forward, kept firing, though he knew his target to be fast-dying by then.

Only when Hadencourt leaped out at him did Drizzt drop Taulmaril and respond, drawing his blades as he turned.

Hadencourt's arm swept across, his bracer throwing forth a volley of explosive shuriken.

And Drizzt's scimitars swept across to counter, blades very near the devil's arm, very near the source of the shuriken, thus blocking each as they spun forth, and before they could gain any separation. Each of those missiles exploded almost halfway between Hadencourt and Drizzt, thus inflicting as much damage and disorientation on the devil as on the drow.

With a snarl of rage, Hadencourt brought forth his great trident, swinging it across like a slashing sword to drive Drizzt back a couple of strides, then turning it deftly in mid-swing so that he could stab it straight out.

Drizzt dodged left, the trident just missing. Then left again he went as the spearlike weapon thrust forth a second time, then back to the right to avoid a third stab.

He slapped at the trident with each pass, his blades sparking as they connected with the hellish metal.

Growling with rage, wild with fury, Hadencourt, like Dahlia had done across the way, came on.

But Drizzt Do'Urden was no legion devil, no foot soldier, and he kept one step ahead of the devil's thrusts, dodging and parrying, letting the malebranche's rage play out. And all the while, the warrior Drizzt waited patiently for an opening. The drow knew he was winning, and his smile reflected that confidence.

But the malebranche was gone in an instant, and in its place stood the legion devil Dahlia had knocked aside with the lightning powers of Kozah's Needle.

Drizzt wasn't ready for this magical trick, but the legion devil surely was—yet another testament to the coordinating telepathy and battlefield acuity of the malebranche. Suddenly facing a different manner of opponent entirely, Drizzt hadn't the time to reorient his defenses. A shield swept aside the drow's scimitars and the legion devil stabbed for the drow's heart.

Dahlia scored a clean hit against the side of her battered opponent's head, staggering it. She glanced at the one behind her, writhing on the ground in its death throes, defeated by the barrage of Drizzt's magical arrows. She noted the devil she'd shocked . . . then gasped in surprise as it disappeared, to be replaced by Hadencourt himself.

Her surprise cost her the initiative against her opponent, and the legion devil, wounded and stunned as it was, came on ferociously, sword slashing back and forth and driving Dahlia backward. She watched it, she measured its attacks and stayed just ahead, and she watched Hadencourt, as well, so near, and truly she feared that the malebranche would soon join in.

She fell away, back and left, as Hadencourt charged . . . right past her.

Drizzt turned aside, the devil's sword grazing his mithral shirt— and had he been wearing anything less than that, he surely would have been skewered. The fiend reacted to the failed attack and retracted its blade quickly, but not fast enough as the quick-stepping drow slid forward.

Drizzt ducked low, dropping into a deep crouch. He knew the devil had but one counter: a desperate backhanded swipe. The sword went over his head harmlessly, leaving him a perfect opening to stab the devil under the ribs, perhaps even to score a complete victory over his resolute foe.

But he didn't take it. Noting movement ahead, Drizzt instead rushed back farther, the legion devil turning desperately to keep up . . . oblivious to Hadencourt's swinging forearm a few strides behind it.

Using that lesser opponent as a shield, Drizzt avoided the shuriken barrage. The legion devil jerked spasmodically as the spinning missiles invaded its back and exploded. Under that brutal assault, the fiend couldn't hold any measure of its defensive posture, and the drow struck hard.

The fiend stood dead on its feet, tilting and about to fall over, its face locked in a hateful stare at Drizzt, when the malebranche arrived right behind it, swatting it aside with no regard whatsoever for its condition.

On came Hadencourt, his great trident stabbing hard and slashing viciously, forcing Drizzt back and to the side. The furious malebranche pressed on relentlessly, driving the drow ever backward, and with attacks too forceful and potentially devastating for Drizzt to even think of countering.

"Where are you running, fool?" Hadencourt taunted.

Drizzt had no verbal jab to counter that. As he'd known his advantage previous, so he recognized Hadencourt's now. He thought of the trees, the higher branches, and he let his gaze slip up there once or twice, trying to get Hadencourt to believe that he meant to add another dimension to the battlefield. His retreat was more than a ruse, however, for he could hardly believe the ferocity of the malebranche, and he found it hard to achieve any counters against Hadencourt's great trident, let alone any effective ones.

So he backed and Hadencourt came on. Drizzt managed a last glance at Dahlia, who had not yet regained even footing against her legion devil opponent.

Suddenly, things were not going well.

Drizzt stumbled back against a thick tree and managed to roll around it just in time to put it between himself and the thrusting trident. He came right back out, hoping the weapon might have gotten snagged on the tree.

But Hadencourt was ready for him, and Drizzt had to dodge back to the other side as the devil filled in the space where he'd been standing.

Drizzt darted out to his right, back the way they'd come, then reversed to the left with great speed.

Hadencourt kept up, though, and more dangerously, so did the malebranche's deadly trident, putting Drizzt on the very edge of absolute catastrophe.

The fiend slipped up, trying too fast for a kill, and as Dahlia knocked aside that awkward thrust, she turned the tide of the battle yet again. Now back in balance and with the shock of Hadencourt fading, she had only the one legion devil standing in front of her, and standing uncertainly, with a hole blown into one leg from Drizzt's magical arrow. The battered fiend somehow managed a modicum of balance, but even so, had one arm drooping from the beating Dahlia had given it.

Dahlia knew she would win here, knew that this foe was nearing its end. But as she worked her way around, turning the devil with her so that she could witness Hadencourt's charge, she didn't feel nearly as confident regarding her companion's chances. She watched the other legion devil fall under Hadencourt's barrage, thanks to a clever turn by Drizzt, but her hopes lasted only the moment it took the mighty malebranche to close the gap to Drizzt, immediately putting him on the defensive, and with no sign of Hadencourt's overwhelming advantage easing. Dahlia gasped aloud as Drizzt went around the tree, and Hadencourt stabbed the trunk so powerfully the elm nearly broke and fell over.

That gasp, that distraction, cost her, and almost dearly, for the legion devil was not similarly distracted and came on with a slash, which Dahlia blocked, but then with a shield rush, too sudden and too near for Dahlia to dodge.

Wisely, the elf didn't try to brace against the battering shield, but instead gave ground willingly, even flying to her back, but in a controlled manner that allowed her to complete the roll and come back to her feet.

The legion devil never slowed, though, and so paced her.

But Dahlia had expected that, and in her roll, she rejoined her staff into a singular unit, and when she came over, rolling only to her knees, she planted the end of that eight-foot staff in the ground beside her and held on tightly.

The legion devil's breath blasted out as it collided with the other end of that metal pole, the tip catching it right in mid-chest. It was not a fatal blow, surely, and nothing from which the legion devil couldn't quickly recover and still hold the advantage over the kneeling female.

Except that Kozah's Needle wasn't a simple metal pole, and the lightning energy that Dahlia had built up after her first release mostly remained, and the cloud that Dahlia had summoned was still above her head, teeming with energy.

A lightning bolt came down to her call, blasting into Kozah's Needle, transferring through the metal staff and taking the weapon's pent up energy with it. A great arc of power burst out the staff's other end into the unwitting legion devil's chest.

The beast flew away, ten strides or more. It landed feet first, but only for a brief moment as it continued to soar backward, crashing to the ground, sword flying from its grasp.

Dahlia leaped up and charged across. When she arrived, the legion devil was still on the ground, still jolting wildly from residual energy. In full stride, she planted the tip of Kozah's Needle under the fiend's chin and threw herself fully behind it, even lifting off the ground as she drove the weapon home.

She heard the crack of bone and felt the fiend go limp, though one limb or the other still twitched from the lightning.

Dahlia spun around and recognized immediately that she couldn't get to Drizzt in time to help him.

Hadencourt had his back to the tree, and both the malebranche and Drizzt knew that the drow couldn't exploit that to begin any type of offensive counter to the stabbing and slashing of the huge trident.

Drizzt, though, did use Hadencourt's position to his advantage. He had one trick remaining, and now he executed it, calling upon his magical anklets to speed him. He leaped and spun to his left, daringly going right past Hadencourt, whose slash with the cumbersome trident couldn't quite catch up to the sprinting drow. Out Drizzt went farther, and Hadencourt kept going in his turn, trident continuing its pursuit as the devil let go with his left hand and opened wide with his right, reaching far to the side like a hunting bird circling from on high.

He might have continued that turn, rolling off the tree, might have kept up to Drizzt and maintained his advantage.

But Drizzt knew better and his sly smile showed it, showed Hadencourt as surely as the thunder of hooves revealed the truth of the drow's long and seemingly desperate dodge.

Hadencourt turned his gaze just in time to see the last speeding stride of Andahar, head down, horn in line.

The unicorn hit the malebranche at full speed and with tremendous force, rattling the tree behind Hadencourt, pinning the devil and puncturing him, the horn driving right through to hit the tree bark behind him.

Drizzt leaped forward and caught the trident's shaft, preventing the devil from bringing it back to wound his beloved steed, but he needn't have bothered, he realized, for there was no strength left in

Hadencourt's grip. Indeed, the malebranche simply dropped his weapon. Hadencourt stood there transfixed, arms out wide, fingers splayed open and twitching as if trying to grasp the empty air.

Andahar's hooves continued to pound, the unicorn driving in even harder, twisting and thrashing its horned head around. The malebranche's mouth hung open wide in a silent scream, and his eyes showed the hatred in his black heart, showed a promise to Drizzt that the battle might be over, but the war between them had just become eternal.

But to that, Drizzt, who felt more alive than he had in centuries, only returned a wide and sincere smile and taunted, "I know a balor who would join your vendetta. If you could bring yourself to align with such a creature as Errtu, I mean."

Staring hatefully, Hadencourt melted away from the Prime Material Plane, back to his haunt in the Nine Hells.

CHAPTER

12

THE QUIET ALLIANCE,
THE LOUD CONSEQUENCE

J ELVUS GRINCH WAS NOT A MAN TO SHY FROM A CHALLENGE.
He'd risen to become one of the leading voices in Neverwinter
through his toughness, his courage, and his indomitable will. But
he shied away now, flinching and all but covering his head with his
strong arms, for the angry reaction had caught him by surprise, a
complete inversion of what he'd expected. And Herzgo Alegni was
not one even stout Jelvus Grinch wanted as an enemy.

Nor did the other citizen leaders of Neverwinter, all sitting behind
Jelvus, as Herzgo Alegni had commanded them.

"The Walk of *Barrabus?*" Alegni repeated over and over again,
shaking his head and moving from a helpless grin to an outraged
grimace with every syllable.

"We thought it fitting," Jelvus Grinch dared to reply.

"I think it idiotic," Alegni snapped back.

"Barrabus the Gray's work in the assault inspired us," Jelvus said.

"And all of it was choreographed by . . . *me,*" said Alegni, poking his
finger against his own massive chest. "Have you so soon forgotten the
role I played? Go out," he bade the man, pointing to Neverwinter's
gate. "Go among the scar of battle and view the many bodies cleaved
fully in half. Only one blade on that field was mighty enough to do
that, and only one arm strong enough to wield that blade."

"Yes, yes, of course," said Jelvus Grinch. "And your actions are
neither unknown nor unappreciated."

"I will find my name attached to some great structure in Neverwinter?"

"If you wish, of course. A market square, perhaps."

"That bridge," Alegni insisted.

"Bridge? The Walk of Barrabus?"

"Never speak that name again," Alegni replied, calmly, too calmly, the threat obvious and undeniable. "Once it was called the Winged Wyvern Bridge, then, too briefly in the days before the cataclysm, the Herzgo Alegni Bridge."

Jelvus Grinch's face screwed up with surprise. Few alive knew of that brief moment of Neverwinter lore.

"Yes," Alegni explained, "because the Lord of Neverwinter in the day of the cataclysm knew well the friendship and alliance of Herzgo Alegni, and he was so grateful for my service to his city that he changed the name of Neverwinter's most notable and famous structure. I didn't immediately explain this indiscretion to you. It's a new day in Neverwinter, and so I decided to show my value to you who have come here to rebuild. Barrabus the Gray is *my* man, who serves at *my* pleasure and *my* suffrage. A man I can kill with merely a thought. He came to you because I sent him to you, and of no accord of his own. Do you understand that?"

Jelvus Grinch swallowed hard and nodded.

"He's my man, not his own," said Alegni. "If I tell him to kill himself, he will kill himself. If I tell him to kill you, you will be dead. Do you understand?"

Another hard swallow preceded the next nod.

"I command a sizable Shadovar force," the tiefling said, lifting his gaze from poor Jelvus Grinch to address all of the gathering. "You have met our wretched enemies, these Thayans and their ghoulish minions with ghoulish designs. I alone can protect you from the withering fingers of Szass Tam, and I will do so."

He paused and turned his glare back to Jelvus Grinch directly, and finished with a simple edict, "The Herzgo Alegni Bridge."

"A bright day will dawn for this land in a time of darkness," came a voice from the gathering, and all eyes turned to see a disarmingly comely woman with curly red hair and a warm and open face.

Several others whispered, "The Forest Sentinel," with great reverence, prompting Alegni to regard this innocuous-looking woman more carefully.

"We have hoped and prayed that one would stand above, and lead us to banish the old evil and open a path to new horizons," the woman, Arunika, went on. "Are you that one, Herzgo Alegni?"

Herzgo Alegni straightened and his massive chest swelled with confidence that he was indeed, or surely could be.

"The Herzgo Alegni Bridge!" another man from the gallery shouted, and many others chimed in their agreement.

Alegni looked to Jelvus Grinch, who eagerly nodded.

The Netherese lord paced around, basking in the glow of approval, then assured them all, "Szass Tam's agents will be driven from this land at the end of my sword. Your city will thrive again. I'll see to that, but on your lives, you will not forget my role."

It started as a small clap, a single set of hands—the red-haired woman's hands, Alegni noted, this one they had called the Forest Sentinel—then joined by a second, and within a few heartbeats, the leaders of Neverwinter called out for Herzgo Alegni with a full-throated "huzzah!"

Jestry stood in the firelit chamber, naked and sweating, covered in hot oil. He didn't cry out in pain, for the aboleth was in his mind and wouldn't allow him to feel that pain. The creature chased down every sensation of pain before it could come to fruition, numbing Jestry, distracting him, keeping him in a state of emptiness.

These mental bindings were much easier, after all.

Not far from Jestry, a cauldron hissed and bubbled. A pair of gray dwarves hustled around it, stoking the flames, pouring in more oil. A third dwarf slave, wearing thick gloves and carrying long tongs, scrambled up and down a small ladder near the cauldron, reaching in to pull forth the treated, leathery strips.

Whenever the dwarf caught one, he jumped down from the ladder and ran to Jestry—there was no time to tarry and let the umber hulk hide cool. He set one end of the long strip against the naked man, right where the last one had ended, and tightly wrapped it around his body, pulling hard with each turn.

The oil beneath the treated strap sizzled, Jestry's skin bubbled and burst as he melded with the enchanted and magically treated leather.

"It will heighten his resistance to lightning energy," the slimy servitor who stood nearby quietly whispered to Valindra, who watched with great amusement.

And turn the blades and dull the thud of Dahlia's staff, Valindra telepathically replied. She didn't specifically impart, but was thinking that they should do this to all of the Ashmadai.

Through his servitor, the aboleth disavowed her of that notion, filling her ear with watery whispers explaining the realities of such an unusual ceremony as this. "Five hulks must die for one human to be armored, and in any typical situation, those five would be more valuable by far. Your human champion will not live long, and will never again know a moment without great pain. Were my master to release him from possession now, the agony would kill him. He will be Sylora Salm's champion only through his zealotry, his willingness, his happiness to die for his cause."

"But he will hate her for this," Valindra reasoned as the dwarf's wrapping reached Jestry's crotch. "For never again will he know Sylora's touch, her kiss and her charms." She gasped, giggled, and blurted, "He is neutered!"

"His focus is singular now," the servitor explained. "He's Sylora Salm's champion and will fight for her until his death. Nothing else will matter to him."

"How long can he live in this state?"

"A few moons, perhaps a year."

Valindra continued to marvel at the process as she watched this Ashmadai warrior become something more, something unique and dangerous. The wrappings went tight around his belly, circling up to his chest, to his neck. She wondered about his head and face—how complete would the skin armor suit be?

The smell of burning hair as the treated umber hulk hide wrapped around him showed her, for when the slave dwarves were done, only Jestry's eyes, nostrils, ears, and mouth remained uncovered.

The servitor moved away from her, moving up to the transformed warrior, for now the aboleth had to focus completely on Jestry, she realized, had to deceive the man so that he could shrug through the agony and hold to his purpose.

One of the dwarves came up to the lich and motioned for her to leave. "Ye best go in the other cave for a bit," he explained. "It's to get loud in here, don't ye doubt."

Valindra looked at him with disdain, even disgust, but she heeded his words and glided out into the antechamber, where several other Ashmadai guards waited.

"Where is Jestry?" one woman asked.

In reply, a shriek of agony came from the other room. It went on and on, changing in tone from a high-pitched, pain-filled wail to an angry cry to a roar of utter defiance.

"What have you done to him?" another Ashmadai asked angrily.

Valindra stared at him and said nothing for many heartbeats. The zealot, for all his rage, shrank back from that withering glare.

"Would you like to learn first-hand the answer to that question?" Valindra calmly replied, and the man, for all his dedication, for all his willingness to die for his cause, shrank back even more.

After a long, long while, the screaming in the other room at last abated, and the servitor arrived at the door to inform them that the "dressing" was complete. Soon after, Jestry shambled out of the room, walking stiffly, rolling his hips to throw one leg out in front of him. His breathing came in gasps, and his eyes showed more red than white, for in his agony and screaming he'd exploded many blood vessels.

"It's done?" Valindra asked him.

He grunted a response that sounded affirmative.

"And you are?" the lich pressed.

"Jestry, Slave of Asmodeus, Champion of Sylora Salm," the living mummy recited.

"And you're tasked with?"

"Killing Lady Dahlia," came the simple response, and the man-beast paused as if considering the words, then clarified with simply, "Killing."

Behind Valindra, that same obstinate Ashmadai sighed in apparent disapproval.

"Show me," Valindra bade Jestry. "You claim to be a champion. I would see proof."

Jestry tilted his head, curious.

Valindra motioned to the Ashmadai.

"He questions the judgment of Lady Sylora," Valindra explained. She smiled widely when she saw the Ashmadai's eyes pop open as he realized the game she was playing. "He thinks you have done her a disservice by becoming such a warrior."

Jestry grunted and faced the Ashmadai directly.

"I don't question Jestry!" the man pleaded. "I questioned the source of his pain-wracked—"

"He thinks you too weak to suffer the torment of the transformation," Valindra taunted.

The man started to argue that point as well, distancing himself from any criticism of Jestry, but he needn't have bothered, for when Valindra, the confidante of Sylora, added, "Show him," Jestry pounced.

The Ashmadai was ready for the charge, setting his spear-staff tight on his hip to intercept the leaping Jestry—and indeed, Jestry's chest slammed into that sharp tip full force. Against cloth armor, leather armor, even sturdy chain mail, such a defensive maneuver would have ended the fight before it began, with the spear tip plunging into the attacker's chest. Against Jestry, though, against the umber hulk hide that had been treated by artisans and wizards alike, the spear couldn't penetrate. The force of Jestry's charge fully overwhelmed the strong Ashmadai, barreling him backward and to the floor.

Jestry had been a strong man before the application of his new "skin," the strongest of the Ashmadai in Neverwinter Wood. Now he was stronger by far, and much heavier than a normal human, and he had little trouble subduing the man, using just his weight and one arm. His other hand grasped the Ashmadai's head and yanked it to the side, pressing down on the man's cheek.

The mummified warrior had no idea why he did what happened next. Never would he have considered such an action prior to that day.

He didn't even realize what he'd done, hardly even heard the screams, until he was standing again, the Ashmadai thrashing on the floor in front of him, holding his ear—or at least, holding the spot where his ear had once been.

That ear was in Jestry's mouth, and the champion chewed it, savoring the taste.

Across the way, Valindra laughed.

Jestry had been given mighty armor, and greater strength. But it was the internal gift of the aboleth ambassador, Valindra realized even if Jestry had not, that would prove the most important. For now he was something beyond a mere warrior.

Now he was without inhibition.

Now he was bound by nothing but the need to gain victory.

Now he was possessed of a hunger that could not be sated.

Now he was feral.

"I'm called Arunika," the woman explained when she stood at Herzgo Alegni's door.

Alegni had been granted a room at the finest inn in Neverwinter, one with a balcony that overlooked the bridge that had been named, yet again, in his honor. He wouldn't be in the town often, perhaps, but a room, this room, would forever be waiting for him.

"They called you something else," Alegni replied, his gaze roving up and down the human woman's form.

"The Forest Sentinel," she answered.

"You're a ranger, then?"

"An observer," she corrected.

"More than that, from what I've heard, for you live outside the city walls, and survive quite well, it seems."

"I have my ways . . . my knowledge," she coyly replied. "Knowledge is power, they say."

"I recall you hinted I was the one destined to save Neverwinter."

Arunika's continuing smile put him strangely off balance. "I said that we hoped for one who would step forward and lead us to defeat the Thayan menace," she corrected him. "Even with the Thayans driven from the wood, there's no guarantee, no mention at all, that Neverwinter will be saved, is there?"

The tiefling narrowed his eyes as the woman widened her smile. Was there a hint in that knowing grin that this creature believed Alegni and his minions might subsequently destroy Neverwinter after defeating Sylora Salm?

"Are you going to invite me in?" Arunika asked.

"Why would I?"

"Would you have my words of insight and wisdom spread wide throughout Neverwinter, then, by keeping me out in the hallway?" Arunika asked innocently. "Where any passersby might overhear?"

Herzgo Alegni leaned out the doorway and glanced left and right. Then he stepped aside.

Arunika moved in comfortably, the ease in her step conveying that she was not the least bit intimidated. That struck Alegni profoundly. What young human woman wouldn't be intimidated walking into the private den of a hulking Netherese tiefling?

"Did your 'knowledge' assure you that I wouldn't hurt you?" he asked, only half joking.

"Why would I bother wondering such a thing, and why would you think to?" Arunika sat, comfortably draping her arm over the arm of a divan set near the balcony door, half turning to gain a better view of the city below. "You're ambitious, and you desire great power." She swung around to regard Alegni as he closed the door. "Surely that's no secret. And you're no fool—that much is obvious as well. You understand that knowledge is indeed power, and there's no one who knows more of the situation in Neverwinter than I. Not even Jelvus Grinch, who often seeks my counsel."

Herzgo Alegni spent a long while lingering by the door, looking across the room at the woman. She didn't appear exotic in any way, hardly the look he would expect from one playing at such dangerous games. Surely she understood that Jelvus Grinch would consider her his personal trough of information, working for him above all others. How might he view her unannounced, uninvited visit to Alegni's private room?

Did this unremarkable human female wish to get in between a possible power struggle involving Grinch and Alegni?

And if so, Alegni wondered, was her appearance here confirmation that she intended to throw in with the Netherese lord? Or was it, perhaps, a choreographed deception orchestrated by Jelvus Grinch?

Alegni approached her, his every step resonating with intimidation. "Who sent you?"

"I came of my own accord," she replied casually, and she looked out through the glass doors once more.

"Grinch?" Alegni demanded.

When Arunika didn't immediately reply, he grabbed her tightly by the arm, turning her around to face him, then roughly lifted her to her feet and glared down at her. The woman barely reached his mid-chest, the discrepancy in their relative sizes and strength so glaringly obvious that Arunika should have been thoroughly flustered.

But her smile appeared sincere.

"Understand this, Herzgo Alegni," she calmly replied, "I don't answer to Jelvus Grinch. He doesn't tell me what to do or where to go, and he knows well not even to try. I answer to myself alone."

"Because you use your knowledge to chart the way to the future you desire," Alegni reasoned. He tightened his grip until the woman showed a hint of a grimace.

But she didn't stop smiling.

"Are you a sorceress or priest, then?" Alegni demanded.

"Not the first, and certainly not the second," she replied with a carefree laugh. "Though I admit I'm not unaware of the ways of magic. What

I am," she added as Alegni began to bend over her, "is one who understands the nature of things, the ways of people. Most of all, I observe."

Alegni backed off a bit. "And you know more of the Neverwinter region than anyone else?" he asked, echoing her boasts.

"I do."

"Your claims of my role here were predicated on more than observation."

Arunika shrugged. "If the Thayans, the old evil, prove victorious, then what matter what I told Jelvus Grinch and the others?"

Now Alegni put his hands to his hips.

"If they don't win out, then of course someone will take the lead against them," Arunika explained. "Why not Herzgo Alegni? I see no one around more capable or prominent."

"Are you saying you made your claim for my sake?"

"There's more to it than that," Arunika replied. "But it seemed prudent to bolster your cause, for your sake, as you said, but also for the benefit of Neverwinter. Our enemies are formidable."

Herzgo Alegni really had no answer. He stepped to the side and looked out through the door to the carved image of the wyvern that marked the Herzgo Alegni Bridge.

To his surprise, Arunika rose and moved right beside him, putting her arm on the small of his back.

"What do you think of the bridge?" Alegni asked.

"It's the most beautiful and impressive structure in Neverwinter," she replied. "It's hard to believe it carried any name other than your own."

Alegni turned on the woman, towering over her.

She didn't back away, but tilted her head back, slightly parted her lips, and closed her eyes, inviting him.

It was an invitation Herzgo Alegni did not resist.

Arunika left Alegni's room much later that evening. She didn't reveal her true form to the tiefling during their lovemaking.

Nor did she tell him of the Abolethic Sovereignty, or of her relationship with Sylora Salm, or a million other little details that might have given the Netherese lord pause in his decision to couple with her.

Or in his decision not to kill her.

232

"A new pet?" Valindra asked when she caught up to Sylora just outside the perimeter of the Dread Ring. Beside the sorceress, flipping somersaults in the air and waggling its arms stupidly, was a small imp, a bat-winged little hellion whose smile might have been meant as disarming, but seemed more of a warning, somehow.

"A messenger from Arunika," Sylora explained. "I assume that your meeting with the Sovereignty ambassador went well."

"You assume? Or you already know?" Valindra asked, looking to the imp, who grinned wider still, that pointy-toothed smile almost taking in its batlike ears. It flapped its leathery wings and flipped over backward, landing easily back in place.

"I've been told that my champion is well prepared for the trials ahead."

Valindra nodded. "And you have heard that the ambassador plans to support our cause with a strike at Neverwinter?"

"It pleases Arunika greatly," Sylora explained with a wry smile. "Apparently the Netherese have now claimed a leadership role in the city. They'll fill the role as the great protectors of Neverwinter, so they say. The new citizens are even naming landmarks after them."

Valindra smiled at the delicious irony. Right after these Netherese proclaim themselves as protectors, the city would be battered to its core.

"They will find their city is built upon less than solid ground," Sylora said.

"Will we join in this attack?"

"Only as a diversion," Sylora replied, "to lure the Netherese from within the city."

She turned away from Valindra then and back to the Dread Ring. She whispered a few words, then bent low, reaching into the ashen circle. When she turned back around, she held one of the Ashmadai scepters, a spear-staff, except that this one was more black than red, coal-colored and shot through with red steaks that appeared like living veins.

"An enchanted weapon?" Valindra asked.

"It draws power from the ring," Sylora answered.

"For your champion."

"Of course. A little added pain for Jestry's opponents."

Jestry appeared, hulking toward her. He wore a cape and a kilt, but his mummy wrappings were all too clear to see. He wasn't moving as awkwardly as before. The wrappings had melded more fully with his skin, and the tightness and stiffness of the treated hide gave way to a more normal gait. He walked right up to Sylora and stared at her, unblinking, those parts of his face that were visible betraying no emotion.

"Does it hurt?" Sylora asked him, and she sounded compassionate.

Jestry shook his head.

"Do you understand how powerful you have become?" Sylora asked.

The mummified champion smiled.

"You will kill her," Sylora assured him. "You will serve as my great champion. All will fall before us—the Netherese will be driven from the forest. Szass Tam will know of your exploits, I assure you."

"When we are done, will you restore me?" Jestry asked, struggling with each word as if the wrappings on his face had not loosened enough for him to properly formulate the words.

"I'm told that it won't be necessary," Sylora reached out and gently stroked Jestry's face. "You will grow fully into your new skin. All of the sensations will return."

Jestry's hand snapped up to catch Sylora by the wrist, and he held her hand against his face for a long while.

"I have another gift for you." Sylora held up the enchanted staff-spear.

Jestry's eyes gleamed with hunger. He let go of Sylora's arm and stepped back, taking the weapon in both hands.

"Go and practice with it," Sylora bade him. "Learn of its new powers."

Jestry looked at her curiously.

"Go," she repeated. "Valindra and I have much to discuss."

Jestry nodded obediently, turned, and ran off.

"You know his wrappings will not become like his old skin, of course," Valindra said when he was gone. "The process is lethal. Jestry has barely months to live, if he's fortunate. A year or so if he's unfortunate."

"He will serve me well long after that," Sylora assured her.

Valindra looked at her, then at the Dread Ring. "The scepter," she reasoned. "You're attuning him to be fully raised into undeath."

Sylora looked to the forest into which Jestry had disappeared. "I already have," she replied.

Barrabus the Gray didn't scream out, and that was a victory. The wracking pains had him doubled over. Only his white-knuckled grip on the bridge's railing kept him from falling onto the cobblestones and writhing uncontrollably.

"The Walk of Barrabus," Herzgo Alegni said for the twentieth time, and he twanged his fork against the blade of Claw, heightening the sword's punishing waves of retributive energy. The large tiefling walked over and tugged Barrabus's hand from the railing, then threw the man to the ground.

"Crawl!" he demanded. "Crawl the length of the bridge, and perhaps I'll rename it again—no, another one, perhaps. Yes, we'll call it the Grovel of Barrabus. How much more fitting that will be!"

Barrabus could only look hatefully at his master, and couldn't respond because he simply couldn't pry his own teeth apart.

"How dare you?" Alegni asked, and he kicked Barrabus in the ribs.

The man hardly reacted to that impact, though, for the pain of the blow was nothing compared to the vibrations of that awful sword.

Alegni stepped back, sighed, and grabbed the tines of the fork, silencing it and halting the waves. The pain immediately ceased. Sweating, Barrabus crumbled lower to the bridge, gasping for breath, his face pressed against the stones.

"What am I to do with you?" Alegni said, his voice full of regret and sadness—and how Barrabus wanted to cut out his heart for that phony empathy! "I bring you glory and power, and you repay me with this treachery."

Barrabus growled and forced himself over onto his back.

"Ah, yes, I know," Alegni went on. "Don't bother repeating your excuse that the citizens insisted. You knew, and you allowed it. You knew my designs on this magnificent bridge. You were the agent who first facilitated the name change I desired. No, deny not the truth. You wanted to wound me. You knew your barb wouldn't stand, but you decided to play the game anyway."

All signs of empathy gone, the angry tiefling kicked Barrabus hard in the ribs once more. The man grunted in reply, rolled up to his side, and curled defensively.

"Was it worth it?" Alegni asked him.

Yes, Barrabus thought.

"Was it?" Alegni asked again, and when no reply came, the tiefling turned and started away. "Come along," he ordered coldly.

Barrabus rolled onto his back and took a few deep breaths. Then, before he could think it through—to do that would have been to warn the awful red-bladed sword—he threw himself over backward, tucking and rolling, coming to his feet and launching himself after Alegni.

He flipped his belt buckle free, the magical implement instantly transforming into a dagger, and moved to throw. He thought himself successful, thought his rash actions had eluded Claw just long enough to allow him one strike at that wretched Alegni.

But the wall of agony came on like a charging bull, stopping him in his tracks, freezing his muscles in place—and he realized he hadn't come close to letting fly the knife.

Claw caught him, inside and out, and mocked him with its power. All strength flew from his every muscle and he simply crumpled where he stood. He couldn't speak, he couldn't roll over, he couldn't breathe. Nothing worked—he couldn't even blink. It was as if all that was Barrabus mentally had been decoupled from all that was Barrabus physically.

This is death! he hoped. Oh, how he hoped.

But it wasn't, and Barrabus gradually felt himself becoming whole again. He rolled onto his back and looked up to see Herzgo Alegni staring down at him. Before he knew what he was doing, Barrabus's knife hand went up to hover above his own face. He felt the compulsion, and couldn't deny it.

He brought the blade down to stab at his cheek, and when the blade slipped into his skin, he dragged it down to his chin.

Images of cutting off his fingers, his toes, his genitals, flitted through his thoughts, and he knew he couldn't deny Alegni's sword if it had ordered him to do any of those things.

His hand inched down toward his crotch, his bloody blade moving with purpose. He lifted his arm, blade pointed down, as if to plunge it home.

Under command of the sword, Barrabus held that humiliating and terrifying pose for many, many heartbeats.

Herzgo Alegni laughed and walked away.

The tiefling had barely gone a couple of strides when an explosion rocked Neverwinter. As the noise dissipated, cries from the wall told them that the city was once again under attack.

"Come along!" Alegni demanded.

The man pulled himself up from the ground. He felt drained, as if much of his life force had been stolen from him, and in his thoughts, he heard the voice of Herzgo Alegni's sword, *You are alive at my suffrage alone.*

Barrabus instinctively countered that it was not a blessing, but a torment, but sarcasm was wasted on Claw.

He should have died many years before. He'd lived two lifetimes, but he hadn't died. He remained vibrant, strong, and quick as ever.

The sword wouldn't let him die. That weapon, which could steal a life force with the slightest cut, which could drive a spirit into oblivion, denying an afterlife, could reverse its murderous tendencies. He was alive at the suffrage of that sentient magical weapon.

But the cost!

He staggered along after Alegni, gradually regaining his agile gait. He caught up with the tiefling in sight of the wall, and another fiery explosion ignited just in front of that barrier, showing the dark silhouettes of ducking guardsmen.

"It would seem that our friends have returned," Alegni muttered to Barrabus and the others who had gathered near him.

"Out by the trees!" one woman on the wall called out. "The zombies have returned!"

"Along with the lich," said a quieter voice, and Effron appeared then as if materializing out of the shadows. "Valindra Shadowmantle," he explained.

"How many?" Alegni asked.

"A veritable horde of the zombies," Effron explained. "And Valindra and Sylora Salm and a handful of Ashmadai."

"Sylora has come to face me?" Alegni grinned wickedly at that thought. "Does she really believe her magic can withstand the power of Herzgo Alegni?"

"I don't know she knows who Herzgo Alegni is," said Effron, drawing a scowl from the tiefling.

Alegni reached into his pouch and produced a gauntlet, black and red, and slid it onto his sword hand. This was Claw's matching piece, designed to dull magic to protect the wielder of the powerful sword from the weapon's telepathic intrusions. Alegni preferred not to wear it, for it dulled his mental connection with the magical Claw, and he believed that his closeness with his weapon helped to keep him alive, particularly when the dangerous Barrabus was around.

But the gauntlet also worked to minimize external magic, and the sorceress Sylora would be hard-pressed indeed to truly wound Alegni while he wore such an artifact.

The tiefling looked to Barrabus, his face showing his eagerness for battle.

"It's a ruse," the battered and bleeding Barrabus said.

Alegni scowled in reply.

Barrabus shook his head. "They want us to come out after them, to be sure," he said. He called up to the wall, "Do the zombies approach?"

"At the trees!" came the shout back.

"They're luring us out there," Barrabus said to Alegni.

"What do we care?" the tiefling replied. "More likely, they're trying to lure the feeble citizens of Neverwinter, who wouldn't be able to win if not for their strong walls. Sylora Salm doesn't understand the power that's arrayed against her."

Neither do you, Barrabus thought, but wisely didn't say.

"Let's go and slaughter some zealots," Alegni called, and he started for the gate, Effron beside him. Barrabus and the handful of Shadovar who had accompanied them to Neverwinter followed in close order.

"Go out to the camp," Alegni bade Effron. "Tell our warriors to come on in full. Swing them wide of Sylora's position, so she will not escape."

Effron nodded and melted back into the shadows.

"I do not wish to send my forces outside our walls," Jelvus Grinch said to Alegni, hustling to catch up to the tiefling.

"No one asked you," Alegni snapped back at him. "Stay within and cower. I'll rid you of this menace."

The men at the gate worked fast at Alegni's approach, swinging one of the two doors wide, and Alegni and his entourage went through without fanfare.

"They'll throw their magic at us all the way," the tiefling leader explained to his forces. "Do not waver, do not falter."

He'd barely finished speaking when the ground beneath them rolled suddenly and black tentacles sprang forth, grabbing at their ankles and legs.

Alegni swept them aside with his mighty sword. Barrabus took a different tactic and pulled forth his obsidian figurine, tossing it to the ground at his feet. The statue became a steed, a nightmare, and Barrabus wasted no time in vaulting atop the skeletal horse's back. Knowing that Effron and the others would come in from the south, his right, Barrabus ran the nightmare off to the left in a wide circuit.

Alegni just kept walking, his foot soldiers in his wake. Claw swept aside the tentacles with ease. When eldritch missiles came soaring out of the tree line at him, the tiefling just held up his gauntleted hand and absorbed the magic with no more than a slight sting, as if he'd caught and crushed a bee.

"Come out, Sylora," he taunted as he approached the tree line.

Instead of Sylora, Barrabus, riding his nightmare, burst out of the trees, bidding him to turn around.

Alegni looked at his slave curiously for just a moment then realized Barrabus had figured something out.

A ruse.

The umber hulks came through the dirt and cobblestones of Neverwinter as easily as if they moved through water. One burst through the floor of a home, its shoulders pressed tightly against the low ceiling.

Both the husband and wife in that home already had their weapons in hand, ready to go out and join in the defense of the town. To their credit, both attacked the umber hulk before it even registered their presence.

A sword banged against the creature's side, an axe dived into its shoulder, actually cutting through the thick hide just a bit.

For a moment, despite their shock at finding a ten-foot tall, monstrous creature in the middle of their home, the settlers dared believe that the close quarters would work in their favor against the lumbering beast.

But the umber hulk swung its powerful arms, filling the room with its sweeping bulk. It drove the husband and wife aside, tossing them like dry leaves in an autumn wind, and worse, when those mighty arms connected, they broke the house's stone walls apart.

The ceiling came down, and the collapse didn't bother the umber hulk at all.

It had the couple scrambling, though, blocks of stone and wooden beams tumbling all around, and in their distraction, the beast caught them and crushed them.

Out into the city it went, where three of its brethren were already causing havoc. Screams echoed from all around as the hardy settlers tried to organize some defense against the hulking beasts. Several men and women did manage to come at one of the umber hulks in a coordinated manner, and managed some stabs and chops at the brute.

But the umber hulk broke apart the nearest building, hurling heavy stones at its adversaries, destroying their coordinated defense. Cleverly, the beast focused its throws, driving one woman out to the side, too far from her comrades.

A giant claw caught her and lifted her into the air, crushing her chest then sending her flying, a human missile, right into the next defender in line. That man tried to catch her instead of simply dodging, and went tumbling to the ground with her. Only then did he realize his efforts were all for naught. The woman was already dead, her chest thoroughly crushed.

He pushed her aside and scrambled to his feet, just in time to meet the attack of a second umber hulk.

Their line defeated and depleted, the defenders were washed away.

Barrabus guided his nightmare at a full gallop back through Neverwinter's gate, carrying Herzgo Alegni behind him. They quickly recognized the threat that had materialized within the walls, and Barrabus sent his mount charging to the nearest area of battle, and the obvious, huge, monstrous centerpiece of that fight.

Following Alegni's command, Barrabus brought the nightmare right past an umber hulk, just a few feet to the side—enough for Alegni to leap from the mount, fall into a forward roll, and come around to his feet with a mighty sidelong strike of Claw.

The umber hulk, which took the blows of other defenders with hardly a shrug, didn't even try to block.

But Alegni wasn't any defender, and Claw wasn't any ordinary weapon. Alegni's strike drove hard into the side of the beast, crushing and tearing through skin and bone, and the beast let out a mighty roar of pain, surprise, and rage.

Alegni's weapon grabbed its victim even more profoundly, the devious magic of Claw biting at the very life force of the umber hulk.

Horrified, the creature thrashed and swung, and Alegni agilely leaped back, taking his sword with him and bringing a moment of relief to the beast. Just a moment, however, for Alegni leaped right back in, thrusting his sword behind a swinging arm, plunging the blade squarely into the umber hulk's chest. Alegni twisted it around and the sword attacked the beast's life force with renewed hunger.

In drove Alegni, ignoring the beast's arms as they swung back at him, accepting the heavy blows while he reached for the umber hulk's heart.

A moment later, the umber hulk stood transfixed, its arms out wide, its great mandibles clacking together as if trying to form some sounds to explain this unimaginable turn of events. Soon the whole of the great beast trembled and shook violently in its helpless death throes.

Herzgo Alegni went hunting for another victim.

Barrabus the Gray was not suited to fighting umber hulks. He knew that, of course. He depended upon speed and precision, measuring the reactions of his enemies to afford him openings through which he could deliver quick, killing blows.

Umber hulks, however, didn't bother reacting to the strikes of a sword and dirk. The misdirection of a man like Barrabus wouldn't turn a monstrous umber hulk.

Still, when he saw one of the monsters wreaking destruction at one square, scattering villagers and tearing apart the buildings, Barrabus found himself charging in at the beast. He rolled off the back of the nightmare as it neared, landing easily and running along behind the magical horse.

That steed charged right into the hulk, slamming the monster hard and knocking it back a stride. The nightmare reared and kicked its fiery hooves into the beast's face, and the umber hulk clawed and swatted with abandon, finally driving the hellish horse aside.

Just in time to catch a flying Barrabus.

The man leaped up at the beast, stabbing hard with his sword and scoring a hit right between the umber hulk's snapping mandibles. Barrabus fell short of the monster, as he'd planned, and darted out to the left, stabbing the creature hard in the side with his dirk as he passed.

The umber hulk swung around, batting at him, but never quite catching up to him. Its heavy arm connected on the nearest building, smashing the wall and sending chunks of stone tumbling.

Barrabus avoided them and used the tumult to run back out the other way, where he launched a flurry of strikes against the distracted brute's back. He hit the umber hulk a dozen times, but could score only minimal damage against the thick hide and sheer bulk of his enemy.

More importantly, though, Barrabus had made the creature furious and it pursued him with a singular purpose. He wouldn't allow it to catch up to him to join in battle once more, however, for when those settlers nearby saw that one of their comrades had the umber hulk's full attention, and noted, too, that it was Barrabus, their hero from the previous battle, they found their courage and came on in support.

Like a hive of stinging bees, they nipped and stabbed at the umber hulk, over and over again. Following Barrabus's lead, and heeding his commands, they stayed ahead of the monster's increasingly desperate lunges and swings.

On and on it went, and finally, the umber hulk dived down to the ground and burrowed away, digging deep through the cobblestones and into the soft earth below. Barrabus actually went into the hole after it, scoring many more vicious stabs at the retreating monster's feet and legs.

When finally he simply let the umber hulk burrow away, leaving him in a trench a dozen feet below the city square above, Barrabus blinked many times and wondered what in the Nine Hells he might have been thinking.

As he ascended, he did so to a growing chorus of elation, and indeed, when he exited, he found that some of the folk were cheering him for his actions in the square.

Mostly, however, they cheered for Herzgo Alegni, and despite Barrabus's hatred for the tiefling, he couldn't honestly claim that those cheers were misplaced. Not at that moment, at least.

Alegni fought a second umber hulk, his mighty sword hacking at the beast with abandon. Its skin hanging in torn flaps, the umber hulk tried to keep up with the relentless cuts, tried to turn around in pace with the surprisingly quick Alegni.

But the tiefling had gained an advantage and he would not surrender it. Claw, that terrible sword, inflicted heavy damage with each strike, damage that went beyond the torn skin and muscle, broken bones and spurting blood, damage that reached right to the heart of the umber hulk's existence, the core of its soul.

The creature turned, and turned some more, and turned yet more as it screwed itself down to the ground, where Alegni finished it off with a great overhead chop, splitting the beast's skull in half.

"You should have finished the task with the cataclysm," Szass Tam scolded Sylora. The sorceress had just informed him of the new information Arunika had supplied regarding the heroic exploits of Herzgo Alegni. "He gains strength and alliance with the villagers."

"I struck at them hard," Sylora countered.

"You?"

"The Abolethic Sovereignty—and I count their alliance as my victory."

"Fair enough," Szass Tam admitted, but he chucked his disgust with every word. "Some villagers were killed, but once again, the Netherese became their heroes, did they not?"

Sylora lowered her eyes. She couldn't answer that.

"It was a good attack," Szass Tam unexpectedly concluded. "Many of the villagers were killed—I sense their souls feeding the Dread Ring now. And not one of our zealots was slain, not a zombie destroyed. Now we must convince the settlers that the reason you attack them is their alliance with the Netherese."

"Arunika," Sylora reasoned, and Szass Tam nodded.

"She can be quite persuasive, I'm told," the archlich said.

"I need more Ashmadai," Sylora dared to remark, and to her surprise, Szass Tam nodded once more.

Sylora breathed easier, her mind already concocting the lies she would feed through Arunika, already thinking of new ways to wound the settlers, to turn them against the Netherese.

But her relief proved short lived.

"You took from the Dread Ring," Szass Tam stated.

Sylora looked up at him with surprise.

"I feel its power diminished, stolen by you."

The sorceress shook her head, trying to make sense of it, for Szass Tam's tone had taken a darker turn—and that usually meant someone was going to die, horribly.

"I didn't . . ."

"Into a scepter, perhaps?" Szass Tam remarked, and Sylora understood then.

"J-Jestry's weapon . . . yes," she stammered.

"You took from the Dread Ring."

"I asked the Dread Ring for strength," Sylora protested.

"Strength it provided, to its own detriment."

"Master, I . . ." Sylora started, but stuttered and shook her head, trying to figure a way out of this.

"Jestry's weapon, you say?" Szass Tam prompted her, and she jumped on that sliver of hope.

"My champion, yes! He is being prepared to—"

"*Your* champion?" the archlich remarked.

"*Our* champion," Sylora corrected. "Your champion. Jestry of the Ashmadai. I've strengthened him. With the help of the aboleth ambassador, I've molded him into a warrior above all other Ashmadai, a warrior worthy of Szass Tam."

"You stole from the Dread Ring."

"I strengthened his scepter, creating a weapon truly fitting a champion of Szass Tam," Sylora explained. "He will face Dahlia."

"Dahlia?"

"She returns, and brings with her a powerful ally." Sylora swallowed hard and considered whether or not she should complete her tale, as the spirit of Dor'crae had relayed it through Valindra

Shadowmantle. But she realized by Szass Tam's posture that she had no choice but to reveal it all.

"Hadencourt is gone," she explained. "Dahlia and her drow companion destroyed him and his devil bodyguards. She knew he was Ashmadai. She knew he was allied with me. She's fully a traitor now, and intends to defeat me and our mission here, and so, yes, Master, I dipped Jestry's weapon in the Dread Ring and prayed for it to lend the weapon some of its power. If Dahlia is successful, the Dread Ring will be imperiled, and that we cannot have."

Szass Tam let her words hang in the air for a few moments before finally replying, "You chose well. Dahlia must be destroyed. Do not fail me in this."

"More warriors?" Sylora dared to remind him. "That Ashenglade will be fully garrisoned?"

Szass Tam nodded. "Presently," he said. "Prove to me that your . . . that *my* champion is suitable." For dramatic effect, he raised his skinny, almost skeletal arms up high, the voluminous sleeves of his great robes sliding back from his dark skin. "Finish this unpleasantness with Dahlia. Oh, my disappointment in that one! I will have her before me—dead or alive, it does not matter!"

He ended with a flourish and the ash lifted up around him, obscuring his increasingly insubstantial form as he melted into thin air, returning to Thay.

Then Sylora did breathe easier. She hated those moments with Szass Tam. Even when she had nothing but good news to deliver, as when she'd revealed Ashenglade to him, she could never be quite sure what his reaction might be. Many claimed he was unstable, insane, and perhaps that was true, but Sylora equally suspected that Szass Tam used his unpredictability to his advantage. She was never balanced when speaking with him, never prepared for what might come her way, never certain he wouldn't kill her for some reason or another, for some excuse she hadn't even considered.

Yes, she realized, he really was her master.

CHAPTER

13

THE POISON IN THEIR HEARTS

DAHLIA WATCHED THE COLD WATER BREAKING LEFT AND RIGHT as she dipped the cloth into the stream. Beside her, Drizzt picked at one of the wounds where a broken piece of barbed quill had stubbornly stuck. His entire right arm was covered in blood again. He flexed his hand and clenched his fist, pushing even more blood forth from the many wounds.

Dahlia rubbed the soaked cloth over the drow's arm, washing away the majority of the blood and revealing his wounds to be a series of punctures rather than one long cut.

Drizzt held his arm up, turning it in the sunlight. He motioned to Dahlia, who moved the wet cloth near enough for him to bite it. He pushed the small knife into his forearm. He grimaced and twisted, then retracted the blade, dropped it, and reached back to his arm to remove the stubborn quill.

The drow let go of the cloth and sighed, shaking out his hand before dipping his arm into the cold stream.

"Wretched little beasts," he remarked, staring at the quill for just a moment longer before flicking it into the stream.

"How many wolves have said the same of porcupines?"

"I know of few porcupines who find the courage to chase wolves through the forest."

"Perhaps they're wiser than devils, then," Dahlia quipped, but while that brought a smile to Drizzt's lips, the woman couldn't quite manage one.

"Hadencourt is gone," Drizzt assured her.

Dahlia nodded absently.

"The threat is passed. Our road to Neverwinter Wood, and Sylora Salm, is clear."

Again she nodded, but it was clear she was hardly listening. She didn't look at Drizzt either. Her gaze roved the shadows of the trees clustered along the riverbanks.

"Sylora is prepared for us," she said. "We'll not have the element of surprise in our favor. Hadencourt was her agent."

"We don't need to continue," Drizzt replied. "We can turn aside now. The whole of the North is open to us."

"No," Dahlia stated flatly.

"We can return another time, not too far in the future, then," Drizzt offered. "Perhaps now that Hadencourt and his minions are gone, we'll regain a measure of surprise. Perhaps if we delay, just a bit, Sylora will let down her guard."

"No," Dahlia said. "There never was a chance to surprise her, and I was a fool to think otherwise. Sylora Salm is a seasoned veteran of Thay and a great disciple of Szass Tam. Hadencourt merely reaffirms what I already knew: Sylora Salm has eyes all around her, and now that she's warned of our intent, she'll never let down her guard."

"What do you know?" Drizzt asked, sensing that something more was going on, particularly from the way Dahlia kept looking into the shadows, as if she expected some devil or other monster to charge out at them then and there.

"Dor'crae," Dahlia admitted. "He's still around, or will be again presently. I'm certain of it. He can find us and we cannot know of his presence."

"As I said, we could turn aside—"

"No," Dahlia cut him short.

Drizzt watched her for a while, trying to read her eyes as she continued to stare off into the forest. There was little caution to be found there, and quite a bit of seething anger. She hated Sylora, of course, but it seemed to the drow that there was something more than that.

"Are you always so eager to kill?" Drizzt asked quietly, though there was nothing quiet about the implications of such a question.

Dahlia kept staring off into the distance then suddenly snapped her head around to consider the drow.

"Sylora, Beniago . . ." Drizzt remarked. "Do you know only one manner of negotiation?"

Her face tightened with anger, but it didn't hold. She seemed sadder and more wounded then, and Drizzt regretted his off-hand remark.

"What anger drives you?" he pressed on anyway. Drizzt rose from beside the stream and paced toward her, but took a circuitous route around her. "She's beautiful. She's accomplished—a skilled warrior, a hunter, a tactician."

He continued to circle. "She's young and can command the world at her feet. Every road is open to her, yet she ever chooses those trails that will lead her to the greatest danger."

"Does Drizzt Do'Urden shy from a fight?" she asked.

"Do I hunt the wolves in the forest?"

The porcupine reference did bring a bit of smile to Dahlia's fair face.

"For one who avoids trouble, your blades carry the smell of much blood," Dahlia retorted. "And for all of your bluster now, are you not walking that same dangerous road beside me?"

"I have my reasons."

"I know your reasons," Dahlia replied. She grabbed Drizzt's hand as he moved around her and pulled him down roughly so she could kiss him.

He didn't resist.

Drizzt moved to the top of the ridge overlooking the stream. He saw Dahlia below him, splashing water on her face. He looked at her curiously for just a moment, for something seemed . . . different. Then he realized her braid was back, and as he considered the water dripping from her shining face, he recognized that mesmerizing woad pattern of bluish spots.

His initial reaction was to pull back. Before he even considered the elf's exotic look, his instincts made him react negatively to this harsher appearance. He was surprised by his response, for he'd previously found Dahlia's exotic hair and woad enticing. And still she was beautiful—he couldn't deny that. This was a more dangerous look, but wasn't that, after all, what Drizzt's life had become?

Hadn't danger been his choice, his preference?

He closed his eyes and imagined the "softer" Dahlia, tending his arm, her hair bouncing lightly around her shoulders, her face clean and fresh and unblemished. He opened his eyes and looked upon her again, considering the change that seemed to come over her at a whim.

Drizzt remembered his midnight ride to Luskan and back, the exuberance of the danger, the thrill of the hunt. Those emotions better accompanied this incarnation of Dahlia. Even though she'd worn the softer look when they ventured into Luskan, it was this impression of Dahlia that helped Drizzt take the risks and enjoy the experience with little regard for the consequences. This incarnation of Dahlia was not vulnerable, was hardly delicate.

As he trotted down to join his lover, it occurred to Drizzt that perhaps he'd become as paradoxical as she.

"Have you ever been in love?" she asked without looking back at him as he neared.

The question stopped him in his tracks.

"Tell me about her," Dahlia said.

Memories of Catti-brie swirled around his thoughts, and it occurred to him that he would likely tell Dahlia of Catti-brie in a different way, with different emphasis and different tales, if she'd been wearing her softer guise.

She looked up at him and wore a smile, though it was lost in the mesmerizing swirl of her woad. Perhaps she meant it to be a warm smile, but he couldn't tell.

"It was a long time ago," he managed to reply.

Dahlia laughed at him. "I'm not jealous," she assured him.

"I know." His voice was flat.

Dahlia's smile disappeared, replaced by a pensive look then a slight nod of understanding. "Tell me of the dwarf, then. Of this King Bruenor Battlehammer. I knew him only for a short while, but he intrigued me. How long did you know him?"

"More than a century," Drizzt replied, and he found he was indeed more at ease then. It would be far easier to speak of Bruenor than of Catti-brie, particularly to Dahlia. "Perhaps closer to two centuries."

"From afar?"

"My closest friend."

"For a hundred and fifty years?" Dahlia asked incredulously, and her smile returned, this time reflecting astonishment.

"Would that I had him beside me for another hundred," Drizzt said.

"Instead of me?"

The suddenness of her question again threw the drow off-balance. He had to think about the answer—and wondered how he might phrase his impulsive thoughts even if he could sort them out.

Dahlia laughed again, relieving the tension. "Beside me, perhaps?" she offered.

"I'll tell you of him and let you decide," Drizzt replied, glad for the out.

"And of your lover?"

Drizzt felt his face grow tight.

Dahlia reached down and retrieved her wide leather hat and plopped it on her head, adjusting her braid so that it curled around her shapely neck and ended at the top of her cleavage.

"Come," she said as she rose. "The road lies before us and I wish to hear your tales of King Bruenor."

Drizzt moved down to the stream and vigorously shook his wounded arm in the cold water. He hustled to catch up to Dahlia, drawing a bandage from his pouch as he went. By the time they reached the road and he lifted his whistle to summon Andahar, he'd wrapped the arm from above the elbow all the way to the wrist. For the rest of that day as they rode, he clenched and unclenched his fist, battling the tingles of the residual devilish poison, and his bandage soon enough showed more than one red stain from the renewed blood flow.

Drizzt didn't care about that inconvenience, however, for he told the tales of Bruenor, as Dahlia bade him. Those stories, happy and thrilling and filled with love and friendship, forcibly battled a different type of poison within the heart and soul of Drizzt Do'Urden.

They set their camp long after the sun had disappeared below the horizon, and were off again before the light of dawn. Andahar carried them effortlessly. Soon enough, they came to the northern reaches of Neverwinter, but on Dahlia's insistence, they didn't venture into the settlement. They set their camp just northeast of the town.

While looking for some wood for their small fire, Drizzt heard a rustle of leaves, a footstep. That alone didn't concern him too greatly—the Neverwinter Guard was likely around the area, and they were not enemies, after all. But as he moved around to investigate, using all the stealth that marked the night as the time of the drow, Drizzt quickly grew more concerned, for whomever he followed showed himself to be quite practiced at the art of avoidance.

The drow at last spotted his quarry, and when he did, he understood why it had taken him so long to locate the source of the noise that had brought him deeper into the forest. The moon was full and bright, after all, and Drizzt's drow eyes could cut through the shadows on a night like this as easily as in full sunlight. Any normal traveler, even a city guard, should have been easy to spot. But now, finally, when Drizzt discovered the source of that footstep, he forgave himself for not locating this one earlier.

The man—or woman, he couldn't tell—was of the Shadowfell, a shade who blended into the darkness beneath one wide-spread elm so easily Drizzt for a moment wondered if he were watching a Netherese lord shift back into that dark realm.

He spotted his prey again, and knew then that it was indeed a man, heavyset and powerfully built. Again Drizzt took up the silent pursuit, moving as invisibly as the other, and far more quietly with his practiced steps and full understanding of the forest floor. He smelled the campfire before he spotted it, and moved more quickly. He counted at least three more shades, all in armor and strapped with weapons.

He recalled what Dahlia had told him of the turmoil in the wood and recognized the war party for what it was.

Drizzt soon enough melted into the night and trotted back the way he'd come.

To his surprise, he found Dahlia on the edge of their camp, her staff already broken into flails and looped over her sash belt on either hip, within ready grasp.

"Shadovar—" Drizzt started to say.

"I know. I smell them," Dahlia said.

"A handful," Drizzt explained, nodding his chin toward the distant camp. "Just over those hills. We can swing off to the west, down near to the coast and . . ."

He stopped talking when Dahlia simply walked away from him into the forest, straight as a killing arrow in the direction of the Shadovar encampment.

Drizzt watched her curiously. "We need not fight them," he called after her, but she didn't slow.

"Aren't the Netherese the enemies of the Thayans?" he asked when he caught up to her.

"Mortal enemies," Dahlia replied, but she didn't stop her march.

"So Sylora Salm would wish us to do battle with this group?" Drizzt asked, hoping to shake Dahlia free of the almost trancelike state that had come over her. Even in the dim light, he could see the rage simmering in her sparkling eyes. She had her weapons off her belt by then, and clutched them so tightly that her skin, appearing pale even in the starlight, seemed brighter around the knuckles, as if white hot with anger.

"If we battle with the shades, do we not do Sylora's bidding?" he asked again.

Dahlia stopped and turned to face him directly. "The Netherese and the Thayans vie for control of Neverwinter Wood," she admitted. "Yes—are you pleased with yourself?—Sylora Salm would want this group slain, would want all these foul grayskins slain."

"Then let's go the other way," Drizzt took a step back toward their own camp, already a considerable distance behind them.

But Dahlia's chuckle denied him. "Not everything in my life is about the desires of Sylora Salm," she said, continuing on her way.

Again Drizzt caught up to her, to find her expression no less resolute than before.

There would be no reasoning with her, Drizzt realized. Over the hills and through the valleys, Dahlia's path remained straight in the direction Drizzt had pointed, toward the Shadovar encampment.

Drizzt had little first-hand knowledge of the Empire of Netheril and little experience with the minions of Shadowfell. He tried to sort this out, for he knew he wouldn't let Dahlia go into this fight alone. He was more than glad to accompany her in her mission to kill Sylora Salm, both because of the devastation Sylora had wrought on the city of Neverwinter and for the loss of Bruenor. Given that decision, did it matter if Drizzt and Dahlia's actions now would be to Sylora's temporary benefit?

Drizzt had no love, no friendship, and not even the benefit of the doubt for the Shadovar and their foul designs.

"There are at least four," he whispered to Dahlia.

They were getting fairly close to the camp. Dahlia stopped and looked down at his scimitars. She smiled when Drizzt drew them, then she nodded and started to run.

Over the hill, they spotted the campfire, and Dahlia didn't slow.

Drizzt remained a few strides behind, easily pacing her with his anklets and superior lowlight vision, and because of both, he was even able to match her strides while keeping himself fairly well concealed. He put away his scimitars and took up Taulmaril instead.

He spotted one Shadovar in the low branches of a tree, but apparently Dahlia didn't. She continued right under the perch.

The Shadovar leaped down at her and flew aside with a shocked and pained shriek as Drizzt drilled him with a lightning arrow.

Dahlia skidded to a stop and spun around just long enough to snap a double-strike, left and right, into the face of her wounded attacker, cracking his skull.

On she ran, the camp in sight and now full of activity.

"Down left!" Drizzt called to her.

Into the firelight went Dahlia, to learn that Drizzt's estimate of their enemies had been low, for even with the fallen Shadovar outside the camp, five Shadovar stood in front of her.

She did as Drizzt had instructed, a sidelong roll to her left, and a pair of arrows soared past her, cleanly removing the middle opponent from their rough semicircle.

Dahlia came up engaged with the pair on the left, and as the two from the right moved to surround her, another arrow flashed through, driving them back, and a dark form came leaping in, scimitars glowing and spinning.

Dahlia furiously pressed her momentum at the pair in front of her, her flails whirling out wide and slamming in powerfully at her opponents. She had them on their heels and meant to keep them there, relentlessly assaulting, left and right, overhand and underhand.

The Shadovar to her left flank managed to stab at her, but her left-hand flail intercepted with a backhanded block, the top pole flipping right over to wrap the sword. Her right hand came across to similarly slap and wrap the sword, and before the Shadovar could retract, Dahlia yelled and threw both her hands out wide, each flail pulling free in the same rotation, spinning the blade and thus tearing it from the swordsman's grasp.

Dahlia rotated her left wrist, sending the flail in a spin, and clipped the Shadovar in the face as it came around.

Dahlia retreated from the other Shadovar at the same time, half-turning and dropping her right foot back behind her left, and with her new alignment, she brought her right hand across in front of her, bending her wrist once, twice, thrice, and snapping that second flail like a whip, the flying pole biting forth to jab the Shadovar hard in the face.

At the same time, Dahlia shifted her left hand under the right, working her weapon in a circular defense, right to left then back to the right, keeping the other Shadovar at bay.

She whip-snapped three times again, but only the first two connected as the dazed Shadovar tumbled away.

Dahlia came up straight against her lone opponent, and just to keep him off balance, reverted her two weapons into one long staff again. She noted then the recognition on her enemy's face. This Shadovar knew her, knew Dahlia as Sylora's champion.

And so he knew, too, that he was doomed.

Drizzt swept the two swords aside, his own blades ringing a tune on the one to his left with a backhand block then a forehand, and back and forth.

"Dahlia!" he called as he drove farther out that way, past the woman's back.

The fighter to Drizzt's right pursued him, and was caught completely by surprise as Dahlia threw her staff out behind her, catching it high along the shaft and stabbing back hard, jabbing the Shadovar squarely in the throat.

Drizzt finished his drumbeat on the sword of his other foe by stepping forward suddenly as he struck one last time, his blade slashing the Shadovar's forearm. His sword went flying wide and the Shadovar fell back, grasping its arm.

But Drizzt didn't follow, leaping back to his right, a sweeping backhand slashing out in front of him to bite at the other dazed warrior. His forehand followed, right below the level of the first strike, and the drow ranger threw himself around in a complete circuit. Once again, the backhand led the way, now just below the last strike, then a forehand, lower again. And around Drizzt continued to a third double strike.

Drizzt leaped back to the left. The other Shadovar had recovered his sword. To the drow's right, his last opponent stood very still, arms stretched out wide. This Shadovar, too, dropped his weapon, though he was obviously not aware of the motion.

Six lines of blood appeared from his neck to his belly.

He sank to the ground.

The remaining Shadovar in front of him turned and fled.

Drizzt glanced back at Dahlia and winced at the sight. She had that last Shadovar down by then, and drove her staff like a spear against the fallen warrior's head, again and again.

"Dahlia!" Drizzt called. He'd never seen her acting so viciously. "Dahlia!"

She finally glanced at him, but quickly looked past him to see the fleeing Shadovar moving into the forest.

"No," the elf said with a growl.

She charged past Drizzt, shouldering him aside and nearly to the ground in her haste.

"Let him go," Drizzt implored her, but too late.

Dahlia sprinted to a large tree, planted her staff, and vaulted up to the branches. Drizzt followed her progress by the rustling and shaking leaves, and couldn't help but be impressed by her arboreal prowess.

Then Drizzt spotted the fleeing Shadovar, some distance away and running through the trees, stumbling often.

The Shadovar came up straight then leaned forward in a sprint, but too late.

Dahlia dropped upon him.

Drizzt shook himself from his spectator's trance, glanced around quickly to confirm that the four Shadovar in the camp were all dead, and sprinted off, calling for Dahlia to spare that one that they might garner some information.

He stopped calling out as he neared the scene and saw Dahlia bending over, her flails pumping furiously. By the time he came up beside her, he had to look away. She'd beaten her enemy's head to a misshapen mess of blood and gore.

"Dahlia," he said, loudly but not sharply.

A flail hummed in the air, spinning and striking down, pulverizing bone.

"Dahlia!" he yelled.

She couldn't hear him. Drizzt looked for an opening so he could get near to her without getting clipped, and quickly enough so he wouldn't give her the opportunity to turn on him with those battering weapons. Dahlia seemed beyond rational to him at that moment, her face a mask of rage, and indeed, she grunted and growled with every vicious beat.

Drizzt truly believed that she might lash out at him.

He slid his blades away, measuring her movements, recognizing her rhythm. Down went her left arm, to the other side from him, and up went her right.

Drizzt dived across her back, slipping his right arm underneath Dahlia's raised arm and clamping his hand behind her neck. As he landed on her back, driving her to the side, she instinctively tried to slap back at him with her free left, and that gave Drizzt the chance to loop his left hand under her left elbow.

He had her trapped, one arm up high, the other pulled back like a chicken wing, and as she continued to stagger to her left under the weight of his assault, it was an easy enough task for Drizzt to slip his left foot to the side of Dahlia's left foot and trip her up. He made the fall as easy as he possibly could, but he had to keep his weight upon her as she thrashed and screamed in protest.

"Dahlia," he kept saying against her insistent chorus of "Let me go!"

"He's dead," Drizzt assured her. "They're all dead."

"I want to kill him more!"

Drizzt blinked in shock and tightened his hold, fully immobilizing the woman. He brought his lips to her ear and whispered, "Dahlia."

"Let me go!"

"They're dead. You killed them. Dahlia!"

He kept whispering, and finally, after a long while, Dahlia relaxed beneath him.

Drizzt eased his grip, inch by inch, then slid off her and jumped to his feet, reaching a hand down in an offer of aid.

Still on her belly, Dahlia looked up at him but refused the hand. She rolled to the side, twisted, and put her feet under her. Then she stalked past Drizzt, back the way they'd come. She did slow enough to spit on the mound of gore that had once been a Shadovar head.

Drizzt winced again and stared, dumbfounded.

Such were Dahlia's demons.

But how, and why, and to what end, he had no idea.

CHAPTER 14

UNWELCOME COMPANIONSHIP

THE LESS YOU SAY, THE MORE I'LL TOLERATE YOU," BARRABUS THE Gray said to his hunting companion.

The misshapen warlock replied with a crooked, condescending grin, an expression that was becoming more and more typical of the young tiefling, and one that greatly annoyed Barrabus. The assassin had never been fond of spellcasters—priest or wizard. He didn't understand them, and certainly didn't like fighting them. He'd fought hundreds of duels against warriors, and usually escaped untouched. But whenever he battled a wizard, he knew he was going to get stung. Even the puniest of spellcasters had clever dweomers that would sift through his defenses to bite at him.

Even more than that, Barrabus had never met a wizard who wasn't arrogant, as he'd never met a priest who didn't justify the most heinous of actions by hiding behind his god.

He had no use for either.

Yet here he was, out in Neverwinter Wood beside this Effron creature, whose dead arm hung behind his back and waggled like a boneless tail, and whose strange eyes seemed a testament to a mixed breeding gone absurd. To make his sheer physical ugliness even more profound, Effron was a tiefling, and Barrabus had come to know he'd rather couple with an orc than partner with one of the devil spawn. Truly, this one seemed possessed of everything Barrabus the Gray didn't like, and that only reminded him all the more that he was no longer possessed of free will, that the awful sword, which he'd carried—and foolishly believed he'd dominated—for decades, would truly torment him for eternity.

"Are you afraid I'll alert the zealots to our presence?" Effron said with a snicker. "Ah yes, as Lord Alegni explained to me, you're only truly deadly when you catch your victim by surprise."

Barrabus stopped and turned around to face Effron, his expression grim—but that did little to douse the tiefling's taunting grin.

"I take it you expect me to attack you, then," the assassin said dryly.

"I'm never off guard," the warlock replied.

Barrabus laughed, but coldly. How many times had he heard such a proclamation? How many times had such a claim been the last words ever spoken by a victim?

Oh, but how Barrabus wished that to be the case now! He would love to cut this one's throat out.

"And you cannot attack me anyway," Effron went on. "Lord Alegni wouldn't allow it, would he?"

At what point would Effron's taunting lead him to the breaking point, where recklessness overruled reason, the assassin wondered? He understood the torment he would receive if he killed Effron. The awful sword had made it perfectly clear to him. He hadn't forgotten his turtlelike posture on the bridge—the Herzgo Alegni Bridge—and the unbelievable agony accompanying, indeed facilitating, that humiliation.

But this one . . .

It had occurred to Barrabus more than once that morning, their first day out in the forest together, that Alegni had placed Effron at his side just to provoke him. Perhaps Alegni, who seemed equally disgusted by Effron, knew the warlock would be too much for Barrabus's limited patience, the sword's threats be damned. Perhaps Alegni wanted Barrabus to slay Effron and thus rid him of the troublesome warlock. Then, as an added benefit, he would torture Barrabus—perhaps to death—as punishment.

The tiefling warlock seemed to revel in annoying Barrabus or Alegni, or any of the others at the Netherese encampment, for that matter. He was always flashing that crooked grin.

To what end?

Barrabus saw pain in the young tiefling's face, but he didn't care enough to look deeper.

He did widen his scrutiny of Effron, though, examining the shattered, badly dislocated shoulder and that ridiculous limb hanging limply behind the tiefling. Someone might have done Effron a great favor and killed him in the course of whatever trauma had caused those injuries.

He caught something else then, just a whisper of sound in the distance—the snap of a fallen twig, perhaps. Effron, oblivious, started to speak, but Barrabus waved him to silence with such intensity that even the obstinate tiefling quickly shut up.

Barrabus turned and moved behind the nearest tree, drawing his weapons as he went. When he looked back, he could only sigh, for Effron had not moved, and just stood there, looking at him curiously, and with a bit of amusement, it seemed.

So be it, Barrabus decided, and he turned his attention to the forest beyond. He was glad he was allied with the Shadovar at that moment, because the zealots he easily spotted might have been invisible in the shadows if they'd been minions of Herzgo Alegni.

He turned back again to the warlock, waving to get his attention, then warning him with sharp hand signals that four enemies approached.

In response, Effron just offered that stupid grin, and he tilted back and forth quickly so that his limp arm would flop out to the side in a ridiculous and macabre wave.

Barrabus narrowed his eyes and wished he had enough time to run back there and throttle the idiot. But again, so be it, he decided, and he felt even better about that choice when he considered that perhaps these zealots would kill Effron and save him the trouble. That pleasant thought didn't hold, however, for when Barrabus turned back to the approaching Ashmadai patrol, he realized they'd already noted Effron, and what had seemed like a simple ambush for Barrabus suddenly transformed into something much more complicated.

One large Ashmadai began waving one of those scepters—only this weapon appeared more black and streaked with red than usual—to direct the other three. One of those three slung a bow over his shoulder and scrambled to a climbable tree, while the other two began their approach, moving defensively from tree to tree and brush to brush. One forged ahead, ducking for cover, then motioned for his companion, who sprinted past him to the next point of cover.

They were well trained and well practiced, Barrabus saw that simply from their coordination. He glanced back at Effron again, who maintained his oblivious posture, and shook his head.

Barrabus weighed the movements of the approaching zealots, weighed his options, and found his opportunity. He always preferred to cut the head off the serpent, so as the three continued toward him, two on the ground and one in the trees, Barrabus slid out to the side and began his own advance—but around the foot soldiers.

The one in the back acted like the leader, and so that one became the primary target. Determinedly, stubbornly, even spitefully, Barrabus wouldn't let concern for Effron deter him, particularly since the idiot warlock seemed unconcerned for his own safety.

Barrabus continued to watch the first three for some time, moving past them carefully but soon recognizing that they had spied Effron as their prey. But he knew he needn't be too concerned. Long experience had shown him that once locked in on a potential foe, these zealots practiced pure recklessness, and if Barrabus had been walking upright and singing a song of a Calimport brothel, those leading three wouldn't likely have paid him any heed.

He continued to watch their advance for a short while longer anyway, and he realized deep in his gut that it was mostly because he wanted to witness the death of Effron.

The archer in the tree moved swiftly into position. Barrabus saw him set an arrow. The other two were nearly at the edge of the clearing, and should charge forth at any moment.

With a determined grimace, Barrabus pulled his attention away and turned back to the Ashmadai leader, noting then the warrior's curious armor. He wore spiked pauldrons and had circular spiked metal plates strapped at various points on his body: one over his left breast, one centered on his gut, smaller ones on his hips and legs, and a strangely spiked codpiece. That garb was unusual enough, particularly for the uniformly leathered Ashmadai, but what showed beneath the armor as the assassin moved closer for a better look had Barrabus pausing in puzzled curiosity.

Was he about to battle a mummy? The warrior was wrapped head to toe in strips of some grayish material, like dirty old rags.

The assassin didn't know what to make of it, but as soon as he heard the bowstring's *twang* behind him, he didn't care, and he bolted from the brush.

He came in hard, sword leading in a sudden thrust. He stopped his run with a hop, planting both feet and springing into an airborne somersault. The Ashmadai warrior, surprisingly quick, turned as the assassin flew by, and even managed to prod out with his black and red scepter.

Barrabus parried that easily enough and landed with his sword cleverly underneath the Ashmadai's weapon. As he turned back in, the Ashmadai charged at him as well, and never quite managed to disengage that weapon. Up went Barrabus's sword, carrying the scepterlike staff-spear with it and creating a clean opening in the Ashmadai's defenses. Barrabus waded in happily, dagger set by his hip. He mused that he might be able to get back in time to watch Effron's demise.

The Ashmadai warrior twisted and tried to pull back, but Barrabus was too fast for that, and the turn only opened up a better target: the hollow of the warrior's breast, just beside the spiked metal plate.

The fine dagger, magically enchanted, smoothed by the blood of a hundred kills, caught up to the retreating man and plunged hard.

And didn't penetrate.

Only then did Barrabus understand that the Ashmadai's backward motion was not a futile retreat, but a ploy—and one that allowed the strange zealot to pull Barrabus off-balance and also put them both in a position where the Ashmadai could disengage his weapon. And since the kill shot had seemed assured, Barrabus had no contingencies in mind.

The assassin moved purely on instinct as he felt the staff-spear pull free of his upraised blade, bringing his sword down hard, though he knew he'd be behind the incoming strike, and throwing himself to the side, swinging his opposite hip out even wider. His amazingly quick reaction prevented a solid strike from the scepter, and he accepted the glancing blow and spun away.

Halfway through that spin, he realized he had a problem.

The muscles on his right hip, where the clubbing scepter had struck, began to twitch and contract, and Barrabus stumbled.

Barrabus the Gray never stumbled.

His hip continued to spasm, the skin tightening around the bruise, and a burning sensation ran down the side of his thigh. He'd never felt anything quite like it. It wasn't poison, but more of a magical effect.

A necrotic and withering magic.

The twitching did not diminish—quite the opposite. His leg muscles snapped and released and snapped again, painfully, and Barrabus had to fight hard just to hold his footing.

He stumbled more than once, and couldn't think of executing either a charge or a retreat.

The Ashmadai warrior came on, a grinning mummy.

Effron casually pulled a crooked wooden wand from his belt as he watched the archer in the tree drawing back, the other two crawling in amidst the thick brush.

Those two burst from the underbrush, ten strides away, and the archer let fly.

And Effron tapped the wand to his head, thinned to two dimensions, and thinned again into what seemed like a single line. The insubstantial warlock plunged into a snake hole, sliding into the ground as the arrow flew harmlessly by.

"A caster!" one of the charging zealots yelled as he and his companion skidded to a stop.

That proved to be an expected mistake, from Effron's point of view, and he came back out of the hole, throwing a curse on the warrior to his left as he widened again to his normal form.

The two cried out and came on with fury, waving their staff-spear scepters and crying out for their devil god.

Effron's magic reached out at the warrior to the right. He didn't point his wand at her, but merely offered a sardonic smile. The air between caster and target waved and waggled, like heat rising from a hot stone. A psychic wave rolled out at the female warrior. That wavering air blackened and seemed to roll back up on itself like a coiling serpent, right before it struck her.

She gave a garbled yelp and staggered, her face twisted and torn, her mind scrambled with agony and stinging pulses of magic.

The warlock threw his hand out to block as the other warrior bore down on him, the zealot bending low as if to plow him right over—and why not, the warlock understood, for this one more than doubled his weight.

Except that the warlock had more than one contingency in place for just this kind of attack, and as the warrior struck him, before the fighter could drive him backward, it was the Ashmadai who went flying, straight back the way he'd come, and in that flight, he burst into flames.

Effron, too, went flying, but not from the warrior's momentum. In his circle of study, the magic was known as Caiphon's Leap, and he simply dematerialized—noting the archer's next arrow sailing at him from the tree at just that moment—and walked through a dimensional teleport to reappear right behind the staggering female Ashmadai.

With that one still dazed and stumbling and the other warrior rolling around on the ground, trying to douse the stubborn flames, Effron focused on the archer. Pointing his wand, he threw a black dart of magical energy from its tip. Anyone inspecting that dart closely might think it a flying arachnid.

It struck the archer and nearly dislodged him, but he managed to hold his perch, grimacing and growling in defiance, and managed, too, to fire off another arrow.

This one nearly scored a solid hit, and Effron looked at the missile with great annoyance as it hung from his black robe.

But he dismissed his anger and turned from the archer and struck again at the burning warrior instead, a black bolt, a ghostly bane, flying forth from his wand to slam the man as he tried to stand, knocking him back to the ground.

Effron could hardly contain his grin as he heard the archer cry out again in pain, and as the female warrior finally straightened out enough to charge at him from the other side. The warlock marveled at the archer's aim, for he knew that his cruel and clever missile had hit the mark, and so knew the man to be in excruciating agony.

But indeed the archer's shot was true, the arrow diving at the back of Effron's head.

The Ashmadai gripped his scepter in two hands and swung it as a club, recklessly pushing forward with his attack.

With his hip shuddering with spasms, muscles popping so forcefully he had a hard time standing straight, Barrabus couldn't exploit that obvious weakness nearly as much as he might have hoped. Absent the injury, he could have picked his strikes clearly. As it was, he took what he could get.

The scepter rushed in from his left and Barrabus faded right, snapping his sword up to block, thrusting his dagger hard again against the Ashmadai's chest, then even managing to twist out of the scepter's reach in such a manner that he was able to slash his sword down diagonally across the Ashmadai's neck. He gained some confidence as he came out of the spinning retreat to find that his enemy was not pursuing, to find the mummy staggering under the weight of that strike.

He started back in for the kill, but something in his gut held him back—just enough so that as he neared, he was ready to defend. Fortunately, the cunning zealot revealed his ruse, coming straight in, uninjured, and launching another series of vicious swings.

Barrabus backed and parried, keeping his distance, inspecting his enemy's neck closely. He hadn't marred the wrapping, and the mummy's grin and sparkling eyes told him that his solid sword strike had actually done no real harm. He scanned downward, to find not a hint of scarring on the Ashmadai's chest from his last dagger strike, and the first, which had been a perfect strike with all his weight behind it, revealed barely the slightest of scratches on the gray material.

His weapons couldn't get through.

Barrabus dodged and struck again, sword deftly working around the swinging scepter to crack against the Ashmadai's knuckles. But the man didn't flinch; his grip didn't waver at all, it seemed. And he responded with a backhand and a second violent sidelong slash that he cut short, as if to tease Barrabus by proving that the strike on the hand had done nothing at all, and reversed the swing suddenly into a forward thrust.

Barrabus turned and fled, forcing his wounded hip forward to throw that leg in front of him. He clenched his teeth against the pain—he had no time for pain. Barrabus made good speed as he turned around a thick oak. He thought of stopping there for a sudden strike on his pursuing enemy, but realized such a reversal to be too obvious.

But there was a second oak, blocked from the Ashmadai by the first . . .

Effron smiled at the Ashmadai female standing directly in front of him just as the arrow dived from the tree. Obviously spying the true-shot arrow, she growled and grinned as well, and stabbed hard.

Effron opened his arms wide, not even trying to block her thrust, and paid no heed to the arrow as it plunged into the back of his insubstantial head. The last magical bolt Effron had thrown took the name of "ghostly" precisely because of its effect on the caster.

The thrusting scepter plunged into nothing substantial, just the misty form of the dematerialized, ethereal warlock, and the female managed just a hint of confusion on her face—just one delicious hint. The arrow, too, passed right through Effron, and right into the woman's eye. The resulting splash of gore and blood proved conclusively that she was not similarly ghostlike. She fell straight to the ground, landing hard and awkwardly, but Effron knew she hadn't felt a thing.

Off to the side and in front of him, the other Ashmadai finally managed to pull himself from the ground. The zealot, his hair and eyebrows all burned and smoking, his skin bright red and bubbling in places, turned a hateful glare at the warlock. His breath coming in gasps of outrage, he charged.

Effron spun his wand in the air and threw forth a spinning, shadowy snake that seemed to dissipate to nothingness as it neared the target. Still, the Ashmadai staggered as if he'd been punched in the face. Blood began to run from his shattered nose, and he spat out a tooth as well, but infuriated, he kept coming.

The archer behind Effron cried out again, and this time there was more than simple pain reflected in that scream. This time, it was a scream of horror.

Effron couldn't help but smile at that, at how easily he'd controlled the battle.

The Ashmadai warrior finally caught up to him, and the warlock moved into a defensive posture. Effron seemed at a great disadvantage, wearing only robes, holding only a flimsy wooden wand, and with one useless arm hanging limply behind his back, but the warlock was not without his magical defenses in the form of his enchanted robes, his ring, his amulet, his cloak, his bracers, and his belt. And Effron didn't have to worry about scoring any hits against this warrior. The Ashmadai would take care of that all on his own.

Indeed, as the warrior tried to strike at Effron, that shadowy snake reappeared as a shadowy strangler around the man's neck. He gasped and gagged, his eyes bulging both with surprise and from the brutal force of the tightening magical coil.

Stubbornly, the zealot swung again, his scepter banging against Effron's mangled shoulder. The blow stung the warlock and forced him a step to the side.

But the shadow strangler struck again, and this time the Ashmadai vomited blood. He lifted his scepter to strike again, but it fell from his dying grasp, and he stared at Effron with confusion and hatred, then tumbled over to the side, quite dead.

The strange, mummified warrior charged around the tree, unafraid. He paused just long enough to look ahead, left and right, to try to find his quarry, and when his head turned right, Barrabus came out from behind the tree to his left.

With all his strength, the assassin smashed his sword down atop the back of the warrior's head, and this time, the zealot did move forward—and it was not a ruse—under the weight of the blow. In went Barrabus for a second strike, and a third and a fourth, and a kidney stab with his dagger.

When his rage played out and the Ashmadai warrior managed to stagger far enough away from him, Barrabus didn't pursue. In that confusing frenzy, Barrabus had been tapped again by the awful scepter, this time on the left shoulder. Now it, too, began to spasm. His dagger fell from his grasp and the pain jolted him every few heartbeats.

A few strides away, the zealot turned around, grinning, unhurt by Barrabus's attacks.

Barrabus's leg clenched in a vicious spasm as he bent to retrieve his dagger, and he nearly tumbled to the ground. It appeared as though he'd completely lost his balance, his sword, too, falling from his grasp.

The Ashmadai came charging in.

But despite the pain, Barrabus was not off-balance and helpless. He reached for his sword, or so it appeared, but came up again with a handful of dirt, which he flung into the eyes of his pursuer.

The zealot groaned and fell back. Barrabus retrieved his sword—his other hand, numbed and writhing with spasms, wouldn't let him get the dagger back—and turned and fled, running as fast as he could manage, throwing his right foot forward and fighting for all his life not to let that numb limb buckle beneath him.

A barrage of screams demanded Barrabus's attention, and he winced in revulsion as he noted the Ashmadai archer tumbling down from the tree. The frenetic man clawed and slapped desperately at his own skin as a horde of tiny spiders poured forth, biting their way through from inside the poor man.

"Effron . . ." Barrabus muttered, and shook his head in disgust.

He came into the clearing just as another black bolt flew from the warlock's wand into the male warrior, who was on the ground and seemed already dead.

"Effron!" Barrabus called. He heard the mummy Ashmadai closing in behind him. He turned to meet the charge, fighting defensively, not wanting to be touched by the scepter again. "Effron!"

"I killed three already, and you haven't even finished your one?" the warlock called back, his voice filled with an oh-if-I-must sigh.

Barrabus growled and muttered a stream of curses under his breath. He parried furiously against the spinning and thrusting scepter. Every now and then, he countered with a strike, but he saw little chance of hurting this . . . creature.

"Effron!" So distracted was he by his anger at the warlock, Barrabus nearly took a hit in the head, and one that would have surely killed him, he realized.

A series of black and purple darts spun and danced in the air past Barrabus, diving into the zealot—and the mummified creature staggered just a bit.

"More!" Barrabus yelled, and he took the opportunity to come forward and crack his sword atop the zealot's forehead just for good measure.

"Oh, I'm quite depleted," Effron replied. His voice came from farther away and continued to diminish as he spoke.

A wave of panic nearly swept over Barrabus. The good news was that at last his leg spasms seemed to have ended, though his left arm continued to jolt and jerk wildly.

He needed another diversion, something so he could break away and flee . . .

Even as he thought of that, the zealot in front of him exploded, or seemed to, with black and purple energy flying forth from every orifice. That energy slammed Barrabus, hurting him far more than it hurt the zealot. But at least the magic had blinded the Ashmadai, albeit briefly, but enough for Barrabus to break off and flee.

The zealot came in pursuit, and Barrabus glanced back just in time to see the contagion Effron had put in the warrior explode yet again, and once more the Ashmadai warrior had to pause and take a moment for his sight to clear.

By that time, Barrabus the Gray had melted into the forest, and few were as adept at hiding as he.

Particularly when his life depended on it.

Barrabus was still limping when he finally returned to the Shadovar encampment on the western side of Neverwinter, just an hour before dawn. He stormed past the guards, ignoring their confused expressions, and moved right up to the small home Herzgo Alegni had taken as his own. The assassin didn't even bother knocking, but just pushed through the door—or started to.

"He's not in there," a guard called to him.

Barrabus spun on the man, and nearly toppled over from the shooting pain caused by the sudden movement of his hip. He twisted his grimace into a scowl and forced himself forward to confront the man.

"Where is he?"

"Gone north," said a second guard, coming fast around the corner. "We found a patrol, one of our own, slain in the forest."

Barrabus looked at him skeptically. Shadovar were dying almost every day in the continuing battle with the Thayans, so why would Alegni go out personally to investigate?

"This is different," the first said.

Barrabus looked from one to the other. "Where is that miserable Effron?" he asked.

"With Herzgo Alegni," the first replied. "He arrived two hours ago, and claimed that you had been lost in battle."

"That was his hope," Barrabus muttered.

"He arrived just as the first report of the deaths in the north came back to us," the other explained.

"Where?" Barrabus demanded.

"The fourth patrol route, near the northern road," replied the guard, referring to a location that Barrabus knew well, since it had been Barrabus, after all, who had determined the most appropriate positions for the patrols.

The assassin set off, but he wasn't walking this time. He had suffered the pain and trekked back to the city on foot because he expected that it would loosen up his injured hip and also in the hopes that he might find Effron along the way.

Yes, finding Effron before the fool had returned to Alegni's side had been his deepest desire, Claw's magic and certain punishment notwithstanding.

He dropped his obsidian figurine to the ground and called forth his hellish steed. The black nightmare materialized in front of him, angry as always, pawing the ground with its fiery hooves. Still favoring his left arm, Barrabus climbed into the saddle and thundered away, following the cobblestones around the city to the northern road. The sun was just peeking over the horizon to his left when he found the small trail and turned back to the west, his long shadow standing out in front of him.

Among the trees on the smaller path, he dismissed the nightmare and began to track—an easy enough task given the heavy-footed Alegni.

"Sylora Salm's champion returns," he heard Alegni say a short while later.

"She has two champions, then," came the reply from a raspy, whispering voice Barrabus surely knew. "The one who killed the fool Barrabus was quite formidable."

Barrabus crept up in sight of the pair.

"Barrabus is not dead," Alegni insisted. "I would know of such an occurrence—indeed, I would summon him back to life."

"The sword has the power to do even that?" Effron asked with a wide smile.

"He will not so easily escape his eternal indenture," was all that Herzgo Alegni would admit, but Barrabus knew the truth of it anyway.

"The strange Ashmadai—perhaps it was indeed a true mummy—had him beaten, I'm certain," said Effron.

"And you left him?"

The warlock shrugged crookedly. "I had used the majority of my repertoire, since it was left alone to me to defeat the entire Ashmadai force, save that one."

The assassin stepped out of the brush then, pacing steadily across at Effron and drawing his sword. "Good, then," he said. "Just what I was hoping to hear."

"Barrabus," Alegni remarked, but the assassin paid him no heed.

"Far enough!" the tiefling warrior ordered, but the assassin again paid him no heed.

He did hear Alegni then, however, and in no small way, as that awful sword reached forth into him and twisted his guts into agonizing knots. Stubbornly Barrabus continued, one step, then after what seemed like many heartbeats, another.

"Barrabus. . . ." Herzgo Alegni warned.

"You hate him as much as I do," the assassin managed to spit through his gritted teeth.

"That's not the point."

"Let . . . me . . . do . . . this," Barrabus struggled to demand.

"Yes, do," said Effron. "I have enough of my repertoire left to dispatch this lowly idiot."

Herzgo Alegni shot the warlock a hateful glare then turned his attention fully back to Barrabus. He drew out Claw and stated, "Enough!" and such a wave of disjointing pain swept through Barrabus that he staggered to the side and fell over.

"Such a wonderful blade!" Effron said with exaggerated glee, and he clapped his one good hand against his chest. "Do let me borrow it, that I might play with Barrabus as well!"

Alegni silenced the warlock with a look, Barrabus noted, and he stubbornly pulled himself back to his feet.

"Enough of all of this," Alegni warned them both, and he slid his sword away.

Barrabus closed his eyes and breathed easier, released from the grip of Claw. He knew the sword still watched him, though, in his thoughts, knowing his movements before he executed them. He wouldn't get near that troublesome Effron.

So be it, Barrabus decided. He would find himself alone with the insufferable warlock soon enough. He'd make sure of that. He opened his eyes again and turned his attention back to the situation at hand, with Alegni poking around the bodies of four Shadovar.

"Sylora's champion returns," Alegni said to him when he arrived at the tiefling warrior's side.

Barrabus considered the bodies, their positioning, and quickly concluded that more than one opponent had battled this group. He focused on one dead Shadovar particularly, noting six long cuts across the bloody torso, and he could visualize the brilliant maneuvers that had so fully torn the dead warrior.

He was quite sure he knew the attacker, and in this particular case, it couldn't have been Dahlia and her blunt weapon, of course.

"She's not alone," he said to Alegni, and when the tiefling looked to him, he led Alegni's gaze to the torn corpse, even prodded the body with his foot to accentuate the scimitar cuts. "No staff, not even Kozah's Needle, did this."

"Dahlia is a formidable one," Alegni said, but Barrabus shook his head.

"I know this warrior, Drizzt Do'Urden by name, a drow ranger of great renown. He has sided with Sylora's champion, it would seem, and that should be of no small concern to you."

"I've heard the name," said Alegni. "It's spoken often in Neverwinter. This ranger is one of the great heroes of the North, so they say."

Barrabus shrugged, conceding the point.

"And he would side with Sylora Salm?" the tiefling asked doubtfully. "He of goodly name and reputation would side with the unmitigated evil of Szass Tam?"

"He's often misguided," Barrabus dryly replied. "It's his way."

"And you think him as formidable as Dahlia?"

"More so, and I've battled both. And Drizzt is often accompanied by powerful friends—dwarf warriors and other drow, even more deadly than he."

Alegni nodded grimly.

"Sylora surrounds herself with powerful allies, then," Effron chimed in. "These two, and perhaps some friends, and the Ashmadai beast we battled in the forest, and this Valindra creature."

Both Alegni and Barrabus looked at the warlock curiously, their expressions making no secret of the fact that they thought Effron to be rambling about things he didn't understand.

"But I would say, Lord Alegni, that this returning elf warrior and her staff are the most dangerous to your cause," Effron finished.

"You would say?" Alegni replied doubtfully.

The warlock didn't back down from the claim.

"She's a champion of no small accomplishment," Effron insisted.

"I know of her," Alegni replied.

"Dahlia Sin'felle."

"Yes."

"Except that's not her name, Sin'felle," said Effron, and even Barrabus's interest was piqued by the confidence in the warlock's tone. "Sin'felle is the name she gave herself, a mockery, a joke, a title of shame."

"How do you know this?" Herzgo Alegni demanded.

"We are enemies with the Thayans and the wretched Szass Tam, of course, and so I made it my task to learn all that I might of these foes."

"How do you know this?" Alegni asked again, his voice lower and stronger.

"We share allies with Szass Tam and his devil-worshiping zealots," Effron explained. "With our heritage and their devotion, we share allies in the lower planes, do we not? I know of Dahlia and Sylora because I searched for an answer among Netheril's spies within the Nine Hells, and I was particularly curious about this young and powerful elf warrior who fights so well with the strange weapon known as Kozah's Needle."

"Whose name is not Dahlia Sin'felle," Alegni said sarcastically.

Effron nodded, letting the derisive tone slip past. "Half true, though. Her birth name is Dahlia, but the joke of her surname is clear to see, even for a dullard." He looked squarely at Barrabus as he finished, "Yes?"

Barrabus narrowed his eyes and focused on happy thoughts of being alone in the forest once more with Effron the warlock.

"So you say, and I have no reason to doubt you, it seems, and less reason to care," said Alegni.

"Her true name is Dahlia Syn'dalay," Effron announced, crossing his good arm over his skinny chest defiantly as if that proclamation should carry great importance, which confused Barrabus.

Until he looked over at Alegni.

He'd never seen the Netherese lord blanch in quite that way.

"Syn'dalay?" Alegni echoed.

"Yes, of the Snakebrook Syn'dalay clan," Effron replied.

Something seemed to be passing between the two that Barrabus couldn't decipher.

"I would guess that she is . . ." Effron paused and assumed a pensive expression. "Perhaps in her early thirties." His grin showed confidence that he now held the upper hand in the discussion. "Would you agree?"

Herzgo Alegni continued to stare hard in Effron's general direction, but it seemed clear to Barrabus that he looked right through the warlock, as if his thoughts were focused on another place—likely another time, given Effron's last comment. The powerful muscles on Alegni's arms twitched, his jaw tightened noticeably, and his breath came in forced heaves. Barrabus almost believed that if the morning birds would stop chirping and the wind would stop rustling through the leaves, he would be able to hear Alegni's heart thumping in his massive chest.

"You cannot know this," Alegni said at last.

"Dahlia Syn'dalay," Effron repeated, "who was barely more than a child those two decades ago."

"Who?" Barrabus started to ask, but he realized it might be better to remain outside of this increasingly private discussion.

Neither Alegni nor Effron noted his interruption, though, and neither seemed about to speak any further.

"I will kill her," Barrabus announced instead. "I will kill them both."

Herzgo Alegni and Effron both turned to him, and he noted a quick flicker of appreciation on Alegni's face, though it lasted no more than an instant. "The elf alone nearly killed you," he reminded.

"Nearly, but I understand her tactics better now."

"You just claimed her partner is likely more powerful than she."

"And he is one I know well, and one I know how to kill." Barrabus filled his mind with images of his battles with Drizzt, and remembered his long-ago hatred of the drow, for Claw was still there, hovering around his thoughts, and though his plans were nowhere near to clear in his own thoughts, he had an idea just beginning to brew, and one of which Herzgo Alegni surely would not approve.

Alegni stared at him a bit longer, and Barrabus stood firm, even nodded slightly.

"Take Effron with you," Alegni instructed.

"No!" Barrabus replied, and he turned a hateful stare at the young warlock. "If you wish me to kill Dahlia, then so be it. But I will not go after such a foe with that one beside me."

"He fears that my skills will upstage him once more," Effron quipped, but Barrabus and Alegni paid him no heed.

Barrabus continued to shake his head, slowly, determinedly.

"If you kill her, I'll reward you," Alegni said. "Perhaps I'll even grant you your wish to return to the southlands."

Barrabus nodded.

"But if you bring her to me alive," Alegni continued, his voice thick with anticipation, "I'll reward you more greatly than you ever imagined possible."

"Alive?"

Alegni nodded and issued a little growling noise, so . . . hungry, that his intensity sent a shudder down the unshakable Barrabus's spine.

CHAPTER

15

A BLADE TO THE THROAT

BARRABUS THE GRAY WAS SURPRISED AT HOW EASILY HE CAUGHT up to Sylora's allies—to Dahlia, at least. When he found their camp that night, soon after sunset, the drow was nowhere to be seen. Barrabus encircled the camp quietly a few times, wondering how Drizzt's absence might affect his plans—designs still only just beginning to form. He wondered how he could he work the arrival of Drizzt Do'Urden to his favor, but the answer remained just out of reach.

Not sure how he would react when confronted by the drow ranger, he was glad he saw no sign of Drizzt. Theirs was an antagonism of another era, a bitter bloodlust, never quite a rivalry, never quite an alliance. The mere thought of Drizzt sent Barrabus's thoughts cascading across the years to a time that seemed so long ago, to a place that seemed so far removed from the shadows and ruin of present day Faerûn.

The assassin shook away those distractions and refocused his thinking on the situation at hand. With only an unsuspecting Dahlia standing in front of him, he dared hope he could finish his mission and be gone before Drizzt returned.

Or did he?

Perhaps he truly wished to face Drizzt again. Didn't a small part of the man who had become Barrabus the Gray want to be back in that other time and place? Again, he shook the distraction away.

"This is your chance," he whispered under his breath, and that reminder put him fully back in the present.

He took a deep breath and considered his options. If anyone could defeat Herzgo Alegni, it was surely Drizzt, after all.

So if Barrabus could capture Dahlia and take her back to Alegni, that would likely bring Drizzt against the Netherese lord. Surely Drizzt Do'Urden would never abandon a companion to such a fate.

Of course, a captured Dahlia wouldn't last very long with Alegni. Barrabus winced as he considered the Ashmadai woman he'd captured outside of Neverwinter. He'd brought her back in, put her in a secure place, and given orders to the guards not to harm her.

And that was the last Barrabus had ever seen the woman alive, or even in one piece, for the guards had informed Alegni of his demands. Simply because Barrabus had claimed the captive as his own, Herzgo Alegni had made her death particularly cruel.

He'd do the same with Dahlia, of course—perhaps even more so because she brought the added weight of being Sylora Salm's murderous champion.

So be it, and such an event might even work more to his benefit, Barrabus mused. If the drow understood that Alegni had killed Dahlia in a most horrible way, Drizzt would exact swift vengeance on Barrabus's hated master.

That was Barrabus's hope, then, as he sat just outside the firelight of the small encampment, watching Dahlia's movements as she set the bedrolls and performed other mundane tasks. Yes, a capture would be best. He focused on that as he watched her building a fire, and reminded himself of the difficulty presented by either task, capture or assassination, though the latter seemed much easier.

He reminded himself that this elf, Dahlia, was fearless and could fight.

He had to take her fast, without a struggle. He scanned the camp, noting that Dahlia had her weapon broken into flails and within easy reach on her hips, looped under her sash belt. To the side lay a fallen tree, propping the backpacks and bedrolls, and farther beyond that, slung over a low branch were saddlebags—rations, likely—and beside those, hooked on a broken limb, a green cloak, one side of it fairly shredded.

Barrabus glanced around and stealthily moved to the side. He retrieved an armful of kindling first, then got the cloak, apparently without attracting any attention. He donned the cloak and pulled the hood low over his face.

Still, fearing that wasn't enough, he went into the firelight, bent low, and turned sidelong, even walking backward more than forward, clutching the pile of kindling up high to help shield his identity.

"Drop it there," Dahlia instructed, pointing to the side of the fire and showing little interest in what seemed to be her returning companion.

Once he'd set events into motion, Barrabus rarely second-guessed himself. But he was doing so now, trying to anticipate every moment, and fearing that his desperation to be rid of Alegni had made him reckless. This was Drizzt Do'Urden and Dahlia he'd tracked down, not a pair of ridiculous Ashmadai zealots!

The whole plan seemed absurd to him suddenly, and he wondered if he should drop the kindling and run off into the forest night.

He did drop the kindling, but then he struck, sword and dagger out and swinging.

To his surprise, Dahlia was ready, her weapons coming into her agile hands and going into sudden blocks and counters. He had the initiative, but not the surprise!

How could that be?

He went at her furiously, knowing that his advantage, slim as it might be, would prove short-lived.

In those few heartbeats of battle, his desperation to win multiplied a hundred-fold because of the implications it held against Alegni, Barrabus the Gray fought better than ever he could remember. He worked his sword in a brilliant overspin, dodging Dahlia's blocking flail, and bore forward, accepting a stinging hit from the elf's other weapon but getting in close in exchange. His dagger moved up for a finishing position against the elf's throat. He would have her surrender, or he would have her life.

Except that a dark form dropped from above, landing just behind him. Even as his dagger climbed up to score the victory, a scimitar crashed atop his skull, staggering him to the side. Before he could come up straight and offer a defense, Drizzt worked that blade and the other inside Barrabus's arms, one tip coming in against the would-be assassin's throat.

So he would die, and Alegni would bring him back and torment him all the more. Or perhaps, Barrabus wondered in that last breath, the Dread Ring would catch him first and animate him as a zombie.

Better that!

Dahlia had warned Drizzt quite succinctly and repeatedly about the Netherese champion, the stealthy killer. That was why Drizzt had doubled back several times after they'd entered the area, and particularly after their battle with the Shadovar patrol.

So when Drizzt had ostensibly gone off that night to gather firewood, which they didn't need, the drow had actually climbed a tree and slipped from branch to branch to get back near the campsite.

He saw the sudden movement of the murderer executing a brilliant overspin defense, and saw Dahlia taken back and nearly overwhelmed.

Perhaps she would have been beaten, but Drizzt wasn't about to let it come to that.

In short order, he turned the tables, and had Barrabus the Gray helpless and about to die.

In short order, Drizzt looked into the eyes of the Netherese champion, facing the man the moment before his scimitar plunged home.

But he didn't strike—he couldn't strike. Paralyzed by a flood of memories that nearly knocked him from his feet, not by any countering move, but by the simple truth of the moment, Drizzt gaped. The skin tone was wrong, of course, being grayer than Drizzt remembered it, but the overall impression, the way he moved, his features . . .

"Artemis Entreri," Drizzt whispered in shock. He wondered if he was just fooling himself, if the spectacle of Beniago's too-familiar dagger had begun Drizzt thinking about his old nemesis.

The drow's blade dipped precipitously—enough so that Barrabus, had he been thinking of a counter, might have broken away.

"Artemis Entreri," Drizzt whispered again, shaking his head, wondering if this might be the assassin's son—or great, great, great grandson, more likely.

The Netherese champion, this Barrabus the Gray, smiled as if in admission of the absurdity of it all.

"It cannot be," Drizzt said, more forcefully, and he reset the blade against the assassin's throat and forced him back against a thick tree.

"Finish him!" Dahlia insisted, but when she moved forward, Drizzt's free arm snapped out to the side to hold her back.

"Well met, again, Drizzt Do'Urden," said Barrabus the Gray. He looked down at the scimitar, chuckled, and added sardonically, "As well met as ever, it would seem."

"Who are you?"

"You spoke my name—twice," the assassin replied.

"He's deceiving you!" Dahlia insisted.

"Though it's a name I've not heard, and have not used, in many years," the assassin continued, though he barely got the words out as Drizzt pressed him more tightly with the scimitar, prompted by Dahlia's warning.

"The name I spoke was that of a man who would be dead for more than half a century, even if he lived a very long life."

"Life is full of surprises," the assassin replied flippantly.

Drizzt tightened the blade, drawing some blood.

"How fares Jarlaxle, who betrayed me to the Netherese?" the assassin asked, dropping his sword and dirk to the ground.

That name gave Drizzt pause, for of course, the last time he'd heard of Artemis Entreri, the assassin had indeed been traveling with Jarlaxle.

"Is this your new bride?" Barrabus asked, turning his gaze to Dahlia. "She fights well—better than Catti-brie . . ." He went up on his toes as Drizzt moved the deadly scimitar in even tighter, drawing a grimace in addition to more blood.

"Never speak that name," Drizzt warned.

"When I had Catti-brie captured, before we ever met, did I harm her?" the man asked, and with that, Drizzt knew.

Beyond any doubt, he knew.

The shocked drow stepped back, despite the protests of Dahlia.

"You should be long dead," he said.

"So should you," Artemis Entreri replied. "I killed you in a crystal tower, in single combat."

Drizzt's mind flew back to that moment. Jarlaxle had arranged the duel, in a magical tower chamber full of obstacles—props for the showdown between mortal enemies. Drizzt believed he had the fight won, but Entreri had countered with some magic against which Drizzt, caught so unprepared, had no practical defense. Entreri's claim was correct: He had killed Drizzt in that tower the last time the two had crossed paths, and crossed swords, and only the intervention of Jarlaxle and his companion, a mighty mind-mage from Menzoberranzan, had brought Drizzt back from the edge of oblivion.

Drizzt had felt deceived by the psionicist's intervention in that personal duel, and felt it again as he recalled that long-ago day. Apparently Jarlaxle had deceived Entreri as well, for the assassin's surprise that Drizzt remained alive seemed genuine enough.

"You beat me fairly?" Drizzt had to ask, a wee bit of his pride forcing the question despite their more pressing issue—like what he and Dahlia might do with the likes of a captured Artemis Entreri!

"I beat you because that wretch Kimmuriel lent me his strange psionic power, and he did so without my asking."

"You admit it?"

Entreri held up his hands helplessly.

Drizzt didn't know what to think, what to feel. This was Artemis Entreri before him, of that he had no doubt. And yet, strangely, he was not prepared to strike at the assassin. He had no intention of killing Entreri. Drizzt couldn't yet sort through his feelings at seeing this man who should be long dead, but he recognized those feelings clearly, and if he denied them, he would be a liar, to himself above all others.

He was not unhappy to see Artemis Entreri. Quite the contrary, Drizzt Do'Urden felt somehow relieved, wistful even, to find a remnant of those long ago days standing in front of him. Perhaps it was the recent loss of Bruenor, the last of his old friends, the last of the other Companions of the Hall, that granted Artemis Entreri more leniency than he deserved, and which facilitated more charity than seemed reasonable and sensible, than seemed perhaps even safe, from Drizzt.

"What are you doing?" Dahlia demanded, and her voice became more desperate as Drizzt slid his scimitars away.

"Why are you here?" Drizzt demanded.

Artemis Entreri rubbed his throat and considered the blood on his fingers. He glanced over at Dahlia again and said with complete calm, "To kill her."

He looked back at Drizzt again, shrugged, and laughed in a self-deprecating way. "That's what I've been told to do, at least."

"Care to try?" Drizzt asked.

Entreri laughed again and asked, "Why are *you* here?"

"You expect me to tell you?"

"No need," Entreri assured him, and he nodded his chin at Dahlia. "Sylora Salm's champion and I are acquainted, and since Sylora and my master have become mortal enemies, so I'm charged with defeating her champion. You're here to serve Sylora, which surprises me." He ended with a little laugh.

Drizzt gave a quick glance over at Dahlia, who remained stone-faced.

"I wouldn't expect Drizzt Do'Urden to fight in support of Szass Tam, Sylora's master," Entreri went on, and now there was a level of taunting entering his tone. "The archlich of Thay, who hates all living creatures. Does Mielikki approve of your choice, or have you seen enough of the world's darkness to dismiss the pretty lies of gentle souls?"

Again Drizzt looked back at Dahlia, and this time he nodded ever so slightly. Dahlia's expression remained tight and she shook her head, again slightly, in response.

When Drizzt turned back to Entreri, the drow was grinning.

"I come not to serve Sylora," the drow explained, "but to kill her."

The assassin tried unsuccessfully to hide his surprise by laughing at him.

"Sylora facilitated the death of Bruenor Battlehammer," Drizzt said, stealing Entreri's doubting mirth.

"You have chosen your companion poorly, then," Entreri said.

"I battled beside Dahlia against Sylora's minions in Gauntlgrym," Drizzt replied. "Dahlia is no friend to the sorceress of Thay, nor to Szass Tam."

"Nor to Shadovar dogs," Dahlia added, spitting every word, and if she were trying to intimidate the man she knew as Barrabus the Gray, her words had an opposite effect.

"I'm fortunate that I'm no Shadovar, then," he said lightheartedly.

"Any Netherese will do," Dahlia assured him.

"I'm fortunate that I'm not Netherese, then," came the quick retort.

Dahlia narrowed her eyes and studied him curiously, her gaze scanning all areas of his exposed gray skin.

"They pay you well, then," Drizzt reasoned. "Ever was Artemis Entreri for sale to the highest bidder."

He was surprised by Entreri's reaction, the assassin's face tightening into a grimace, and Drizzt knew immediately that Entreri's relationship with the Netherese was not a bargain of gold coins. Entreri had claimed he served a master, but Drizzt understood then that it was not by choice.

Entreri stared hard at him.

"What is it?" Drizzt asked.

Entreri didn't blink.

"If not gold, then what?" Drizzt demanded. He draped his wrists over his sword hilts, a poignant reminder of who held the upper hand. "Why would Artemis Entreri serve the Nether—" He stopped and considered Entreri's earlier words, a claim that Jarlaxle had betrayed him to the Netherese. Instead of continuing with the line of reasoning, Drizzt looked into the eye of his old enemy and asked, simply, "Why?"

"Because he has my sword," Entreri admitted after a long pause.

"Khazid'hea?" Drizzt asked, and he was a bit confused, for as far as he knew, that sword was still in the possession of the dark elf To'sun Armgo, who lived in the Moonwood in the Silver Marches.

Entreri considered him with a bit of obvious puzzlement, then nodded, as if realizing something. "You wouldn't know of Claw," he explained. "Charon's Claw, actually. Truly a mighty blade, greater by far than Khazid'hea."

"And you wish to have it back, so you serve the hateful Empire of Netheril?"

"I wish it destroyed!" Entreri countered angrily, but that fast melted into resignation. He laughed helplessly. "I'm its slave. The Shadovar lord in Neverwinter holds the sword, my sword, and it has taken power over me." He looked over at Dahlia. "And so I'm compelled to kill you," he explained with a shrug. "Nothing personal."

His flippant remark had Dahlia advancing a step, her hands going to her weapons, before Drizzt intercepted her.

"He would prefer death," the woman protested.

"Indeed!" Entreri agreed, and Drizzt looked at him curiously.

"If you could," Entreri explained.

"He just had his blade to your throat," Dahlia reminded the assassin.

"But the sword would just bring me back to fight you again," Entreri went on, ignoring her. Again he looked past Drizzt to Dahlia, and this time, there was more sadness than cleverness showing on his face.

"You're a slave to a sword you once possessed?" Drizzt asked.

"If I don't work to its ends, I'm tormented." He shook his head. "You cannot imagine the torment, my old nemesis. It would do your mother proud."

Drizzt scrutinized him closely and understood from the assassin's truly helpless expression—a visage that seemed so out of place on the face of Artemis Entreri!—that the assassin was not exaggerating.

"And its ends include killing Dahlia?" Drizzt asked.

Entreri shrugged. "That's part of it."

"Then you die," Dahlia interrupted, but Drizzt continued to hold her back, and he silenced her with a look.

"Does Dahlia truly matter?" Drizzt asked, drawing confused expressions from both of the others. "Or is she a means to an end?"

"What are you plotting here?" Dahlia demanded, but Drizzt ignored her.

"She's an obstacle in my master's way," said Entreri.

"But not the goal?"

"An obstacle to the goal," Entreri replied, and Drizzt grinned, catching on.

"Then help us to kill Sylora," Drizzt reasoned, and Dahlia's gasp did not deter him. "Is that not the greater prize your master seeks?"

Entreri answered with a nod as he considered the reasoning, and the possibilities.

"Killing Dahlia, who vows to kill Sylora, wouldn't please your master, then," said Drizzt.

"You would ally with us?" a skeptical Entreri asked. "I witnessed your work on the Shadovar patrol north of Neverwinter."

"Ally with a Shadovar, a Netherese pig?" Dahlia replied, equally incredulous. "Never that!"

"Artemis Entreri is neither," Drizzt assured her. "Why not, then?" he asked both of them.

"It's often claimed that the enemy of my enemy is my friend," Entreri replied with a shrug.

"Are you still my enemy?" Drizzt asked him.

Entreri laughed a bit as he considered that. "I grew bored with you more than a century ago. To think me your enemy would be to think I care about you one way or the other."

"And for me?" asked Dahlia. "You just admitted you plan to kill me."

"That can wait."

"The enemy of my enemy will be my enemy again?"

Entreri smiled wickedly. "We shall see."

Drizzt turned from him to Dahlia. "It's settled, then?"

"I intend to kill Sylora," Dahlia stated flatly. "And I intend to kill any who try to hinder me from experiencing that pleasure."

"And what of those who would aid you?" Entreri teased.

Dahlia turned and walked away.

"Well met again, Drizzt Do'Urden," Entreri said to the drow, and he motioned down at his dropped blades.

Drizzt glanced at Dahlia, then, and despite himself, shook his head.

"I will not kill her," Entreri promised. "Nor you."

Drizzt eyed him with clear doubt.

"I hate my master, while you merely bore me," Entreri said.

"And Dahlia?"

"She's my counterpart, the champion of my master's enemy, as I am my master's champion. And so we were tasked with our battle, a proxy battle. It really is nothing personal."

"So you would say," Drizzt started to reply—started, but the words caught in his throat as Artemis Entreri came forward suddenly, reaching to his belt as he lunged. That buckle became a knife and that knife beat Drizzt to the drow's throat.

A heartbeat later, Entreri looked into Drizzt's lavender eyes, stepped back, and dropped his knife, which showed no blood. He held up his hands. "Now you can trust me," he said.

It took Drizzt several heartbeats to even sort out what had just occurred, and he silently chastised himself for allowing his guard to slip, for forgetting the continuing danger presented by the skilled Artemis Entreri. He could have been murdered, then and there, because his heart had been looking backward, and no doubt doing so with a stilted view of what had once been.

He looked at Entreri then, standing unarmed and at ease. He looked down at Entreri's buckle knife, an ample weapon with which Entreri might have cut out Drizzt's throat.

Drizzt chuckled and turned away from Entreri once more to follow Dahlia. He chastised himself again for being so foolish, but he applauded himself, or was greatly relieved at least, that he'd been right. The fact that he was still drawing breath proved he'd been right.

This man from his past was not his enemy.

Artemis Entreri.

Artemis Entreri!

The name resonated deeply within the soul of the assassin. His given name, that long ago moniker that had seemingly been lost to the ages, as the person who had once been Artemis Entreri had likewise been lost to the ages.

His thoughts went back to a long-ago day in Calimport, a day Entreri had come to cherish as the moment of his escape. Not from Drizzt Do'Urden, whom he'd thought dead. Not from Jarlaxle and the drow elves, for he was certain they would return for him, and they had. Not an escape from Herzgo Alegni, surely, a tiefling who likely wasn't even born at that time.

Nay, on that long-ago day, Artemis Entreri had escaped from the man who had proven to be his greatest enemy, his most dangerous foe.

On that long-ago day, Entreri had found a moment of mercy, and mercy on a priest no less, in exchange for a promise that the priest would behave according to his professed tenets, which promised benefit to the poor of the desert port city.

On that long-ago day, Artemis Entreri had escaped from himself, his past, his self-loathing.

And he'd come to look at life differently, for just a short time, until the drow mercenaries of Bregan D'aerthe returned.

All of those memories flooded through him in a burst of confusion.

The irony that it had been Drizzt Do'Urden who had revived the name of Artemis Entreri, and who had revived something else, something far more profound, was not lost on the assassin.

He noted that the drow kept his hands on the hilts of his blades as he walked off to catch up to Dahlia, and Entreri had no doubt that, should he retrieve his own blades now and go after Drizzt, he would again face that legendary barrage of spinning scimitars.

But Entreri had no such intention, of course. He'd assured Drizzt of his intent by surrendering the lethal advantage, and even before that, Entreri had known from Drizzt's eyes, from the moment of the drow ranger's recognition of him, that Drizzt had not been saddened by the sight of him.

Artemis Entreri was glad of that expression, and not simply because his own foolish plan had failed, and if Drizzt had thought different of their meeting, or had not recognized him, he would surely have been killed. No, it was more than that, much more. Indeed, Drizzt couldn't begin to know the level of relief that flooded through the tormented man even then.

And as an added benefit, a plan was truly formulating in Entreri's thoughts, a way to be rid of Sylora, then use the moment of joy to facilitate an introduction between Herzgo Alegni and Drizzt Do'Urden, and with the lovely Dahlia thrown in against Alegni as well.

In that moment, Artemis Entreri, a man who had for decades been known as Barrabus the Gray, felt something he'd not experienced in those same decades:

Hope.

CHAPTER 16

ALL SIDES AGAINST THE MIDDLE

H E'S JOINED WITH MY ENEMIES?" HERZGO ALEGNI ASKED WITH obvious doubt, and he half-drew his sword, trying to find some hint of confirmation from the sentient blade. He stood on his namesake bridge in Neverwinter, the sun low in the western sky in front of him.

"Perhaps, perhaps not," Effron replied cryptically, drawing a glare from Alegni, who was in no mood for such games.

"Barrabus has joined forces with the drow and Dahlia," Effron said. "It would appear the Thayan sorceress's champion returns as her mortal enemy."

"Why should I trust you?"

"Why would you send me to follow Barrabus if you weren't going to believe my report?" the warlock shot back.

On Alegni's command, Effron had used his spells to covertly follow the assassin into the forest. A creature of shadow, both because of his heritage and training, even the clever Barrabus failed to notice the surveillance. And from afar, Effron had witnessed the exchange between Barrabus, the elf, and the drow.

"Perhaps Lady Dahlia seeks alliance," Effron offered.

"Dahlia, who murdered my patrol," Alegni reminded him sourly, and Effron quickly backed away. "Barrabus has joined forces with Dahlia after she murdered my patrol! And more than a dozen other Shadovar besides."

"I didn't mean that the fool Barrabus should go unpunished," Effron was quick to reply. "Perhaps after he kills Sylora, you can remind him of his failings."

Herzgo Alegni turned away and walked to the edge of the bridge to regard the last colors of daylight. The simple truth of it was that if Barrabus brought him the head of Sylora Salm, he would hardly punish the man.

A grin widened on Alegni's face as he considered his stealthy champion, and remembered all of those times over the last decades when Barrabus the Gray had exceeded expectations so completely Alegni had to work hard to keep from openly marveling at the man.

If Barrabus returned to him bearing the head of Sylora, and the head of her champion, Dahlia, as he expected would likely happen, then Alegni would surely reward the assassin.

Of course, if Barrabus failed him, whether he was killed or not in the attempt, Herzgo Alegni could use Effron's startling information as an excuse to torment the man even more.

For an instant, Alegni almost hoped Barrabus would fail. Only an instant, though, for defeating Sylora Salm was surely the greatest prize of all, and one that would gain him accolades from his superiors in Shade Enclave, would perhaps silence even the wretched Draygo Quick for a while.

The Netherese lord glanced back at Effron as the light diminished in the west, and that dimness seemed somehow to help complete the crooked and misshapen warlock's form, to make him seem more substantial and less . . . defective.

In that moment, Herzgo Alegni wished he didn't have to loathe this one so greatly, wished that the mere sight of Effron didn't turn his stomach so.

When Herzgo Alegni walked onto the bridge that bore his name, the villagers of Neverwinter typically avoided that route. There were two other bridges, after all, though neither matched the grandeur and width of this one, and even though Alegni and his band had been declared heroes of the city, few were comfortable around the tiefling, and fewer still would dare to interrupt him in any case.

So when a small form, a woman it seemed, bending low against the wind and with her red cloak and hood pulled tight, stepped onto the bridge and headed his way, Alegni eyed her curiously, then with grinning recognition.

She didn't slow.

"Take a different bridge," Effron called out, and lifted his wand at the approaching figure.

Herzgo Alegni grabbed the young warlock by the forearm and forcefully pushed his arm back down. Effron looked over at him in shock, but Alegni shook his head.

The woman neared, and pulled back her cowl, showing her curly red locks.

"Welcome, Arunika," Alegni greeted.

"What news, Herzgo Alegni?" she replied. "Your posture tells me that the word is good."

Alegni laughed at that. Arunika had told him she was an observer, after all, and that knowledge was her true power.

"Have you met Effron?" Alegni asked, deflecting her inquiry. "A warlock strong beyond his years."

Arunika glanced at him with that inviting, disarming smile of hers, and Alegni's face screwed up with surprise when he saw Effron— Effron the insufferable!—return that look with a sincere smile and open expression of his own.

Alegni glanced back at Arunika and scrutinized her in a different light then.

"What news?" Arunika pressed. "You just came in from the forest, I've been told, and came straight to speak with our guardian here." She motioned at Alegni, and flashed him a rather wicked smile and a wink.

Effron seemed truly flustered, and that, too, had Alegni off-balance. When ever before had this cynical and smart young tiefling ever teetered in disarray?

"It's no news as of yet," Alegni answered, and Arunika looked at him doubtfully, and a bit, he understood, as if she'd been wounded by his lack of trust.

Herzgo Alegni thought back to the night before, to their amazing tryst.

"Hopeful signs, though," he said. He glanced over at Effron and waved the warlock away, then turned to face Arunika more directly. When Effron didn't immediately depart, Alegni cast him a sour glance.

"We may have found unexpected allies in our battle with the Thayans," Alegni admitted to Arunika as Effron shambled off the bridge. "Her champion returns from the north."

"Her champion? Would that not bolster—"

"*Former* champion," Alegni corrected. "This warrior, Dahlia, returns with a vendetta against Sylora, it would seem, and brings beside her a drow ranger of great renown."

"A drow ranger? Drizzt Do'Urden?"

"Yes, and now my man Barrabus has joined with them on their path to rid us of Sylora Salm. If they succeed, if they can behead this Thayan beast that has infected Neverwinter Wood, we will claim a great victory."

Arunika stared at him for a few moments, then matched his hopeful grin. "That's quite a trio of power," she said. "And likely, Sylora's champion will know of the Thayan defenses and how to get through them."

"Barrabus almost rid me of the witch by himself," Alegni agreed. "With those two beside him, I've no doubt that Sylora Salm will soon be dead. Barrabus is an annoyance, to be sure, but a useful one, else I would have destroyed him long ago."

"It's good that you didn't, then," said Arunika. She paused for a few heartbeats then smiled once more and turned to leave. As she lifted her hood back in place, she whispered, "Will you join me later that we might celebrate this hopeful news?"

Herzgo Alegni had every intention of doing just that, whether Arunika invited him or not.

Sylora sat in her chamber in the tree-tower, impatiently tap-tapping the crooked wand on the chair's arm. She looked across at Arunika's messenger, the imp hopping back flips in front of the hearth for no apparent reason.

The sorceress had already known that Dahlia and the drow ranger were on their way. She'd communed with devils of her own, and so had learned of Hadencourt's fate. Sylora understood the power of the malebranche and its ever-present allies, and so she understood that Dahlia had found a capable companion indeed to have so defeated that troupe.

But now, with the news from Arunika, Sylora understood that the danger had grown substantially.

The sorceress stood up quickly, and the imp responded by halting its spinning for a bit and staring at her curiously. "Where is she?" Sylora asked, pacing over and throwing another log on the fire.

"In Neverwinter, silly wizardess," the imp replied.

"Not Arunika!" Sylora snapped back, though she realized the imp already knew that and was just being clever.

"Dahlia on her way . . ." the imp started, but Sylora cut the tiny creature short with a glower.

"Not Dahlia," Sylora said evenly. "I know where Dahlia is. You just told me where Dahlia is."

"Then why ask, Lady of Silly?"

Before Sylora could respond—and she intended to respond with a killing bolt of Dread Ring energy—there came a shuffling noise from the stairwell, and both the sorceress and the imp turned to watch Valindra enter the room. Another form lurked behind her on the stairs, in the shadows.

"We should strike the city this night," Valindra said, her voice surprisingly clear, her eyes remaining focused. "They're battered from our first assault and even more so by the damage and carnage caused by the ambassador's umber hulks. They're vulnerable and we shouldn't let them get their footing back on solid ground."

As impressed as she was by Valindra's clarity of thought and expression, Sylora shook her head throughout the speech. "Not yet."

"Delay favors the Netherese."

"It cannot be helped. We have more pressing business." Sylora looked over at the imp.

"Dahlia again?" Valindra asked with clear exasperation.

Sylora had to pause and consider that for a bit before responding.

Valindra's mental instability seemed fast fading. The ambassador had been working on Valindra quite extensively, helping her as the drow psionicist had aided her in the early days of her affliction. Only more effectively, Sylora knew. She was thinking in leaps now, instead of merely reacting to the situation in front of her, and more importantly, she sold her advice with more than mere words but with emotion and even cleverness, like the dramatic effect in her response to Dahlia.

"Don't underestimate her."

"As Hadencourt did?" Valindra asked. She'd been at Sylora's side when they received the news of the malebranche's defeat. "He's a devil, Sylora, and so thought himself so elevated above the mere mortals he could act foolishly. So he did, and so he's paid for his mistake."

"As you do now," Sylora warned.

"Not at all," Valindra replied with confidence. "I've witnessed Dahlia's martial prowess and know it to be considerable. I also know I can defeat her. Magic is stronger than the blade . . . or than that stick she spins with such abandon. I would think Sylora Salm would know that."

"She has an ally, a ranger of great reputation."

"And you have me."

"She has another ally," Sylora went on, again turning to the imp. "The Netherese champion has joined with her. Those three, at least, are coming for us, and we must expect that Barrabus the Gray will bring along Shadovar reinforcements."

"I do not fear them," Valindra announced.

"But nor will I ignore them," said Sylora. "They are coming. They are likely nearing our position even now. And so we'll prepare for them. Keep the Ashmadai close—double the guards at the walls and let the zombies roam the forest near to Ashenglade. You watch them, Valindra. You see through their eyes. We'll know when these would-be assassins come into our fortress, and we will destroy them.

How much weaker will the Netherese be when their champion's head is returned to them?"

"Or when their champion is raised by the power of the Dread Ring and turns to fight against them?" Valindra replied, and that brought a grin to Sylora's face.

Valindra turned back to the stairwell and lifted her hand and beckoned, silently calling. "As you requested," she said when the crinkled ashen zombie crept in through the door.

Sylora had indeed asked Valindra to bring along one of their undead pets, and she suppressed her revulsion at having the diminutive thing in her private room. With every step, the wretched little creature left ashen footprints, and the smell of burned flesh was a perpetual condition for these monsters. A decade had passed since the cataclysm, and still the zombie legions reeked with the foul aroma.

Behind the sorceress, the imp snorted and let out a little shriek.

Sylora ignored the tiny devil, focusing on the zombie and the sensation in her wand because of the proximity of the creature. She'd felt this before, but from afar, and now with Ashenglade's first round of construction completed, the wand, the Dread Ring, had compelled her to further investigate.

She reached out to the zombie and closed her eyes.

Soon she was seeing through the undead creature's eyes.

Sylora could inhabit it at will, could see through it, could hear through it, could control its every movement. She almost unleashed the creature's continual fury, then, for in looking back at herself, in looking past her meditating form, she noted the imp, its face a mask of disgust, its long and pointed tongue hanging out and flicking with distaste. Through the zombie's ears, Sylora heard the curses muttered under impish breath.

Sylora moved back fully into her own consciousness, and slowly turned to face the impudent little imp. "You don't approve of my pet?"

"Wretched disgusts me, it does," the imp whined.

"This is a child of the Dread Ring," Sylora explained.

"Let it fall dead and bury it deep!" said the imp.

"You try my patience," Sylora warned. "Only because of Arunika's favor do I not punish you for such words."

"Arunika! Arunika is not my mistress! I'm indebted to her, but I'm free when done with you!"

A wry smile widened on Sylora's face, telling the imp that perhaps it should not have admitted such a thing. "You insult the zombie, you insult the Dread Ring," she said.

"Wretched disgusts me!"

"And if I allow the zombie to act on your insults?" asked Sylora. She felt the wand thrumming in her hand, the power building with her intent and her understanding now that she didn't have to put up with the impudent little beast.

The imp's long tongue flicked and sent a line of spittle at Sylora's feet. "I go!" it announced.

"You do not!" Sylora demanded sharply. "First you must battle and defeat this child of the Dread Ring you have so callously insulted." She glanced over at Valindra, letting the lich see her grin, but that brought more puzzlement to Valindra's expression than anything else.

Sylora recognized that and wasn't surprised by the lich's reaction, given that Valindra hardly understood what was happening either. But something surely was happening, within the wand and deep in her subconscious, and the sensation she received from the Dread Ring was of power and pleasure, like a building climax.

The imp spat on the floor again and cursed Sylora.

She invited the release.

The ashen zombie beside Valindra exploded into a puff of black smoke and ashes, and before any could spread wide or descend to the floor, the wand drew them in, hungrily eating the zombie's remains.

Sylora's eyes closed in a fit of power and pleasure, and she let the decomposed zombie flow through the wand, bursting back out in a black spray that struck the imp and sent it flying backward into the wall. It howled in pain as wafts of smoke began rising from all around it.

"What have you done?" Valindra asked happily, but Sylora ignored her, couldn't be bothered with her at that moment as she, too, tried to sort out the magic she'd just enacted.

The imp came forward, but slowly, its movements sluggish as if it was in thick mud or tar. It was the ash, Sylora realized, hardening around its joints and skin. The imp tried to spit, attempted to stick out its tongue, but Sylora saw the black goo covering the creature's mouth press forward.

The magic fully encased the creature except for one eye the imp had managed to close before being struck, and that the imp had opened quickly enough to avoid the hardening black coating. That eye revealed the creature's hatred for Sylora, a red gaze of sizzling and seething flame.

The diminutive beast kept approaching, and Sylora was too mesmerized to even realize she should retreat, or strike again.

But it didn't matter. The imp turned aside and dived into the fireplace. It rolled around on the logs and slid its limbs under the hot coals, burning the black goo from its body. The fire didn't bother a creature of the lower planes, after all. In moments, it was free, and it shot one last hateful look at Sylora, full of indignity and dire threats, then rushed up the chimney and out of Ashenglade entirely.

"That show was worth the cost of a zombie," Valindra said coyly.

Sylora turned to her and held forth the crooked, blackened wand Szass Tam had given her. "There's more," she said with both conviction and confusion, for she knew there were indeed more and varied catastrophes she could conjure with the magical energy of the ashen zombies, though she wasn't quite sure what those disasters might be.

Sylora's eyes sparkled at the possibilities.

"You can channel the power of the Dread Ring," Valindra reasoned, and Sylora nodded.

"It's intoxicating," the sorceress admitted.

"More powerful than your own practiced magic?"

Sylora considered that for a few moments, then nodded once more. "I had thought my time here near its end," she admitted. "One last strike at the Netherese and the settlers of Neverwinter, one added massacre to complete the Dread Ring, and I would move along to another place, another mission."

"But now?"

Sylora was too lost in the sensations of the wand to catch the undertone of concern in Valindra's voice, or to even consider that she hadn't made her impending departure a secret, or that her departure would place Valindra Shadowmantle as her heir apparent in Neverwinter Wood.

Valindra's question remained unanswered as Sylora fell deeper into the connection to the Dread Ring, trying to sort out the powers it might now afford her. She wasn't quite sure.

But she intended to find out.

CHAPTER 17

INTO THE HIVE

"I T'S NEW TO ME," DAHLIA WHISPERED. SHE LAY ON A GRASSY KNOLL, Drizzt to her right and the man she'd known as Barrabus the Gray farther to her right, beyond the drow.

"It's a very recent addition," Entreri replied, though Dahlia had aimed her remark at Drizzt. She hadn't spoken a word to Entreri since the fight of the previous day. "I've been scouting Sylora Salm for some time—all through your journey to Gauntlgrym. I've been near to her, looking over her shoulder, and I've seen nothing like this fortress before. Not a hint that any such thing existed."

"It reminds me of my homeland, strangely," Drizzt added.

He couldn't help but make that comparison. The centerpiece of the grand fortress was a treelike tower, obsidian colored, set on the side of a rocky hill. If some wizard graced that tower with purple faerie fire, it could well be set in Menzoberranzan to hide among the stalagmite mounds that served as homes for the various drow families.

The whole of the fortress also showed that same otherworldliness as Menzoberranzan. The obsidian-black walls were not of mortared bricks, but seemed as if they'd simply lifted up from the ground, pressed forth by magic, in a single piece. Gate towers—perhaps they were gate towers—showed at various points, looking much like smaller versions of the treelike tower on the rocky hillside that dominated the place. Other structures showed, usually abutting the walls, and those, too, were obviously created and not constructed: large blackened boulders, roughly shaped to resemble squat stone buildings, like barracks and other necessary structures. One on the far side of the fortress was open faced, a forge burning within. Another appeared as no more than a stone lean-to, and under its sheltering wall lay a rack of bows, piled quivers of arrows, and a host of those Ashmadai staff-spear scepters.

"The Dread Ring did this," Dahlia said, nodding as she figured it out. "Sylora, or perhaps Valindra, has found a way to tap its power." She looked over at the other two. "That's no small thing."

Her companions looked at her with curiosity.

"I lived in Thay for most of my adult life," Dahlia explained. "I've witnessed a fully thriving Dread Ring—several, in fact. It was no secret among we who served Szass Tam that the archlich derived his power from that primary source, and his power was beyond anything you have witnessed, I assure you."

"She's trying to scare us," Entreri deadpanned to Drizzt. "Are you so certain she's truly allied with us against Sylora Salm?"

Drizzt's amused snort disarmed Dahlia's angry retort before she could begin to utter it. In response, the elf woman narrowed her eyes even more and shifted her gaze from Entreri to Drizzt, allowing him to be the source of her ire if that was what he so desired.

"If you're scared, then please do leave us," she said.

"I've been many things in my long life," Entreri replied. "I don't believe that 'scared' has ever been one of them."

"Until now," Dahlia said.

"Including now."

"Then you're a fool," said Dahlia.

"If you're scared, then please leave us," Entreri shot back. "I'm going over that wall to find Sylora Salm, and finish her at last."

He shifted up into a crouch and moved along the ridgeline to view the fortress from other vantage points. Dahlia started to follow, but Drizzt held her back and let Entreri get some distance away.

"He's not our enemy in this," the drow reassured her.

"How do you know? He's a long-lost friend, then?"

Drizzt almost fell over at the sheer irony of that statement, given his turbulent past with Artemis Entreri, a man he'd battled, had hunted, and who had hunted him, both with the intent of killing the other.

But there were other times, Drizzt recalled whenever he came to question the assassin's motives. Trapped beneath Mithral Hall before King Bruenor had reclaimed and civilized the place, Drizzt and Entreri had fought side-by-side for their common good. Trapped in Menzoberranzan, slaves to the drow, Drizzt, Entreri, and Catti-brie had likewise fought together for their common good.

Artemis Entreri was a violent man, hardly a friend to Drizzt Do'Urden, but he also was, above all else, a pragmatic survivor. It was in Entreri's interest to see Sylora Salm fall. Drizzt believed that, so he didn't doubt Entreri's loyalty to him and Dahlia in this matter. And hadn't Entreri proven that when he'd surprised Drizzt in the first moments of their meeting, when he'd lunged forward, bringing his knife to a hair's breadth from Drizzt's throat? If Artemis Entreri had meant to kill Drizzt, Drizzt would have died then and there.

But still, despite that moment and despite his instincts even before the further evidence of alliance, the thought had occurred to Drizzt more than once in the last day that he was fooling himself, that his judgment was clouded because Entreri represented the last shred of that distant past of which Drizzt didn't want to let go. The Companions of the Hall were gone, Thibbledorf Pwent was gone, Jarlaxle was gone, and only Drizzt remained—only Drizzt and Artemis Entreri.

That notion came to him again in that moment, on the knoll overlooking the impressive fortress of Sylora Salm, and again, as with every time previous, Drizzt allowed the reasoning to play through its logic in his thoughts. But even before he came to the same conclusion as the previous times, Drizzt knew in his gut that it was so. He glanced over at the assassin, lying low again and studying the fortress and the many Ashmadai zealots moving around inside of it.

Drizzt knew he would be glad to have Artemis Entreri fighting beside him when he, too, went over that wall.

"When the sun sets," Drizzt promised Dahlia, and a quick glance to the west told them that was nearly upon them. "We would do well to determine where Sylora will be found before all daylight has flown. The tower, I would guess."

"The tower," Dahlia answered without hesitation. "Sylora is vain above pragmatic, and confident above cautious. She wouldn't allow anyone to gain a seat above her, whatever the risk of identifying herself."

"Unless she was trying to ensure that she could not easily be found," Drizzt replied. "She's surrounded by enemies. Wouldn't she be wise to—"

"If Sylora was the slightest bit afraid of the Netherese, or any others, she wouldn't have built this . . . place," Dahlia interrupted, shaking her head.

"Vanity above prudence?" the drow asked.

Dahlia nodded. "She's in that tower."

They lay in wait while the shadows lengthened around them, the light quickly fading.

"The darkness won't protect us from those guards," Entreri said some time later, the night growing thick. The assassin slid over to join the other two and pointed down at the wall. Drizzt and Dahlia could just make out the forms, a group of sentries. In the dim light, Drizzt at first thought them goblins, or kobolds, perhaps. But as he watched them more closely, he realized they didn't move in the least. They just stood there, perfectly still, not swaying, not moving their arms, nothing.

"The ashen zombies," Drizzt said.

"Darkness won't slow them," said Entreri.

"They sense life, and need no daylight to see us," Dahlia agreed.

"Where do we want to breach the wall to find the best route to the tower?" Drizzt asked of Entreri, who had been sliding all around, after all, studying the black-walled fortress from many different angles.

"Very near to where that bunch is gathered," Entreri replied.

Drizzt glanced down the other side of the ridge, then brought forth his onyx figurine and summoned Guenhwyvar to his side. He whispered to the panther, and Guenhwyvar sprang away. Drizzt drew his blades and motioned for Dahlia and Entreri to follow him back behind the ridge.

There, the drow climbed a skeletal tree, high enough to see the wall, and the panther, as Guenhwyvar approached the cluster of zombies. The cat growled and struck, tearing the head from one, then darted back up the hill with the others in pursuit. There followed a bit of commotion atop the wall, as living guards tried to see what was happening.

As Drizzt had instructed, Guenhwyvar circled back around to ensure that she would be clearly seen by the guards. She growled at them before running up the knoll and over the ridge, past Drizzt as he dropped down from the tree, past Entreri and Dahlia.

The scrambling zombies came in pursuit, and right into three waiting warriors, four blades, and a pair of spinning flails.

Only heartbeats later, the trio lay at the ridge-top again, looking down at the wall, which had gone quiet once more, the Ashmadai resuming their patrol routes. Again Drizzt whispered his instructions to the panther.

"It's a dozen feet, perhaps," Entreri said. "No more."

Drizzt produced a fine elven cord from his pack and tossed one end to Entreri. "I'll brace," he explained.

Sylora Salm opened her eyes and was almost surprised to find herself back in her chamber in the tower. She'd been watching the fight in the forest through the eyes of one of her zombie minions—a creature that had met a sudden and shocking end at the decapitating swing of a scimitar. She started to shake her head, but nodded instead, conceding a bit of respect for what she'd witnessed.

"They're coming," she explained to Jestry and Valindra, who were in the room waiting for her to return. "They're in the forest nearby, already fighting our minions."

"All three?" Jestry asked.

"It's rather amazing," Sylora admitted, "and somewhat amusing." Her expression revealed her honest surprise. "Truly, I believe Dahlia the least of these three warriors, and by no small margin."

Valindra seemed as if she didn't know what to make of that, but Jestry nodded, though he seemed a bit removed from appreciating the weight of that statement.

Yes, they wouldn't truly understand, Sylora reminded herself. Jestry had little personal knowledge of Dahlia's considerable martial prowess, and while Valindra had witnessed Dahlia fighting in Gauntlgrym, that was in the midst of a larger, frenetic battle, and at a time when the lich was hardly in her right mind.

"True, they're formidable," Jestry replied at length. "We know the reputation of Barrabus the Gray, of course, though few thought him the equal of Dahlia from what I've heard."

"I would disagree," said Sylora. "She's quite his equal. But, yes, they are quite formidable. More than I expected."

"Then why would you let them get so close?" Jestry asked.

Sylora shot him a glare.

"It's a valid question," Valindra put in, and Sylora turned her glower her way.

"We're surrounded by warriors," Sylora said, "but understand that I hope Dahlia and her two companions get much closer." She held up the wand as she spoke. "You have brought a group of zombies close by, for my . . . use?" she asked Jestry.

"More than a dozen," he replied. "Just to the side of the hill, as you instructed."

"Yes, I can feel them," said Sylora, and she brought the wand up to tap it against the side of her head. She whispered something the others couldn't hear, and waved the wand.

"An even dozen remaining now," she explained as a burst of ash came through the wand and filled the air around Sylora.

Rather than fall to the ground, the individual ash particles dissipated and became a grayish, translucent cloud that encircled Sylora, forming a semicircular, bubblelike shield in front of her.

"Valindra, call some more zombies nearer to the tower, so that I can access their life forces as needed," she commanded, and Jestry looked at her as though wounded that she'd not assigned him the task.

"You will wait in the cave near the entrance to the tower," Sylora said to him. "You are not to leave. You will meet Dahlia if she gets close."

"I'll kill all three!" Jestry declared.

"You were constructed to defeat Dahlia," Sylora replied sharply. "Do not forget that. Your ring, the wrappings, the weapon I've given you . . ."

"You just claimed her to be the least of the three," Jestry argued.

"When you're done with Dahlia, then you may destroy the others," Sylora agreed. "But only when Dahlia is defeated and dead."

Jestry straightened and didn't reply.

"Do you understand?" Sylora prompted, and she tapped the wand against her face again to convey a clear threat.

The mummy-wrapped zealot nodded. "Dahlia will die."

Sylora responded with a wide grin. "Oh, they all will," she replied.

Sylora waved them away and moved back to the small, descending stairway to the balcony, heading down so that she could look out over Ashenglade. She reached into the wand again, seeing the world through the eyes of various zombies, looking for a vantage point from which she might again spy her enemies.

She didn't find anything then, but no matter.

They were close, and they were coming.

The trio of would-be assassins spent another few moments watching the patrols along the wall top, looking for the optimal moment of approach. Just a few moments, though, for none of these three had ever been known as overly cautious.

Drizzt led the way down the slope and across the open ground. He ran right to the wall, spinning around and throwing his back against the lava stone, crouching and cupping his hands down low as he did.

Just a few running strides behind, Entreri sprinted right up to the drow, planted his foot in his cradled hands, and leaped as Drizzt threw him, easily grabbing the wall top and scrambling up.

Drizzt went right back into position, expecting Dahlia next, but she hardly needed him, charging the wall with her long staff held out in front of her. Even as Drizzt turned and began to climb, with Entreri bracing the rope from above, Dahlia vaulted beside him and rose above, landing on the wall top with a graceful inversion and roll, catching the crenellation with her hand and setting her feet firmly on the parapet. She spun around and broke down her weapon into the more manageable flails before Drizzt gained the wall only a couple heartbeats later.

Artemis Entreri pointed to a building to his left, then to his right, then dropped, caught the wall with his hand, and swung down, hanging for just a moment before silently dropping to the ground. Similarly, Drizzt dropped to his right, and headed for the back wall of the structure Entreri had indicated, as Dahlia went off to the left.

Entreri split the middle, moving along the wall of the left-hand building, which looked quite like a blackened and enlarged boulder. Drizzt moved to the corner and watched him, and heard, as Entreri no doubt heard, some talking from in front of Dahlia's position.

Drizzt motioned to Dahlia to hold her place, and glanced back at Entreri.

The assassin put a hand up, open, signaling for Drizzt to stay put, then folded his fingers one at a time into a fist, and Drizzt understood he was calling for a five-count pause.

Then he disappeared around the corner.

By the time Drizzt had silently counted to five and moved to the spot where Entreri had been, the assassin came back around the corner, dragging the body of an Ashmadai woman.

Drizzt slipped around the front corner and retrieved the assassin's other victim, dragging him, too, out of sight.

Dahlia came by him as he did, moving to the next structure in line.

Silently, signaling with their hands, the deadly trio hop-scotched, structure to structure, to the inner wall. They almost made it without further resistance, but as Drizzt sprinted out in front across the small clearing between the last structure and the wall, he noted movement far down to his right. For a moment, he sucked in his breath, thinking their stealthy approach at an end. But then he saw that the pair were not Ashmadai, and weren't raising an alarm. The withered, charred zombies were hardly interested in proper tactics.

Instead of throwing his back to the wall, the drow dug in, pulling Taulmaril from his back and setting an arrow in one fluid motion. He thought better of taking the shot, though, figuring the flash would surely alert any and all Ashmadai in the bailey, perhaps even those within the second wall. When he considered his companions, who even then came out to join him, weapons drawn, he realized he didn't need the bow.

He put it back and drew out his blades instead. "Zombies," he whispered to his companions. "Only zombies."

Both Dahlia and Drizzt understood the meaning behind that remark. Like Entreri, they used misdirection, deception, and deceptive coordination to throw their opponents off balance.

Such tactics were pointless on zombies.

But these three didn't need them.

The horde of undead came on, outnumbering the companions five to one at least, a host of withered, charred arms reaching to grab their intended prey.

Those arms went flying to the ground as Drizzt and Entreri waded in, blades flashing. Dahlia followed them into the mob, her long staff stabbing between them, or rolling over and outside one or the other to drive back a zombie that had moved too close. Her weapon wasn't as effective on these particular creatures as those of her companions, and so she found her place in setting the enemies up for the other two: batting aside a blocking arm so that Entreri's sword could stab home or lifting up one zombie shoulder high, the creature grabbing the staff as she went, so a sidelong slash from Drizzt's scimitar could disembowel the undead beast.

They tried to be as quiet as possible, and indeed they were, other than the sound of metal cracking on bone, or the *splat* as Dahlia's staff crunched down on a rotting face.

Not quiet enough, however. Soon, they heard a commotion from the other side of the wall, a call to arms.

"They'll be waiting for us," Entreri said, cutting down another undead monster.

"Perhaps," said Drizzt, and he fell back from the fighting, motioning for Dahlia to take his place.

The drow pulled out his bow again and rushed back to the spot between the last two structures they had crossed between. He dropped down to one knee and leaned forward, turning Taulmaril sidelong and bringing it as low as possible. He took aim at the first wall, many strides away, angling his shot so the lightning arrow flew just above it as it exited the bailey.

He rushed back, shouldering his bow. Seeing Entreri finishing off the last of the zombies, he threw his back against the wall and produced his fine rope once more.

He held Entreri and Dahlia back for just a few heartbeats, however, until a greater commotion began to stir far down to the other side of the compound.

"The cat," Entreri said, for indeed, Drizzt's shot had been the predetermined signal for Guenhwyvar to join in the fray, and far to the side so that she would serve as a powerful distraction.

The panther flew over the wall with a great leap, clearing it cleanly. The sentry she'd targeted only noted her at the last moment, for barely a heartbeat had passed between the time Guenhwyvar had first charged from the brush and sprang.

That sentry almost got his arm up to block, though of course such a defense would have afforded him no protection against the power of the panther anyway. The cat was past him too quickly for that raising arm to even touch, and the Ashmadai flew from the wall, his head and throat ripped ear to opposite collarbone, as Guenhwyvar continued past. He hit the ground in a heap, not even crying out, other than a strange gasping groan as the air was blasted from his dying body.

Guenhwyvar twisted around in her descent, fast approaching a stone building. With great agility, she managed to swing sidelong, planting her claws and scrabbling wildly so that she barely brushed that structure as she ran along.

Shouts rose up all around her. Answering those, a group of Ashmadai guards rushed out of an alleyway, leaping into the path of the charging panther.

Guenhwyvar roared, the low rumbling of the cry echoing all around the fortress and the forest beyond, and guards fell all over each other trying to get out of the way. Guenhwyvar blew through them, biting one, clawing a second, and knocking two others aside. Several running strides later, the panther still had one zealot clamped in her jaws, and only then felt the strikes as the frantic woman pounded her scepter down against the great cat's muscled shoulder.

Guenhwyvar let her go, then, and she fell away, rolling and grabbing at her mauled thigh.

The panther cut down the next alleyway right in front of a group of zombies. With a twitch of her powerful muscles, she leaped over them and continued on, calls of warning and sounds of pursuit mounting all around her.

From the balcony of her tower, Sylora knew the location of the trio. Even then she looked through the eyes of another zombie, one down the wall from the three. She controlled this one and wouldn't let it advance to be chopped apart.

She saw the drow with his back to the wall, holding Dahlia and the Netherese champion back—no doubt waiting for the mounting distraction they had summoned on the other side of Ashenglade. There, too, Sylora had noticed the large black panther, but paid the cat little heed.

The panther was a diversion, nothing more. The real threat lay here, with these three.

The drow cupped his hands, signaling the other two to move.

The sorceress thought to consume her zombie and create a new trick, a ring of woe, on the ground at the drow's feet, to sting him and the others, to show them that they were puny creatures indeed against the might of Sylora and her Dread Ring.

She resisted the urge.

"Not yet," she whispered aloud, though she was the only one up there on the balcony. "Let them come closer, where they cannot turn back."

She watched them go over the wall, Dahlia with her staff, the Netherese champion with help from the drow.

Then she released the zombie and sent her thoughts careening around the inner wall, seeking a new host from which to view the continuing battle more clearly.

Dahlia flew over the wall, this time beating Entreri. Both were on the ground in the inner bailey by the time Drizzt scrambled over. This area was more open, with only a couple of small structures between the companions and the treelike tower that stood beside a cave opening on the side of a rocky hill, the place they suspected to be Sylora's abode.

"Be quick!" Dahlia warned. "Sylora may strike at us from afar!"

Her words seemed prescient indeed, for at that very moment, they all noted a form in the branchlike balcony of that treelike tower, one Dahlia surely recognized, even from afar.

She started to sprint for Drizzt and Entreri, but pulled up short, taken aback and genuinely surprised as the pair ran off, shoulder-to-shoulder, across the open ground and straight for the tower. Dahlia felt like an outsider suddenly, as if her two companions shared some bond she couldn't understand.

And indeed they did, for not only had the unlikely pair battled against each other so many times in the long distant past, they had battled side-by-side, as well. A century might have passed, but it hardly seemed to matter in that desperate moment. For time had not blurred the reflection each of these warriors saw in the other. They, their skills, their challenges, and mostly their fears, remained inexorably linked, Drizzt to Entreri and Entreri to Drizzt.

They understood each other, they knew each other, and most of all, they knew each other's fighting maneuvers.

Like one four-armed, four-legged beast, Drizzt and Entreri charged out into the open, and they were set upon immediately by a host of Ashmadai zealots.

Just before they met the lead of that counter-charge, Drizzt stopped fast and Entreri rushed past him, right-to-left.

So, too, did the nearest Ashmadai ahead and to Drizzt's right, one who had been coming in straight at Entreri, turn to follow the assassin's cut, and so when Drizzt rolled around Entreri's back, the enemy wasn't ready for him.

Drizzt hooked his right scimitar inside the man's left arm, pulled it free of the scepter, then stabbed with his left and brought the right one back with a sudden backhanded slash.

The drow kicked the wounded zealot back into those coming in behind, and reversed his rush, ducking low.

Entreri back flipped right over him and the two zealots he'd intercepted both came on, but both looked up at him as he somersaulted—so neither were prepared for the drow, coming out of his crouch with upraised blades.

Despite her urgency, Dahlia almost stopped short again at the sight, and when Entreri landed in perfect balance and came around just in time to cut a backhanded parry with his sword, step forward, and dispatch the next zealot with his dagger, the elf woman heard herself gasp.

Dahlia prided herself on her fighting skills, and indeed they were magnificent. She'd respected the skills of both of these warriors individually, of course—that was more than a small part of why she'd chosen Drizzt Do'Urden as the next diamond stud to grace her ear—but now, amazingly, the two together seemed even greater than the sum of their considerable parts.

Dahlia kept close enough to the pair to enjoy the reprieve offered by their destructive wake as they waded across the field. When one zealot ran out wide to flank Entreri, Dahlia was there, meeting him with the blur of her flails. She slapped at him, left and right, above and below, and had him dodging and twisting every which way to try to keep up with her movements. He didn't even realize how off-balance he'd become until Dahlia sent one of her weapons spinning up under his extended arm, caught its flying pole as it came around with her other hand, and sent her victim flipping head over heels to land hard on his back.

He made the mistake of trying to get right back up instead of curling defensively on the grass. The woman, who couldn't have remained behind to finish him off had he so curled, took that one opening to smack him across the skull and lay him low.

Dahlia turned back to see Sylora up on the balcony lifting her wand.

Drizzt saw the sorceress as well. "Dahlia, to me!" he yelled, then called to Entreri for cover.

The assassin moved in front of him in a blur, sword and dagger spinning wildly, driving back the nearest zealots with pure fury.

Trusting that Entreri could hold the line as Dahlia rushed forward to replace him, Drizzt fell back fast into a backward roll.

Drizzt managed a wry grin as Dahlia reacted perfectly, leaping over him as he extricated himself.

He was still grinning as came around, with his bow in his hands and with an arrow already set on the bowstring.

The sorceress above couldn't have anticipated such a movement, and with the stunning grace and realignment of the drow, she seemed to interrupt her spellcasting for just a heartbeat.

That momentary delay gave Drizzt all the time he needed to beat her to the strike. In the blink of an eye, he launched an arrow at her face.

But Sylora smiled and barely flinched. The shot soared true, but the lightning arrow fell short of the mark, slamming into some shield the sorceress had around her. Sparks flew, arcing out to the sides and up and down, but none going forward into Sylora.

Despite the failure, Drizzt wouldn't let up, and so he sent bolt after bolt at the balcony, the sheer fury of the assault driving the powerful sorceress back.

The line of devastation held true for several shots, but then Drizzt was forced to alter his tactics, bringing the bow down lower with every other shot to blast aside an advancing Ashmadai.

Still, Drizzt grinned all the wider as he did. Dahlia and Entreri had begun a dance of their own. They went back to back, blades and poles working brilliantly to open paths. They turned shoulder to shoulder in perfect unison to overwhelm one zealot who found herself out alone as her comrades moved to try to flank the devastating pair.

Drizzt rushed to catch up, calling for them to keep him clear. His focus was back above again, and had to be, his missiles crashing into the balcony, ricocheting around the overhang to keep the mighty sorceress at bay.

More zealots came in at them, but Dahlia and Entreri proved up to the task of driving them off. Their coordination improved with each new turn, and as they came too far under the overhang for Sylora to pose much of a threat, Drizzt, too, could join in.

He shouldered his bow and drew his blades, thinking to do just that, trying to sort out how he might best complement the fighting pair, when the puzzle solved itself.

Dahlia, too consumed by her hatred of Sylora, apparently, seemed less than interested in the zealots. Entreri executed a crossover strike, moving in front of her and stabbing an Ashmadai hard with his sword. As that one crumbled, the appropriate action for Dahlia would have been to fall back to her right, around the assassin, to protect his right flank.

But as the zealot in front of her fell away, the others posturing and angling for a better lane of attack, Dahlia saw the path to the cave clear in front of her and charged from the throng.

Entreri let out a yelp, for he was left obviously vulnerable. Only Drizzt's quick action saved him. The drow, legs speeded by his magical anklets, rushed up beside Entreri just in time to parry a stabbing scepter, and even then he had to lunge so far forward that had the

Ashmadai been a more proficient warrior, he could have retracted and changed his angle of attack to hit the drow instead of the assassin.

But that zealot wasn't so good, and Drizzt was able to get his feet balanced back under him in short order. Then it was the zealot who was still off-balance from the hard parry. He did manage to realign his scepter in some semblance of defense, but he needed much more than "some semblance" against the likes of Drizzt Do'Urden.

The drow's blades smacked at the scepter left and right, went over and under and back around in such a dizzying blur that the zealot couldn't seem to distinguish one from the other.

In a few heartbeats, the overmatched Ashmadai swung his scepter haphazardly, awkwardly, so busy trying to keep up with the whirling scimitars he seemed to forget the purpose of the dance. Eyes down at the blades, trying to sort out the movements, the poor fool didn't even see the killing blow, and his eyes went wide with shock indeed when Icingdeath came in hard against the side of his neck.

Other zealots replaced him, but they found themselves against Entreri instead of Drizzt as the two quickly rotated around.

In that turn, Drizzt caught sight of Dahlia at the cave opening, and he sucked in his breath to see her locked in battle with a strange-looking Ashmadai, wrapped like a mummy in some grayish hide and holding a scepter that showed as much black as the typical red. His worry only multiplied.

Entreri caught sight of her as well.

"Not that one, Dahlia," the assassin whispered.

CHAPTER

18

THE SUM OF THEIR PARTS

Dahlia didn't recognize Jestry. She did guess from his initial attack and defense routines that this opponent was more skilled than the vast majority of Ashmadai, though she almost immediately realized he was no match for her. She worked her flails furiously, slapping them hard against the scepter every time the strangely-armored Ashmadai tried to come at her, or simply to keep him on the defensive. Impatiently, she found an opening and took it, expecting her strike to finish him. Hard against the side of his head went her right-hand flail, a solid blow that should have snapped the zealot's head to the side.

Should have.

And in anticipation of exactly that consequence, Dahlia put her left hand into a high, backhanded roll up and over her head so her other flail would score a second strike following the first.

That first strike didn't jolt the Ashmadai as she had expected. Indeed, the man's head barely moved, and his attention wavered not at all. But his hands moved, taking advantage of Dahlia's overconfident follow-up maneuver by stabbing his scepter straight ahead.

The agile elf managed to twist to her right behind that backhand to avoid the brunt of the blow, taking just a grazing touch and barely drawing a scratch. In exchange for that, Dahlia managed a third strike, again against the side of the zealot's head, and again, to no avail. Even caught by surprise, she thought she'd won the round.

She went right back to her furious spins and strikes, trying to get back to level footing with the zealot and figure out a better method of striking him. She couldn't believe the strange hide wrapping had so utterly defeated three solid hits by Kozah's Needle.

Then she found a second problem, a far worse one. The muscles where she'd been grazed contracted suddenly, painfully, causing her to lurch back and to her left. She staggered and stumbled, right back to her original position, where she managed to stand straight once more, wincing against the pain.

Her left hand led, the flail spinning up and over, down against the scepter, while she rolled her right-hand weapon over top to bottom, catching the pole in her armpit. And there she held it, tightening her muscles expertly while pulling mightily against the hold.

She bided her time, left hand working furiously, and the left side of her ribs aching profoundly. On one such spasm, Dahlia lurched.

The zealot leaped forward, stabbing hard.

But Dahlia's lurch had been voluntary, and enticing. She side-stepped and the zealot missed badly, opening his defenses in the process.

Out snapped the right-hand flail, a sudden and brutal, spearlike thrust that drove into the zealot's chin with tremendous force. The man's head snapped to the side, and he staggered away under the sheer weight of the blow.

But he didn't fall, and if the strike had seriously injured him, he didn't show it. With a feral growl, he came right back after the woman, fighting wildly, seeming more angry than hurt.

And now Dahlia was angry, too, for she heard Sylora up above, calling out—to Valindra, it seemed—and the sound of that voice surely drove Dahlia on, her frustration mounting against this zealot who was preventing her from reaching her prize!

She took a different tack then, repeatedly cracking her flails together as she worked them furiously around and against the scepter. She felt the tingle of power with each strike as Kozah's Needle began to build its charge. In a matter of heartbeats, she'd cracked the metal poles together more than a dozen times, and her hands began to feel the prickles of mounting power. But she held on and continued to grow that explosive energy, determined to reduce this fool to a smoking husk. Again and again the flails clanged together.

A second zealot dashed in at her from the side, but Dahlia noted the movement and merely flipped her wrist over, her right-hand weapon cracking against the thrusting scepter, driving it back behind her. And she turned as it did, her left hand coming around to crack the zealot in the head. Unlike the mummified opponent in front of her, this one wasn't so well-armored, and the heavy blow opened his skull and sent him flying away.

Knowing the strange one to be coming fast in pursuit, Dahlia finished her spin, her hands working furiously as she did. She came to face him once more, and held not a pair of flails, but a single eight-foot staff.

"Drizzt!" she called, fending off the Ashmadai's attacks. "Drow! Lend me an arrow!"

"Entreri!" Drizzt called to his nearest companion.

But even as he spoke the name, the assassin yelled back, "Go! Go!"

Entreri rushed in front of him, sword and dagger working in a blur to drive back the attackers, giving Drizzt the room to disengage just long enough to draw Taulmaril once more and set an arrow. He leveled and let fly, the lightning missile speeding just past Dahlia's shoulder, aiming for her opponent's face.

It never got there, intercepted by the power of Kozah's Needle, drawn into the staff, which was already tingling with energy.

Dahlia wasted no time, spinning the staff up above her head and around, and promptly thrusting it into the chest of the mummified zealot. That physical blow did little damage, of course, but Dahlia cried out in victory, the win all but assured, as she let loose the tremendous lightning energy pent up in the weapon.

Drizzt nodded grimly as crackling arcs rushed along the length of the staff, diving into the zealot, cascading along his form with sharp crackles. All around him the lightning danced, gradually coalescing down his right arm and at his right hand—more specifically, at a ring he wore on his right hand. The lightning sparked and snapped and rolled around the circle.

And turned around.

Scimitars back in his hands, Drizzt's eyes widened with surprise and shock as Dahlia went flying backward, arms and legs flailing, staff flying from her smoking grasp.

"Go! Go!" the drow yelled at Entreri.

Drizzt stepped in front of the assassin, his scimitars intercepting the scepters of the two Ashmadai pressing in, opening just enough of an avenue for Entreri to run free to the cave.

He heard Sylora above him, but pressed from every side now, Drizzt could only grimace against the implications of her chant. His hands worked in a blur, over and around, as he spun to drive back the two he'd been fighting. Drizzt dropped low and kicked out to painfully straighten the leg of one of Entreri's foes as the woman tried to come at him from behind.

Up Drizzt sprang, his blades spinning horizontal circles up high and out wide, working down to block, working back up high to drive one or another of the four back yet again. He found his rhythm and when one of the frustrated zealots threw his scepter at Drizzt, the drow's blade was in line, not to block, but to deflect the weapon. It flew into the face of the zealot behind him.

That one fell away and the one who threw the spear followed it by leaping wildly at Drizzt, trying to tackle him to the ground. That zealot did indeed hit the ground, face first, clutching at the five stab wounds the drow had expertly inflicted before nimbly ducking aside—and doing so with such control that he used the falling Ashmadai to block the view of the zealot opposite. He came over that descending form so quickly and so furiously that the surprised zealot never got her weapon up to block the scimitar thrusting true for her throat.

She did manage to scream, at least, but that was abruptly cut short.

As more Ashmadai rushed to crowd in around him, Drizzt found a moment to glance at Dahlia. She was on her feet again, her braid dancing like a living serpent atop her head. She'd retrieved her staff, but was obviously shaken and confused. The strange Ashmadai bore down on her with great advantage.

And Entreri had not gone to her!

Drizzt spied the assassin scrambling off to the side, along the rocks at the base of the tower, apparently seeking a way in. The dark elf called out to him, but didn't finish the thought before the ground around him roiled suddenly, turning black and with a strange smoky ash wafting from it. The Ashmadai nearest Drizzt cried out first from the burning pain.

And Drizzt felt it too, acutely, such a sting as if his pants had been lit on fire. Only his bracers saved him then, his feet working fast enough to extract him from the devilish black ring of ashen energy.

Hardly thinking of the movement, the drow had simply leaped out of the ring of woe as efficiently as possible, and that moved him farther from Dahlia, back out from the cave entrance and the rocky hill. He got a better view of Sylora Salm at least, standing above him, twenty feet above on the balcony.

She held a strange wand, a broken branch, it seemed, and she smiled wickedly. In that moment, Drizzt felt as if all of this had surely been for naught, as if he and his companions had been fools indeed to think they could go against the magnificence that was Sylora Salm.

Back at the smoking ashen ring, a pair of zealots burst from the growing cloud of withering blackness, reaching for Drizzt.

Their faces were no more than skinless skulls, their reaching hands skeletal, and both crumpled dead to the ground before they ever got near.

But Sylora kept smiling.

Dahlia's skills and warrior instincts superseded her surprise and got her back to her feet and back in a fighting pose before the mummified champion could truly exploit the explosive turnaround.

But it was worse than mere surprise. The blow had hurt her, and her muscles trembled so violently she could hardly hold onto her long staff. Dahlia wanted to break her weapon back into flails, or perhaps into a tri-staff, that she might pry the zealot's weapon away, but she didn't dare, for fear of dropping Kozah's Needle altogether.

The wound inflicted by the zealot's scepter had not abated, either, her gut muscles tightening painfully. She didn't know how long she could fend off this ferocious opponent. She was beginning to understand that she was beaten.

That understanding only got worse when, in one parry and dodge, she looked past her opponent to the back of the cave and saw a grinning Valindra Shadowmantle looking back at her. The lich held her larger, redder scepter, and more than once pointed it Dahlia's way. But she didn't enact any of its powers, or her own. She simply seemed to be enjoying the show.

Valindra didn't intervene because she knew she didn't have to, Dahlia thought, for even though her sensations were returning, her grasp growing steadier on the long staff, she could hardly hope to defeat this strange Ashmadai.

In a single fluid movement, Drizzt sheathed his blades, took up his bow, and sent a stream of arrows at Sylora Salm.

They struck that strange shield in front of her and burst into myriad multi-colored sparks, one after another. The drow could only hope he was doing some damage to that magical defense, at least, wearing it thinner with each explosive strike.

He caught sight of Sylora moving her hand, her wand, behind that barrage, and he fell back as the two Ashmadai who'd fallen dead at his feet leaped up suddenly, animated by the sorceress.

Drizzt turned his bow at them, but before he could fire off an arrow, the two leaned toward the balcony and seemed to elongate, then to fly off as they became insubstantial black smoke.

Drizzt spun his bow up and let fly, filling the area in front of Sylora with yet more sparks. From that field of explosion, though, came a responding missile, black and large and flying fast at Drizzt. Again the magical speed of his anklets saved him as he threw himself aside, both from the missile and from yet another Ashmadai coming in at him from behind.

That unfortunate woman caught Sylora's missile instead, and it covered her in what seemed like thick soot. In moments she began to writhe and scream out, throwing herself to the ground as if on fire.

Drizzt sent an arrow, then a second and third, up at Sylora, then turned and shot dead the screaming Ashmadai, purely out of mercy.

He moved with every shot, having no intention of catching any return fire from Sylora.

All the dead Ashmadai around him began to rise up, and all the remaining living Ashmadai backed away.

The zombies didn't come at him, though. One after another they leaned toward the balcony and were stretched upward, reduced to black smoke, and absorbed into Sylora's wand.

Another missile flew down from on high, striking the ground in front of Drizzt, creating another ring of woe, perhaps ten feet in diameter.

The drow moved aside and kept up his fire. Then he moved again from a third ring of woe, then a fourth. He recognized that Sylora was surely cutting him off from the cave, from Dahlia, with an overlapping line of rising ash energy. The powerful sorceress didn't stop there but created more deadly rings, driving Drizzt back, herding him like an animal to the slaughter.

He growled and continued his missile response, increasing the speed of his shots so incredibly that it seemed as if the bow reached forth with one long missile. The balcony exploded and sizzled with such a rain of sparks that to a distant onlooker, it might have appeared as if all the wizards of Faerûn had joined in a great fireworks celebration.

Drizzt kept glancing at Dahlia, wanting to help her, but not daring to interrupt his flow of arrows, not wanting to even allow Sylora to see the battlefield in front of her.

He was almost out of room to move.

On the rocky hillside at the base of the tower, Artemis Entreri quickly deduced that there was no way into that treelike structure. He also found a host of enemies waiting for him, a cluster of ashen zombies, standing and swaying.

To his surprise and relief, they didn't attack, and to his further astonishment, one after another burst into smoke and flew up at the distant balcony lip, as if it had been dismantled and sucked in by some giant vortex.

Not one to pause and reflect on good fortune, Entreri scrambled up the front of the hill, and was nearly stabbed as a zealot appeared from behind one of the many large rocks, spearlike scepter thrusting hard.

Across came the assassin's sword, just quick enough to drive aside the thrust. But the Ashmadai tiefling rose up above him, on the rock he'd been scaling, and thus gaining the advantage.

Except that this was Artemis Entreri.

Entreri cried out and fell back, turning to run, and the predictable zealot leaped at his back.

Entreri spun and swept his sword across, deflecting the scepter. He fell aside as he did, the man frantically trying to twist and grab at him, and catching instead a stabbing dagger right in the heart.

With a groan, the Ashmadai continued by, and Entreri cut him chest to groin, gutting him as he tumbled past.

A second Ashmadai replaced the first, coming straight up in front of Entreri, who had his back to the open drop now. The zealot stabbed wildly as if trying to force Entreri from the ledge, and at one point, the man cried out, thinking victory at hand as Entreri bent far backward, balancing precariously.

But when the zealot dropped his shoulder and bulled forward to finish the task, even diving so he would go with his victim, Entreri twisted to the side and dropped into a low crouch. He came up fast, shouldering the man from the ground, and turned and launched him into the open air.

Then he ran on, up the hillside, angling for the top of the cave.

He ran out of room, but mostly, Drizzt was just running. He sprinted to the edge of one ring of woe, and having no choice as another ashen black missile streamed out from the balcony at him, he leaped over it.

The smoking strands reached up at him and bit at him hard, stinging his legs, and he landed wobbly, but still managed to snap off another ineffective shot at Sylora.

But now Drizzt was back in open ground, and as he shook off the latest burns, he started to run around, buying himself more time. First he concentrated on those Ashmadai nearby, lowering Taulmaril and sending out a stream of arrows to drive them away.

Then he went back to Sylora, continuing his spark barrage to keep her from spotting him clearly. Finally, he turned his attention to poor Dahlia, who fought frantically, but lost ground against the strange opponent she faced.

Drizzt winced as she barely dodged a high swing of the Ashmadai's scepter, then shook his head in frustration as Dahlia properly responded and slammed the man—to no visible effect.

The zealot's next swing clipped her, just a bit, as she spun, and she even turned around enough for Drizzt to catch her profound grimace of agony.

He couldn't get to her. He had no clear shot, but he had no choice, either. He leveled the bow and let fly as Dahlia spun to the side, and to his relief, she didn't come right back the other way, and to his greater relief, her staff didn't catch that missile.

The arrow struck true, square in the chest of the mummified Ashmadai, slamming him hard, and he staggered backward, almost into the cave.

Only then did Drizzt see another figure deeper within the shadows, and he surely recognized Valindra Shadowmantle!

He let fly again, and a third time, though he had to roll aside to avoid another ring of woe, then had to dive again as a more direct missile nearly caught him from above. Both of his shots soared past

Dahlia and the Ashmadai and into the cave, though he couldn't tell if he'd scored any meaningful hit on Valindra or not.

What he did see, to his dismay, was that his earlier direct hit on the Ashmadai apparently had inflicted no serious damage. The man again pummeled Dahlia, who kept cringing and lurching, and seemed barely able to block his barrage.

Drizzt couldn't help her!

He had no choice but to turn his attention back to Sylora, to match her assaults with an overwhelming volley. The sparks, even if they did no more than somewhat blind the sorceress, were his only defense, and eventually getting through that magical shield, his only hope. As it was, Sylora had already littered the field with the black circles of destruction. The Ashmadai at the perimeters of the fight began throwing rocks, and a few even had bows.

For a moment, Drizzt considered that he might have to flee the field, and if Dahlia fell near the cave, the drow expected he would have no choice but to run away.

Drizzt knew they'd been baited, brought to a place in which he and his friends could not win.

Their enemy was, perhaps, too powerful for them.

But the despair could not take hold. Unexpectedly at that dark moment, Drizzt felt as if he was upon Andahar, riding from Luskan through the dark night. Exhilaration replaced dismay, and pure energy replaced fear.

He moved faster, diving and rolling, coming around to let fly behind to drive back an Ashmadai, then back forward, one, two, three shots to blind Sylora, if not actually hurt her. On one turn, he noted a host of zombies and he let fly at the group as well. But then he noted that they were not approaching, and a heartbeat before another black volley came at him from the balcony, one of those charred little creatures broke apart into flying ash and soared up to Sylora, as if it was one of her arrows.

He didn't understand, and he didn't have time to sort it out. Better to shoot the zombies, perhaps, or the Ashmadai?

He just kept his stream of shots and his continual movement, dodging rings and stones and arrows, trying not to wince when he glanced at Dahlia and her desperate struggle.

They would win, he believed. He was riding through the dark Luskan night and he would prevail.

There was no other choice.

"How do I hurt you, you beast?" Dahlia asked, accentuating her question with a spin of her staff and a straight, hard stab that jabbed the zealot in the chest, again to little or no effect. Her voice was raspy, her abdomen knotting and clenching from the withering wound.

But she wasn't twitching from the residual effects of her own lightning anymore, at least, though her braid had unwound itself in the process, leaving a thin shock of long black and red strands splayed around her otherwise bald head. Worse for Dahlia, she couldn't feel several of her fingers, and worse still, one of her eyes flickered and closed from the newest wound wrought by the zealot's powerfully enchanted scepter.

Despite all of that, the elf warrior broke her staff in half as she retracted it, then spun out those two poles, one in either hand, and broke them fast into flails. She didn't expect the weapons to be any more effective than the long pole, but she hoped her whirling display would buy her more time.

She couldn't win. She knew that.

"Shoot him again, Drizzt," she whispered desperately.

She ducked low as the scepter whipped across up high, then cut her counter short as the zealot retracted and stabbed for her belly once more. Then she jumped up high as his real attack swept in, a low cut aimed at Dahlia's legs.

She'd expected it. If he could but touch her legs with that withering scepter, the resulting cramping muscles would likely render her incapable of escaping.

And that's exactly what Dahlia was thinking about: escaping. As the scepter passed beneath her tucked legs, she still maintained enough of her balance to spin her weapons up and over, smashing them down atop the zealot's wrapped head.

He ignored the strikes and brought his scepter sweeping back the other way.

Dahlia moved as if to jump again, but instead stepped back—and it was a good thing she took that second route. The zealot stopped his swing midway through and lifted the scepter straight up. Had Dahlia leaped as before, she would have surely collided with it on her inevitable descent.

Now he faced her again, his eyes shining, his smile peeking out between the tight wrappings.

It occurred to Dahlia then that either of those places, eyes or mouth, might prove to be her best opportunity, but before she could even think through that proposition, she let out a cry of surprise and fell back as a form came leaping down.

She recognized it as Barrabus, as the man Drizzt named Entreri, and for a moment thought he was leaping at her. His hands were up high and wide, one holding his dagger, the other a knife. He crashed onto the zealot's back, and even that didn't bring the monstrous Ashmadai to the ground.

But down came those hands, faster than the zealot could react, dagger plunging into one eye, knife into the other.

How the zealot howled and spun around, feet moving every which way, arms waving crazily. The scepter fell from his grasp as his sensibilities fled.

Entreri hung on, riding him like a wild horse.

Around and around the zealot spun, slapping and lurching, and finally throwing the assassin aside.

Out came the knife with Entreri's tumble, though he'd lost his grip on the dagger.

There it stuck, protruding from the mummified zealot's left eye.

Entreri hit the ground in a roll and drew his long sword as he came back around to his feet.

"Come along!" he ordered Dahlia, and he rushed right past the still-spinning zealot and into the cave, not even pausing to retrieve his dagger.

Dahlia followed, slowing only long enough to glance back at Drizzt and to smack the zealot one last time across the side of his head. Convulsing weirdly now in his death throes, he fell to the ground as she passed him by.

"Valindra first!" Dahlia cried when she saw Entreri cut to the left, to the base of the tower.

But when she entered the cave, she blinked. It was a shallow cave with no apparent exits or hiding spots, but the lich was nowhere to be found.

Drizzt cheered and almost laughed when Entreri came down upon Dahlia's foe, and the precision of the assassin's strike reminded Drizzt all too keenly of how deadly a foe Artemis Entreri could be. The killing blow had to be perfect, and so Entreri had been perfect.

The drow took immense satisfaction in his decision to be merciful, to allow Entreri to travel beside him and Dahlia.

Still, his own situation remained precarious. He was fully thirty paces out from the treelike tower, nearer to the wall than he was to Sylora or his companions, who had disappeared into the cave.

Ashmadai enemies lined the wall, and the continual volley of stones and arrows had Drizzt paying them more heed than Sylora—something he knew would certainly spell his doom.

He had to leave, to move to the side enough, at least, to get out of Sylora's line of sight. But then what good would he be to his companions?

A familiar roar sent shivers through his spine, and sent the Ashmadai opposing him into a desperate frenzy.

Guenhwyvar—always and ever Guenhwyvar—arrived on the field just opposite the wall from Drizzt, charging at the Ashmadai line with abandon, ignoring the slings and arrows and chasing the zealots from their perches.

With full confidence in his panther companion, confidence built on a century or more of experience, Drizzt turned back to the distant sorceress with full force. As he dismissed those enemies behind him, he navigated the ground to move nearer to the tree. Sylora could fill in the few safe spots, he understood, but he saw, too, that the initial rings of woe were dissipating, leaving behind blackened areas of absolute death, but areas, perhaps, that he might cross.

If he could pick his way carefully and prevent the sorceress from filling in the gaps in the outer areas of agony, he might indeed get to the cave.

His hands worked in a blur then, a solid line of missiles flying forth, nearly every shot true. He could no longer see Sylora, so great was the spark shower. When no further black missiles reached out in response, it occurred to him that she might even have retreated into the tower.

Or dare he hope that one of his arrows had penetrated the strange bubble and struck her?

Drizzt nodded, but didn't slow the barrage for another few heartbeats.

He started forward tentatively, picking his way across the field.

Even as he entered the short stairwell leading up to the base floor of the tower, Entreri was met by a howling Ashmadai guard, stabbing at him furiously with the sharp end of his scepter.

Such straightforward ferocity was no way to battle Artemis Entreri. He easily deflected the thrust aside with his sword then expertly snapped that sword back out straight, taking the man in the shoulder. And when the Ashmadai overreacted, spinning aside and throwing his weapon up and over—and missing badly as Entreri swiftly retracted the sword ahead of the parry—the assassin calmly stepped forward and drove his dagger under the man's ribs.

The zealot howled and lurched over, and was surely doomed, except that neither Entreri nor his companion cared at all about him. The assassin slammed him on the back of the head as he bent, then grabbed his collar and yanked him forward and down the stairs.

Dahlia added a crack with a flail as he tumbled by, but like Entreri, her focus remained in front of her, not behind.

Up they went into the first floor then rushed along the stairway to the second. From there they could see the balcony, now empty, and the spark shower from Drizzt's continuing barrage as the missiles struck the shield Sylora had left behind.

Despite that explosive assault, Entreri moved toward the balcony, and the small stairway leading to the tower's third floor. There he fell back, dodging a blast of black ash as Sylora filled the space with a ring of woe.

The assassin tested it, but backed off again as the smoke bit at him painfully.

"The other way," he told Dahlia, nodding to the stair across the second level.

"She's up there?" Dahlia asked, not moving other than to reform her singular long staff.

Entreri looked at her curiously, and tried to push her toward the stair.

But Dahlia avoided him and moved toward the balcony instead, though she motioned for him to continue across the room.

The assassin glanced back as he reached the stair, and smiled wide. Dahlia rushed to the edge of the smoking area, planted her staff against the base of the wall opposite the short stair, and leaped forward, twisting and pushing off as she came even with the opening. With great agility and strength, the elf woman hung there, her momentum lost, and as she started to descend, she lifted her legs higher to the side and pushed off with all her strength, lifting herself up the side stair.

Entreri sprinted up the short stairwell and burst through the door, to find himself facing Sylora Salm and her crooked wand.

Dahlia was there, too, having cleared the blackened area.

"All my enemies in one place," Sylora said. "How convenient."

Dahlia responded by thrusting the end of her staff at the woman's mouth. The attack seemed true, but the weapon hit a barrier, a brown semicircle glowing in front of her at the impact.

Sylora laughed and whipped her small wand in front of her, and from that wand came a series of black darts, spinning through the room.

Both Dahlia and Entreri curled defensively, but both got hit. Many darts flew, and those small missiles brought forth painful bites indeed.

"Go!" Entreri demanded of Dahlia. He leaped at Sylora, as did Dahlia, sword, knife, and staff stabbing hard.

And all, weapons and attackers, were easily repelled by the barrier.

Down below, from the balcony, they heard a different cadence of explosive missiles.

"The barrier can be broken!" Dahlia surmised, and though Sylora hit them again with a rain of darts, on they came, their only defense a brutal forward assault.

Indeed, behind the globe, Sylora appeared genuinely concerned, and a bit disoriented by the sheer ferocity of their attacks.

The strikes didn't diminish until something flew past Dahlia, making her instinctively duck. She called out to Entreri as she did, and he, too, had to dive aside, his dagger not quite catching up to the small fiend as it fluttered past him. The devil's strike, however, did score, its whiplike tail lashing out at the assassin and cutting him painfully across the shoulder.

Up into the air went the creature, above the next rain of Sylora's darts—and that barrage had Dahlia and Entreri staggering back under the weight and sting of the assault.

But Arunika's imp hadn't been hit. Its skin hanging in burned strands from Sylora's earlier encasing ash, it understood the sorceress's defenses more keenly than the others.

Sylora hardly even seemed aware of the creature as it flipped over the top of the bubble and dropped down upon her extended arm. With clawed feet and hands, it grabbed at her forearm and hand, at the wand, and when she pulled back against it and slapped at it with her other hand, the imp bared its fangs and bit down hard on her weapon hand.

It lifted its head, two severed fingers hanging from its mouth, and tore the Dread Ring wand from Sylora's weakened grasp. Away it leaped, stinging her with its tail as it flew free of her desperate grabs.

Time seemed to stop then, a sudden, shocked pause from the three remaining in the tower room.

"Oh, now you die," Artemis Entreri promised, rising from his knees against the far wall, Dahlia beside him.

But Sylora Salm wasn't out of tricks. She threw her cloak up over her head, and as it descended, she transformed into the likeness of a giant raven.

Dahlia yelled in protest and struck at her. Entreri, too, managed a stab.

But neither scored a mortal, or even a serious hit, and the raven dived from the room, down the short stair, and out the tower balcony.

Drizzt leaped high, clearing the last line of still-smoking rings, on his way to the cave.

As he landed, though, he heard a sound from above, a peculiar sound given the circumstance and location: the whinnying of an angry horse.

That noise turned his attention back the other way, where he saw a large crow, a human-sized bird, fly out from the balcony, soaring into the night.

Drizzt leaped back the other way, drawing an arrow in mid-flight, and he landed and dropped to one knee, leveling his bow and letting fly.

The lightning arrow streaked off into the dark night, and sparks flew along with feathers as it struck home. But the crow kept gliding, disappearing over the wall and into the night beyond the strange fortress.

A second form came out from the balcony, and Drizzt nearly shot it, until he recognized it as Entreri's nightmare steed, the assassin and Dahlia astride it.

The amazing hell horse dropped down gracefully from twenty feet, and somehow landed gently enough so that its two riders weren't launched from its back.

Drizzt's jaw hung open, his stunned expression reflected on the faces of a pair of Ashmadai watching from the wall, as the nightmare thundered away in pursuit, flames flying from its hooves. It ran along the wall to the open gate then charged across the outer ring, Drizzt following its progress by the shouts of the defenders still out there.

Drizzt started back toward that wall, but noticed Dahlia's wide-brimmed leather hat and paused just long enough to scoop it up and put it on. Then, blowing his whistle loudly, the drow leaped the next ring, and sprinted around a third. He lined himself up with Andahar's approach, and waved the mighty unicorn past him. He leaped up and grabbed Andahar's mane as the galloping steed charged on.

In a few heartbeats, Drizzt was out of the fortress, with no pursuit apparent other than a growling panther leaping over the wall down to his right. He spotted Entreri's steed, the flaming hooves bright in the night, and bent low over Andahar's strong neck, urging his mount along, and gaining ground with every stride.

As he neared, it became apparent to Drizzt that Dahlia was guiding the mount in front of him. Entreri sat in the saddle, but she whispered into his ear continually. Entreri's nightmare ran with conviction, as if they knew where they were going, though the raven was nowhere to be seen.

Drizzt didn't question it. He put Andahar in line behind Entreri's nightmare and instructed the unicorn to follow.

Dahlia glanced back at him and nodded. When the trail cleared a bit and allowed for it, she held her staff out wide and up high, and again motioned to Drizzt.

The drow ranger grinned as he figured it out. He clamped his legs tight around Andahar's flanks, stood tall, and took up Taulmaril.

Kozah's Needle swallowed his first lightning arrow. Dahlia nodded, and kept the staff up high and out wide.

Drizzt let fly again, then a third time, the powerful staff feasting on the lightning energy. Drizzt could see little arcs of power jumping along its length, and Dahlia grasped it with her other hand as well.

Still she kept the staff up high, though, and pumped it emphatically. Drizzt let fly again, then a fifth time, and sparks leaped higher and thicker along the weapon's length. Dahlia's mostly-unwound braid once more began to dance with residual energy.

But she called for one more, and so Drizzt let fly again.

The trees thickened around them and Dahlia wisely brought the staff in closer, and lower. Drizzt settled in his seat, placed his bow across his lap, and urged Andahar on.

Valindra Shadowmantle slipped out of the crack in the stone at the back of the shallow cave and reverted to her normal three-dimensional form. The drow and his shining white unicorn were out of sight by then, but Valindra followed their progress out of Ashenglade by the tumult of Ashmadai zealots calling out their locations.

Valindra glided out of the cave and onto the ravaged field. A few of the rings of woe still smoked with dark energy. The lich moved to one and dipped her toe in. As she suspected, it was Dread Ring energy, necromancy, and so to Valindra it felt like a warm bath in oil-scented waters.

The cries around her muted. The drow was out of the fortress then, she knew, and galloping away in pursuit of Sylora the Crow.

Valindra knew where Sylora had gone, and expected that Dahlia did, as well.

She pondered her next move, but became distracted when a small form flew down at her and landed on the ground beside her.

"Wretched creature!" Arunika's imp snarled, waving the crooked wand. "I hope they make her suffer before they kill her!"

Valindra grinned at him then held her hand out for the wand.

The imp shifted away.

"Give me the wand now . . . Greeth! Greeth!" Valindra ordered.

Her eyes spun crazily and the imp's bulbous eyes widened. Suddenly the diminutive creature couldn't scramble fast enough to hand the wand over to the terrifying lich.

Valindra took it and brought it up in front of her eyes, issuing a little mewling sound as she did, as she connected to the comforting power of the Dread Ring.

"Shall I inform my mistress that you're the new Thayan leader in Neverwinter Wood?" the imp asked.

Valindra didn't even hear the creature, her focus locked on the sudden sensations of the roiling power. Sylora's overreach had hurt the ring, she knew, and badly.

"Shall I inform my mistress that you're the new Thayan leader in Neverwinter Wood?" the imp repeated.

"Be gone," Valindra replied, staring at the wand the whole time, feeling its power as she rolled it around her fingers. "Tell her— Ark-lem!—that I'll speak with her presently."

The infusion of power tickled her, and mostly tickled Valindra's thoughts. Images of Arklem Greeth flooded her. With this power, surely she could reclaim her beloved. And surely, once she'd resurrected him, he would help guide her from the tumult within her head. Maybe she wouldn't need the Abolethic Sovereignty's ambassador anymore. Valindra hated letting that piscine creature into her deepest thoughts, emotions, and secrets.

The imp fluttering up in front of her eyes pulled the lich from her contemplation, and as it sped away, sputtering curses, Valindra realized that it had likely asked her a question, likely repeatedly, before leaving in such a huff.

Valindra dismissed the creature from her thoughts—her increasingly scrambled thoughts. So much possibility! So great a promise of power! And the notion of Arklem Greeth at her side once more!

"No, no, I mustn't," the lich told herself.

Then she nodded as she considered her course and knew where she must go, and what she must ensure. She fell into her magical powers, preparing to leave, but stopped short and considered one other thing she might want to bring along.

There he was, crumpled on the ground just off to the side.

Only when she stood on the edge of the Dread Ring did Sylora Salm understand the depth of her error, the travesty she'd wrought.

Basking in the power of the wand and the connection it offered her, Sylora had taken more than the life force of a few ashen zombies. Indeed, those rings of woe, and maintaining that magical shield against the barrage of arrows, had stolen power from the Dread Ring itself, and no inconsiderable amount.

Blood oozed from her shoulder. The drow's arrow had wounded her critically, perhaps mortally. She needed the Dread Ring's power again, she knew, to heal herself.

But dare she pull more from it? Could she?

The implications of the depleted grayness before her struck the sorceress profoundly. She could almost picture Szass Tam within that smoking ring, could almost see the look of unmitigated anger on his withered face.

He wouldn't forgive her this time, she knew. After more than a decade, she had at last failed him.

Perhaps she could retreat belowground. Perhaps the Sovereignty would take her in.

Her thoughts spun as she sought a way out, and the desperation of her situation was brought home vividly when she heard the sound of approaching riders.

She turned and put her back to the Dread Ring. Whatever fears she had of Szass Tam's response seemed distant then, as the immediate necessities became clear. Sylora closed her eyes and tried to connect to the power behind her, asking the Dread Ring for still more.

Entreri eased up on his nightmare's pace as he noted the form in the clearing beyond the last tangle of trees. Drizzt did the same as he brought his unicorn up beside the nightmare, though neither steed seemed overly comfortable with the other so near.

It was indeed Sylora, all three riders saw.

"The Dread Ring is right behind her," Dahlia warned.

They crossed through the tangle and into full view of the sorceress Sylora, and the smoky tendrils of darkness behind.

Drizzt let fly an arrow, but alas, the sorceress once more had enacted a magical shield in front of her.

Not so great a shield, Drizzt and the others realized, though, as the sorceress winced in discomfort and staggered back a step.

Drizzt broke Andahar to the left and set another arrow to Taulmaril, but behind him, before the unicorn had gone three running strides, Dahlia struck next.

As Entreri pulled his nightmare up short, Dahlia cried out for Sylora to "Defeat this!" and used all the momentum of the stopping mount to hurl Kozah's Needle, spearlike, at her foe.

His jaw hanging open in surprise, Drizzt watched as the long staff slammed into Sylora's thin bubble shield and exploded into such a display of arcing lightning and thunderous reverberations that the night itself was momentarily stolen.

Andahar neighed, pawed the ground, and reared up, but Drizzt clamped his legs tighter and held his balance.

And when the explosion of pure energy roiled and coiled and slammed Sylora, sending her flying backward through the air, the drow was ready. Another lightning arrow soared off, flying true to its target. Then a second missile from the right flank joined the first, a large black missile, as Guenhwyvar leaped high and long and crashed into Sylora as she descended into the smoking Dread Ring.

They landed out of sight, within the black fumes, with a roar and a shriek, both primal, followed by . . . silence.

Drizzt looked to Entreri and Dahlia, Andahar and the nightmare pawing the ground.

And all three companions breathed easier when Guenhwyvar walked back out of the ring.

Dahlia slipped down from the nightmare's back and walked forward to retrieve Kozah's Needle, which lay on the ground right in front of the blackness. She picked it up and casually continued, not even looking back, but walking right into the intimidating smoke.

"Dahlia!" Drizzt called.

"I'm not following her," Entreri said.

Dahlia found Sylora Salm some dozen long strides into the Dread Ring. She lay on the black ground, twisted weirdly with one leg up behind her head and one of her arms beneath her. Blood flowed from her left shoulder where Drizzt's first arrow had struck her, from her right side where his more recent missile had struck, and from deep claw marks on the side of her face and throat.

But those were the least of her wounds, for Kozah's Needle had broken through that magical shield to open the center of her chest. Even in the dim light, Dahlia could see the woman's heart. It still beat, just once, then again after a long pause.

"Finish me," Sylora said, her voice thick with pain.

Dahlia bent over so her face was very near to Sylora's.

"Please," the doomed sorceress mouthed. "Finish me."

Dahlia reached down as if to comply and Sylora closed her eyes.

But Dahlia instead just roughly pulled the crow cloak out from around Sylora, jarring her to the side and drawing a gasp of profound agony.

With a last smirk at Sylora, Dahlia threw the cloak around her own shoulders and walked back out the way she'd come.

"She's dead," Sylora Salm heard Dahlia announce to her companions, followed soon after by the clip-clop of hooves receding into the forest.

EPILOGUE

They ran on for a long while, putting leagues behind them, Entreri's nightmare and Drizzt's unicorn gliding effortlessly through the forest night. Finally, in one moonlit clearing, Entreri pulled up his fire-breathing, fire-stomping mount and slipped down from the saddle.

"So, in the end battle, we didn't need your help at all," Dahlia pointed out, flipping down to the ground beside him. She grinned as if a great weight had been lifted from her shoulders.

"You'd prefer to be dead outside Sylora's tower?" Entreri asked. "I understand."

Andahar trotted into the clearing then. Drizzt dropped from his mount and walked over to join the pair, leaving the unicorn a safe distance from Entreri's nightmare. He wore a curious expression— jealousy perhaps?—as he scrutinized Dahlia and Entreri.

"We're done here," Dahlia announced to Drizzt.

"Valindra Shadowmantle remains—"

"I don't care. Not for her, not for this war. This was a personal grudge between me and Sylora Salm, and Sylora Salm is dead."

"And I don't care about Sylora Salm, other than how killing her might benefit me," Entreri replied.

He and Dahlia exchanged intense stares.

"And me?" Dahlia asked. "Would you still wish to bring my head to your master?"

"You just said you were leaving, so what would it matter?"

"It might matter to me," Dahlia replied, and Entreri laughed. He never stopped staring into Dahlia's blue eyes.

"What's your next move?" Drizzt asked the assassin, abruptly and pointedly. "Where will you go?"

"Back to Neverwinter, as I am bound," Entreri replied, and he gave a helpless shrug. This was a critical moment, he realized, and he knew he hadn't thought any of it through quite thoroughly enough. He had no idea how to pivot now, how to coax Drizzt and Dahlia to go back with him and rid him of his burden.

"Perhaps with Sylora dead and Dahlia gone, Alegni will be done with me, and I can return to the south in peace," he said.

"Who?"

Dahlia's voice, like her expression, went stone cold. It caught Entreri by surprise.

"Who?" Entreri echoed.

"*Who* will be done with you?" Dahlia said.

"Alegni."

"What is his name?" Dahlia demanded.

"Aleg—"

"His whole name."

"He's a Netherese lord, a tiefling Shadovar named Herzgo Alegni," Entreri slowly replied, enunciating every syllable clearly, scrutinizing Dahlia as he spoke.

He saw it, then, the profound pain that flickered behind Dahlia's eyes—primal, beyond anything any physical cut could ever inflict.

"What is it?" Drizzt asked, and Entreri glanced his way just long enough to realize that the drow didn't recognize the depth of Dahlia's profound agony.

Dahlia swayed and seemed as if she might fall over.

"What?" Drizzt asked again, coming up to support her.

"Apparently she's acquainted with my master," Entreri started to say, but Dahlia cut him short by spitting in his face.

Drizzt grabbed her by the shoulders and held her back. "Dahlia, what is it?" he insisted, keeping his face right in front of hers, trying to bring her back from whatever emotional ledge she'd walked out onto.

"Speak his name again," Dahlia said to Entreri.

"Herzgo Alegni."

"Your master, your friend."

"Hardly. My slaver, my hated enemy," Entreri assured her as she pressed against Drizzt, trying to get at Entreri.

That seemed to calm Dahlia, so much so that when Drizzt shook her and forced her to look at him again, she said, "Had I known that Aleg . . ." She stopped and swallowed hard, and seemed incapable of even speaking the name.

Entreri couldn't believe his good luck. He did indeed recognize the profound pain in Dahlia's eyes and knew that in simply speaking Alegni's name, he'd inadvertently made the important pivot needed to lure these two into his personal battle.

"Had I known he led the Netherese, I would have remained at Sylora Salm's side," Dahlia said to Drizzt.

Drizzt glanced over his shoulder at Entreri with obvious concern.

Entreri hardly noticed, and didn't return the look, for now it occurred to him that even being here at this time might well be aiding his hated master. Alegni had the sword, and the sword had Entreri. It could access his innermost thoughts and memories at any time.

Entreri leaped back up upon his nightmare steed. "I'm not your ally in this," Entreri announced to them. "Though I would love to see Herzgo Alegni dead."

Drizzt started to respond, but Entreri didn't wait, kicking his nightmare into a leap and gallop, off into the forest night.

Drizzt spun to face Dahlia, who all but collapsed into his arms.

"I'll kill him," she said coldly, without emotion, but when Drizzt lifted her face to his, he saw tears flow down her delicate cheeks.

She was still alive. She couldn't be! No one should have suffered this amount of pain without expiring.

So much pain, indeed, that Sylora Salm had not even realized that she was still alive for a long, long while. But now she realized the truth of it, and that alone made her realize her pain had subsided a bit.

Sylora gasped and coughed. The Dread Ring was healing her!

She moved her leg back under her, straightening once more, and as her body shifted, she saw her guardian, Valindra Shadowmantle, standing just to the side, holding Sylora's crooked wand, aiming it Sylora's way. Valindra called upon the powers of the Dread Ring to heal Sylora's mortal wounds.

"Valindra," she mouthed, barely audible, though the lich smiled and seemed to hear. "Thank you."

Valindra cackled loudly. "Thank you?" she echoed. "I only keep my enemies from having the pleasure."

Sylora looked at her curiously—more curiously when another form moved up beside Valindra.

The Thayan sorceress understood her doom, in Jestry's eyes—or eye, for Artemis Entreri's dagger remained deeply embedded in the other. That one visible eye socket, the orb gouged out by the knife the assassin had later retrieved, flickered with red flame, with the energy of undeath. Sylora had attuned him to the Dread Ring with the scepter she'd created for him, and now the ring had done its job, had brought him back into a state of powerful undeath.

And the creature wasn't looking upon the broken sorceress fondly.

Valindra cackled louder and spun away, gliding into the dark and smoky night.

Jestry towered over Sylora, reaching down to grab her roughly. He easily lifted her into the air.

Then the powerful undead creature bent her in half backward, shattering her spine, folding her like a brittle parchment. She screamed with her last dying breath, before Jestry slammed her broken form down into the ground and began to stomp on her with his heavy wrapped feet, a thousand times.

The imp growled and twisted and pushed, but to no avail against the strong strands of the magical web that held it up high on the wall.

"You didn't think I would allow a creature such as yourself to fly in and out of Neverwinter freely, did you?" Effron said, pacing in front of the diminutive devil.

"You err, warlock," the imp insisted. "My mistress—"

"Arunika," said Effron, and his recognition seemed to put the devil back on its clawed heels a bit.

"My mistress is powerful, and intolerant of—"

"Shut up," Effron said quietly, but with such a threat in his voice that the imp complied.

"I don't intend to hurt you," Effron explained. "As long as you understand that you now work for me, and for Herzgo Alegni, as well as for your mistress."

"I am of the Nine Hells, not the Abyss," the imp said with a little snarl.

"And I can send you back there, in pieces."

The two stared at each other for many heartbeats then Effron said simply, "Tell me of the events in Neverwinter Wood."

Later on the next morning, Effron found Herzgo Alegni on his namesake bridge, as usual, and recounted the strange but promising news of the previous night's events.

"Sylora Salm is no more," Alegni said smugly when the warlock was finished. "Perhaps Draygo Quick will allow me to leave this place at long last."

"Our enemies have been dealt a serious wound, but they are not gone," Effron pointed out.

"Led by an insane lich," said Alegni.

"More sane every day, from what I can determine, and she's being aided, perhaps by Arunika."

Herzgo Alegni looked at him curiously.

"I don't know all of the details," Effron admitted.

"Then learn them!"

Effron nodded.

"Now Barrabus rides with Sylora's champion and her powerful drow ally," Alegni mused.

"Artemis Entreri," Effron corrected, and when Alegni looked at him with surprise, the twisted warlock clarified, "His name is Artemis Entreri."

Herzgo Alegni laughed and walked to the bridge railing, staring out over the running river as it wound its way to the sea. "I'd forgotten that name," Alegni admitted. "I've not heard it in decades. Nor had he, I would assume." He glanced over his shoulder at Effron. "He's still mine, you understand, and so his name remains Barrabus."

"They're unpredictable, and powerful," Effron warned.

"Quite predictable," Alegni corrected. "Barrabus will try to get his new friends to come after me."

Effron grinned as he mouthed "Dahlia Syn'dalay" with open malice.

R.A. SALVATORE

R.A. Salvatore was born in Massachusetts in 1959. His love affair with fantasy, and with literature in general, began during his sophomore year of college when he was given a copy of J.R.R. Tolkien's The Lord of the Rings as a Christmas gift. He promptly changed his major from computer science to journalism. He received a Bachelor of Science degree in communications in 1981, then returned for the degree he always cherished, the Bachelor of Arts in English. He began writing seriously in 1982, penning the manuscript that would become *Echoes of the Fourth Magic*.

His first published novel was *The Crystal Shard* from TSR in 1988 and he is still best known as the creator of the dark elf Drizzt, one of fantasy's most beloved characters.

His novel *The Silent Blade* won the Origins Award, and in the fall of 1997, his letters, manuscripts, and other professional papers were donated to the R.A. Salvatore Library at his alma mater, Fitchburg State College in Fitchburg, Massachusetts.

THE ABYSSAL PLAGUE

From the molten core of a dead universe

Hunger
Spills a seed of evil

Fury
So pure, so concentrated, so infectious

Hate
Its corruption will span worlds

The Temple of Yellow Skulls
Don Bassingthwaite

Sword of the Gods
Bruce R. Cordell

Under the Crimson Sun
Keith R.A. DeCandido

Oath of Vigilance
James Wyatt

Shadowbane
Erik Scott de Bie

Find these novels at your favorite bookseller.
Also available as ebooks.

DungeonsandDragons.com